The MISFIT & The BEAST

VERA BROOK

THE MISFIT & THE BEAST
Copyright © 2023 by Vera Brook

All rights reserved. No part of this book may be used or reproduced in any manner without written permission, except in the case of brief quotations embodied in critical articles or reviews.

This is a work of fiction. Names, characters, businesses, organizations, places, events, and incidents either are the product of the author's imagination or are used fictitiously. Any resemblance to actual persons, living or dead, events, or locales is entirely coincidental.

Cover design by Vera Brook.
Background image by Sascha Duensing.

First Paperback Edition: June 2023
Published by Felix Press LLC.

To all my readers

Vera Brook

Chapter 1

I wished for the sun this week. So, of course, on Monday morning, rain hammers on the roof of our rental townhouse as I slip out of my bedroom and hurry down the creaky staircase, my school backpack hanging over my shoulder and an oversized plastic bag in my hand. Nothing is ever easy, right? I keep forgetting.

I flip on the light in the kitchen and drop my backpack on the spare chair. There are exactly three chairs in our kitchen, and none of them match the white, fake-distressed table: a dark wood chair with a curved back that Mom favors, a light oak with a red pillow that I always sit on, and a teal plastic spare. They came with the house, and after a year of living here, I barely notice the clashing styles. It's all temporary, anyway. Until we fix up the duplex, pay off the loans, and get back on our feet.

Where to put the bag, though? I don't want Mom to see it.

I cross to the odd door next to the fridge, open the brass latch, and throw the bag inside, then lock the door again. It's a back staircase to my bedroom, narrow and steep, a quirk of the old house, although I never use it.

It's already 6:47 a.m., as the glowing clock on the microwave informs me, so I busy myself with making coffee. I fill up the electric kettle and scoop up the grounds into the French press. As the coffee brews, I peer out the window.

Sheets of rain slash against the glass panes, blurring the view of our small backyard. A lone linden tree stands in the corner of the overgrown lawn. Tangled vines cover the tall fence.

But my favorite is the rose bush near the window. It's as tall as me, with stalks as hard as the iron frame that supports it, and viciously sharp thorns. The roses themselves are dark and scrunched, the ugliest I've ever seen, almost as if the plant had a mind of its own and didn't care to be admired or loved. The bush is tough and healthy, though, despite our negligence and sore lack of gardening skills, so we leave it alone.

I hear a knock and a whir, and Mom walks into the kitchen, the wheels of her suitcase catching on the uneven floor boards.

She smiles and sniffs the air. "Good morning, honey. Is that coffee?"

I pour her a cup, add a splash of milk. Then grab bread and pop two slices into the toaster. "What jam do you want on your toast? Raspberry or orange?"

"Just coffee is fine. Thanks."

Mom is wearing her travelling pantsuit and holds a dull metal case, which she puts on the counter. She's a medical sales rep, on the road every other week. The case holds whatever devices and samples she's selling this time.

"Mom, you need to eat," I protest.

But she only sips her coffee. "I'll grab something later."

I sigh. She'll go through a drive-through, get another coffee with extra milk, and call it lunch. She forgets to eat even when working in her own kitchen, never mind driving halfway across the country. But we've had this conversation too many times before.

Through the drumming rain, I can hear the rumbling of trucks on Highway 15, which connects to Interstate 80 a few miles north of town. I hate the idea of Mom driving in this weather, but sales reps don't make their schedule, and her boss is too cheap to pay for a bunch of flights.

"So I'm driving you to the office, right?" I ask, and I bite into my toast. Since I got my license last winter, my mom leaves her Corolla with me and takes a more presentable company Lexus.

Mom sets her cup down. "Oh, honey. No. Didn't I tell you? I have to take our car. A new policy."

I stare at her. "But—"

I almost blurt out, *I need it for the play!* The

director is gone this week, so no rehearsals yet, but we're doing the set build, and I have the costume meetings, and they're all in the evenings. No school bus to get me there or back after hours.

But I bite my tongue. Mom doesn't know I'm involved in theater, or about my clothes making, and I want to keep it that way.

"I'm sorry, Abby." Now Mom looks worried. "Is it the SAT prep course after school? Because I could ask Mrs. Smith to drive you."

Mrs. Smith, our neighbor next door, is a retired pharmacist and the nosiest person I've ever met. The last thing I need is for her to take interest in me and report back to Mom.

"No, no," I quickly say. "I'll get a ride. It's no problem."

A familiar red jeep springs to my mind, the leather seats and rolled down windows promising freedom and adventure, but I push the thought away. Who am I kidding? It's never going to happen. He barely knows I exist.

My appetite is gone, the toast dry like sawdust in my mouth, but I force myself to finish. I'll need the fuel to get through the day. Just the thought of begging people to pick me up and drop me off, over and over again, makes me bristle. Acting friendly is exhausting. It's not that I don't want to make friends—I do. But it's not friendship if I'm always the one asking favors and have nothing to offer in return—it's charity. I'd rather walk the three miles to school and back.

Mom frowns, her worry predictably escalating into guilt, and I know what she's going to say even before she speaks. "Are you sure you're going to be okay by yourself, Abby? I'll be gone an entire week. Maybe I should cancel."

I resist the impulse to roll my eyes. We've been over it before, a recurring theme ever since Mom got offered the job and we moved here for it. And we both know my answer. "I'm going to be fine, Mom. I'm almost seventeen. I can take care of myself." I glance at the microwave clock: 7:05 a.m. "But I need to run to catch the bus."

"I can give you a ride," she offers meekly.

But I shake my head, already tying my sneakers and grabbing an umbrella. The new high school is in the middle of nowhere, surrounded by woods and farmland. With the morning traffic, the detour would cost her a good hour.

"I'm okay, Mom." I glance at the door to the back staircase. I still need to grab the plastic bag. "You've got everything? Water? The charger for your laptop?" I ask casually.

Mom pales and looks up toward her bedroom. She forgot the charger on the last trip, and had to borrow one from a client in the middle of her presentation. She fretted about it for days. "I better make sure."

I kiss her cheek. "Drive safe, Mom."

I wait until she disappears up the stairs before I retrieve the bag, shrug on my backpack, and rush into the rain.

Chapter 2

Market Street, the town's main thoroughfare, looks like it's going through a car wash.

I turn into it and race five blocks, past a bank, a movie theater, and a bunch of shops and restaurants, blinking against the rain. I all but give up on the umbrella as I duck under low tree branches and try not to trip on the cracked slabs of sidewalk lifted by the roots. I clutch the bag in front of me. The last thing I need is to spill the contents.

The last building on Market Street, on the corner with Highway 15, is the old high school. It's been empty for a year, the doors chained shut and the brick walls crumbling as if in shame or grief. The bus stop to the new school is in the back.

I make it on the bus at the last moment, my awkward load and dripping umbrella earning me a stern look from Mr. Brown, the driver. He waves me in with his prosthetic hand, and I hustle to an empty seat, ignoring the curious and pitying looks people throw me. Most upper classmen drive to school or share rides with friends. I have the rare and dubious distinction of being a junior who takes the bus. Thankfully, half of the seats are empty, so I don't have to talk to anyone.

Mr. Brown steps on the gas, and the bus shudders and lunges forward.

The movement jostles me before I can brace myself. My shoulder slams into the window, and the wet umbrella swinging from my wrist hits my kneecap like a hammer, before proceeding to drip all over my shoes, which are soaked anyway. I wince and swallow a curse, but I never let go of the bag. I slide it onto the seat next to me, water pooling and streaking on the plastic, then changing direction and bending outward as the bus makes a sharp turn and we merge into morning traffic on Highway 15.

We roll past a supermarket, a car dealer, an antique barn, a gas station, all blurred by the rain that shows no sign of relenting. Finally, Mr. Brown makes another sharp turn, this time to exit the highway.

We pass a few ranch homes overlooking a large, briskly flowing creek. And then the sidewalks vanish, and we're on a country road—nothing but tall, green corn stalks shivering in the rain. The fields stretch and roll in all directions, dipping where some stream cuts through the land, and climbing to the edge of the forest in the distance. An occasional dirt road, a rusted mailbox, or a wooden barn are the only sign that people live here. It's a rain-washed picture of central

Pennsylvania.

The bus turns again, and we follow a new blacktop, one narrow lane in each direction, slick with rainwater. A ditch runs along the asphalt on both sides, the dirt turning to reddish mud. And beyond that—tall weeds, and thick, tangled brush.

We are about to make the last turn—into the large parking lot and the bus loop in front of the school—when we pass him.

A tall figure in the opposite lane.

His head is bent, the hood low over his eyes, his hands deep in the pockets of his sweatshirt.

I've never seen anyone walk on this road before, but that's what he's doing.

He walks the edge of the blacktop, but stays the course without stepping into the ditch, unmoved by the constant traffic of SUVs and minivans that squeeze past him, the most doting parents driving to work after dropping off their kids.

Somehow, the sight of him touches me deeply. I don't know why, but it does.

My chest tightens and I shiver, as if it was me braving the lousy weather instead of him. And for a moment, it *is* me—water drips into my eyes, my sweatshirt and jeans cling to my skin, and my toes turn to ice inside my soaked sneakers.

Irritation rolls over me. Why should I care? I don't

even know him. He must be a new student, or I'd recognize him. Plus, I have my own problems. But for some reason, I can't look away, can't stop watching him. My head swivels after him as the bus gets ahead, as if some invisible thread connected us.

And then he looks up, dark eyes under thick brows meeting my gaze—and his expression is so harsh, so hostile, my breath catches.

What are you staring at? His eyes flash with warning. *Mind your own business.*

My face turns hot, and my head snaps away from the window.

The back of the seat in front of me has a deep, diagonal slash across it, like a vicious knife wound. Foam pokes through it like torn flesh.

I keep my eyes fixed on the tear until the bus lurches to a stop and students push past me to the door. I'm the last to get up from my seat, still reeling from that glare. *What's your problem?* I want to confront the stranger. I want to block his path, yank back his hood, and look him in the eye as I yell at him. *I haven't done anything to you. And you already hate me?*

I don't get rattled easily, so the fact that a guy I don't even know can get to me like this is maddening. I'm furious with him, but even more furious with myself. *Come on*, I scold myself silently. *Pull it together.* All my hopes and dreams are pinned on this semester. I won't get a second chance if I slip up.

I nod goodbye to the driver and step out of the bus and onto the wide sidewalk, clutching the bag close. It's not worth opening the umbrella, so I lower my head and hunch my shoulders against the onslaught of water, planning to make a run for the main doors. But as if by magic, the rain eases to a light drizzle.

I glance over my shoulder toward the student parking lot, and my heartbeat quickens.

Because it's exactly the person I wanted to see—jumping out of his shiny red jeep and strolling in my direction.

Thick, wavy blond hair frame a strikingly handsome face. A white shirt stretches across broad shoulders and grey slacks hug long legs and narrow hips. A stylish brown leather bag. And up close, I know he has a perfect sun-kissed tan and his eyes are the deep blue of the ocean.

Jordan.

He's not strolling toward me, of course. I doubt he even sees me. He's heading inside the school, same as everyone else, streams of students from several parked buses joining with student drivers into one river of bodies that flows into the building through the open doors.

And it's a good thing he doesn't see me, because my shoulder-length hair is still damp and plastered to my face, and my sweatshirt and jeans are far from dry either, with wet splotches in random places. Not my most attractive look, to say the least.

I turn and rush inside the school ahead of Jordan, not caring if I splash through puddles.

I wipe my shoes on the giant doormat between the two sets of glass doors, and dive through the crowd of students in the side hallway to get to my locker next to the biology lab. I set the bag down and fumble with the lock combination, the umbrella banging against the metal. The stupid lock gets stuck all the time.

"Hi, Abby. What's in the trash bag?" a voice chirps, and I spin around to see Tammy.

"It's not a trash bag," I snap, although I realize it is. An oversized trash bag was the largest bag I could find. *God.* I hope Jordan didn't notice that. The lock finally pops free, and I yank the locker door open and stuff the bag on the bottom. "Just some costume options I found."

Tammy has a heart-shaped face and a purple pixie cut. She claps her hands together, beaming at me. "Awesome! I can't wait to see them."

She's a year ahead of me, a senior, and has been on the crew for every theater production since her freshman year. Last fall, for *A Midsummer Night's Dream*, she worked the lights. But this year she's on costumes with me, and apparently happy to let me make all design decisions, even though it's my first play. I should be flattered, but to be honest, it makes me nervous. I can't imagine trusting anyone so easily.

"They may not work out," I say defensively.

I almost close the pesky lock before I remember the umbrella still dangling from my wrist. I hang it inside the locker, then push the door shut. The hallway is emptying around us, students hurrying to their classes. Mine is at the opposite end of the building. I have to go. I'm already turning in that direction.

Tammy smiles and moves out of my way. "You've got Physics, right?" She's good at reading clues and has an uncanny memory. "Well, see you at the set build at 5. It'll be fun."

I stop. *The set build.* I'm planning to stay after school and use the wait time to do homework. But I still need a ride back...

Before I can force my tongue, suddenly thick and useless in my mouth, to say the words, Tammy's smile widens. "If you ever need a ride, just let me know, okay?" she says cheerfully.

I blink at her, incredulous. I didn't even have to ask. "Are you sure?"

"Absolutely. You live downtown. It's practically on my way. See you later, Abby." And Tammy glides away to her own class, whatever it is, just as the bell rings.

I've got a ride. I let the relief sink in, a smile stretching my lips. Then I rouse myself and run in the opposite direction, back toward the main hallway. Physics lab is on the other side, and I'm already late.

The collision almost knocks me down.

I trip, caught in a half spin—but strong hands grip me and steady me, breaking my fall.

My head spins, and for a second, I imagine brilliant blue eyes peering at me, and I gasp, thrilled and mortified. I've run smack into Jordan and… he caught me.

But the daydream clears. It's not Jordan.

Somber dark eyes under heavy brows frown at me, the voice gruff and unfamiliar.

"Whoa! Slow down. Where's the fire?"

Chapter 3

It's the boy who was walking in the rain earlier—the one who glared at me—although he's not glaring at me now. Still, I shake his hands from my arms, and take a step back, my heart pounding.

"Watch where you're going," I snap. Where did he come from, anyway?

The thick brows go up. "Me?"

"Yes, you!"

He's pushed back his hood, and in the harsh halogen light, his face is pitted with acne. His straight dark hair sticks out in all directions. But it's dry, which confuses me. Shouldn't it be dripping wet, or at least damp, like mine? Until I realize his dark sweatshirt is a waterproof jacket. Smarter than using an umbrella. His jeans are soaked, though, and his heavy work boots so thoroughly coated with mud, it's hard to tell their color. So I guess we're even.

A slip of paper lies on the muddy floor by his boot. He bends down and picks it up, shakes out the water.

I recognize the slip at once. Less than a year ago, I stood where he's standing, the same piece of paper in my hand. It's his class schedule. So he really is a new student, joining a week late. Still, better than six weeks into the semester, like when we moved here.

He glances at the slip, then his gaze locks on my face, as if waiting for something.

I stare back, unnerved but determined. I didn't forget he glared at me for no reason. If he wants my help, he'll have to ask for it. We stand like this, smack in the middle of the building, for a long moment, the tension prickling my skin like static.

Then, without another word, he glances around, orienting himself, and heads down the side hallway.

I frown. Does he know where he's going? But I'm already late for class, so I follow a safe distance behind. At least he walks fast, wherever he's heading.

Except he stops in front of the Physics Lab. *Great.* He's in my class.

The door is closed, and I can hear Mr. Miller's animated voice inside, which means the lecture has started. He's my favorite teacher, but he speeds through his slides, and I need to take good notes for the college subject tests later. It's bad enough that a new student got to class before me.

I throw the newcomer an impatient look. *Come on, go in already. What are you waiting for?* But he surprises me again. He pulls the door open and steps aside, letting me enter first.

I hesitate. Why would he do that?

But Mr. Miller, who likes to pace up and down as he lectures, is already waving me in. "Abby? Come in, come in." Then he spots the newcomer and waves him in as well. "Cory Brennell? Welcome."

Cory.

He's behind me when we step through the door, and I suddenly want to turn around and see how the name fits. But we're both caught in the projector beam, and the whole class is staring and murmuring, so I slip out of the spotlight and escape to the safety of my seat near the wall.

Cory starts to follow me, then stops, looking at the teacher. He stuffs his hands in the pockets of his jacket, and moves awkwardly from foot to foot, squinting against the brutal light as he waits to be released. I can see his clenched jaw and the tense line of his shoulders all the way from where I sit. Looks like he dislikes being on the stage as much as I do.

"I'm glad you made it, Cory," Mr. Miller says kindly. "Go ahead and pick a seat. We have a lot to cover, so I won't make you introduce yourself."

"I appreciate that," Cory mutters, and walks to the seat in the back of the room.

"Thank you for your help, Abby," Mr. Miller says to me with a smile, and my body flushes hot with embarrassment.

He thinks I helped Cory find the classroom. Maybe even that Cory and I are friends.

I half expect the gruff voice to correct him, but only a sullen silence flows from the back row. Should I say it, then? Tell everyone that Cory found the class on his own, with no help from me, and that we're definitely not friends?

I glance over my shoulder, half expecting to meet another glare.

But Cory is looking straight ahead, disinterested. Did he even hear what Mr. Miller said? Or he heard it, but he doesn't care?

I should be relieved, but instead I'm annoyed again. I spin back to my desk and grab my backpack, pull out my pen and notebook. Mr. Miller resumes his lecture, and I tune out the ongoing whispering and concentrate on taking careful notes.

The class goes by fast, and I forget all about the rude newcomer.

Then the bell rings, and Mr. Miller turns off the projector. "All right. That's all we have time for today," he says with a sigh, as students spring from their seats and rush for the door.

If it was up to him, we'd have five hours of Physics daily, so he can rave about all the new discoveries and applications, and take us on tours of university labs and industry projects, instead of only rushing through the dry basics. Mr. Miller believes Physics can save the world.

"Stay curious and keep up with the readings! I'll see you on Wednesday," Mr. Miller calls out, as students flee from the room. Then he adds, "Cory? A word, please."

I'm still furiously scribbling in my notebook. Mr. Miller drops plenty of helpful tips for the college tests, if you know what to listen for. But they're not on the slides, and if I don't write them down, I won't remember a thing.

From the corner of my eye, I see Cory's dark jacket as he passes my row of tables. I break off mid-sentence, grab my stuff, and get to my feet. I need to get out of here.

"You're Walter Brennell's grandson, aren't you?" Mr. Miller asks Cory.

"Yes, sir."

"The best electrician and handyman in the county, if you ask me, and honest to a fault. Saved my skin multiple times. I'm sorry to hear about the accident." There is genuine concern in Mr. Miller's voice. "A broken hip, huh? That's tough. How is he doing?"

"Doing all right. He's still in the hospital."

The back of the classroom is empty. Everyone else is gone. I drop my gaze and hurry down the only aisle, acutely aware that I'm eavesdropping on a private conversation.

Do they even know I'm here? Cory's back is to me, hiding me from view.

"So you're on your own," Mr. Miller says.

I'm about to slip past Cory and out the door, when he moves a step, from foot to foot, blocking the aisle and my way out.

My face warms. I'm stuck behind him.

I thought his jacket was black, but now that it's dry, it's dark green. I contemplate the tense line of his shoulders, his long, dark brown hair. He smells of the forest, and overturned dirt, and the rain. So different from what Jordan smells like...

I shake myself and clear my throat. I can't stay here. "Excuse me."

Cory doesn't flinch or startle. He simply turns to me, his dark eyes inscrutable, and moves out of my way.

But Mr. Miller throws out a hand to stop me. "Abby! Oh, good. I'm glad you stuck around. You can help me with my pitch."

Oh, God. He makes it sound like I stayed behind on purpose.

"What pitch?" Cory asks, and now he sounds wary, like he suspects a trap.

But Mr. Miller plunges in with all his enthusiasm. "*The fall play!*"

Of course. I'm such an idiot. Mr. Miller is our production mAnager, a volunteer role on top of his regular teaching duties, second only to the play's director. He's a major theater fan. How could I forget?

There's no stopping Mr. Miller now. Words rush from his mouth, propelled by his inexhaustible energy. "You see, Cory, your grandfather generously helped out with the set build for… oh… at least two decades. And when I say, helped out, I mean, he ran the show. And without him, we need help pretty badly." Hope shines in the teacher's eyes. "So let me ask you this, and please be honest. How are your carpentry skills? Did Walter Brennell teach you any of his magic?"

Cory's shoulders relax a fraction, but his expression remains guarded. "I do okay."

"I knew it!" Mr. Miller exclaims. "You'd be surprised at how many people can't hammer a nail without injuring themselves. Not to mention handling any power tools. You can imagine the accidents there!" He shudders.

"I don't have to imagine," Cory says. "I've seen them."

Mr. Miller blinks, taken aback, then realizes that focusing on the negatives may not be the best way to entice participation, so he changes tactics. "Well, my point is, we train everyone on the crew the best we can, including safety rules. But any prior experience is precious. We already have excellent people on lights. And we're lucky to have Abby on costumes. But we're still short-handed on the set crew."

Cory looks at me, the same unnerving, unreadable expression in his eyes. "So you've done it before?" he asks me.

The question catches me by surprise. "In my previous school. I was too late for the crew call here last year," I blurt out, and instantly regret it. This is way more information than I want to share, and none of his business. "I can tell you it's a lot of work. Lots of evenings and weekends. You have to be really committed," I add icily.

Mr. Miller frowns, misinterpreting my curtness. "Sorry, I know it's late, and you both need to run to your next class. So without further ado, Cory... how would you like to join the crew and experience the magic of theater? We'd love to have you."

Say no, I urge him in my head. I can't believe this is happening.

"Sure. I'll do it," Cory says.

Mr. Miller beams. "*Excellent!* The set build kicks off at 5 pm today. Come at 4:30 if you can. I expect a few more new folks, so I can run the whole group through basic training." He turns to me. "Am I forgetting anything?" Then back to Cory. "Anyway, if you have any questions, Abby is a great person to ask."

As soon as Mr. Miller turns away, I rush out the door and into the hallway. My next class is Calculus, up on the second floor, and I can't be late again.

But the by-now-familiar gruff voice stops me. "I do have a question."

I spin around, exasperated. Is he messing with me? He must be, because no one else gets under my skin with as little effort, although I have no idea why. "What is it?" I snap.

"What's the play?" he asks.

I almost smile. That's easy. "We're doing *Beauty and the Beast*." The dark, romantic drama, closer to the original fairy tale, not the silly musical.

"Never heard of it," Cory says. "Is it any good?"

"It's one of my favorites," I say.

He nods. "Okay." And then he walks away, hands back in his pockets. His boots leave muddy footprints on the floor.

I watch him for another moment. Who hasn't heard of *Beauty and the Beast?* Or was he messing with me again? It's extremely aggravating that I can't tell.

Chapter 4

It's lunch break, and I'm at my locker again, fumbling with the lock. For some reason, my best costume ideas always come at the worst possible time, like in the middle of a Calculus quiz. I need to grab my sketchbook, so I can draw them in the cafeteria before they are gone.

"Come on, come on," I mutter, frustrated.

"Do you want me to open it for you?" a gruff voice asks, and I don't even have to turn around to know it's the new guy again. Cory.

"I've got it," I say, without looking at him. How would he open it, anyway? It's not like I'm going to give him my combination.

"The notch must be shallow," he says. "Go slower and don't press so hard on the dial."

I don't answer. Did I ask for his advice? But I turn the dial more gently, and the lock releases. I pull open the door, stuff my backpack on the shelf, and grab my sketchbook. Then I push the door shut and snap the lock back on before I reluctantly face Cory.

I should thank him, but instead, I hear myself say,

"Are you following me?"

"Do you want me to?" he asks. His tone is matter-of-fact, no hint of a smile, giving away nothing about what he's thinking.

I narrow my eyes at him, indignant. "No!"

A group of girls pass us on their way to the cafeteria. Their eyes flicker from me to Cory, and I catch curious looks on their faces, which irritates me even more.

I don't know them, but I'm pretty sure they're on the soccer team. The competitive sports are a separate universe from theater, and I can think of only one person who's equally comfortable and welcome in both worlds.

To my horror, I hear his voice now.

"Be nice," Jordan Lockwood says, and I freeze, too mortified to look behind me. Did he witness my exchange with Cory, and is talking to me?

But the angry rattling that accompanies the voice can only be Mr. Dodd, the school custodian, with his wheeled bucket and mop.

"Nice? Look at all the mud he dragged in," the custodian grumbles. "This is a school, not a barn! We wipe our shoes here."

Emotion flashes in Cory's eyes, his jaw clenching, but it's gone before I can identify it, his coarse features unreadable again. It takes me another second to make the connection. It's Cory's muddy boots that set off Mr. Dodd.

I have no choice but to turn around. This is a disaster, and I'd give anything to be as far away from this spot as possible. Why did I stop by my locker at all? I should've gone straight to the cafeteria. I grip my sketchbook as if it could protect me. *Stupid, so stupid.*

But Jordan meets my eyes and smiles, and it's like stepping into a warm sunshine. All my irritation melts away, replaced by a happy daze, and all I want is to drink him in. We only had one general meeting so far, and the cast don't usually socialize with the crew, so I doubt he knows who I am. But he will.

Jordan is the Beast, the male lead in the play, and eventually, I'll have to meet with him to work on his costume and mask. The thought fills me with dread and delight. Jordan isn't the only reason I volunteered for the crew, but he is right there at the top.

A screech of the wheel yanks me out of my reverie, as the custodian pulls his bucket to a halt.

"What if someone slips and falls, huh?" He glares at Cory accusingly. "Who's going to get blamed for that?" Mr. Dodd spins the mop around, and dirty water sloshes inside the bucket, dangerously close to spilling over Cory's boots and my sneakers.

I reflexively step back, but Cory doesn't budge.

Jordan puts a calming hand on the old man's arm,

his voice warm and full of deference, an irresistible combination. "You're absolutely right, Mr. Dodd. But you saw the rain out there. Not everyone has access to reliable transportation. Things can go wrong, no matter how hard we try, and we can never truly know what someone else is going through. So kindness is always better than punishment. Wouldn't you agree?"

It's like the resentment drains from the old man, and Mr. Dodd suddenly looks sheepish. "True, true. We do the best we can, and that's all we can do. Just don't want anyone to get hurt on my watch. Not you either, son." That last part with a glance at Cory.

I watch the transformation in awe. This is what Jordan does—his gift, his magic. I've only seen it on stage so far, from a distance, but it's even more enthralling up close.

Although something about the scene makes me uneasy too. I can't quite put my finger on it, but it's there. Like hearing a wrong note in a sweet melody—I'm aware of the false sound but could never explain it, wouldn't even know where to start or what words to use.

Mr. Dodd's truck is a rusted ruin, held together with wire and tape. He always parks it in the back of the building, in the far corner of the lot, hidden behind the trash bins. The engine sounds like a dying animal, choking and spitting. I also heard rumors that Jordan's father, who owns the largest real estate firm in the county, hires the custodian for odd jobs, to help him out.

"I'm sure he'll be more careful in the future," Jordan assures the custodian, with a pointed look at Cory.

This is Cory's cue to speak up. A simple thank you would do. Jordan has already done all the work for him.

But when I turn to look at him, Cory's face is a cold mask, his jaw set and his lips a tight line, and he's studying Jordan with an intensity that makes my skin crawl. The custodian hurries away, the rattling of the wheels fading as the bucket rolls down the hallway. And Cory never says a word.

What did I miss?

Jordan's perfect mouth twists with displeasure. But honestly, I don't blame him.

"See you later, Abby," Jordan says to me, and I'm so stunned by this, my breath catches and my knees go weak. By the time I find my voice again, Jordan is gone.

Cory is still here, though, watching me with a frown, and suddenly I can't stand him. "Why do you have to be so rude? He was helping you!" I hiss, putting as much venom into the words as I can.

Cory only scowls. "*Helping me?* Is that what he was doing? And maybe he was helping this poor old man, too?" Then his eyes turn hard. "If that was *helping*, I never want to find out how he *hurts* someone."

A chill runs down my spine, even though the comment makes no sense—or maybe because of that. Jordan hurting someone? The idea is ridiculous. He may intimidate people, sure, because he's so good at everything he does. The uncontested male lead in all the school plays. The president of the student council. Straight As in all his classes and a perfect SAT score. He even gave a solo martial arts demonstration once. He trains with a personal trainer, since we don't have a team.

But people admire Jordan for that. Not hate him or hold a grudge.

No. This isn't about Jordan, I decide. Some people just drag in darkness with them like mud, bring it with them wherever they go, and ruin everything. I don't know what Cory's problem is, but I'm too mad to argue with him, and I'm definitely not going to just stand here and let him bash on Jordan.

So I turn on my heel and stalk away, the sketchbook clutched to my chest, even though I have no idea anymore what I wanted to draw.

Chapter 5

Unlike during lunch, when it's milling with students and buzzing with conversation, the cafeteria after school is an oasis of calm. A large open space under a high ceiling, it has cream walls and a two-tone tile floor like a chessboard. Two dozen round tables take up the middle, framed on one side, parallel to the main hallway, by high counters for people who prefer to stand, and by a row of booths on the other side, along the wall window.

Thankfully, I'm the only person here, killing time before the set build. I sit in the last booth, which overlooks flower boxes at the edge of the patio. I wish I knew the names of the flowers. They make me think of wildflowers, sturdy more than pretty. Anyway, it looks like they survived the rain, and I'm glad. The ground is still wet, but the sun is out, peeking through the clouds.

I chew on a cereal bar and sip my water as I try to make progress on my Physics homework, the pen dancing in my fingers over the page. But today, as much as I respect Mr. Miller, my mind is too restless to focus on Newton, classical mechanics, and endless pairs of bodies exerting equal but opposite forces on each other.

Finally, I give up. Anyway, the natural light pouring through the window is too good to waste. I close my workbook and pull out my polaroid camera. I stick the workbook in my backpack and drop it on the opposite seat, where it hits the wood with the exact same force and at the precise moment that the wood hits it.

I slip out of the booth and lift a large plastic bag from the floor and onto the seat next to my backpack. It's the same bag—okay, the same *trash* bag—that sat on the bottom of my locker all day. I grab a paper napkin from a dispenser and carefully wipe my table and the one in the booth next to it. Then I open the bag.

Inside are two stacks of carefully folded clothing, all lucky thrift store finds from my personal collection. I pick up the first stack and set it down in the corner of the table. I peel off the item on top—an embroidered white shirt that might suit Beauty when she does her house chores—and spread it on the second, empty table.

I make a few adjustments: straighten the sleeves, smooth out a wrinkle. Then I climb onto the seat, my polaroid camera in hand, to snap a photo.

It takes me a good minute of turning and bending before I'm ready to take the shot. The camera hisses and spits out a square print, and I watch anxiously as the image emerges. It's fine. Good, actually. Polaroid is pricy, but I adore it. It would be cheaper to take photos with my phone and print them in a CVS, but the closest one is two miles away from my house and four miles from the school. Too far to walk.

After I'm done with the embroidered shirt, I fold it neatly, and drop it off on the first table. It goes in the opposite corner: a new stack. Then I grab the second piece—a knee-long flowery skirt—and repeat the photo-taking process.

We already have some of the costumes for *Beauty and the Beast*. The theater program has a small collection of gowns and coats and hats and such, most of them donated by past student actors, but a few purchased or custom made for a specific performance. I've been in the storage room briefly, but today, Tammy and I are planning to really dig through it, to find pieces we could use.

My plan is to photograph all of them with my polaroid, so Tammy and I can brainstorm the outfits for all the characters in the play.

I muse about the story as I work, caught up in the timeless magic of it, scenes and images fleeting through my mind.

In the original tale of *Beauty and the Beast*, Beauty's merchant father loses his fortune, and he and his children—four daughters and two sons—are forced to relocate to the country, where they have to work for a living, a banishment of sorts. Unlike her older sisters, who are vain and lazy, too busy lamenting their lost dowries and missed marriage opportunities to be of any help around the farm, Beauty is humble and industrious, and adapts to her new life graciously.

The father learns that a ship with his merchandise has arrived, and sets out on a journey to claim it and restore family wealth. But he runs into legal trouble and returns empty-handed—a cruel fate taunting him and undoing his plans again. Distraught, he loses his way in the forest, on the verge of dying from cold and hunger, when he wanders into a magnificent but empty castle. He warms himself by the fire, eats the dinner on the table, sleeps in the bed, and in the morning, new clothes wait for him, although he never sees the owner of the castle and his benefactor.

Alas, on his way out, the father makes a grave mistake: he picks a rose from the garden—the only gift his beloved daughter Beauty asked for—and provokes the Beast's wrath. The rose happens to be the fearsome monster's most valued possession. Now he will only spare the merchant's life if one of his daughters comes to the castle and dies for her father's crime, and she must come willingly. And Beauty does just that...

Tammy finds me in the cafeteria just as I bend over

the table to photograph the last outfit—a pair of loose, striped capris in earthy colors that might work for one of the Brothers' hunting outfits in the play.

"You have a polaroid camera. That's so cool!" Tammy exclaims. Another girl hangs a few feet behind her. She has a freckled face, and her long auburn hair is in an elaborate braid around her head. Tammy grabs her hand and pulls her toward me. "Abby, this is Zoe. She wants to help out with the costumes, and she can also do hair. She's really good. Mr. Miller is okay with adding her to the crew, if you're okay with it."

"Of course!" I say, and my hand reflexively goes to my own unruly hair. I'm lucky if I can get it to stay in a ponytail for gym class. "Nice to meet you, Zoe." Then inspiration strikes me. "Actually, do you mind if I take a picture of your hair? This style might work for one of the Sisters."

Zoe grins, and glances around her. Even her throat and arms are freckled. "Sure. Where do you want me?"

"Umm. Here in front of the wall is good. A plain background. Let's take one from the front first," I instruct, and Zoe poses for the camera. "On three. One, two, *three*." Zoe holds still, and I snap the picture. The camera hisses, and the print slides out.

Tammy reaches for the print, delighted. "Can I see it?"

I hand it to her, and turn back to Zoe. "One more

from the back. And... one, two, three." I catch the print as it comes out.

Tammy glides toward Zoe and slips her arm around her waist, pulling her close until their heads touch, facing me and the camera. Zoe giggles. "Take one of both of us?" Tammy asks.

I smile. "Sure. On three? One, two—" In one fluid motion, Tammy and Zoe turn to each other and kiss on the lips. "—three," I finish, my own face warming. I didn't realize they are a couple.

I offer them the print when it's ready. Zoe snatches it, and they both lean over it, eyes bright.

"I love it," Tammy says.

"I love you," Zoe counters. And they kiss again. A real kiss.

My mind conjures Jordan's perfect face, his blue eyes looking straight at me, and longing slashes through me like a knife. I quickly turn to the booth and busy myself with packing the two stacks of clothes into the bag, so we can take them backstage.

"There they are!" Tammy exclaims.

And I turn around to see a small group gathered in the main hallway. For some reason, my eyes go to Cory first, which is annoying, so I quickly move my gaze to Mr. Miller. A few other students are there too, but I don't know them. It must be safety training for new crew members.

"Are you ready?" Tammy asks me. "We could walk with them."

I'm not thrilled by the idea, but I cover it with a smile. "Sure. Go ahead. I'll catch up."

Tammy and Zoe start walking, their fingers linked together, while I take my time putting away my camera and prints, zipping up my backpack and shrugging it on, and finally pretending I'm still packing the bag.

It works. When I turn around, the hallway is empty. *Good.*

I slip into the wings of the theater and into the storage room. I start moving the heavy-duty, roll-n-lock costume racks, my nose wrinkling at the strong scent of Febreze and dry cleaning.

The racks are organized by play. *Beauty and the Beast* will have its own rack, which sits in a flat, oversized delivery box at the moment, waiting to be assembled. But it takes two people, so I'll wait for Tammy to help me.

Inside the racks, the costumes hang on hangers or lie folded on shelves, each protected by a clear garment bag and labeled with the character who wore it. Head coverings and other accessories are stored in plastic boxes on top. One whole section holds smaller set pieces and props. The large painted backgrounds are stored backstage, suspended from the ceiling like carpets.

I wish the light was better in here. The yellowish lamps hanging from the ceiling muddy the true colors and aren't great for photographs. But one costume catches my eye and makes my pulse quicken. I grab it off the rack and slip it out of the plastic to inspect it more closely.

It's a man's tailcoat with a matching vest and a lace neckerchief. The coat is wide in the shoulders and tapers at the waist, the fabric a rich, dark blue velvet with gold buttons and stitching.

Yes. It's perfect for a cursed and brooding fairy-tale prince who lives alone in a gloomy castle. And I know someone who will look stunning in it.

Like on cue, voices and footsteps drift from the stage. People are arriving for the set build. It's one time when actors and crew mingle as equals, wielding hammers and paint brushes.

I can't help myself. I hang the tailcoat over my arm, so I have an excuse, then I slip back into the wings and scan the stage.

And there he is, the lights catching the gold in his hair as he enters.

Jordan is wearing dark jeans and a gray t-shirt, and he brought a black metal toolbox the size of a small coffin. The box looks incredibly heavy, but he carries it in one hand, the muscles in his arm as perfectly defined as if sketched by an artist.

He sets the box down on a raised platform not far from where I'm lurking in the wing, although he still hasn't seen me, and instantly, a small crowd of admirers gathers around him.

Marie, who plays Beauty, gets there first, graceful like a dancer. She's wearing a black top and tights that show off her gorgeous olive skin and slender figure, and match her long, black hair. I feel a sting of envy, although I don't think there's anything romantic between her and Jordan. It's just not fair for anyone to look so beautiful without any effort.

Marie's faithful entourage is right behind her. The three actresses who play the Sisters, and the makeup guy, Luke. A few more cast and crew members hurry over, including Adam and Neon. Adam is on lights. Neon is Jordan's understudy for the Beast, although they must do it just for the experience, since it's unthinkable that Jordan would miss a show. He is the star the audience comes to see.

Marie brushes the shiny lid of the toolbox with her fingertips. "Jordan, this looks like a treasure chest," she croons in her singsong voice. "Look at the lock!"

Jordan laughs, playing it up. "Are you ready? Do you want me to open it? *Are you sure?*"

His audience starts to chant. "*Open it! Open it!*"

"Open what?" Mr. Miller walks onto the stage, followed by more students. His eyes widen when he sees the toolbox. "Jordan, you're spoiling us."

The training for new recruits must be over. I reflexively scan the group for Cory, but don't see him. Maybe he already quit. That might be best.

"Hey," a voice whispers behind me, and I jump. But it's only Tammy.

"Sorry," she says, keeping her voice low. The wing hides us in the shadow. "What's happening?"

"Just... Jordan," I blurt out.

"Right," Tammy huffs. "Okay, well, Zoe and I can get started on the rack," she says. "We don't need any fancy tools for that."

I frown. That's harsh. But before I can defend Jordan, Tammy turns and is gone. She's the only person I know who's not a fan of him, and I don't think it's just because she's gay.

Well—she and Cory. He doesn't seem to like Jordan either. But he's new and doesn't know Jordan, so that doesn't count.

The smile fades from Jordan's face, and he pats his pockets. "I think I left the key in the car."

The response is a collective groan of disappointment.

"You're kidding! Nooo…"

Then someone's phone chimes.

"The wood is here!" Skyler, a senior with buzzed brown hair and lots of earrings, glances at the message, then slips the phone back in their pocket. Skyler is our production designer, and Mr. Miller's right hand on the set.

"Great. Thanks, Skyler," Mr. Miller says. "All right, everyone! There's going to be plenty of boards to carry. So if your hands are free, we're going this way."

The stage quickly empties as the cast and crew cheerfully follow Mr. Miller out the side door. I spot Cory in the back of the group, eyeing the toolbox. Only Jordan turns in another direction, leaps off the stage to the floor and jogs down the aisle between the rows of seats toward the main theater entrance. Toward the student parking lot and his jeep, no doubt.

I glance at the tailcoat I'm holding. The light is so much better on stage. But I need my camera. I run to the storage room to get it.

"I'll be right back," I tell Tammy and Zoe as I dig in my backpack for my polaroid. They are almost done assembling the rack. Impressive.

Back in the wing, I hang the tailcoat on a hinge that makes the wing wall movable, and take two steps back onto the stage, just far enough to take a photo. I lift my polaroid to my eye to frame the shot.

"*What. The. Fuck!*"

I almost drop my camera, shocked by the hateful edge in the voice even before I spin around to see the person.

Jordan's mouth is twisted, and his eyes blaze with anger. "Who did this? Who opened it?"

I stare at him, utterly dumbfounded. I barely recognize him. Then the meaning clicks, and my eyes jump to the toolbox.

It gapes open like a horrible mouth full of gleaming metal, the lid pushed all the way back.

Someone unlocked it.

Jordan sees me and stalks closer.

"Was it you?" he growls.

I flinch and shake my head, still numb. "No."

Jordan wheels around, scanning the stage, his blond hair in his eyes and his nostrils flaring. Then he turns back to me and grabs my arm. "Well, did you see who did it?" he hisses through clenched teeth.

The pressure of his fingers on my skin—not the gentle touch I always imagined, but rough and demanding—takes my breath away. Then my own temper flares, and I wrench my arm from his grip.

"No, I didn't see," I say. And technically, it's true. Although I instantly know who did it.

Maybe if Jordan asked me nicely. I certainly don't owe any loyalty to the lock picker. But I don't respond well to threats either.

"Okay. I know you didn't. I'm sorry," Jordan says in his normal voice, and runs his hand through his hair to smooth it. "I just don't like it when people don't respect my stuff, you know? These tools are very expensive. I could get in trouble with my father if anything went missing."

"Then don't bring them here," I say, more confused than ever. Does he think there are thieves among us, waiting to steal from him?

Jordan's eyes narrow for a second, then his face relaxes. He looks at the dark blue tailcoat hanging from the hinge, and walks over to it. Passes his hand over the velvet.

"For me?" he asks, his blue eyes searching mine. When I nod, he takes the coat off the hanger and shrugs it on. He doesn't bother with the vest or neckerchief, but I can tell the costume fits him perfectly. He strikes a pose, his eyes locked on my face. "You were going to take a picture?"

"Sure." I dutifully snap a photo of him, concentrating on keeping my hands from shaking. The camera hisses like a snake, and the print slides out. I put it away without a glance. I already know he's gorgeous in it, and the costume is just right.

Jordan smiles, takes off the coat, and hands it back to me.

"I love it. Thanks, Abby," he says in his stage voice, way louder than necessary, just as Mr. Miller and his helpers return.

Cory is right there in the front, lugging a stack of

rough wooden boards. His eyes brush the open toolbox, then slide from Jordan to me, and he frowns.

I grab the blue tailcoat and the hanger and flee from the stage.

Chapter 6

It's almost 9 p.m. and completely dark by the time Tammy drops me off after the set build, true to her promise. Zoe insisted I ride shotgun so I could give directions, but she climbs into my seat as soon as I get out of the car. She and Tammy wave goodbye and drive off grinning at each other, and I can't help feeling I crashed their date, even if they are sweet about it.

I use the side door in the alley, fumbling with my key, and step into the dark kitchen. I lock the door behind me and switch on the lights. The house is eerily quiet, except for the hum of the fridge and the buzzing cicadas in the yard. I kick off my sneakers and drop the house key into a chipped ceramic bowl on the counter, so I don't have to look for it in the morning.

I pull out my phone and reread the text Mom sent me earlier, although I already replied. *I made it to Chicago*, she wrote. *The drive wasn't bad. I hope you had a good day at school. Don't stay up too late. Love you.*

I sigh. She sent it after 6 p.m., so she was on the road for almost twelve hours. She's not a complainer, but I can read between the lines. *The drive wasn't bad* means the rain was truly nasty, and she probably hit a traffic jam in the city. The reminder to go to bed means she's exhausted, but she'll stay up to research the clients and polish her presentation anyway. And the comment about school basically translates to: stay focused and study hard—your future depends on it.

Mom has my whole career planned out for me, and she's tireless in keeping me on track and cheering me on. The plan includes me acing the college prep tests two months from now, getting a scholarship to a great college to major in biology or neuroscience, and then on to some prestigious medical school, preferably to become a neurosurgeon like Dad, although she's flexible on the specialty.

I have a completely different plan, but she has no idea, because, basically, I don't have the guts to tell her. Instead, I pretend to go along with her plan and lie about everything else.

At least for now. Mom has enough on her mind, and she works harder than anyone I know. I don't want her to worry.

This reminds me I still have homework to finish. I dig out my Physics workbook and the calculator. Then I fix myself a bowl of ramen noodles, add some spinach, and sit down to the table to eat and work, careful not to spill the broth on the pages.

When I'm done, I wash the bowl in the sink, and move on to the Calculus problems. I'm halfway through when I remember the design idea I never had a chance to sketch. The Beast's hands! I push the problem set aside and grab my sketchbook.

I found a pair of monster gloves in storage, part of a costume from some old zombie play. But the thick, fake fur makes them hot and itchy, and the long plastic claws are hard enough to scratch. Plus, the colors are all wrong, the claws white like bleached bones and the fur almost black.

I can do better. Pick softer, lighter materials in shades of brown to match the rest of the costume and the Beast's mask, when I have it. The gloves will be another piece for my portfolio—designed and made by me.

They'll feel nice on Jordan's hands. My gift to him.

Jordan.

The thought of him sends a jolt through me, and I dig in my backpack until I find the polaroid photo of him in the tailcoat. I lift it to my eyes, and my face warms. Jordan is looking straight at me, his blue eyes intent and a smile pulling on his lips. As if he, too, had a secret, and was about to share it with me.

Then my gaze stops on his hands, thumbs tucked under the collar of his coat, as he poses for the photo. He has beautiful hands, with long, graceful fingers. But when I look at them, I feel a phantom pressure on my arm—a hard grip just above my elbow.

The spot is sore when I press it through my sweatshirt. Slowly, reluctantly, I pull up the sleeve.

The first time Jordan touched me—and he left a bruise? My heart sinks. It seems… impossible.

Then another memory flashes through my mind. Strong fingers closing on my arms to keep me from falling. Cory's hands, when I collided with him in the hallway.

Of course! The marks are from Cory, not from Jordan. This is why Jordan's touch felt rough, when it wasn't. It's all Cory's fault.

I recall the glare on the newcomer's face when he saw me on the bus, and I'm suddenly restless. I slip Jordan's photo inside the cover of my sketchbook and tuck the book away in my backpack. I get up and pace the kitchen, the crooked floor boards treacherous under my feet.

Why would anyone walk to school when it's pouring like that? Why not take the bus? And where does Cory live, anyway?

I cross to the counter and fill up the electric kettle. I open the cabinet and grab the first tea box from the shelf, fish out a tea bag and drop it in the mug.

As I wait for the water to boil, I peer out the back window into the backyard. But all I can see is dark outlines of the rose bushes, the linden tree, and the fence, with my own reflection superimposed on them.

Maybe there is no bus. If you live within a mile of the school, you're supposed to walk.

The water boils, and I pour it over the tea bag. I let it steep as I gaze out the window again, trying to see further this time.

Five blocks of two-story houses divide my backyard and back alley from Highway 15. If I listen carefully, I can hear the traffic on it even at this hour, an odd truck rumbling past or a car breaking for red lights. Past Highway 15, more houses line Market Street and the intersecting streets for several more blocks. But beyond that and a few small shopping and medical centers, the residential development gives way to rolling fields, brisk streams, and patches of forests.

And farms.

Is that where Cory lives? On a farm? He must. I picture dirt roads and tall corn stalks swaying in the rain. The work boots and sturdy rain jacket make sense now.

I think back to what Mr. Miller asked him. Cory's grandfather is in the hospital. What about his parents? Maybe I missed it? But then I remember something else Mr. Miller said. *So you're on your own.*

Cory is alone?

I imagine an empty house, nothing but dark fields

and even darker woods stretching in all directions, and a starless night sky pushing down like a lid—and a shiver runs through me.

By the time I remember my tea, it's already lukewarm. I lost track of time. I drop the tea bag in the trash and force the tepid liquid down my throat, annoyed with myself.

Maybe I can still do some sewing tonight—for my own project, not for the play. I keep my sewing machine hidden in the back staircase. A basic Singer model with 24 stitches. It was all I could afford with the SAT prep course money from Mom.

But it's already 12:03 a.m., as the microwave clock reminds me. If I don't go to bed, there's no way I'll make it to the bus on time tomorrow.

I grab my backpack, turn off the kitchen light, and climb up the dark stairs to my bedroom.

ଔଛଛ

The next morning at school, I confront Cory in the hallway. I get straight to the point but keep my voice low. This is between him and me. "You picked the lock on Jordan's toolbox," I say.

"So?" He doesn't even try to deny it.

I shake my head. "So what was the point?"

Cory only shrugs. "The point? How about this:

That lock is useless, and the whole box is shiny, overpriced junk. And I bet he doesn't even know how to use the tools."

I bristle on Jordan's behalf. "You don't know that. Maybe he does. And anyway, it's his business."

I start walking. I'm done with the conversation. But apparently Cory isn't, because he falls in step with me.

"I see it's your business too," he says flatly.

"Yes. You know why?" I spit out, wheeling around. "Because *you* weren't there, so *I* got yelled at." I don't know why I tell him this. It's not really what happened. Jordan didn't mean it. It was a misunderstanding.

My words hit a nerve, though. Cory skids to a halt and leans closer, his eyes intense and the look of disbelief on his face. "He yelled at you because of the stupid lock?"

"Don't worry. I didn't tell him who did it," I say.

Cory pulls back and his face darkens, the acne scars reddening painfully. "Why not? You should've told him. I can handle it," he says hotly. "I don't need you to cover for me."

"Fine," I snap, my blood boiling. *Cover for him?* Why would I ever cover for him? I wasn't covering for him yesterday either, or not intentionally. I glance around me, regretting I ever spoke to him at all. We're standing in front of my locker, and he's blocking my way. "Now can you move? I don't want to be late."

Cory just looks at me, then turns and walks away.

                                        ଔଓ

I assume the topic is closed. But when I arrive on the set build later that day, I discover I couldn't be more wrong.

Stacks of wooden boards line the stage today, and rolled up design drawings stand against the wall. We're starting to build the set pieces.

Tammy, Zoe, and I work in the back, hurriedly photographing a few more costumes we found in storage, before we help out with building the set. Tammy hands each piece to Zoe, who stands on a stool behind a primed particle board, and Zoe dangles the garment in front of the board which serves as background, while I quickly snap a photo.

A group of actors mill around the stage, next to but separate from a larger group of crew members. They are all idle and chattering excitedly. But Mr. Miller and Skyler sit side by side in two metal chairs, working on their laptops, only looking up now and then.

What are they waiting for? I wonder. Then I realize Jordan isn't here yet. That must be why.

I see Cory scanning the aisles of the theater, as if looking for someone too. He stands by himself, his face tense. Then he looks my way, and I swiftly turn my head.

But my intuition is right on target.

The moment Jordan strides onto the stage and sets down the toolbox on the raised platform, Cory walks up to him and points at the box.

"Let me know if the lock jams *again*," he says, not loudly but not quietly either. "I'm happy to help."

The chatter on the stage cuts off as if snipped with a pair of scissors, and all the heads turn in their direction.

Jordan holds perfectly still for a moment, his eyes on Cory's face, assessing him. Then he smiles and says casually, "Thanks. I'll keep it in mind. What's your name again?"

"I'm Cory. And you are?" Cory asks.

I stare at Cory. What is he doing? He already knows Jordan's name. Everyone does. Is he trying to prove something? Or just showing off? Either way, it won't work. He'll only make enemies.

Jordan only laughs. "Right. You're new here. I'm Jordan." Then he adds in his character voice, a low, gritty growl, "I'm the Beast."

I expect them to shake hands. But they never do. They just break eye contact and walk away from each other. The strangest introduction I've ever seen, if that's what it was.

I glance past them. Skyler is still typing on their laptop, a look of total concentration on their face.

But Mr. Miller closes his laptop and crosses to Jordan. He claps Jordan on the back, beaming with his usual enthusiasm, and apparently unaware of the exchange with Cory.

"All right, everyone!" he calls out. "We're all here, and we've got a lot of work to do. So let's get started! Skyler or I will come by each group to explain the job."

Everyone gets to work, and I breathe with relief. Maybe Cory's stupid stunt was harmless. Nobody knows he opened the toolbox except Jordan and me anyway. So what does it matter?

Until Jordan's eyes brush my face. He's not smiling anymore. It matters to him.

And now he thinks I had something to do with it.

Chapter 7

The next day at lunch, Heather spots me and waves me over before I can slip past her table and make my escape. "Abby! Come sit with us."

Heather is in my Biology class, a junior like myself, and if my mom could pick a best friend for me, it would be her. I'm pretty sure she declared pre-med in kindergarten, and hasn't strayed from the rigorous and meticulously put together schedule of courses, research projects, and enrichment activities ever since. Both of her parents are cardiologists.

"Hey," I say brightly, as I slide into the chair and set down my lunch tray, although my stomach is already in a knot, and I doubt I'll be able to eat a single bite. Heather always has this effect on me. "How's it going?"

Heather doesn't waste time on pleasantries. And neither do the other three students who sit with her—two girls and a boy. They're all in my AP Biology class, and I should know their names, but I don't.

"Abby, you're taking the SATs in November, right?" Heather says. "Can I ask you a question about your strategy for the reading part?"

I swallow. This is why I avoid Heather. The SATs are two months away, and while I bought a used copy of the massive prep book, I haven't opened it yet. "Sure," I say.

"Do you read the passage first and then the statements, or do you read the statements first? Or do you just skim the passage, read the statements, and then go back to the passage and read the relevant parts?" When she's stressed or excited, Heather's speaking speed is rapid-fire, the words rattling as they drop from her lips.

I miss the second part altogether, because just then Cory appears in the hallway. He scans the lunch crowd as he walks. When he sees me, he gives a slight nod, and I nod back before I think better of it. Then panic cuts through me. What if he wants to sit here? But he doesn't turn into the cafeteria. He keeps walking toward the back of the building. Where's he going? Doesn't he eat lunch? But I'm relieved.

"Abby?" Heather prompts.

"I read the passage first," I say, grasping for the easiest answer, since I lost my train of thought.

Heather frowns. "That's what Ethan said his tutor told him to do." She glances at the boy at our table accusingly. He must be Ethan. "But the instructor in my prep class told us to read the statements first. So now I don't know what I'm supposed to do." Heather sounds genuinely upset by this.

The other girl noticed Cory, though, and she turns to me with a sudden interest, as if I was an insect she was told to dissect. Her dark brown hair is in a high ponytail that bounces when she moves. Sarah. That's her name, I remember.

"So how do you know Cory?" she asks me.

"Who?" the third girl pipes up. She has glasses and strawberry blond hair that just brushes her shoulders.

"The farm boy," Ethan cracks. "I heard they don't even have the internet. But they have cows and pigs. Can you imagine the stink?"

I flinch. So I'm not the only one who figured out where Cory lives. But I didn't expect the offhand cruelty. They don't know anything about him. It's just... mean gossip.

"Gross." The girl in glasses makes a face. Laura. No—Lauren. "Stop it. We're still eating," she scolds Ethan.

I don't point out that we're all eating today's special: ham and pineapple pizza.

"So how do you know him, Abby?" Sarah presses.

"I don't," I say, and feel a sting of shame but ignore it.

Sarah smiles as if she scored a point. "He just nodded at you."

"Isn't he doing the fall play with you?" Ethan says, and I remember he's in my AP Physics class too. Great. "It's *Beauty and the Beast* this year. Mr. Miller can't shut up about it."

Sarah chuckles. "*Beauty and the Beast?* No way. The one with the singing teapot, and the broom in love with the candle holder?"

"No, that's the Disney musical," I correct coolly. "We're doing the dramatic version."

"So what, the farm boy plays the Beast?" Lauren giggles.

"Are you kidding?" Ethan scowls at her. "*Jordan Lockwood* plays the Beast. It's the leading role."

"Ahh... Jordan." Lauren sighs, her gaze unfocused and her lips parting.

But Sarah turns to me again, sharp as ever. "Who do *you* play, Abby?"

"No one," I say. "I'm on crew. I do costumes."

A collective smirk of laughter. Then Lauren's eyes widen. "Wait. So you help Jordan change into his... whatever he's going to wear. Nice."

"I wish I had time for theater," Sarah says bitterly. "It sounds fun." And the implication is clear and cuts me deeper than all the hurtful comments before: theater is for losers with no serious ambitions—a big waste of time.

Sadly, my mom would probably agree.

Heather returns from her private ruminations. "Guys, what about the essay part? How are you prepping for that? I'm doing a full practice test every weekend, but I haven't done any essays yet."

This is it for me. I feel like a slacker, guilt burning under my skin. Maybe I shouldn't bother taking the SATs at all. I'll only humiliate myself.

I pick up my tray and get up to leave, my pizza untouched. "Sorry but I've got to go. I'll see you in class."

"If you want to do a practice test together some time, let me know," Heather offers.

"Thanks, I will." And I walk away as fast as I can without running.

Chapter 8

At least the set builds are productive—my only source of any sense of accomplishment this week, since I'm behind on everything else. By Friday, under Mr. Miller's ever-patient and encouraging supervision, and with Skyler's wicked organization skills, we've already gotten a lot done. But we have a list of set pieces to construct today, including the most important one—the staircase and the gallery room inside the Beast's castle.

Skyler showed us their designs. The finished, painted set will be breath-taking, a dark, gothic dream. But for now, the staircase and the attached platforms are only a bunch of plain wooden boards stacked around the brightly lit stage. A different group is building each part. The sound of drilling and hammering echoes through the theater. You can smell the wood.

When Mr. Miller divvies up the work, he deliberately mixes actors and crew, so we can get to know each other and bond before the show. That's what he calls it: bonding.

I work with Adam (lighting) and Harper (the

Witch) on the baluster for the staircase. Adam is gracious and easy-going, accepting whatever task he gets, even if it requires kneeling uncomfortably to drill the holes. Harper is pretty much his polar opposite, huffing and grinding her teeth when the bars don't line up.

Our bonding sounds something like this:

"All right, hold it steady," Adam says.

"I've got it," I say.

"Wait, the damn thing is off," Harper says.

I keep wishing I was in Jordan's group, or even in a group working close to him. Too bad he's at the far end of the stage. I can't even see him. A tall, skeletal frame of the staircase in progress blocks my view.

I don't think Jordan looked at me once in the last two days—not even when he walked right past me. Is he mad at me? Part of me wants to pull him aside and explain I had nothing to do with the picked lock on his toolbox. But I'd never have the nerve to approach him.

Anyway, maybe I'm only imagining that he's avoiding me. We're all busy, trying to get as much done as we can before the rehearsals begin on Monday. Mrs. Adams, the director, is back tomorrow.

Although it won't be the same after that. The set build will only be on the weekends, and cast and crew will barely interact. Two different worlds. Me in one, Jordan in the other.

And it's all Cory's fault.

I turn around to find him. And there he is, only a few yards away.

He and Neon are working on the staircase. They lift a long, heavy board, each holding one end, and smoothly lay it on the bottom rise. Then Neon holds it in place, while Cory hammers in the nails. It's just the two of them, but they work fast.

"Okay, I need coffee," Harper announces next to me. "I'll be right back." She uncrosses her long legs and gets to her feet. She's almost 6 feet tall. "You want anything from the vending machines?" She looks from me to Adam.

I shake my head. "I'm good, thanks."

"Nothing for me," Adam says, "but a break sounds good." He gets up and stretches his arms, rolls his neck. Then glances over his shoulder and saunters off down the side ramp connecting the stage to the audience seating.

Neon catches up with him, throws their arm around his neck. They walk out the side door together, laughing.

I stand up as well, trying to get a glimpse of Jordan without being too obvious about it.

Instead, I see Cory lifting another long board from the top of the stack—except now he's doing it by himself.

Don't, I urge him in my thoughts. *It's a two-person job. Wait for Neon.*

But of course, he can't hear me. He grips the board in the middle, and gets it a few inches in the air... before it slides to one side, and he has to drop it.

He never makes a noise but a grimace of pain twists his mouth, and I see him gingerly turn his hand and look at it.

I hesitate only for a heartbeat.

I get to his side in five quick strides. I try to be discreet. Something tells me he wouldn't want to advertise an injury.

"Let me see it," I whisper.

"See what?" He actually tries to hide his hand behind his back.

Is he serious? I'm in no mood for games. I reach for his wrist. "Come on, I saw what happened. Let me see your hand, Cory," I demand.

Maybe it's the sound of his name. But he stops twisting away from me and lets me catch his wrist. I lift his hand to examine it.

A whole row of splinters sticks out of the side of his palm, the skin scraped raw around them.

"Ugh!" I clench my teeth. I can almost feel the throbbing burn myself.

"I'm fine," Cory protests, and tries to pull his hand back like he's embarrassed by it.

But I don't let go of his wrist. "No, you're not. These could get infected. Come with me."

I need a first aid kit. Mr. Miller likes to keep a few of them around. I spot one on a table and pull Cory in that direction. There is a tug of resistance, but then he follows me. I grab the kit and keep walking, my fingers still closed on his wrist. We slip into the wings.

"Where're we going?" Cory says, and now there is a note of curiosity in his voice.

"Just here." We're in the back wing, mostly hidden from view, but one of the spotlights fills the nook with bright light. I point to a bench. "Sit."

"Really, it's not a big deal," Cory mutters, and again I get the sense it's not the pain that bothers him, but something else. But when I sit down, he huffs and sits down next to me.

I let go of his wrist long enough to fish out an antiseptic spray and tweezers. Then I reach for his hand again, lift my foot onto the bench, and prop his wrist against my bent knee, so I can see the splinters better.

Cory has strong fingers with blunt and not very clean nails. Is that why he's self-conscious? Or is it because of me—because he doesn't like me? Either way, I don't care right now.

"This is going to sting," I warn, and I lightly mist his injured hand with the antiseptic. I glance at Cory's face, but if it hurts him he gives no sign. He just watches me. So I spray the tweezers as well and get to work. "Hold still."

At least the splinters are big and stick out enough for the tweezers. I carefully pull them out. All but one. I can see it, but it's lodged too deep, the skin around badly scraped. I turn Cory's hand slightly, adjusting my grip on his wrist, but the tweezers won't work.

"Shoot," I groan. "I need a needle. I have a sewing kit—"

"I've got it." And Cory disengages my fingers, brings his hand to his mouth, and works the splinter out with his teeth. He spits it out away from me.

I grab his wrist again. The splinter is gone. "Or you can do that," I say, irked.

Does it mean he didn't need my help at all? He could've removed all of them himself? To think of it, he told me he was fine. I sort of forced my help on him. Why did I do that? It's my turn to feel self-conscious.

I hand him the antiseptic without looking up, my face warmer than I'd like it to be. "Spray your hand again."

He does, while I dig in the first aid kit for a band aid. The only band aid large enough comes preloaded with antiseptic ointment—and I mean, plastered with it, judging by the thickness. "Okay, more antiseptic won't hurt," I comment, as I put the band aid on. I'm starting to feel like an idiot.

I let go of his hand, drop the spray and the tweezers back into the kit, crumble the band aid wrapper and slip it into my pocket. And then I finally risk looking at him, half expecting him to be laughing. "Okay. How does it feel?"

But Cory's expression is serious, his gaze locked on my face, and I notice for the first time the specks of green in his eyes. His eyes are hazel, not brown. There is a thin scar on his upper lip, and another one above his brow. I never noticed that before either.

"Better," he says. "Thanks, Abby." And the way he says my name sends an odd rush of warmth through me.

I jump to my feet, unsettled, and Cory stands up too.

Metal clatters against the bench and hits the floor.

Cory quickly bends to pick it up and slips it back into his pocket. But he uses his injured hand and his grip is clumsy. I catch a glimpse of a circular bracelet and a short chain.

"What is it?" I ask, my throat dry and all the warmth gone from my body.

"Nothing." Now he's the one looking away. "We should get back."

But I already know what it is.

Handcuffs.

The moment we step back onto the stage, we turn

away from each other. I drop off the first aid kit on the table before hurrying to my work area. Cory crosses to the staircase he's building and picks up a hammer in his injured hand as if nothing happened.

Neon isn't back yet, and neither is Adam. Harper sits on the edge of the stage, sipping her coffee and chatting with the actor who plays Beauty's Father. Her back is to me.

I sigh, relieved no one noticed my absence, when someone touches my shoulder.

"Hey, you okay?" It's Tammy. She scans my face and frowns. "You look like you saw a ghost."

"I'm fine." I manage a smile. "Are there ghosts here? I want to meet them."

Tammy laughs. "Me too! They must have horror stories to tell." Then she takes my elbow and steers me toward her work area. "Come see the spectacular masterpiece we made. Your life will never be the same."

She's working with two actors who play Beauty's Brothers. Their names are Nate and Mike, I think. They are attaching a sixth leg to what looks like a massive table lying upside down. A platform of some sort? I'm drawing a blank.

"Behold the gallery room. Can you see the majestic splendor of it?" Nate gestures dramatically at the thick wooden legs. And when it's clear I don't, he clutches

Mike's arm as if drowning. "She doesn't. She doesn't see it. We're doomed! *Doomed!*"

Mike grips him back, swaying as if they both stood on the edge of some abyss. He stares at me beseechingly. "Take pity, fair maiden. You must look with your heart! Not with your eyeballs!" His eyelids flutter, and a real tear flows down one cheek.

Then Nate and Mike both crack up laughing.

Tammy rolls her eyes. "Actors. This is what we have to put up with." But she's grinning too.

Then I turn my head and see Jordan smiling at me.

So he's not mad at me. Maybe he already forgot the whole business with the toolbox.

My heart leaps with happiness, and I smile back. Although a sting of pain is there, too, like a splinter.

Chapter 9

Saturday morning feels like summer, which technically it still is, since it's only the middle of September. The day is warm and sunny, not a cloud in the sky. The backyard is lush with green.

I stand on the curb in front of my house, waiting for Tammy and Zoe to pick me up. I'm in a t-shirt and jeans, and the sun feels good on my face and arms.

Today, the actors have a read-through at the school, and I wish I could be there to watch. But it's literally the whole cast sitting in a circle and reading their lines, and the director wants to keep them focused and the stage quiet. So the crew are not invited.

Instead, we're going to the Mega Thrift Store in Mifflinburg to hunt for some things we still need for the play.

I don't have to wait long. Tammy pulls up in her silver Honda.

"Hey, Abby!" She turns to me with a smile as I settle in the back seat.

"Hey," I reply. "Thanks for picking me up."

"Sure." Tammy exchanges a look with Zoe, her

eyes shining with mischief, and I tense.

I'm always wary of surprises. They usually mean bad news. Like when Mom told me we're moving out of state. Or when I first learned that Dad was leaving.

"So we were thinking," Tammy continues, "we should take the scenic route. You know, past the school and through the back roads. It won't take much longer. What do you think?"

Cory.

That's the first thought that pops into my head. That's where Cory lives. Tammy must have seen me with him, and this is her way of letting me know. Or maybe she thinks I want to drive by his house.

"Why?" I ask, careful to keep my voice neutral.

Another conspiratorial look is exchanged, and now I'm really getting nervous. They're up to something. God, they don't think we're going to *stop by Cory's place*, do they? No way.

Zoe's cheeks turn pink. "Okay, don't laugh. But we were hoping to take some pictures. All these green fields! I got a new phone for my birthday, and it has a really good camera. Would you mind if we stopped?"

Photos. They want to take photos, that's all. I relax. "Oh, I don't mind at all. The weather is perfect, actually."

"Great!" Tammy exclaims, and I notice she and Zoe are wearing matching t-shirts. *I'm with her*, each t-shirt says in a cheerful cursive, and the arrows point at each other.

"I love your t-shirts, by the way," I say.

"Right?" Zoe beams. "Tammy found them online." And Tammy and Zoe do this thing when they turn to each other at the same time and kiss. And then Tammy drops her hands on the wheel, shifts into drive, and we're off.

We drive to Highway 15 and follow the school bus route from there. Except we don't turn onto the new blacktop. We stay on the main country road and keep going.

The fields are beautiful, the corn stalks a rich, vibrant green, and the occasional meadows sprinkled with wildflowers. But I'm absorbed in studying the road we're on.

The road has two lanes and isn't much wider than the blacktop that leads to the new school. There is a little more room to walk or bike on both sides, and no ditch. But the road winds like a snake, and sometimes cuts between two hills, and then the bike lane abruptly ends, blocked by steep, rocky slopes on both sides. And, of course, there are no street lights anywhere.

Is this the road Cory walks on? I can't help but wonder. All the set builds this week ended well after nightfall, but I doubt Cory asked anyone for a ride. So how did he get home in the dark?

"How about right there? Pull over!" Zoe points to a gravel patch on the side of the road up ahead, and Tammy turns into it, the wheels crunching on the stones. She parks the car, and we get out.

A meadow gently slopes away from the road toward a creek, wild grass with yellow, purple, and blue flowers. Tall oaks, maples, and pines line the edge of the creek on the other side—the edge of a small forest. Birds chirp, insects buzz, and the air smells fresh and sweet.

"I hope we're not trespassing," Tammy says.

I glance around us. We passed a dirt road a while back, but there's none nearby. No bridge to cross the wide creek either. And the gravel patch is an invitation to park your car.

"I think we're fine. I don't see any signs, and we're not going to stay long."

Zoe skips into the meadow, the phone already in her hand. She spins to me and aims her camera. "Hi, Abby!" She snaps the photo of my frowning face.

I hurry to take the camera from her. "Okay, my turn." I prefer to be the photographer.

Zoe pulls Tammy closer, and our photo session begins. My models pose in earnest for a while, and then dance, jump, and goof around in the sun, while I snap one photo after another.

Zoe wasn't lying about her camera. I'm impressed

and a little jealous. The colors are crisp and true, and there is a portrait mode that blurs the background. Nothing like my old, glitchy phone.

"Ahh, I just want to roll on that grass!" Zoe laughs. "My dog would go bonkers here."

"I want to lie down and take a nap like a cat," Tammy counters.

"Do it!" I say, suddenly inspired. "I mean, lie down on your backs. I have an idea."

I direct them to lie down with their heads close together and legs pointing in opposite directions, as if upside down, while I hold the camera over them.

I feel a bit guilty about the wildflowers we are crushing. But the pictures are going to be worth it. I can't even take the credit. It's just Tammy and Zoe. They're great together, and I'm happy for them.

For some reason, I picture Cory laying on the grass, looking up at me. I think of his eyes. I bet the specks of green in them would look even greener out here.

I blink the image away, dismayed at myself. It's not like I want Cory here. I don't. Why would I? He's rude, annoying, and just... weird.

I picture Jordan instead. His blue eyes would blaze like sapphires in the sun. I imagine lying next to him, his arm around me and our faces moving closer...

Yeah, right. Like that's every going to happen.

"We should get going," I snap, taking my frustration out on Tammy and Zoe.

They get to their feet without protest, and pick the grass off each other as we walk back to the car.

When we get back in the car, I hand Zoe her phone. She looks at it with longing, clearly tempted to see the photo roll. But she only sighs and puts the phone away.

"Later. No distracting the driver."

Tammy blows her a kiss, and we pull out of the gravel patch and get back on the road.

ଓଽଠ

The Mega Thrift Store stands smack in the center of a dying strip mall—the main attraction, twice as tall as the other shops and services around it. Three times taller if you count the corner restaurant that burned to the ground last year.

We pause in the entrance between two sets of doors, next to the shopping carts. I turn to Tammy and Zoe, and we go over the list we put together earlier. "Okay. Number one. We need men's shirts for the Brothers. Cheerful, natural colors like yellow, pea green, or salmon. Patterns are okay. Medium or large."

Zoe and Tammy nod, although they seem nervous.

"Number two. The Witch. It could be a top and long skirt, or a long dress. Dark but probably not black.

We already have the cape, and it has a purple lining."

More nods. But something is definitely going on. Are they worried about the time?

"And number three. The Beast's Servants. They're half human, half creature. We need long shirts or tunics in earth colors. Also, scarves." I put away the list and pull out the envelope from Mr. Miller. "One last thing. Here is our budget."

Tammy takes the envelope and counts the cash. "Eighty dollars? That's it?"

Zoe frowns. "That's not much."

I'm detecting a strong skeptical vibe, and I'm not sure why. "Eighty dollars is enough. You'll see." Then I get it. "You've never shopped in a thrift store?"

"Nope."

"Never."

I smile and grab a cart. "Okay. I know it's a little different from a department store. But think of it as treasure hunting."

I love thrift shopping. It takes some persistence. But if you go in with an open mind and look past the flashy junk and the general aura of melancholy hovering over the crowded racks and etched into the bare walls, you can find real treasures. I always do.

Zoe still hesitates. "But all these clothes are used. Other people wore them and sweated in them."

I sigh. "First of all, not all the clothes are used.

Some are brand new, with the original tags still attached. Second, all the clothes are washed or dry cleaned. Even the new ones. It's going to be fine. I promise. Ready?"

Tammy and Zoe lock arms and grab one cart between them. "Ready."

Inside, we find two aisles that are promising, and we start moving down them side by side. Tammy and Zoe in one aisle, and I in the other. We browse the racks as we go, the hangers scraping, although my costume crew are still reluctant to touch the clothes.

Maybe if I distract them...

"Hey, so the set build is really coming together," I say, and I'm not faking how impressed I am. "Mr. Miller and Skyler keep us on top of things."

Tammy and Zoe exchange a look, and Tammy says, "Yeah. Wait until Skyler needs something from you. If you're late, or they don't like what you did, they won't be shy about letting you know."

"I heard them yell at the new guy," Zoe says.

"Cory?" I ask, instantly alert. At least she didn't call him the farm boy.

Zoe nods. "Yeah. I guess he didn't hand in the parental consent form yet, and Skyler is in charge of them. They were really on his case."

A chill runs through me. *Parental consent form.* I handed in mine on time. But it's not Mom's signature on the form.

"Are you serious? Skyler needs to lighten up." Tammy shakes her head. "He already missed the first week of school because the school board took too long to review his paperwork. Like they were looking for a loophole not to admit him."

I stare at her. This doesn't make sense. "What do you mean, 'not to admit him'? We're a public high school. If he lives in the district, they *have* to admit him. No?"

Tammy blinks, surprised by my intensity. And honestly, so am I. Where did this come from?

"Yes, in theory," Tammy say carefully. "But in practice, there's all kinds of politics involved." She bites her lip and trails off.

"What politics?" My mind is racing. Tammy's mother is active in the PTA, so Tammy has insights into things I'm clueless about. I feel bad for pressuring her, but I need to know. "I won't repeat it to anyone," I assure her.

Tammy winces, clearly reluctant to elaborate. "Well, you know. It's the district culture. We're very strong academically. Very competitive, too. So they're not thrilled about any student who could pull down the average or... cause other problems."

I think of the picked lock on the toolbox. I think of the handcuffs.

"What other problems?" I ask, my throat suddenly tight.

"Honestly, it's really sweet of Mr. Miller to get Cory involved in theater," Zoe pipes in. "Maybe that'll help. Co-curriculars always look good in your records."

"Look at this!" Tammy yanks a green-and-orange paisley shirt off the rack and flips it on top to show me and Zoe. "Would that work for the Brother costume?" She touches the front, then checks the size. "Medium, and the fabric is nice."

I frown, my mind still on Cory. Tammy and Zoe both know something they aren't telling me. But it already feels like I'm drilling them, and it's not like I can force them to tell me. You can't force someone to trust you.

I wish I could tell them about the lock and the handcuffs. At least tell Tammy. It would be a relief to get it off my chest. But it doesn't feel right. I know they wouldn't intentionally pass it on, but if they let it slip, I can only imagine what the school gossip mill would do with the information.

I do need to know, though. I'll have to ask Cory directly. Maybe the explanation is simple, and I'm worrying for nothing.

Although what simple explanation could there be for a student carrying handcuffs in his pocket? It's odd. Worse—it conjures the worst cautionary tales and news stories about psychopaths. People who look perfectly harmless, even friendly, and then snap one day and do horrible things. Hurt or kill others. My stomach twists just thinking about it.

"You don't like the shirt?" Tammy asks. "Too busy?"

I shake myself. Looks like my tactic worked. My costume crew is thrift shopping.

"No, I like it!" I quickly say. "It's not too busy at all. The pattern will blur with distance. The rule is twenty feet. Put it in the cart, and let's keep going."

Tammy looks pleased. But I catch a glimpse of concern in her eyes.

She knows where my mind went.

Chapter 10

When I get back home, it's already afternoon, and a pile of homework waits for me. Physics, Calculus, and I really need to get started on the SAT prep. Mom gets back tomorrow.

It's a good thing Tammy took the loot from the thrift store with her, so that distraction is out of the way. We found most of what we need, but not everything. We'll have to try another thrift store some time. My costume crew sounded cautiously excited about it.

My stomach growls, so I make a quick sandwich and toss a tomato salad, adding way too much salt because I'm not paying attention.

I eat standing up while I gaze out the window. The salt tingles on my lips. Half of the backyard—the half near the house—is still washed in sunlight, the grass a brilliant green and bees buzzing around the rose bush. But the tree's shadow covers the other half, stretching and creeping closer as the sun moves lower in the sky.

I want to grab my books and a blanket and go outside. I know better, though. I wouldn't get much done. So I spread out on the kitchen table and force my mind to focus.

It's dark outside by the time I finish my Physics and Calculus homework and put the notes away. Now the thick SAT prep monster stares at me. I gingerly page through it, and my heart sinks. The previous owner wrote all over it. There are rushed circles around the answers and scribbled notes in the margins. *Dumb question. What the hell is this word? I hate this so much.*

I grind my teeth. The used book was cheaper. At least the markings are in pencil. But now I'll have to erase them.

I close the book in disgust. I need a break. I grab my laptop and open the browser. The page I want is already bookmarked.

A gallery of beautiful action shots greets me. Kids my age and slightly older rehearsing on stage, sketching designs, building sets, setting up lights, mixing sound, writing. In one photograph, cast and crew stand in a long row across the stage, grinning and holding hands as they bow for the audience after the show.

It's the online portal for The New York City Academy Summer Theater Program. I click on the image representing the Costume Design track, then on the Apply tab in the sidebar.

Your application is in progress, a message informs me, and there is my name and address, and a list of items still missing. The costume portfolio is at the top, followed by a personal essay, school transcripts, recommendation letters, and financial aid form.

This is my dream and my goal. A 6-week residential training program in the city, studying with the best theater professionals, doing what I love the most. If you get in, you get a full scholarship, including room and board. I could never afford it otherwise. But the bad news? Admission is ultra competitive. My portfolio must be outstanding and my recommendation letters stellar.

This is why *Beauty and the Beast* is so important. It's my ticket there.

A soft knock makes me jump.

I freeze, listening. There's no way I'm letting anyone in when I'm alone in the house at night.

But it's only a moth, beating its wings against the window, attracted to the light inside. The wings flutter for a few more moments, then become still.

I get up and lean close to the glass to study the moth. It's the color of ash, with wings like velvet and faint brown markings. I wish I could let it in, but it would only burn against the lamp, and I don't want it to die. I tap on the window to scare it away, but it doesn't budge, as if glued in place.

Fine. Stay there if you want. But you're not getting inside.

I close my laptop and pull the SAT prep book closer. Then I grab an eraser and get to work.

The moth is still there when I finish. I leave a small light on in the kitchen when I go to bed.

I dream of being inside the school building. Of walking and then running down the empty hallways, as someone keeps knocking on the door. I'm alone, searching for them. I try door after door, but they're all locked. Sometimes the knocking gets softer, sometimes louder, leading me in circles. But I never find the person, never learn if they wanted to be let in or let out.

☙❧

On Monday, I pack a sandwich for lunch—easy after the grocery shopping with Mom the day before—so I don't have to wait in line in the cafeteria. Instead, I perch on a bench in the side hallway, hidden from view, my lunch and water bottle in my backpack, waiting.

I need to talk to Cory.

When he finally walks by, I almost lose my nerve. He's heading for the back of the building again. Where's he going? The curiosity wins out, and I follow.

He's wearing a messenger bag today, a strange black thing with lots of open pockets. He gets to the solid back door, pushes it open, and walks out. Just like that. No hesitation, not even a glance around him. Like it's perfectly fine, and he knows exactly where he's going.

 I pause at the door. It's a utility door. Students never use it, so I don't know where it leads. I try to visualize what's on the other side. The delivery deck for the cafeteria? The trash bins?

 Oh, whatever. I push it open and step outside.

 Bright sunlight hits my face, and I shade my eyes with my hand, blinking. I forgot how sunny and warm it was. Another summer day. It feels nice.

 Off to my right is the staff parking lot, and beyond that, the soccer field enclosed by a tall wire fence. On my left is a storage shack overgrown with vines. But in front of me, past a narrow sidewalk and a short stretch of mowed grass—nothing but open fields.

 I spot Cory's leg sticking out from behind the shack. He's sitting with his back against the wall, facing away from the school.

 I take a deep breath and walk over. I make no effort to be quiet, so he knows I'm coming.

 "Hi." I step in his line of vision, not sounding nearly as confident as I hoped.

 He's eating an apple. He slowly gets to his feet. He's facing the sun, and his eyes are bright and fixed on me.

"Hi. What's up?" And he waits, studying me with a strange look on his face, wary but also curious.

The look unnerves me.

"Why don't you eat inside? Why do you come out here?" I ask, working up my courage to ask what I really want to know.

He shrugs. "Because I can. Because it's nice out." He's still watching me. "What about you? Why did *you* come out here?" he asks, and now a smile is pulling on his lips.

"I have to ask you something," I say, and my heartbeat quickens, my nerves taut as wires.

He takes another bite of his apple and tosses the core away. His eyes grow serious.

"Okay. Ask."

I need to know about the handcuffs. I think back to the set build, to the splinters in his hand, to the metal clattering on the floor. His hand seems fine now. The band aid is gone.

But another question pops into my head at the last moment. "Why did you glare at me?"

Cory's eyebrows go up. It's not what he expected. "Glare at you? When?"

"When you were walking to school in the rain. On Monday."

Cory frowns. "Wait. Were you the one who almost ran me over? Or the one who swerved into my lane to splash me?"

"No!" I protest, my face warming. Someone did that? Jerks. "I was on the bus. I didn't do anything to you."

Cory looks confused. "On the bus? Then why would I—?"

I narrow my eyes at him. "I don't know. But you looked right at me!"

Cory shakes his head. "Abby, I didn't see you on the bus. It was raining too hard." He swallows, like the next part is somehow difficult. "I would remember if I saw you. *Trust me.*"

"Why?" I snap, a second before I realize it was a compliment.

Cory's cheeks darken, and he looks down at his shoes. "Just because."

I don't know what to say to that, or how I feel about it. What am I even doing here? I should go back in, and eat my lunch inside. But I can't seem to leave.

I walk over to the storage shack and lean with my back against the wall, a few feet away from where Cory is standing. I turn my face to the sun and close my eyes.

Cory doesn't say anything, but I feel the wall give a little when he leans back against it.

I open my eyes, shrug off my backpack, and sit down, my back still against the wall. Cory's bag sits on the ground between us. A second red apple sits in the pocket.

I look over at him. "You have another apple."

Cory chuckles, a crooked smile brightening his face. He slides down until he's sitting too. He picks up the apple and offers it to me. "It's yours."

"Hmm. I don't want to steal your lunch." I dig out my lunch box and put one of the sandwiches on the paper napkin for him. "I'll trade you."

He looks at me for a moment. Then he nods. "Okay. But I'm getting the better deal here."

We trade. I set my sandwich aside and lift the apple to my nose. I inhale the sweet scent. "It smells delicious," I say. "What kind is it?"

Cory shrugs. "No idea. There was no label on the tree."

"You have an orchard on your farm?" I blurt out.

Cory shoots me a look. "Just a few trees. And it's not really a farm."

Why did I have to mention the farm? I feel terrible. "I'm sorry," I say.

"Why? Don't be. I'm not offended," Cory says. "I wish it was a farm. I wish I knew how to work the land. But I don't." He sounds sad about it.

I bite into the apple. The flesh is even sweeter than the scent. When I'm left with a slender core, I shake out the seeds into my palm and get to my feet.

Cory watches me, his eyes bright again. "What're

you doing?"

"What does it look like? I'm going to plant those. So generations of students can sneak out here at lunch and enjoy mouth-watering apples. Your anonymous gift."

Cory laughs. I've never heard him laugh before. His laugh is rough and warm at the same time, just like his voice. I like it.

I walk past the mowed grass and into the field. I pick up a short stick. Then I kneel over a spot that looks good and make a hole in the ground.

When I glance up, Cory is next to me, a bottle of water in his hand. He smiles. "Okay. One seed per hole. So they have the best chance."

I smile back and open my palm. There are three seeds. "You do it."

He plucks one seed from my hand and drops it in the hole I made, then fills in the dirt and pours water over it.

We find two more spots, a few yards away, and repeat the process, marking each spot with a small rock.

The school bell, when it rings, sounds like it's coming from miles away.

We run back to the storage shed to get our stuff. I put my sandwich back in the box, but Cory chews on his while we hurry to the back door.

I pull the handle—but the door is locked. *No way.*

We have to run to the main entrance and be buzzed in?

Cory doesn't look worried, though. "One sec." He swallows the rest of his sandwich and reaches into his pocket. A tool flashes in his fingers while the other hand grabs the door handle.

And the door opens.

"See you, Abby." Cory smiles at me when we step inside, and we part ways and rush to our classes.

But my mind swarms with questions again.

Chapter 11

After school, I take the bus home. I don't want to leave. I'd love to stay for all rehearsals, even though it'll be weeks before we finish the costumes, and I'm not really needed on the set until then.

But Mom is home this week—which is to say, at the office, but back around 5 pm—so I have to be careful. If I push my luck and stay after school every day, she might get suspicious. So I'm waiting till Wednesday. That's when Jordan's scenes start, and I couldn't miss that.

From the bus window, I scan both sides of the blacktop for Cory. But he must have stayed behind. Some students use the library computers after school, because of the fast internet. Or maybe he takes a different route back? I still have no idea where he lives. Anyway, I don't see him.

When I walk into my kitchen, a bowl of apples stand on the counter. I forgot we bought them at the supermarket. Bright red, they beckon for me to sink my teeth into them and taste the sweetness. But when I lift one to my nose, I'm disappointed. There is no scent at all, the flawless, smooth skin as odorless as wax.

I put the apple back in the bowl. I've lost all desire to eat it.

I spread out my school work on the kitchen table. I have a desk up in my bedroom, but the light is so much better here.

I'm reading the introduction in the SAT prep book when the key turns in the lock and Mom walks in. I quickly flip the pages to about one third into the book. This is about where I should be if I kept up with the prep course. I grab a pencil to make it more believable.

"Hi, honey." Mom puts her computer bag on the chair and leans over me, her lips brushing the top of my head. She scans the page I'm on and smiles. "Oh, good. So the course is helpful? Have you done a practice test yet?"

I swallow and keep my eyes down. I'm not taking the course, but she doesn't know it, and I don't think I could lie to her face. I rake my mind for answers and grasp at the first one. "I'm going to do one with Heather this week. A full practice test, and then we'll go through the answers."

Mom squeezes my shoulder encouragingly. "Great. I'm glad. It's all practice, Abby. There's no magic."

"I know."

Mom walks over to the sink and pours a glass of water. She sets it on a coaster in front of me. "And how was school today? Did you get back your Physics test yet?" she asks.

The Physics test. Another risky topic. I think I did well, but I'm never sure.

"Not yet," I say. "Mr. Miller is still grading them. He always gives a lot of feedback."

This is true. But Mr. Miller is also busy with the play, although Mom doesn't know that either. I don't think she's even aware we have a theater program in my high school. She was out of town when I went to see the show last year, and I never mention the topic. It's better if she doesn't remember I used to do theater in my previous school. The fewer questions she asks, the fewer lies I have to tell.

Mom pours herself a glass of water and turns to the window to admire the backyard.

I watch her, guilt and dread rolling in my stomach. I can't keep all these secrets forever. At some point, very soon, I'll have to tell her the truth.

But not yet. I'm not ready yet.

Mom's phone rings, and she glances at the name. "It's the contractor," she tells me before picking up. The conversation is short. "Yes... That's right... Great, I can meet you there in ten minutes."

Mom hangs up and turns to me. "I'm going to run to the duplex and talk to the contractor. I shouldn't be long."

I get to my feet. "I want to come with you."

Mom smiles, pleased but surprised. "Are you sure you have time?"

"I'm sure." I can't quite meet her eyes. "I want to be there and listen. I can take notes too." I cross to the cabinet and dig in the drawer until I find a small notebook and a pen.

"Thanks, honey. That's a good idea." Mom gives me a quick hug. "Let's go then."

She stuffs a thick folder into her large purse, and we cut through the backyard and exit through the back door in the fence into the back alley. The duplex is only two blocks away, and I can see the edge of the roof from here.

The contractor is already waiting for us outside.

I pictured a guy, but it's a woman. She's wearing a flannel shirt and dark jeans, with a tool belt around her waist and a large flashlight in her hand. Her long graying hair is in a braid down her back.

She shakes Mom's hand, and then mine, her grip firm and her skin rough like sandpaper. "I'm Amanda. Good to meet you both," she says in a smoker's voice, then turns to the house. "That the place?"

The brick duplex isn't much to look at, the gray paint peeling, the blue shutters hanging askew, and the red roof badly patched. Inside, the two house units are mirror images of each other, attached by one wall—

both two-story high, with three bedrooms, two bathrooms, and an attic.

Mom bought the property in auction when we moved here, sinking all her savings into it and taking out a large loan besides. The idea was to fix it up, rent out one unit, and live in the other. But then we discovered the busted electrical wiring, and it's been one delay after another ever since.

Mom unlocks the front door on the left, and we go in.

Amanda flips on her flashlight, and the beam is brighter than daylight. She sweeps it across the foyer and the living room, illuminating every dusty corner, missing floor board, and crack in the wall.

Mom sighs, and the brief, hushed sound conveys months of frustration.

It doesn't make sense to fix the superficial issues if the walls may have to be ripped out to replace the wiring. So we haven't been able to make much progress. But the loan payments keep coming.

"All right. Let me see the circuit board first," Amanda says, and we head down to the basement.

Mom starts down the stairs ahead of me, and I see her shudder. She's afraid of spiders, and there are lots of them in the basement. But she clutches her purse in front of her, keeping her hands close to her body, and she keeps going. She never lets her fear stop her.

Sparks of anger dance on my skin, and I think of Dad.

Neurosurgeons are in high demand, a kind of aristocracy among medical doctors, so his salary was always several times higher than what Mom made as a staff scientist, even though they worked in the same medical research center.

So when Dad left her—or left us, I guess—he offered her money. Alimony for her, and child support for me. But she refused.

She actually asked me if I wanted it. It was about two years ago, and I was fourteen.

I said no—an easy decision. I didn't want anything from him, then or now.

He's my father, and we lived under the same roof for fourteen years, but I barely knew him, even before he divorced Mom and moved to New Zealand to chair a Neurosurgery department at some big hospital and marry another doctor. I didn't know him because he was never there. Always working evenings and weekends, or away at international conferences—a stranger who on rare occasions sat down to dinner with us, his phone always by his hand.

It was always just me and Mom. Mom dropping me off and picking me up, Mom attending school events and asking if I did my homework, Mom cooking dinner and taking me to a doctor.

We don't need him or his money. Or at least I don't.

Sometimes I think Mom still loves him and misses him. She quit her research job after he left, gave up on all the projects she worked so hard to start. She never told me this, but I suspect she just couldn't bear to stay there, to work in a place where everything reminded her of him, never mind people talking behind her back. Instead, she got the travelling job, so she's always on the move, never in one place for long. And when she comes home from a trip, she always glances around with this hopeful look on her face, as if searching for someone. And I think she's searching for Dad—hoping he's back, reading a journal and drinking coffee at the kitchen table, waiting for her.

But I don't know any of this for sure. Mom and I never talk about him.

The basement is partially finished, with a cement floor, some built in shelves, hookups for washer and dryer, a large sink, and a counter. A fine layer of dust sticks to every surface.

Amanda sets her massive flashlight on the counter, like a lamp, and uses a smaller penlight to examine the circuit board. She flips a few switches on it, then pulls out a device from her belt and measures something in the nearest outlet. She tries another outlet, frowning. Then she puts her device away.

"Can you tell me what the problem is?" Mom asks anxiously. We've been through this before, and never got a straight answer.

Amanda doesn't answer right away. She scans the walls and ceiling, as if tracing the wires inside. Then she turns to Mom. "You said the county inspector flagged the electric on his report? Can I see the report? Do you have it with you?"

"Of course. I have it right here." Mom pulls out the thick folder and digs through the documents.

But I touch her arm. "No, Mom. Wait." I turn to the contractor. "We want to hear what *you* think first. *Your* professional opinion." I glance back at Mom. "I mean, that's the point, right? We already know what's in the report, and it's useless."

Amanda narrows her eyes at me, but I meet her gaze head on.

She gives a huff. But I have a feeling it's not me she's annoyed at. Something else bothers her.

She stares at the wall for a moment, thinking. Then she asks, "Has anyone offered to buy this place since you got it? Approached you to take over the loan and such?"

"I don't..." Mom starts to shake her head, then her eyes widen. "Yes!" She checks the folder again and pulls out a printed letter. "This company. Last spring. But we turned them down. We're not interested in—"

Amanda takes one look at the letter, and her eyes harden. She cuts Mom off mid sentence. "You want my professional opinion? *Sell it.* Just... let them have it."

Mom blinks. "What? Why? I don't understand. Is the damage so bad?"

Amanda shakes her head, and her expression softens. "It's not about..." She stops herself. "It'll just make your life easier. Trust me on that. Real estate is a tough business, and you're swimming with sharks here." Then she adds. "I can't help you. I'm sorry."

She picks up her big flashlight, and we follow her up the stairs.

In the foyer, Mom pulls out her checkbook, ready to write a check. "Thank you anyway. How much do I owe you?" Her hands are shaking.

Amanda winces. "Nothing. Let's say it was a free estimate. Just think about what I said." She turns off her flashlight, and instantly, it is dusk. "Sometimes we just can't win." She turns to leave.

I'm really mad now. This isn't right or fair. We need to know what the problem is before we can make any decisions, like to sell the house.

"Wait!" I step in front of the contractor, blocking her way. "If you can't help us, and won't even tell us what's going on, or *whatever*, is there someone else we can ask? Someone who will tell us the truth?"

My face burns, but I clench my jaw and stare

Amanda down.

"Abby!" Mom exclaims.

But Amanda only looks from me to Mom. "Yes. There is one person. Ask Walter Brennell."

Cory's grandfather.

I speak before I think. "We can't ask him! Walter Brennell's in the hospital. He broke his hip."

Shock registers in Amanda's face, and the lines crisscrossing her face deepen with concern. "Is that true? My God. I didn't know. That's awful."

When we step back outside and into the street, evening is falling. "Thank you again for your time," Mom says to Amanda.

The woman nods and hurries away to her truck.

Mom closes her eyes and takes a deep breath. Then she looks at me. "We have to figure out dinner. What do you feel like?"

"Let me take care of it." I'm suddenly desperate to cheer her up. "I already know what to make. But you have to stay out of the kitchen."

Mom smiles at me. "I have the best daughter in the world."

I turn away to avoid her eyes, and hook my arm with hers for the walk back.

Oh, Mom. If you only knew... I'm a terrible daughter.

Chapter 12

"Abby!"

Mr. Miller calls my name, and I walk to the front of the class to pick up my test. It's Tuesday morning. My Physics class.

"Thank you," I mutter, and I hurry back to my seat before I turn the test over to see the grade.

I got an A minus. *Good work*, Mr. Miller scribbled at the top, and he drew me a smiley face.

I slide the test and my notebook into my backpack, and I lean back in my chair, so relieved my muscles feel like cotton. An A would be better, but I was dreading a C, since I was mostly guessing on the last problem. I'll have to review the answers later. The class is almost done.

"Ethan," Mr. Miller calls. "Samir... Jada... Gwendolyn... Hajin..."

He only calls first names and never goes in alphabetical order. The last few students hurry to the front to get their tests—and then the bell rings.

"All right. Thank you, everyone, and see you on Thursday," Mr. Miller says, his hands empty. But one more test sits on his desk, and a chill goes through me when I realize whose name he never called.

Cory's.

I glance over my shoulder to where he sits in the back row. He meets my eyes, no emotion in his face. But he must be anxious too. Did he fail the test? I hope not.

"Cory, a word," Mr. Miller says.

Everyone else is gone, and I already packed my books, so I have no reason to linger. I walk out of the classroom on wooden legs and turn down the hallway.

But I can't leave. I take two steps and stop. I scoot closer to the open door, the wall hiding me from view, ready to eavesdrop shamelessly. Mr. Miller's teaching voice makes it easy, but Cory's voice is quieter and harder to hear. I sharpen my focus, desperate not to miss a word.

"Great job, Cory! Especially the last problem," Mr. Miller says, and I almost laugh in relief. *Great job?* That means an A, for sure. "Am I correct in guessing you've covered some of that material already?"

"Some of it," Cory says, and he doesn't just sounds modest but... embarrassed. "I had a lot of time."

"And what better way to spend it than on Physics?" Mr. Miller exclaims. "So what's your favorite unit so far, Cory?"

This time, there is no hesitation. "Electricity.

Electric circuits."

"Terrific! You're weeks ahead of us." I can just picture the delight on Mr. Miller's face. "So now I have to ask," the teacher continues. "Are you thinking of electrical engineering, maybe, going forward? Or maybe electronics—computers?"

"Maybe," Cory responds, but now his voice is hollow, almost dejected.

I wish I could see his face. He should be happy. It's obvious Mr. Miller thinks highly of him. I would be thrilled if it was me.

"And how is your grandfather doing?" Mr. Miller asks.

"Umm. He's going to need a hip replacement."

"I'm sorry to hear that. Give him my best, please." Mr. Miller says, then adds. "I just want you to know, Cory. If you ever want to talk, my door is always open. All right? Again, great job on the test."

"Thanks," Cory says.

Panic grips me. I can't be here. He'll know I was listening. But which way should I run? The hallway is empty on both sides. *Quick, I need an excuse.*

Too late.

Cory strides out the door. His eyes widen when he sees me. "Abby. Hey."

"Hey."

I should explain myself. Anything but: *I was*

waiting for you. Or: *I was worried.* Anything but the truth.

Cory scans my face, frowning, and the realization dawns on him. It doesn't matter what I say or what lie I try to hide behind. He's just figured it out on his own.

I brace myself for a smug or snarky comment. But he only smiles, like I handed him a gift.

"What do you have next? I'll walk with you," he says easily. "I need to learn the classrooms."

It's a weird response, but I'm grateful. "I have Calculus." It comes out as a whisper.

He nods, and his hand brushes my back, steering me in the right direction. "Second floor. I know where it is. Come on."

ಞ

I spend the last ten minutes of Calculus debating with myself if I should sneak outside and join Cory at lunch or not. A part of me definitely wants to, and that part brought extra sandwiches. But the other part is getting uneasy about the whole thing. What am I doing? I have enough going on. It would be smarter to stay away.

I'm still torn and trying to decide when the class lets out.

A section of the second floor hallway crosses above the main hallway like a bridge, with a baluster on one side and a double staircase on the other. Below, a river of students flows down the main hallway toward me.

I spot Cory among them. He walks alone, looking straight ahead. People push past him and bump into him, talking and turning and not looking where they're going. But he ignores them, not straying from his path. The river of bodies turns and floods the cafeteria, but he walks on. Heading for the back of the building.

The moment I lose sight of him, I feel a pull, as if an invisible rope was tied to my waist. And I know I'm going to follow him. Maybe I always knew I would.

He's a strange person. Always apart, somehow, even when he's in a group. Not trying to impress or compete, to win friends or claim the spotlight. He never speaks up in class, and I haven't seen him talk to anyone for more than a few seconds. Like he actually prefers to be alone, or at least it doesn't bother him.

But there are times I know he's holding back. And I can't help but wonder what he's like when the mask of calm detachment comes off—and why he needs the mask in the first place.

Maybe that's why I'm drawn to him. I can relate. I hide behind masks too.

I jog down the stairs and turn, eager to follow Cory outside, when a hand grabs my arm.

"Abby! There you are. Come sit with me." It's

Heather with her thick SAT prep book under her arm and holding her lunch tray. "Are you getting lunch?" she demands.

"It's in my backpack."

"Then come on. There's this one SAT question that's driving me crazy. I have to show you." And she pulls me into the cafeteria.

I glance toward the back of the school, and regret stings me. If I didn't waste time deciding, I'd be sitting with Cory right now.

But I need to study. Heather is doing me a favor.

"Okay. Sure," I tell her. "Where do you want sit?"

I hope Cory brought more than an apple for lunch.

Chapter 13

Beauty's dress is a dream—the dusty pink of the first dawn light, with a fitted bodice and a pinched waist that gives way to a flowing, full-length skirt, the satin layers crossing and overlapping like the petals of a rose. Pink beads pretending to be pearls adorn the short sleeves and graceful neckline, and make the skirt shimmer with every movement. Incredibly romantic.

Marie stands on a wide stool, barefoot and wearing the dress. She examines herself in an ornate standing mirror that must have been a prop for some play. Her long black hair is tied in a loose knot on top of her head, exposing the graceful line of her neck and shoulders.

It's Wednesday evening, and we're in the costume room backstage. Mom thinks I'm with Heather, doing a full SAT practice test. I plan to do one tonight, by myself, so it's not a complete lie. Or so I tell myself.

But right now, I'm kneeling at Marie's feet, pinning up two inches of the bottom layer of the skirt so it ends above her ankles. Tammy is on my right, smoothing out the fabric and making the fold, and Zoe is on my left, handing me the pins. A borrowed tree lamp illuminates our work area, the cord snaking across the floor toward the wall.

"I thought the dress would be yellow," Marie comments. She's chewing gum. "Yellow would compliment my skin tone better, no?"

"Don't be silly. This color looks great on you," Tammy responds, and I'm grateful I don't have to. I'm tired of explaining we're aiming for a timeless, dramatic love story—not the sugary musical version. A sunflower yellow dress would be just wrong.

"You really think so?" Marie doesn't sound convinced. "I never wear pink."

"I know so." Tammy's voice carries authority. "Plus, the final scene is at night, in moonlight, which means blue-tinted light. A yellow dress would look faintly green, like something rotting. Not what you want."

"Ugh." Marie makes a face. "Definitely not."

I glance at Tammy, impressed. How does she know that? Then I remember: she used to be on lights. I wonder why she switched to costumes this year. I'll have to ask her.

We finish pinning up the section of the skirt caught in the bright beam of the lamp.

"Turn, please," I say to Marie.

"You wouldn't have to do that if I could wear

heels," Marie complains, but she obediently turns a few degrees, a new section of her skirt illuminated. "Heels would make my calves look better, and they're so much easier to walk in. *I hate flats.*"

"Sorry, but you heard Skyler," Zoe pipes in. "Beauty wouldn't wear heels. And nobody can see your legs in this dress, anyway."

Tammy makes the fold, Zoe hands me another pin, and I pin another stretch of the hem on Beauty's skirt, the satin cool and smooth like rose petals under my fingers.

But my attention is divided, one ear tuned to the voices coming from the stage. I left the door to the storage room ajar for the purpose.

I can hear the director's booming voice, then Ryan's lower one. Ryan plays Beauty's Father, and they're blocking the scene where he gets lost in the woods and stumbles into the Beast's castle right now.

"Turn, please," I tell Marie, anticipation making my skin tingle.

In the next scene, Beauty's Father will pick a rose from the garden—and face the Beast's fury.

This is Jordan's first scene—the first time the Beast appears on stage—and I wouldn't miss it for the world.

In the original tale, after Beauty's Father steals the rose for her, the Beast is so enraged, he wants to kill him. But he lets the Father go free on the condition that one of his daughters willingly takes his place. And Beauty does. She comes to live with the Beast in his castle.

Afraid and homesick at first, she slowly warms up to the Beast as she gets to know him. She refuses to marry him, though. Until, her greedy sisters trick her into breaking her promise and overstaying her visit home, and the Beast, wounded by her brothers, almost perishes, thinking she betrayed him. Beauty gets back just in time to save his life, realizes she loves him, and agrees to be his wife. Their kiss breaks the witch's spell—and the Beast turns back into the handsome Prince he always was deep down.

And it all starts with a stolen rose and a raging, heartbroken monster…

When I hear Mrs. Adams again, giving director notes to Ryan after his scene, I can't wait any longer.

"Zoe, can you take over for me? Just keep pinning the hem all around." I'm already rising to my feet. "I'll be right back. Thanks."

And I rush out of the storage room. I slip into the wing of the theater, just as the next scene begins, and Ryan snips a fake rose from an unfinished set piece—and faces Jordan.

The two actors wear t-shirts and jeans; the set still looks mostly like a construction site, with plain wooden stairs leading up to a large platform, and barely sketched backgrounds; and there are no light effects yet.

But it doesn't matter. Jordan's presence works the magic.

I watch him from the wing, awed and spellbound, drinking in every expression on his face, every inflection of his voice, every gesture he makes.

The scene ends, and I hear the director's voice, but I tune it out. I'm still inside the castle, watching the Beast rage in pain at losing the one beautiful thing he owned and loved, and I wish I could run to him and console him...

"Hi," a voice yanks me out of my daydream.

I turn, blinking, to see... Jordan.

"Hi," I breathe.

He steps into the wing next to me. "How was I?" he asks.

My breath catches, heat flooding my body. *Gorgeous? Amazing?* I don't trust myself to speak. "Good," I manage.

A small voice in my head warns me to be cautious, reminds me about his bad temper. But that voice has no power over me when Jordan stands so close.

He laughs, then leans against a post, facing me. "So when do I get to transform into a horrifying monster?"

"Excuse me?"

He takes a step toward me. "My Beast mask. When

do I get to try it on?"

"Oh. Soon. I'm working on it."

He moves closer and lifts his hand to my face, fire simmering behind his blue eyes. And for a moment, I'm certain he'll kiss me. I hold my breath, my heart hammering. But he only brushes a strand of hair from my face and smiles.

"I look forward to it, Abby."

He turns his head to glance across the stage, and I reflexively follow his gaze.

Cory stands in the back wing on the other side, watching us.

My face warms, a rush of irritation mixed with guilt. Is Cory spying on me now? I wasn't really going to kiss Jordan—or rather, he wasn't going to kiss me. But what if he was? I don't appreciate the interruption.

Jordan, on the other hand, smiles and raises his hand in greeting. An odd gesture that seems friendly...

Except I see Cory's face darken and his shoulders tense.

Instantly, my chest tightens. *Was it me? Did I hurt him somehow?* The thought bothers me more than it should. I barely know him.

"You made a friend," Jordan observes, his blue eyes on me, and his upper lip curling a little when he says it.

He's not my friend, I almost say, the words ready to

roll off my tongue, the impulse to deny it automatic, like deflecting a blow. But I stop myself.

Instead, I look past Jordan, meet Cory's eyes across the stage, and speak the truth.

"Maybe. I don't know yet."

I think I see a hint of smile on Cory's face. He's standing too far to be sure, though.

But the tightness in my chest eases.

Chapter 14

The theme of the set build on Sunday is painting.

Cans of paint and metal trays with brushes and rollers sticking out of them stand scattered all over the stage, in between the set pieces and backdrops to be painted. Large sheets of tarp protect the floor from drips and splashes. A faint odor of paint drifts through the theater, but I don't mind it.

I'm just happy to be here. I missed the set build yesterday. Another pointless appointment with a contractor. This one wouldn't shut up about renovating the twin kitchens, but dodged all our questions about the faulty electric in the duplex.

And it was Mom's birthday. We celebrated with a chocolate cake and a Wes Anderson movie, and today Mom left for another business trip. Gone before I even opened my eyes in the morning. She was supposed to wake me so I could make her coffee, but she let me sleep in.

I got up twenty minutes before Tammy and Zoe came to pick me up, my hair still wet from the shower when I climbed into the back seat of the car. The set build today was rescheduled to start an hour early, so the paint has time to dry.

It's a full house, more than twenty actors and crew members, everyone with a paint brush or roller in hand. I work alongside Ryan, Marie, and Adam, painting a bunch of free-standing walls. Next to us, Tammy, Zoe, and Harper are painting the wide staircase. We're all using white paint for now—priming the pieces before they are properly painted later to look like the Beast's castle, the merchant's house, or the enchanted forest.

The stage quickly becomes crowded, with people moving about and pitching in wherever needed, and I worry I won't see Jordan again. But this time, I'm in luck. It helps that he's perched on a ladder, painting the top of a tall set piece with Luke, Mike, and Nate. I couldn't ask for a better view.

He looks utterly distracting in a simple t-shirt and sweatpants, his blond hair mussed as if he just got out of bed. My pulse quickens any time he enters my field of vision, and it takes all my willpower to tear my gaze away and get back to painting.

He wears a woven bracelet today, and a part of me wishes I was that bracelet, coiled around his wrist and touching his skin at all times—although the other, smarter part of me thinks the idea is pathetic. He may be nothing like the fantasy I have of him. Still, I can't help myself. He's gorgeous in every way, and watching him is a thrill.

But as the time goes by, I find myself looking around for Cory.

Where is he? I haven't seen him since Wednesday. He missed Physics and wasn't around for the last two rehearsals. I almost snuck out the back door to look for him at lunch on Friday, but Heather found me first. It even crossed my mind he might be avoiding me, but that's silly. Why would he avoid me? He has no reason. More likely, Cory's grandfather needed him.

Finally, I'm too restless to keep painting. I need a break to stretch my legs. I also need some air.

I put my brush down and sneak off the stage and into the main hallway. I turn to the front entrance and start walking, my steps echoing. Both sets of doors are glass, with a small foyer in between. Beyond the glass lies the empty sidewalk, bright in the sunlight. The bus loop is off to my left and the student parking lot off to my right, although I can't see them from here.

I push through the first door, and I'm about to open the second, my palm already pressed against the handle—when I see him.

Sitting on the curb off to the right, his face turned away.

I open the second door and lean outside. "Cory!"

He turns, sees me, gets to his feet and jogs over. And then he's right next to me.

"Abby."

Relief cuts through me like a knife, sharp and quick. *He's okay. He's here. I don't have to worry.*

But now I'm confused. "What are you doing outside?"

"The door was locked. Am I late?"

"About an hour. The set build was rescheduled." I'm still holding the door open, and my eyes brush the lock. "*Wait.* Since when can a locked door stop you?"

Instead of answering, Cory glances upward. I follow his gaze and spot the security camera tucked under the corner of the short roof over the entrance.

I shake my head. "It's not on. It's never on."

"It *is* now," Cory says. "See the red, slow blinking light? It's recording." Then he adds, guessing my next question. "And the other doors might trigger an alarm on the weekend."

I frown, processing the information. Why would the school turn on the security camera now? I have an uneasy feeling it's not a coincidence.

But Cory is still waiting, so I open the door wider. "Sorry. Come in. You're coming in, right?"

He holds my gaze. "If I'm still invited."

"You're definitely invited," I tell him, suddenly anxious he'll change his mind and leave. "I'm inviting you right now. Just… get in."

"Okay."

A smile lights up his face, the thin scar pulling his lips down slightly on one side—and for some reason, I want to lean in and press my mouth to this smile.

I shake the thought and look down, a flutter in my stomach, as Cory steps past me and through the door. I hope he didn't notice. He crosses the small foyer and opens the next door for me.

We start walking down the hallway, and a new worry occurs to me. "You weren't locked out yesterday, were you?"

"No. I wasn't here yesterday. I... couldn't make it. How did it go?"

"I wasn't here either," I say. "It was my mom's birthday."

Cory's face changes for a split second—a grimace like pain, there and gone.

"So what are we building today?" he asks.

His face is relaxed again, but he changed the subject. What was that about? But I don't have the nerve to ask, and we better get back to the set build.

"Not building. *Painting*," I explain. "Come on."

Work is still in full swing when we step on the stage. I catch a few curious looks but ignore them.

I glance around for Mr. Miller, so he can give Cory a job, but I don't see him. The work flow is more freeform anyway, with no stable teams. It looks like my own team—Marie, Ryan, and Adam—have finished priming the set walls and scattered to join other projects. I spot more color paints in use now, instead of just white, and some groups are painting the backdrops.

"Abby! Over here!" Tammy waves to me from the back corner. "You want to paint the forest with us?"

It's sweet of Tammy, but the forest backdrop is already pretty crowded, with several people working elbow to elbow. There's room for maybe one more, but that's it.

I turn to Cory, reluctant to leave him behind. "You want to paint some trees?"

He smiles. "You go ahead."

"Okay."

I'm already turning away when a familiar voice pulls me back.

"You made it!"

Jordan walks up to us, smiling. I forgot all about him. How strange.

He glances at me, then his gaze locks on Cory.

"I did. Thanks. You need any help?" Cory doesn't return the smile.

And I see why. Up close, there's nothing friendly about it, the blue of Jordan's eyes cold like steel. He scowls at Cory, his voice low. "*Help from you?* No. I don't." Then he says loudly and brightly, "Mike might need your help. *Mike!* Where you at?"

Unease sweeps over me. What's gotten into

Jordan? Is this about the toolbox? Is he still mad at Cory about *that?* Nobody even knows Cory picked the lock except the three of us.

Mike comes running, a paint brush and small can of paint in hand. "Yo! What's happening?" He sees Cory and grins. "Cory! It's Cory, right? Come on, man. I need your opinion about something. Help me out?" He glances at Jordan, then turns on his heel and heads for the far corner of the stage.

"Sure." Cory throws me a reassuring look and follows him.

But I don't like it. Something is wrong. I hurry after them.

Mike stops in front of a finished backdrop. I take one look at the painting—and gasp.

It's an old farmhouse kitchen with a cast iron wood stove, copper pots hanging over a wooden table, and a view of a barn and rolling hills in the window.

Mike turns to Cory. "So what do you think?" He cups his chin in his hand thoughtfully as he studies the backdrop, and I realize he's acting. It's a stupid prank. *I knew it.*

Cory glances at him, and I know he's figured it out too. But he's amused instead of upset. "Why are you asking me? I'm not an artist."

It gets eerily quiet on the set, and all the heads turn in Cory's direction.

"Well." Mike pauses like an actor who forgot his lines and has to improvise. "We are aiming for...um... a realistic and accurate depiction of... um... this type of dwelling. And you have the benefit of... um... first-hand experience."

I clench my teeth. I could just slap him. Although this wasn't his idea. I can tell by how his eyes nervously dart around. Someone put him up to it.

I glance over at Jordan. Was it him? I can't quite believe it.

Smirks and whispers travel across the stage.

If I was in Cory's place, I'd be mortified with so many people watching me. And I can tell he's uncomfortable too. But he plays along and examines the painting. "Okay. Let's see. It's very well done. Great detail. But there's one thing."

Mike eagerly leans closer. "What is it?"

"The cast iron wood stove."

Mike stares at the painting in feigned horror. "What about it?"

Cory shakes his head. "Just look at it. Where does the smoke go? *It's missing a chimney.*"

I stifle a laugh. It's the perfect punchline, and the joke is on Mike.

Several people must agree because they chuckle and applaud. "Nice," someone comments.

Then Skyler steps up to Cory, and a hushed silence

falls over the stage again.

"I painted it," Skyler says, and a chill goes through me, even though it's not me who just criticized their work in front of everyone. Skyler just isn't someone you want to mess with.

Mike discreetly slips away. But Cory just stands there, waiting.

Skyler studies the backdrop for a moment, their mouth a harsh line, before they turn to Cory. "You're right. It needs a chimney. Nobody else noticed. Thanks." Then Skyler turns and frowns at everyone else. "Can we get back to work now?"

A loud chatter fills the theater as people grab their brushes and rollers and get back to painting.

I catch Cory's eye and smile at him. He just gave them something new to talk about, maybe even won some friends, and I'm glad.

But Cory's expression is grim.

Chapter 15

After the last class period on Monday, I stand off to the side of the main hallway, letting the river of students rush past me. Some people are half running, the rubber soles of their shoes squeaking urgently, others trace a wavy path. A few even use their elbows to get to the door faster. They're all in a hurry to bust out of the building—to get to their getaway cars and buses, and make their escape. Really, you'd think they were locked up in here for weeks instead of hours. It must be the nice weather outside.

I wait until the main hallway empties before heading in the opposite direction—away from the front door and toward the cafeteria. I have two hours to finish homework before the rehearsal.

Mrs. Adams, the director, wants to repeat one scene from Friday—the Beast courting Beauty—because *the emotions need work,* as she phrased it. Honestly, I'm not sure what she meant. The scene broke my heart just fine the last time. But if she wants Jordan to repeat it, I'm thrilled to watch it a hundred times more.

I turn into the empty cafeteria, digging in my backpack for a cereal bar I clearly forgot to pack. *Shoot.* My stomach is already growling. Maybe I could get some pretzels or chocolate peanuts from the vending machine to carry me through.

"Abby!"

Tammy and Zoe catch up with me.

"Guess what arrived yesterday?" Tammy's eyes shine with excitement.

My heart thuds. "The Beast's mask!"

"Yes!"

We used Tammy's address when we ordered the mask from a theater costume vendor online. I told her it's because the mail person leaves our packages on the doorstep, since we have no real porch, and I don't want the mask to get damaged if it rains. But, of course, that's not the main reason. I don't want to risk Mom finding the package. Or Mrs. Smith, for that matter. My neighbor is probably nosy enough to "rescue" the package no matter what the weather and "accidentally" open it to peek inside. The woman should have been a spy instead of a pharmacist.

"Hold on. It arrived *yesterday?*" I frown at Tammy. "Why didn't you tell me earlier?" I passed her in the hallway at least twice. To think of it, she wore a mischievous grin both time. I should've known something was up. Doesn't she know I've been waiting for this package on pins and needles?

Tammy shrugs, unrepentant. "You had the Calculus test today. I didn't want to sabotage you."

My Calculus test? I'm stunned. How did she know about that? I mean, I probably whined about it a lot, but I didn't expect her to pay attention or care. And she's absolutely right: I'd be hopelessly distracted if I knew the mask was here.

The whole thing is so thoughtful and considerate that I don't know what to say except a glum and awkward, "Right."

Tammy picks up on my mood, and worry crosses her face. "How did the test go? Did you do okay?"

I blink at her, beyond embarrassed now. She knows me too well *and* she cares how I did on the test. I guess it's been a while since I had a friend. How pathetic is that?

"It went fine. I'm just…"

I don't know how to finish that sentence. *Surprised that you care? Grateful for your friendship? Shocked that you know me so well you practically saved me from myself—because I would've totally bombed Calculus picturing Jordan in the mask?* Any line I come up with makes me cringe.

"So where is it?" I ask instead.

"Safe in my car," Tammy says.

Impatience stings me. I thought she had it in her

backpack, but the package must be too big. I turn, ready to head out. "Let's go open it then!"

But Tammy and Zoe exchange an uncertain look. "In the parking lot?"

"Sure, why not?"

Tammy pales. "Um... Some kids are still hanging around. Someone might see it."

"So?"

"It's bad luck!" Zoe shivers. "No outsiders can see the costumes before the play—except *on the actors*. Or the show will flop."

I almost roll my eyes at the silly superstition. But we had a handful of similar magical rules at my previous school, and some theater people took them pretty seriously. It's not something you can argue about anyway.

"Let's go to my house then," I offer, impatient to tear the package open and see the mask. "My mom is on a business trip, so no one will bother us."

Tammy and Zoe brighten.

"Really? Awesome. I'd love to see your place!"

"I can drive us!"

See my place? I swallow, instantly regretting my offer. "Okay, but just so you know... We're in a rental, and it's nothing fancy... It's pretty small and dull, actually..."

It's too late to take it back, though. We're already

walking to the door.

"No worries," Zoe chirps. "My room is always super messy, and I don't even notice. It's like a selective blindness or something."

My room. God, did I even make my bed? Nope, I didn't. Best to not even go up there. We're going to stay in the kitchen.

"I want to see your sewing machine and your whole setup," Tammy says as the three of us jump into her Honda. "I wish I knew how to sew."

I glance around me, but the back seat and the floor of the car are empty. The package must be in the trunk. Then Tammy's comment registers.

"Oh. I'm happy to show you." Of course, my Singer is tucked away in the back staircase together with the costumes I'm working on and all my other sewing projects. How am I going to explain that? Maybe just: not enough closet space? That's true enough.

Tammy executes a flawless parallel parking maneuver and retrieves the package from the trunk. The box is bigger than I thought. I dig out my house key and we step into the kitchen.

My costume crew look around, and I expect disappointment when they see the lackluster cabinets and old appliances, the uneven floor boards and unmatched chairs. But the sunlight falling through the window bathes the room in a golden light, and my guests seem enchanted.

"This is amazing." Tammy sighs. "I love old houses."

"And your backyard!" Zoe exclaims. "Look at those vines! And the roses! Magical."

My attention is on the package in Tammy's hands. I drop my backpack on the chair, and grab a pair of scissors from the drawer. "Let's see the Beast's mask."

I open the package—and shudder.

The Beast's face stares back at me, terrifying and almost alive. Rough, brown fur stretches over the harsh, chiseled lines of the brows, nose, and jaw. Thick lips curl in a snarl, and twisted horns complete the effect. The eyes are empty holes, but it's not hard to imagine the bright blue of Jordan's eyes flashing through them.

I pick up the mask with trembling hands, my heart hammering.

Zoe swallows. "Wow. It's... intense."

"Yeah." Tammy nods. "Definitely a new look for Jordan. Nobody will recognize him."

Jordan.

I turn the mask in my hands, examining it from all sides. A hidden zipper splits the back in two all the way to the top of the head. I work it open and inspect the inside, brushing my fingertips over it. The underside of the fake fur is scratchy, and hardened glue around the cutout eyes juts inward.

I sigh. It's my job to make sure the costume fits the actor and isn't too uncomfortable on stage. But this thing is hot and itchy, and I'm pretty sure it'll be hell to perform in.

"Touch it." I show the inside of the mask to Tammy and Zoe, and they gingerly obey.

Zoe makes a face. "Ugh. This is awful. I'd go nuts if I had to wear it."

Tammy turns to me, frowning. "What do you want to do? It's the best we could find."

I bite my lip. If we return it, the replacement could be even worse. And the mask isn't something I can build from scratch. Not to mention, we're running out of time.

"I can fix it," I decide. "Hold on. I have an idea." I set the mask back on the table, cross to the fridge, and unlatch the door to the back staircase.

Tammy and Zoe are instantly behind me. They peer inside the dark space, giddy with excitement.

"Oh, my God. What's this? You have *a secret staircase?*"

"This is *so cool*. Where does it go?"

I flick on the single light and grab the box with my sewing machine and a bag of scrap fabric. "It goes up to my room, but… I only use it for storage."

Zoe points at the garment bag hanging on a hook.

"Is this Beauty's dress? Is it done?"

"Yes. We should take it back to the school." I finished sewing in the hem last night.

I brace myself for awkward questions as I retrieve my Singer from the box and set it up on the kitchen table, next to the Beast's mask—*Why do you hide your sewing machine in the staircase? Do you do all your sewing in the kitchen, so you have to set up your work space each time?*—but Tammy and Zoe only watch me with bright eyes.

I find a scrap of silk the size of a small towel and smooth it inside the mask. "What do you think? I'd cut out the eyes, of course."

Zoe caresses the silk. "So much better! Jordan will *love you* for it!"

I gulp and look down, my face hot. But she didn't mean anything by it.

Tammy takes the mask from my hands, smiling. "This could work, Abby." She lifts the silk and prods the solid, snarling lips with her finger. "And maybe you could cut a slit for the mouth in the mask. He'll have a microphone. But this would make it easier to breathe."

I nod, smiling back. "You're right. I can definitely do that."

Now that we have a plan, we all relax. Zoe eyes the Singer on the table like it's a cute but wild animal.

I laugh. "Do you want to try it? It won't bite."

Zoe's face brightens, her freckles standing out. "Are you sure? I don't want to break it."

"You won't. Don't worry." I dip my hand in the scrap fabric bag and pull out a square of blue cotton. I fold it in half inside out. "Pull up a chair and let me show you a simple stitch."

I explain the basics and slowly run the machine to demonstrate, first by hand, then lightly using the pedal. I let Zoe finish the other two sides by herself while I instruct her on each step. She's a natural, gently guiding the fabric without bunching it up or stretching it. She's done in three minutes. I cut the thread, turn the fabric the right side out, and hand her the finished project. "Congratulations. You made a pocket."

Zoe squeals with glee. "I made a pocket!" She gets up and offers her seat to her girlfriend. "Tammy, your turn!"

Tammy slides into the chair, grinning, I grab two pieces of cotton this time and slap them together, and we get to work.

Tammy is sewing the second side of the pocket, when a sharp knock on the door makes all three of us jump.

I leap to my feet, my chair scraping the floor behind me, and Tammy slams on the Singer's pedal, but thankfully lets go of the fabric before the stitching needle catches her thumb.

"Who is it?" Zoe whispers.

"I have no idea." Mom, back early from her trip? Who else would come to this door instead of the front one? At least the blinds on the side of the alley are tightly closed. I glance at all the incriminating evidence, and panic licks my spine. "She's going to know," I moan.

Before I can move, Tammy grabs the Beast's mask and Zoe the box, and they slip into the back staircase and pull the door behind them. I'm about to protest I meant the sewing machine, not them, but there is another knock, and I reflexively close the latch.

I open the kitchen door a crack, my heart in my throat.

Mrs. Smith clutches a small empty jar.

"Hello, Abby. Can I bother you for some sugar? I'm having my afternoon coffee, and I ran out."

I stare at her for a moment, my knees weak with relief that it's not my mother. "I'm sorry. But we don't have any sugar. We don't use it." I shift my body to block her view of the table.

A mistake. Mrs. Smith narrows her eyes and cranes her neck to see what I'm hiding. "You don't use sugar? Even when you bake?"

"We... don't really bake," I confess, my face warming. She must see the sewing machine.

"I see," Mrs. Smith says, and I start to close the

door—when she nudges it open and steps inside, handing me the empty jar. "I'll take some milk then. You must have that. I know your mother takes it in her coffee, as do I."

Irritation flares in me, but I bite my tongue. The last thing I need is to give this woman a reason to chat with Mom when she gets back.

"We do have milk, yes. I'll get it for you." I turn on my heel and hurry to the fridge, watching her from the corner of my eye.

Mrs. Smith circles the kitchen table, then leans over the sewing machine and inspects Tammy's ruined project. "You're learning to sew. Hmm." She doesn't hide her skepticism.

I pull out the milk container and fill the jar, splashing some on the counter in my haste. The sooner I give her what she wants, the sooner she'll leave.

"Here you go. Or would you like the whole container? I don't really need it."

But Mrs. Smith ignores my outstretched hand, her eyes narrowing again. "Your mother is away, then. You're all by yourself. For how long?"

I bristle. There's no law against someone my age staying home alone, and I know what I'm doing. But some people frown on it, and others are just bored and looking for an excuse to stir trouble.

"Just a few days. Actually, I'm supposed to call her

right now." I smile, hoping my neighbor takes a hint.

But Mrs. Smith strolls around the kitchen, her sharp eyes taking everything in—then she suddenly turns to me.

"You are *being careful*, I hope?"

"What?" I burst out laughing. I can't help it. Does she mean safe sex and condoms? Where did that come from? I've never been on a date or had a boyfriend yet—only secret crushes.

But Mrs. Smith frowns. "What's funny? You're cooking on this horrid old thing." She points to the oven. "Gas stoves should be banned! You need to check and make sure that each burner is off before you leave the house or go to sleep at night." She glances up to inspect the ceiling. "At least your smoke detector is working. Fire is no laughing matter, young lady."

She snatches the jar with milk from my grip—when a noise makes us both freeze.

A shuffling step and a muffled groan inside the staircase.

Mrs. Smith's gaze swings in that direction—then back to my face. "What was that?"

"Nothing. I didn't hear anything." But my blush betrays me. For someone who lies a lot, I'm really not good at it.

"I see. Well. Thank you, Abby." A smile lights up Mrs. Smith's face, her eyes shining like a fox's when it spotted its prey. But she finally turns to the door and walks out.

I open the freezer and put my face in, the cold air blissful on my hot skin. Then I unlatch the back staircase. Tammy and Zoe spill out of it, giggling.

I glare at the gas stove like it has Mrs. Smith's face on it, and I remember I'm starving. "Are you hungry? I could make ramen before we go back for the rehearsal."

"Yes, please!" and "I love ramen" are the replies.

I turn the burner on high out of sheer spite, the flames blackening the pot I'll have to scrub later. But I feel a little better.

Chapter 16

We leave the Beast's mask behind when Tammy drives us back, since I want to make the improvements before presenting it to Jordan. But Beauty's dress is finished, so we take it with us. Zoe gestures me into the front seat while she climbs in the back. She holds the dress lovingly the whole time, the hanger in her lap and the puffed up garment bag stretching across the seat like some sleeping fairy creature.

We make it back to school a good twenty minutes before the rehearsal time, but muffled voices drift into the hallway from the theater.

I feel a pinch of regret. I don't want to miss anything. "Do you hear this? It's coming from the stage. Did they start early?"

Tammy cocks her head, listening, then her face brightens. "It's Neon and Patricia!"

The understudies for the two leads—the Beast and Beauty. "They rehearse on their own?"

"You bet. They have to learn all the scenes. You should go watch." Tammy gives me an encouraging smile and points to the theater entrance. She really knows me too well.

"They're really good." Zoe waltzes with Beauty's dress pressed to her front. "It's like a different play when they perform it."

A different play? That piques my curiosity. She says it like it's a good thing, but how could that be if Jordan is already the perfect Beast?

"I won't be long," I promise. We're supposed to check the head coverings, but my crew can start without me.

I crack open the door and slip inside the theater. The house is dark, the only light directed at the two actors on stage. I tiptoe to a middle row, slip into a corner seat, and settle down to watch.

Zoe was right—the acting is great.

Neon and Patricia are both in jeans and t-shirts, her long brown hair gathered in a loose braid. They have no microphones, and the tight spotlight on them plunges the rest of the stage in inky darkness, the set design as simple as it gets. But within moments, I'm pulled into the scene, my body shivering and my eyes stinging as I'm in turn the Beast and Beauty, Beauty and the Beast, caught up in their strange, heart-wrenching courtship.

I also see what Zoe meant about this being a different play when the understudies perform it. Patricia's Beauty moves and speaks with a quicker, sharper rhythm than Marie's Beauty. But the biggest difference is the Beast. Neon's character has no simple gender, just like the actor, and their depth comes from pain and longing instead of rage. I've never imagined the Beast this way, but it works.

In fact, I'm so moved by the scene I almost forget myself and applaud when it's over, clenching my hands together to muffle the first, impulsive clap.

But I'm not the only audience. As soon as the actors stop, the spotlight moves up and down, the colors shifting and blending artfully. It's Adam—using the lights to cheer for Neon.

Neon blows a kiss toward the tech booth up in the balcony, their face aglow with happiness. They and Patricia join hands, and both actors take a deep bow in front of the dark theater.

Then someone really is clapping—each clap loud and sharp like the blow of a hammer.

"Very nice," a voice says, and Jordan saunters onto the stage.

"Thanks," Neon says brightly.

But Jordan ignores them, and walks up to Patricia. "How would you like to run through the scene with me?"

Patricia flusters, her confidence a moment ago vanished, the willful, self-possessed Beauty reduced to an awkward, star struck fan. "I… Sure… I mean if you have time… That would be great…"

Neon stands frozen, as if uncertain what to do. No—as if waiting for Jordan to acknowledge and include them.

But when Jordan finally turns to them, disdain laces his voice. "Do you mind? *You're in my way.*"

I suck in a furious breath—and at the exact same moment, someone huffs angrily behind me.

I spin around, squinting at the dark rows of seats, and spot a familiar silhouette in the back row, off to the side.

Cory.

How long has he been here? Is that where he hangs out before the rehearsals? Alone in the dark, empty theater? I guess it's another thing we have in common.

Neon still doesn't move, their jaw set in silent defiance.

Jordan advances a step, and I watch with disbelief as his hand rolls into a fist. Is he acting? He must be. "Maybe you didn't hear me…"

"You don't have to be rude," Neon says.

"*Boo!*" Jordan leaps forward, and Neon stumbles back and nearly falls, startled.

The spotlight over the stage flashes red with warning.

Jordan looks up at the tech booth, shading his eyes with his hand. "Adam? I liked the previous light better. Is there a problem?" He's smiling but his voice is all ice.

Neon looks up at the balcony too and shakes their head. *Don't.*

The flashing red light continues for another moment—Adam venting his anger and punishing Jordan like some invisible god of violent weather. But he must know it's pointless and Jordan doesn't care, because the regular spotlight returns.

I watch Neon hang their head and walk off the stage in defeat.

Jordan turns to Patricia with a brilliant smile. "Okay, Beauty. Let's take it from the top. Ready?"

They start rehearsing the scene, and my stomach turns in disgust. The changed emphasis on certain words, the faces too close together, the unnecessary touching.

Jordan is flirting—I'm sure of it.

"Abby?" a voice whispers.

I spin to my right to see Cory. He sits in the row behind me, leaning forward, his crossed arms resting on top of the third chair from me. When did he switch seats? I didn't hear a thing.

"If you don't want to be seen, you better go. They're about to turn on the lights."

How does he know…? But there's no time. I take his advice and slip to the entrance in the back. I'm barely through the door when the lights brighten and I hear voices and footsteps—the actors and set crew arriving for the proper rehearsal.

I stop the door with my toe, careful to stay out of view while I listen in, a morbid curiosity coursing through me.

"Jordan!" The director's voice rings with praise. "How incredibly sweet of you to rehearse with Patricia!"

"Not at all," Jordan responds, and it's scary how convincing he sounds, an even mix of surprise and modesty. "I should be thanking her. She's helping me become a better actor."

What? They barely started the scene.

And then it hits me—Jordan timed it that way. He never cared to help Patricia, or even to finish the scene. He just wanted everyone to see how kind and generous he was—the main lead rehearsing with a humble understudy.

When in truth, he acted like a selfish and cruel asshole.

I remove my toe and let the door close behind me, cutting off the lights and muffling the voices. I march down the hallway and push through the door that leads backstage. I don't feel like watching the rehearsal anymore.

I'm about to head straight to the costume room and busy myself with the work. But a question occurs to me. Something I need to check.

I slip into the back wing and cautiously peer out. Not at the stage, though. I look right past Jordan and Marie and scan the audience.

Cory sits in the middle of the theater, clearly visible in the half lights.

I knew it.

He warned me to leave—but he stayed put. Now Jordan knows Cory saw him barge in and kick out Neon. Is that what Cory wants? Why? I can't decide if it's brave or stupid.

I spin around and hurry to the costume room, away from both of them.

Chapter 17

I decide to skip the rehearsal on Tuesday too, and on Wednesday after that. That makes three rehearsals I missed in a row.

When I first tell Tammy and Zoe I'm taking the bus home and won't need a ride, they stare at me, clearly worried. The classes just ended, and we stand outside.

"Are you sick?" Tammy scans my face as if looking for symptoms.

"You do look a like flushed," Zoe observes. "Do you have a fever? Headache? Sore throat?"

I look a little flushed? As soon as she says it, my cheeks warm. "I'm not sick. Really. I just want to finish the mask for the Beast." But Tammy and Zoe are still frowning, unconvinced, so I sigh and add sheepishly. "And I have a ton of homework and SAT prep to do. It's such a lame reason, I know."

That does the trick. My costume crew mates radiate sympathy. Tammy puts her arm around me, and Zoe squeezes my hand.

"It's not lame. This stuff is important too."

"Seriously. Don't beat yourself up. There's plenty of rehearsals left."

"Thanks, guys." I'm genuinely touched.

I don't know which of us moves first, or where the force vectors originate, but we all lean in and pull closer—and end up in a group hug. My first ever.

I disengage myself awkwardly. "Sorry, I'm going to miss the bus…"

"Go, go!" From Tammy. "Let me know if you need anything."

"Take care, Abby." From Zoe. "Don't forget to hydrate!"

I'm not sick, I want to protest, but I bite my tongue. It doesn't matter. Kindness is still kindness, and I'm both grateful and a little overwhelmed. I wave to them and run for the bus.

CR80

The real surprise awaits me when I run into Jordan just before the rehearsal on Thursday—after my return from the brief, self-imposed banishment.

"Abby." Jordan intercepts me backstage on my way to the costume room. "We missed you at the last three rehearsals."

I blink, insanely flattered. I didn't think he'd even notice my absence. But he not only noticed—he kept track.

"Oh." I lift the box I'm holding. "I was working on your mask. It's finished. I have it right here."

"Really?" Jordan glances at the box and smiles.

But his eyes quickly swing back to my face, and he's watching me a little too carefully, and an alarm goes off in my head. *Caution.* Did he really miss me? Or is he trying to find out about Monday—if I was in the audience when he barged on the stage to insult Neon and flirt with Patricia, and then acted all perfect in front of everyone else?

He must know Cory saw him. Cory made sure of that.

And to think of it—so did Adam. And Neon. And Patricia. How come Jordan didn't hold back when they were watching? Doesn't he care what they think of him? Does he split people into two groups: one group he wants to impress—and the other he can treat like dirt, because they don't matter to him?

I wonder which group I'm in.

Then I think of Cory. And suddenly I understand him in a whole new light.

Maybe the whole point of Cory's stunt on Monday—and the ones before that, all the way back to the picked lock on the toolbox—was to call Jordan out and to defy him. It was like Cory telling Jordan again and again: *I see what you're doing. But you can't put me in a box—I'll smash out of it. If you don't respect me—watch out. I'll fight you and annoy you and get in your face until you do.*

"...Abby? Did you hear me?"

"I'm sorry, what?" I look up from the box in my hands. I was staring at it.

Jordan tosses his blond hair impatiently. "I said I want to wear the mask in the next scene. Surprise Mrs. Adams."

I gulp, my thoughts racing. "What about the mike? You don't want to test it first?" But I set the box down on the floor, open it, and take out the mask.

"Right. The mike." A guy on set crew walks out of the wing, and Jordan snaps his fingers to get his attention. "Hey! Get the sound girl. I need a mike. Tell her to bring it back here ASAP."

The crew guy frowns, but he turns on his heel and takes off. I make a mental note to learn his name. I'm ashamed I don't know it.

Jordan turns to me in the same bossy manner. "Where's—?"

"Here." I hold up the mask, my stomach in a nervous knot. What if he doesn't like it? What if I made it worse instead of better? I modified it quite a bit.

But Jordan's eyes widen in awe, and a low whistle escapes his lips. He grabs the mask and examines it. "Damn. This in incredible."

The flattery sends a jolt of pleasure through me, even though Jordan seems no longer aware I'm here. All he sees is the mask, and he's staring at it with such intensity, I half expect him to sink his teeth into it and take a bite. But maybe that's why I believe it more than his earlier compliment.

The sound tech comes running toward us, a microphone in hand.

She glances at the mask in Jordan's hands and gasps. "Wow! Is this...?" She turns to me. "Great job, Abby!"

I'm flattered all over again—and mortified that she knows my name but I don't have a clue about hers. "Thanks. We got it online. I just made some changes. I'm sorry—remind me your name."

"I'm Natasha." The sound tech smiles, switches the mike she's holding from hand to hand, and we shake.

"Can you hurry up?" Jordan cuts in. "I want to wear the mask for this scene, and she's going to call us any second."

Natasha frowns. "Did you already test it?" She looks at me, and I shake my head.

"No time. Just hook me up. Come on."

"Okay, boss."

The mike is at the tip of a bendable wire that loops behind the ear before turning into a thin cable that attaches to the battery-powered transmitter. Natasha secures the mike behind Jordan's ear and clips the transmitter to the waist of his jeans, over his lower back.

Jordan hands me the mask. "Help me put it on." At least he didn't snap his fingers at me.

It takes a few tries, but Natasha and I get the mask on and zipped up in the back with the mike still in place inside it. It doesn't help we're rushing, dancing around Jordan and reaching past each other, while he keeps snapping at us to hurry.

"How does it feel? Can you breathe okay?" I get goosebumps just looking at Jordan's face—or the Beast's face.

Jordan turns his head left to right, moves it up and down, like a fighter impatient to get into the ring. "Fine. How's the mike?"

Natasha grabs the back of his jeans and flips a switch on his transmitter. "You're turned on. But I've got to get back to my board to put you through to the speakers." And she takes off for the sound desk, which sits on a raised platform in the back of the audience.

You're turned on? I repress a giggle. I know she meant the mike, but still.

"Act one, scene four!" The director booms. "Beast! Beauty! We're ready for you."

"Showtime." Jordan brushes past me and strides onto the stage, his head bowed.

No *thank you*, no *excuse me*. Like I'm not a person—but only a pair of hands to assist him. So much for missing me.

He stops dead center on the stage, stretches his arms, and looks up.

The audience is a handful of actors and crew, but their reaction is a collective gasp, followed by hooting and applause.

"*Ahhh!* The Beast! My Beast!" Mrs. Adams screams with joy. "Perfect. Just perfect. I love it."

Then Jordan speaks—but I have no idea what he says because his words are obliterated by a shrill, hair-raising shriek that dissolves into banging knocks and hissing static. Even with my hands pressed over my ears, it's the worst, most painful noise I've ever heard, and I feel lightheaded.

Skyler storms onto the stage, gesturing like they're cutting their own throat. "Cut his sound!"

And someone—it must be Natasha—mercifully does.

The silence is bliss, even though my ears are still ringing. I want to sink to the floor, stretch flat on my back, and close my eyes. But one look at Jordan, and shock clears my head.

He moved to the far corner of the stage, his back to the director, and is yanking at the mask angrily, trying to get it off. What's he doing? The zipper is still closed.

I rush toward him and grab his arms before he can tear the thing apart.

"*Stop!* Let me help you!"

I manage to open the zipper before Jordan grabs the bottom of the mask and rips it off his head. He's furious, his face red and curses dropping from his lips.

Natasha races onto the stage and catches the mike that swings loose before Jordan can step on it. "*Whoa!* Watch out."

The wire is still attached to the transmitter clipped to the back of Jordan's jeans, and it stretches dangerously when he wheels around to her. "You messed me up," he snarls, keeping his voice low. "It's your job to get the stupid mike to work. You got it?"

Natasha's lip trembles and tears shine in her eyes. "It's not my fault. I told you we should test it first. Didn't I?" She looks to me for support.

"You did." And so did I, although I don't mention it. "Don't worry. We'll figure it out."

"Jordan?" Mrs. Adams calls out. "Is everything okay?"

Jordan scowls at me and the sound tech. "Fine. Later."

He marches off to the front of the stage and addresses Mrs. Adams, his voice considerably sweeter. "Sorry about that. A technical glitch. The mask isn't quite ready yet, so I won't wear it for the scene. I just wanted to show it to you. I hope that's okay."

The director waves it off. "Of course, of course. Let's focus on the performance. Places, please."

What? The mask isn't ready? I stare daggers at Jordan's back, an ache in my chest.

I can't believe he pinned the blame on me. Why would he do that? Why not tell the truth and admit we should've tested the mike beforehand? It wouldn't cost him anything. The director already knows and adores him.

But I badly need to make a good impression—or I can kiss her recommendation letter goodbye.

Chapter 18

That night, a noise startles me awake. I jolt upright in bed, my heart racing, scenes from a restless dream scattering away before I can make sense of them. I grab my phone from the night stand and freeze, holding my breath and listening. Was it the door? Is someone in the house?

But it's only the blowing wind. The strong gusts pummel my bedroom window like angry fists. The glass shakes, and the wooden frame groans, the air hissing and whistling through the cracks.

The next morning, the temperature drops twenty degrees. Even in a sweater, my teeth chatter the whole bus ride to school. The cold doesn't bother Mr. Brown, our driver, who is from Alaska and wears a polo shirt even in winter. He's also known to tease mercilessly whoever asks him to turn the heater on, so nobody does. I'm definitely not brave enough.

I hope Mom packed some warm clothes for her trip. I don't even know her route this time. Is it across the Midwest? Up into New England? She usually stops in several cities to make her sales pitch and check in with existing clients. If she's on the road right now, I hope she has a cup of hot coffee and keeps the heater on in the car.

When I walk into the Physics classroom, Cory's already in his seat in the back row. His eyes find me, and he straightens, a strange look on his face.

I'm already on edge today. Now dread cuts through me, and my feet stop. *He has something to tell me... Something happened... He's in trouble...*

Several students push past me. I'm blocking their way. I drop my gaze and start moving.

My table is in the middle row, next to the wall. I turn from the center aisle into my row just as Gwendolyn, who sits next to me, slides into her seat.

"Someone left me a present. Cool."

She picks up something from the table and tosses it into her backpack.

A red apple.

I stop in my tracks again and glance over my shoulder.

Cory is frowning, but I can't help a smile. I'm pretty sure the apple was for me.

After class, Cory waits for me in the hallway.

"Hey." He sounds grim.

"Hey." I try to keep a straight face but a smile wins out.

"What?"

"Gwendolyn liked your gift. Very thoughtful. It definitely brightened her day."

Cory huffs, and I laugh. But I mean every word, even if I can't eat the apple.

More students pour out of the classroom. Several throw us curious looks, including Ethan, but Cory and I ignore them.

"Okay if I walk with you?" he asks.

"Sure." And we head for the stairs and my Calculus class on the second floor. He already knows the way.

We've just stepped onto the half-floor landing when a student rushes past us, heading down. He's on the wrong side and going too fast, and slams into Cory's shoulder. *Hard.*

Cory spins around, the impact knocking him down a step. But it's me who yells angrily.

"Hey! *Watch it!*"

If Cory had worse balance, he'd be tumbling down the stairs, breaking bones.

The student stops and turns to face us—and it's Jordan.

"Abby." His eyes stay on me, as if Cory wasn't there. "Sorry. I didn't see you."

I'm about to snap, *It's not me you hit*, but Cory speaks first. "That's all right. Apology accepted."

If Jordan planned to ignore him, that plan just fizzled out. Jordan's eyes swing to Cory, his expression resentful. "I wasn't talking to you."

"No? My mistake."

"That's right. It *is* your mistake. Looks like you make a lot of them." Jordan glares at him. "I'd be more careful if I were you. Mistakes have consequences."

Cory's face darkens, and I've had enough.

What's Jordan's problem? Why can't he leave Cory alone? And the part about mistakes and consequences—was that a threat?

"We've got to go." I pull Cory behind me up the stairs, away from Jordan.

It's only when we stop outside the classroom that I realize I'm clasping Cory's hand.

My face warms, and I quickly relax my grip. But Cory's fingers stay wrapped around mine, like he's not ready to let me go.

He leans closer, shielding me from the students who pass us in the hallway. "If he ever bothers you, you need to tell me. Can you do that?"

I blink in confusion. Jordan bothering *me?* Why would he? It's not against *me* he holds a weird grudge.

"Don't worry. He wouldn't hurt me."

The words rush from my mouth, and they come out all wrong, like I'm defending Jordan, when it's the last thing I wish to do. He already hurt me once. He dumped the blame on me when the mask interfered with his mike. Although… it wasn't intentional. And definitely not the same as threatening me or slamming into me on the stairs...

"Jordan... isn't like that."

Cory frowns, and his eyes harden. "No? What *is* he like?"

I stare back. What's got into him? All of a sudden, he's drilling me on Jordan? It's the last topic I want to debate right now. I have to go to class.

I pull my hand from his, and this time Cory lets me go. My skin tingles from his touch, my hand oddly empty without his fingers around it. I stuff my hand deep into my pocket, annoyed.

"I can take care of myself, you know," I snap.

"I never said you couldn't."

We both turn away at the same time.

CB8O

I keep to the costume room during the next two rehearsals, and steer clear of the stage or the audience. I chat with Tammy and Zoe as we work, and I briefly interact with a few actors when they try on their costumes. But I never have to see Cory or Jordan, and that suits me just fine.

Most of the costumes for the play are ready, the new roll-n-lock rack already full. But we still have plenty of checks, adjustments, and final touches to make. The Witch's dress needs to be lengthened to match Harper's height, and more purple accents added to match the lining of the cape. Beauty's Sisters require three unique and over-the-top outfits each, complete with head coverings, fans, purses, and jewelry, since they are all vain and greedy—but the outfits used in the same scene should never clash. And my favorite: the Beast's Servants, half-human and half-creature, who must be able to blend in with the backdrops and disappear when they stand still…

When I'm alone and undisturbed, my crew gone to watch the rehearsal for a while, I tackle my biggest challenge—the Beast's mask.

I thought the job was finished. The mask looked and felt great. But I forgot the sound. Now I need to figure out a way to attach the mike so Jordan-the-Beast sounds as awesome as he looks.

It feels strangely intimate to press my face against the silk that touched Jordan's skin. I close my eyes and inhale, but if his scent lingers on the fabric, it's too faint for my nose. All I smell is the fake fur and the glue, and even those fade away after a minute.

I'm wearing the mask, testing different positions of the mike in front of the antique mirror, when Tammy and Zoe return from watching.

I turn my head to the door—and Zoe shrieks and jumps up.

"Abby! *God!* You almost gave me a heart attack."

"Sorry. How was the rehearsal?"

Zoe is still catching her breath, so Tammy answers for her. "Really good. You didn't come to watch?"

There is a lot packed into that question, and maybe some day I can tell Tammy the whole story. If I tell anyone, it'll be her. But for now, I go for the simplest answer.

"I wanted to finish this."

"And how's it going?"

I smile behind the Beast's mask. "I think I figured it out."

Tammy smiles back, like she can see right though the mask. "That's great. So you're ready to go? The rehearsal is done."

For some reason, Cory pops into my mind. I think of the apple he brought me, of the way his fingers held mine, of the angry way we parted—and unease sweeps over me. A part of me wants to run out there to see him, just for a moment.

"Umm." I take off the mask and the mike, and put them away in the box, stalling as I decide what to do.

"I'm ready!" Zoe eyes the mask warily, then presses two fingers to her neck. "My pulse is still racing. That mask is just… *too real*. It scared the heck out of me."

I stash the box away and grab my backpack. Why

should I look for Cory? If he wanted to see me, he knows where to find me. Anyway, he probably already left.

"Okay. I'm ready to go too."

Chapter 19

Saturday is the last set build, and we're painting again. Darkly romantic piano plays in the background, setting the mood and marking the occasion. Skyler, our production designer extraordinaire, is running the show.

I'm in a group with Natasha. No brushes or rollers today. We use sponges to add texture to the forest trees—blue to the leaves, purple to the bark and the roots. Other groups use the same technique to add shadows to the stone walls, columns, and stairs of the castle.

Cory isn't here. Three different times I sneak off the stage and run to the front door, in case he's late and can't get in. But there's no sign of him.

Instead, I see Jordan sneak up on Marie in the wing, a moment before she steps on the stage. Zoe must have done her hair, because it's up in a lovely, braided knot. Jordan sticks a fake red rose in it and whispers something in her ear, and Marie laughs. But after he walks away, her smile vanishes, and she struggles to get the plastic thorns untangled from her hair.

The whole thing annoys me, and I suddenly

wonder if Jordan and Marie ever dated. They're both seniors and main leads in all theater productions, so it would make perfect sense. Maybe they're together now—just being discreet about it. Is it possible I missed it? Beauty and the Beast do kiss at the end of the play, and I heard rumors it'll be a real kiss…

Now I'm confused. I thought I was over him. But if I was, I shouldn't care what he does. So why does the thought of him dating Marie still bother me?

When I finish my trees, I wander about the stage, admiring the set design. It's hard to believe that these gorgeous backdrops and elaborate set pieces were once plain wood held together with screws and nails. And before that—sketches and diagrams done by Skyler's hand, based on what they saw in their head. Skyler truly had a vision.

Skyler circles the stage, a brush and a small can of paint in hand. They scan each backdrop and set piece from a distance, then walk up to it, dip their brush in the paint, and scrawl a line here or a smudge there with quick, determined strokes. I notice the paint is black.

What's Skyler doing? I have the sickening thought they're destroying the paintings, and I hurry over to stop them, ready to wrestle the brush from them if I have to.

But up close, my error is obvious. Skyler is deftly adding shadows and cracks, and the effect is magical.

Every surface gains depth, every object becomes more solid. A knife lies on a cutting tray in the farmhouse kitchen. It looks so real I want to pick up.

I exhale in relief, and Skyler throws me a look.

"Perfection's fake. Beauty is always flawed. That's what draws us in."

I nod. "The sets are amazing. You should take pictures for your portfolio."

I mean it as a compliment, but Skyler only scowls and turns away. "What for?" they mutter, more to themselves than to me, then jab another shadow on with a swift, angry flick of their wrist.

I blink. Skyler is a senior. Aren't they applying to theater programs? They should. They'll be designing on Broadway one day. But this is the longest conversation I had with Skyler, not counting their stern but helpful comments when they reviewed the costumes, and I don't have the guts to ask them to their face.

What would I ask them anyway? What do you mean, *what for?* You're putting together a portfolio, correct? And planning to study theater production and make it your career? *You're incredibly talented, and theater is clearly your passion, so I hope you won't give up on it, because that'd be a terrible waste.*

Yeah, right. Like I could ever say that to Skyler.

Maybe I'm talking to myself. Although the part about Broadway is only wishful thinking in my case. I wish I had half of Skyler's talent and skills.

I've already made it awkward, and it looks like Skyler's done talking to me, so I walk back to my group. I reflexively glance around for Cory, but he's a no-show today.

Natasha is sponging the same trees, this time with a shimmering, silvery paint. "We're doing a second layer. It'll look like moonlight. Want to help?"

"Sure." I'm grateful for something to do.

"Here you go." She hands me a new sponge and pours some paint into a small tray. "You want to do the tops of the leaves and this side of the trunk. The moon is going to be in the center."

I watch her for a moment, to see how she does it, then I dip the corner of my sponge in the paint. But as I touch it to the backdrop, a noise startles me. Muffled by the music, the sound's so faint, I think I imagined it.

Then I hear it again—a groan and a thud like a body hitting the floor.

Alarm zaps through me. *A fight?*

"...It hurts. I told you..."

I know the voice instantly—Jordan.

My mind goes to Cory. *Are the two of them fighting?*

I drop the sponge and put down the tray, almost spilling the paint. "I'll be right back."

I rush into the wing. The sounds are coming from

backstage.

"Jordan!" I yell as I clear the corner. "*Stop—!*"

The words die on my lips, my face flushing with embarrassment.

Jordan holds a guy in a choke—but it's Mike, not Cory. They're on a beat-up gym mattress, Jordan poised on one knee, and Mike sprawled in front of him. Nate and Harper watch.

It's not a fight. It's a lesson. Jordan is the teacher.

He relaxes his hold on Mike's neck and turns to me with an amused expression. "Abby. I'm sorry. Are we too loud? Mike's still learning to fall silently." He offers Mike a hand, which he accepts, and Jordan pulls him up.

Everyone looks at me, waiting for a response.

"No… You're fine…" I look at the mattress, the floor, my shoes. Anywhere but Jordan's face. "I just thought…"

There's a moment of stillness, and I realize too late it was my chance to leave. Since I didn't take it, they must think I'm staying to watch. And I do want to watch Jordan.

"Okay, Mike." Jordan says brightly, and when I look up, his gaze flickers to me, and he smiles. "Let's try it again—but a little faster."

Mike swallows. "Faster?"

"Like I pissed you off, and you really want to hit

me. Just remember, when I throw you... *don't fight it*. I don't want to break anything."

Mike nods solemnly, and they face each other on the mattress.

I think back to the martial arts demo Jordan gave at the school assembly. His movements were graceful and precise like a dancer's—leaping and spinning, his arms punching and blocking, his legs kicking and swiping. I was spellbound by Jordan and the sheer speed and elegance with which he moved, and so was everyone else. I saw no violence in it—only mastery.

But now that Jordan has an opponent—a target, even if just for practice—a chill runs down my spine. How much damage could his punch or kick do? Or a choke, or a throw? And what was it he told Mike? *Don't fight it. I don't want to break anything.*

Everything happens with a dizzying speed—

Mike clenches his jaw and lunges forward, his fist flying at Jordan's face.

But Jordan isn't there. He sidesteps Mike, catching his wrist and pulling him forward, all in one fluid motion.

Mike ends up sprawled on the mattress, with Jordan's arm hooked around his throat.

"Very good. You see how I used your anger against you? Anger doesn't make you faster or stronger—it just makes you sloppy. It's a great tool."

Mike makes a strangled sound and his eyes roll back in his head.

I rush forward, my foot hitting the mattress, and grab at Jordan's arm. "*Stop!* You're choking him!"

But before I reach him, everything spins, and a strong arm slips around my throat—not pressing down, just demonstrating—while another arm holds me around the waist.

I gasp, too stunned to fight back with Jordan's body suddenly pressed to mine.

"Nobody's choking. See? I'm gentle." Jordan's breath tickles my ear, and I shiver. "The clown was faking it."

Mike steps into my line of vision and flashes me a guilty smile.

"Let go of me." I slam my elbow into Jordan's side with all my force, and he laughs before lifting his arms from my body, like my punch tickled him.

I stalk off the mattress, my heart pounding, and spin back to my attacker, searching for the most cutting insults to throw at him. But he's looking straight at me, a knowing smile on his lips, like he just peered into my thoughts and liked what he saw, and all the words desert me.

"Okay. That's one way to put a choke on someone." Jordan opens his arms and looks from face to face. A gesture of invitation. "Now you get to practice it *on me*. Who wants to go first? Harper?"

I expect a huff of indignation or a sharp *no way*. But Harper only tosses her hair and walks onto the mattress, not surprised or shy in the least.

"If you touch my boobs, I swear I'll kick you in the crotch," she warns, and Mike and Nate burst out laughing.

Jordan joins in. "Duly noted. We better take it slow, then."

I don't care to observe the next part. I turn and hurry away. Jordan calls something after me, but I don't quite catch it, and I'm not about to go back to let him repeat it.

Back on the stage, the work is winding down.

My tree is finished, and my sponge and tray are gone. Natasha gives me an odd look, but doesn't comment.

Skyler stops by each backdrop and set piece for a final inspection. They come to check on our group last, and don't look at me once as they examine the backdrops and standalone pieces that make up the enchanted forest. "Good job. You can help clean up," they tell Natasha and walk away. It takes me a moment to remember Skyler isn't happy with me.

Why do I even try to make friends? I'm really lousy at it.

Luke walks around with one bucket to collect the

wet sponges and another for the small trays to wash. People bring the leftover paint to one spot, and Tammy and Neon hammer the lids back on the cans, sealing them for storage.

"So how is the Beast's mask coming along?" Natasha asks me. "Did you get the mike to work with it?"

"Yes. I think so." I'm only half listening, my thoughts running in all directions. It's like Jordan's arms are still around me, his breath warm on my skin.

"You did?" Natasha sounds surprised. "Well, did you tell Jordan? We could test it right now."

I spin toward her, Jordan's name like a gong that makes me wide awake and on edge. "Why? He can wait."

Natasha frowns at me, then her eyes widen. "You're still mad at him."

"Aren't you?" I snap back. I'm mad at him in ten different ways, for ten different reasons. She has no idea. "He was rude to you too."

Natasha shrugs. "I don't care. He's always like that. He doesn't mean anything by it." A cunning look comes into her face. "But I thought you... *liked him*."

We're bending low over the floor, folding the huge sheet of tarp that protected this part of the stage. I almost lose my balance and put my palm right in a semi-dry splash of blue paint.

"Why would you think that?"

Natasha studies me closely. I'm only making things worse. *The lady doth protest too much.* But I'm desperate to know. What gave me away? Is it only Natasha who noticed—or does everyone know, including Jordan himself?

Natasha smiles. "Well, it's pretty obvious *he likes you.*"

My knees turn to cotton, and I drop down to my hunches. "*What?*... That's... Why do you say that?"

"Oh, come on! Don't tell me you didn't notice. He's always looking at you—or trying to get you to look at him."

"No, he's not." I shake my head vigorously. "I'm sorry but you're wrong."

Natasha rolls her eyes at me. "Okay. Whatever. But we'll have to test the mike some time."

I'm still shaking my head when she carries the tarp away.

Here's the infuriating part: I don't want Jordan to like me—I want to be over him.

And where the heck is Cory?

Chapter 20

Ard's Farm Market is a year-round grocery store, a seasonal farmers' market, and a family restaurant rolled into one. The parking lot has spots for cars as well as poles to tie your horse if you travel in a buggy. All kinds of arts and crafts decorate the brick walls outside and inside the building, and a real farm with fields and not one but two red barns stretches in the back.

Mom orders an Eggs Benny, which comes with two poached eggs, an English muffin with bacon and Hollandaise sauce, and a pile of roasted potatoes. I get a dish called Hay Stack, which has roughly the same ingredients only mixed together and topped with three kinds of cheese, minus the muffin. She drinks coffee, and I sip hot apple cider, which is delicious.

Mom shares the highlights of her trip, and I catch her up on my school, careful to leave out any mention of theater. I expect a question about SATs and the prep course I'm supposedly taking, but Mom surprises me.

"And how is... life? Did you make new friends?"

Friends.

Alarm cuts through me. This is a dangerous

territory.

Cory pops into my mind first. *No good.* Tammy and Zoe? *Not much better.* Marie? Adam and Neon? Harper? All theater people. I don't have a single class with them. I rake my brain for people I know who aren't cast or crew in the play—and come up with one.

"Heather is a great study partner," I blurt out, and inwardly wince at how pathetic that sounds.

Worry crosses Mom's face, but she quickly hides it behind an encouraging smile.

"That's great, honey. One more month to the SATs. And you'll be taking some of the same subject tests in spring, so you can help each other again."

One more month to the SATs. My body actually turns cold at the thought, and I'm not ready to contemplate the subject tests yet. But I manage a nod and a smile.

"Definitely."

It was Mom's idea to go out for breakfast, and I suspect one reason was to let me drive. Ard's Farm Market is on Route 45, about ten minutes outside the borough, with nothing but farms on both sides of the road. I haven't had much driving practice lately, taking the school bus even when she's in town.

"Should we take the scenic route back?" I offer when we get back in the car and start the engine. "It won't be that much longer, and you can relax and enjoy the view."

Mom laughs. "You mean, I don't have to drive? And there's no traffic, no parking, and no schedule? How could I refuse?" She leans back in her chair and sighs contentedly. "Just don't let me fall asleep."

The day is sunny but a chill hangs in the air. I head west on Route 45, then turn on a country road. We pass a farm and a large corn field. The stalks are a tall green wall, but the leaves are edged with brown and yellow. We cross a bridge over a creek and climb a hill, with more farms and fields stretching in both directions. Then the road winds through a forest, and my chest tightens because the maples and oaks look on fire, the fall painting their leaves red, orange, and gold. The fiery colors are gorgeous, but I'm sad the summer is over.

Mom dozes off after five minutes, snoring lightly, and I don't have the heart to wake her. The skin under her eyes looks like someone smudged a shadow there. She got back yesterday, only minutes after Tammy dropped me off after the set build, but stayed up late answering emails. She needs the rest.

My plan is to loop back to town eventually, but I have no specific route in mind, and I'm in no hurry. Mom's old GPS displays the map of the area, our car a moving dot on the single road in view, and I glance at it from time to time. I forgot how much I like driving. It means freedom to drive wherever I want, and there's one place I really want to see...

I never consciously decide it, but suddenly the road becomes familiar. I drove here with Tammy and Zoe to the thrift store. Now I'm heading in the opposite direction, toward the new blacktop and the school.

The farms start, and I slow down. They're all roughly within the one-mile range of the school. But which one is Cory's? And what would I do if I saw him right now?

A dirt road is up ahead. I picture Cory standing there, waving and gesturing for me to turn... I picture myself parking the car and getting out... I picture turning to Mom to introduce him—*Mom, this is my friend, Cory. We have AP Physics together*—and Mom shaking his hand and smiling...

A pickup truck honks as it passes me, and I veer into the narrow shoulder, startled, and almost knock down a rusted mailbox. I silently curse the rude driver, but it's partly my fault. I was going half the speed limit.

Mom stirs in the passenger seat and opens her eyes. "Ah. Look at the view. Beautiful." A dirt road cuts through a farmland to a small house at the foot of a wooded hill. "It's like time stopped here. Nothing changes. You know exactly what the rest of your life will be like." I can hear the mild horror in her voice. She makes it sound like a prison.

I bite my lip. So much for introducing Cory to Mom. It'd be a disaster.

What would I even tell her about him? He's good at Physics and… picking locks. He carries handcuffs in his pocket. Oh, and we planted some apple trees together, but I don't think they'll make it.

I can just imagine the look on Mom's face.

I press on the gas and focus on the road. No more scanning the farms and searching for Cory. I barely glance at the blacktop to school when we pass it.

※

In the afternoon, Mom and I check on the duplex. We still don't have a contractor, so the electric is off, and the twin houses stand empty and dark. But Mom is worried about winter. The water heater is electric, and without hot water, the water could freeze and break the pipes, and we'd have both the electric and the water system to fix. Mom's voice sounds hollow, all the hope drained from it, when she talks about it. We could never afford two huge repairs like that—we'd have to sell the duplex.

We work on one unit first, then move to the other. We wipe the dust from the counters in the kitchen and the vanity in the bathroom. Clean the windows. Sweep the floors in all the rooms.

With a flashlight in hand, I climb into the attic to check for squirrels and other critters that might have moved in, but I only find a few spiders, and I leave them alone. The basement looks fine too, chilly but dry. I ignore the dust down here. We'll deal with it after we fix the electric.

But when I sweep my flashlight across the far end of the room, the beam catches the spikes of a wheel, and I walk over to investigate.

A bicycle hangs on the wall, the handlebars twisted parallel to the front wheel and the seat wrapped in a plastic bag.

Huh. I've never noticed it. I guess it came with the house.

"Mom? You have two copies of the master key, right?" I ask Mom when we're ready to lock up. "Could I have one? Just in case."

"Umm. Yes. That may be good." She flips through the keys on her key ring, slips one key off, and hands it to me. Then she frowns. "But if anything happens when I'm away, you probably shouldn't come here alone."

I work the master key onto my own key ring. "Don't worry, Mom. I'd ask Mrs. Smith to come with me."

Mrs. Smith. I cringe when I remember the last time I saw her. I'm pretty sure she lied about needing the sugar or the milk. It was just an excuse to barge into my kitchen and snoop around. But I know it's what Mom wants to hear.

Mom's face brightens. "Yes! Mrs. Smith is a lovely neighbor, and we're lucky to have her. You can always go to her if you need anything. She's your emergency contact at school too. Did I tell you? It was very sweet of her to offer."

I swallow. So Mrs. Smith talked to Mom. *When?* Before or after Mrs. Smith's surprise visit to our house? They could've run into each other when picking up mail. Or maybe they talk on the phone even when Mom is travelling?

"That's... good to know. Were these the forms we filled out last year?"

I'm blatantly fishing for information here, but the timing is crucial, and this is serious. Between the noise in the back staircase and the weird comment about being careful, I dread to imagine the tale Mrs. Smith might spin for Mom. But if they already spoke, and she didn't rattle on me yet, maybe I worry for nothing.

"Oh, no. I updated the information online." Mom puts her keys away, and I hold my breath, waiting. "Weeks ago."

My blood turns to ice. *Weeks ago.* So before the last trip. Which means the neighbor could call on Mom and give her report any time, and there's nothing I can do about it.

"Yes, it's been weeks since I talked to her," Mom muses as we start walking. "You know, honey, we should really invite her over for dinner."

"*What?* No way." Mom looks startled, so I quickly backpedal. "I meant—*not now*. I'm... I'm so busy. Maybe after the SATs? I could cook!"

Mom puts her arm around me and squeezes my shoulders. "Oh, honey. That's true. You *are* busy. And I'll be away several weekends. After you're done with the SATs, then."

I exhale with relief. "Thanks, Mom."

Then I remember—too late—what's on the weekend after the SATs: the three performances of *Beauty and the Beast*. And how could I possibly miss that?

Chapter 21

On Monday, the Physics class starts and ends, and all I can think of is the empty seat in the back row.

Cory's not here.

After Calculus, I lurk on the bridge over the main hallway, searching the lunch crowd for him. But I don't see him then—or the rest of the day.

I can't risk going to the rehearsals until Mom leaves for her next trip on Thursday. Nobody does full SAT practice tests every day—not even Heather. So after agonizing for half an hour about how to word the question, I text Tammy, *Hey, is Cory there?*

She answers right away. *Hey. Can you make it? I can come get you.*

It's sweet of her, but not what I asked. I text, *Sorry. Can't.*

Now what? Should I ask again? She must have seen my question. I'm restlessly pacing the kitchen, my homework spread out on the table while I'm getting nothing done, when her next text arrives. *Checked. He's not here.*

Thanks, I text back. I feel guilty for being so

impatient when Tammy actually went and looked for Cory for me. Then I remember something. *How did the photos turn out? From the scenic route?*

OMG, Tammy texts. *So great. Didn't we show you? Gahh. Okay if I give your number to Zoe?*

Sure.

Hold on.

Ten seconds later, a stream of photos arrives on my phone. Tammy and Zoe in their matching t-shirts, smiling, dancing, and striking poses in the middle of a green meadow. In the second batch, my models lie on their backs on the grass, upside down and heads together, their eyes bright from looking up at the sky. And in the very last photo—still upside down on a mess of crashed wildflowers—Tammy and Zoe kiss, each nose hitting a chin.

Thank you, Abby!!!! Zoe texts me, and Tammy follows up with, *What she said!!*

And between them, they send me about a hundred heart emojis in all colors and styles.

The photos make me feel better for about five minutes—and then worse. It's totally selfish. But the more I look at them, the more envious I become of what Tammy and Zoe have. Some people are just lucky.

Or maybe it has nothing to do with luck, and everything to do with being brave.

Which I'm not.

※

The next day, I have no classes with Cory, and I deliberately keep my gaze on the floor every time I'm walking down the hallway. That way I can pretend Cory was there, he passed me at some point, I just didn't see him. It's a stupid game, I know. But it helps.

Heather does a wonderful job of distracting me at lunch. With only a month left to prepare, she's so thoroughly freaked out by the SATs that she does try to do a practice test every day. If she can find one. It's getting difficult, since she did so many, and she's reluctant to use the materials from too far back. The huge SAT prep book is always with her, the zipper barely closing on her backpack, and each page has so many pencil notes, it's giving me a backlash.

She also doesn't eat at all, and I almost tell her to take it easy and stop being paranoid, everything's going to be fine.

But who am to give advice? I barely manage a bite of my sandwich. The moment I let down my guard, I see Cory's body sprawled on the forest floor, his throat crushed by an expert choke. I know it's irrational, but I can't shake the awful feeling something happened to him.

Later, at home, I anxiously wait for Mom to get back from the office. Struck by sudden inspiration, I found the address of Cory's farm. It's Walter Brennell's business address, since he works from home, listed under Electricians and Handymen in the yellow pages. I can't believe I didn't think of it earlier.

My plan is simple. I'll make up a lie about some supplies I urgently need for school, so I can take Mom's car and drive to Cory. I just need to see he's okay, so I can sleep tonight. And if he's not there? I have no clue. Call the police? But what if they question me about him? Would I get him in trouble if I told them about the locks and handcuffs?

Anyway. He's going to be there. I just need to see he's okay, and I'll drive right back.

I'm brainstorming a list of suitably supplies when Tammy's text stops me cold.

Hey, Abby. You there? News on Cory.

My heart stops.

News on Cory? What does that mean? The rehearsal just started. Does that mean Cory's there, and Tammy saw him? But if so, why not say, *Cory's here?* Stating a fact. What's *news?* Aren't news usually bad?

I hate this. I'm scared. But I need to know.

What is it? I type with shaking fingers.

Not verified. Zoe heard him talking to Mr. Miller.

About??

Moving. There is a pause. *She thinks Cory is moving.*

My heart sinks.

Moving? Cory's moving? As in: moving away and changing schools? Why else would he tell his teacher about it?

But that's not possible…

I've got to run, Tammy texts.

Thanks, I type, my fingers and my whole body numb.

I thought if I knew he's okay, and not lying dead somewhere in the woods, I could sleep peacefully tonight. But I don't think that's going to happen.

ෆෂා

Cory is in the Physics class the next morning. I'm acutely aware of him, as if my brain somehow tracked his position in real time, even though I'm careful to never look in his direction, to never make eye contact. I'm afraid of what he'd read in my face.

The moment the class is over, I bolt from my seat and rush into the hallway. I don't stop or look back until I get to my desk in Calculus. Cory can't follow me here.

But when Calculus is over, and before Heather can find me, my feet carry me down the stairs and out the back door.

I halt on the sidewalk outside the building, uncertain of what I'm doing. But the door is already locked—too late to change my mind. So I walk to the storage shed, a stubborn determination pushing me forward. I shrug off my backpack, sit down with my back against the wall, and stare straight ahead, waiting.

The sun is out, the air warmer than it was the last few days. The maple leaves in their fiery colors rustle in the wind. The grass field, too, has more brown, rust, and yellow mixed in. A crow flies overhead, cackling at me, before it settles on top of the wire fence that stretches around the soccer field.

"Hey."

Cory's suddenly there, his silhouette a dark shadow in the corner of my vision. He moves so soundlessly I never heard him arrive. But I knew he was coming.

I look up at him. And he studies me, a guarded look on his face, although I can sense a storm of emotions behind it. He's as upset as I am, although it can't possibly be for the same reason.

My heartbeat pounds in my ears, and I don't trust my voice, but I force myself to answer. "Hey."

Cory's shoulders relax a fraction, and he shrugs off his bag and sits down a few feet away. In the same spot and the same distance from me as the last time. The wall gives a little when he leans against it, the motion travelling from him to me like some wordless message. An apology?

But it's not enough. I need words.

I look him in the eye. I need to see his reaction. "You're moving away?"

"Me? No. Why?" Cory's brows knot like he's solving a puzzle, then realization crosses his face. "My grandfather is."

Somewhere deep inside me, the soothing answer registers, my pulse slowing and tension easing from my muscles. But my mind doesn't trust. I must be missing something.

"Your grandfather is moving?"

"He already did. I was helping him."

"But *you're not* moving with him?" I need to hear it clearly, so there's not a trace of doubt.

Cory shakes his head. "No. I'm not. I'm not moving anywhere."

"Good." I didn't mean to say it aloud, but all the breath leaves my lungs in a shuddering sigh of relief, and the word gets caught up in it.

Cory watches me with a strange expression, a grimace of pain battling with a smile. Then he shakes his head again. "Wait. How did you—?"

"So where did he move, your grandfather?" I cut him off. No way I'm revealing my sources.

"With his friend. In the next town. She has a ranch

house. No stairs, so easier for him to move around."

I remember the hip injury. "How's he doing? Is he okay?"

"Better, I think. He was having a rough time. The man doesn't know how to rest or take it easy, even if it's doctor's orders." Frustration rings in Cory's voice, and he runs his hand through his hair. His hair has gotten longer. It almost reaches his shoulders.

That sounds like my mom. She can't be idle or still for long either. Then something Cory said clicks.

"Wait. *She?* The friend is a woman?"

I don't know why I ask that. It's none of my business. But Cory's cheeks darken like he's blushing, and my curiosity flares up like a wild fire.

"I think they've been... seeing each other for a while. Just never lived together. They're both widowed."

I gasp with delight. "So she's *his girlfriend.*"

Cory blinks, surprised by my reaction. "I guess you could say that. Just don't let either of them hear it."

"And he just moved in with her?"

"Until his hip gets better. Yeah. He's already fixing random things around her house, even though Jill absolutely forbid it. It was her one condition when she invited him to stay. You should hear how they fight about it." Cory huffs. "So she may kick him out soon."

He sounds more exasperated than amused, but I

can't stop a grin that pulls on my lips. "*Jill?* Is that her name?"

Cory nods, watching me closely. "You like that story?"

"Don't you?"

He shrugs, but his somber expression lightens. "I love my grandfather, and I want him to get better. But he doesn't listen. And if I go behind Jill's back and help him, I get caught in the middle."

"He asks you to help him fix things in her house?"

"He doesn't ask, exactly. He just... finds something to fix and starts fixing it. And I can't just stand there and *not* help him. I mean, he took me in and vouched for me and everything..." Cory clenches his jaw and looks away, as if he said too much.

All the lightness I felt a moment ago evaporates.

Took him in and *vouched for him?*

I don't understand what that means. Why did his grandfather have to vouch for him? And to whom? The school? Mr. Miller, so Cory can do theater?

"Well, I'm glad you're not moving," I tell him, and I mean it.

Cory turns to look at me. "Yeah?"

"Yeah."

He smiles, one corner of his mouth slightly higher. "Me too."

He kicks at a rock near his shoe, scanning the field

of wild grass in front of us. Then he jumps to his feet and extends his hand to me. "Come on, let's check on the apple trees."

I hesitate, my heartbeat quickening again. But I take his hand, and he pulls me up.

His fingers are warm and strong, and he doesn't let go of my hand until we step into the field. The grass is taller, and we both bend over it, combing through it to check the three spots where we planted the seeds.

"Nothing yet."

I straighten and turn—and find Cory right in front of me.

He holds my gaze and moves closer. "That's okay. We have time." His fingers brush my arm.

He's going to kiss me. The thought pins me in place, both thrilling and terrifying.

Then the school bell rings, breaking the spell—and I take a step back. "No, we don't. We have to go."

So much for being brave.

Cory frowns, a glint of disappointment in his eyes, but he hurries ahead of me to the shed and hands me my backpack.

When we get to the back door, he unlocks it and grabs the handle.

"You weren't at the rehearsal yesterday. Are you coming today?"

Today's Wednesday. Mom's still in town. I shake

my head. "I can't today. But I'll be there tomorrow."

Cory studies me with a worried look, and I realize he must have questions of his own. "Okay. Then see you tomorrow."

He pulls the door open for me, and I step inside.

Chapter 22

Tammy stares at me, incredulous. "You want *me* to do it? To help Jordan test the mask? You're kidding, right?"

I take the Beast's mask out of the box to show her. "The mike is already installed. See? Natasha will turn it on and take care of the sound. You'd just have to watch him put it on and then zip it in the back. That's it."

The rehearsal is about to start, and we're in the costume room.

Tammy crosses her arms over her chest. "Sorry, Abby. I don't deal with Jordan."

I turn to my other crew member and extend the mask in her direction. "How about you, Zoe? You'd just have to—"

But Zoe recoils, her mouth twisting in repulsion. "Nope! Keep this thing away from me! I'm not touching it."

I sigh. If Tammy won't deal with Jordan, and Zoe won't touch the mask, I'm out of options. "Okay. Fine. I'll do it."

"Good luck," Zoe says.

"If he tries anything, *scream*," Tammy says, and I'm not entirely sure she's joking.

Just do it, I order myself. *Get it over with*. I can't avoid the male lead in the play forever.

I rush out of the costume room, clutching the mask and the attached mike to me.

I turn into the wing and run into Marie, her hair in another artful hairdo of Zoe's doing.

Her eyes slide to the mask, and she skids to a halt. "What *is* that? Oh."

I glance down at the bundle of fur and silk in my hands. I could be carrying a dead, partially skinned animal. The dangling wire is the tail.

I smile. "It won't bite, I promise."

Marie chuckles. She brushes the mask with her fingers, then leans closer and sniffs it. "It's soft, and it doesn't smell too awful." She sounds relieved. She points toward the stage behind her. "If you want Jordan, he's right there. *Jordan!* Abby's looking for you!"

I bite my lip. I was hoping to find Natasha first.

Too late. Jordan's already walking in my direction.

"Abby! I thought you forgot about me." The wounded reproach sounds genuine, although I know better.

"Hi, Jordan. I *didn't* forget," I say coolly, to make it clear I mean the choke he put on me.

He only smiles, his blue eyes flashing, and walks into the wing. He points to the bench. "Where do you want me? There? I'm all yours."

My cheeks warm, memories stirring. I sat with Cory on that bench to take out his splinters. I think of the handcuffs dropping to the floor. This space is like a puzzle I still need to solve. I don't want Jordan to intrude. Besides, the wing is too private, and for once I prefer an audience.

I step past Jordan and onto the stage. "We need Natasha to help us."

A few actors mill around, scripts in hand, studying their lines as they wait for the director. But my eye goes to the group of crew members moving the backdrops and set pieces in place.

Cory is among them. He meets my gaze and nods.

Such a small thing, but it's like a balm on my nerves.

"Are we going to test the mask or not?" There's an edge to Jordan's voice now.

"Hold on." I cross to the front of the stage and squint toward the dim theater and the tech booth. I clear my throat. "Natasha? You have a minute?"

The speakers click on, and Natasha's voice fills the stage. "I'm here. Just hook him up and let me know when you're ready."

I narrow my eyes. So she's not coming down?

Thanks for nothing.

I turn to Jordan and hand him the mask. "Okay. The mike's attached outside. So be careful."

He takes it without a word and puts it on, his face and his blond hair disappearing under the brown fur. I hang on to the transmitter, carefully extending the wire so we don't get it tangled. I still need to zip up the mask, but that requires both hands.

"Now the transmitter." This is the part I've been dreading. I move closer and put one hand on Jordan's back. He's wearing a t-shirt. Hard muscles shift under my touch, and my pulse speeds up. "I'm going to clip it to your jeans."

Of course he moves, and I know it's on purpose. The clip bites the air, and I almost drop the device. Jordan smirks.

"It's not funny," I mutter. Now I wish we did it in the wing, where no one could see me fumbling and blushing. "Do you care about this show at all? Or do you want it to crash on the opening night because of a stupid tech issue?"

"So serious. That's what I like about you." But he stops moving.

I clip the transmitter to his waistband but leave the switch off.

"Are you going to turn me on, Abby?" Jordan asks suggestively.

The mask muffles his words, so only I can hear him. But my cheeks still burn.

I reach for the zipper in the back of the mask. "I'm going to zip it up. *Please* don't move." A broken zipper would be a disaster.

"So you can be nice to me if you want to. That's a start. Now, come on—*turn me on*."

Has he always been so obnoxious? I must've been blind. I want to smack him, but I won't give him the satisfaction.

"Get ready," I warn, and I flip the switch on his transmitter, then I turn toward the tech booth and give a nod and a thumbs-up to Natasha.

There is a click—and then Jordan's voice, suddenly sweet and respectful.

"Thanks, Abby. I appreciate it." He bows to me, then turns around to face the audience. "How is the sound? Can you hear me okay?"

The theater is mostly empty, but I spot Tammy and Zoe in the middle section. They cheer and give thumbs-up.

Like on cue, Mrs. Adams bursts through the door and hurries down the aisle, her long scarf floating behind her.

"So sorry, everyone. A flat tire. Can you believe it?" She drops her huge tote on a seat in the front row and turns to the stage. "Now. What was that beautiful sound I just heard? Was that the Beast?"

Jordan steps to the very edge of the stage. "Yes, madam. And I'm going to rehearse in the mask, if that's okay with you."

"Excellent! Let's get to it then." Mrs. Adams pulls out her script and flips to the page she wants. "Act one, scene eight."

I flee into the wing and out of view, but pride fills me. Because his voice is clear and strong, even through the mask. I got the mike to work.

I wasn't planning to stick around to watch. But the moment Jordan and Marie take their places and begin, the heart-wrenching magic of the play wraps around me—and I forget to leave.

In the scene, Beauty begs the Beast to let her visit home and her sick father, promising to return in a week. They argue passionately, and at last the Beast relents and gives her leave. But he suspects a lie—she loathes him and wants to escape—and he secretly vows to end his life if she breaks her promise.

The scene is intense and the blocking complicated. The Beast is in constant motion, restless and despairing as he tries to persuade Beauty to give up her family, as they gave up her, and stay with him. His voice is so full of emotion, and his gestures and head movements so expressive, I forget he's wearing a mask at all—not to mention I'm responsible for it…

I'm entranced until the director stops the scene to give the actors a break.

"Take off your mask, Beast. No need to push it." She gestures to Jordan. "Somebody help him. Who do we have on costumes? Did Abby leave?"

The sound of my name pulls me forward, and I rush onto the stage. "I'm right here."

I step behind Jordan and switch off his transmitter before I unzip the back of his mask.

He takes the mask off, his blond hair reappearing. His face is flushed, and his whole body radiates heat. He hands me the mask and leers. "Careful, it's hot."

I give him a withering look. *Really?* I'm glad I turned off his mike.

He's right, though. The silk lining is warm to the touch from contact with his skin, and I have an impulse to press my own face against it and inhale. But I push the thought away, annoyed.

Jordan unclips the transmitter and hands it to me too, leaning closer than necessary. "I'll be right back. Gotta take a piss." He's back to using his low voice, so he can mock and insult me without anyone else hearing it.

He strides off, and I stare daggers at his back, anger burning in my throat. I flee to the wing, the mask and transmitter in my hands, and stand fuming silently.

I think of what Natasha said. Does he think I like

him? Is that the problem? *I like him*—so he can push me around and get away with it?

By the time Jordan returns, I've made up my mind.

He may be the most talented and best-looking guy I've ever met, but I don't care. I've seen what he's really like, and I want nothing to do with him.

But it's one thing to decide—and another to say it to his face. What words do I use, so he can't laugh it off? So he knows I mean it, and it's not a game?

Jordan grabs the mask from my hands. "Did you miss me?"

That does it. "You need to stop—" but Marie hurries toward us, so I quickly change tracks "—you need to be more careful with it."

"Abby? Tammy had to leave early."

"All right! Where are my Beauty and my Beast?" The director's booming voice fills the stage. "We're still in act 1, scene nine. Let's finish it."

Tammy left? Anxiety cuts through me, and I step out of the wing and peer at the dim theater. Tammy and Zoe's seats are empty.

"But I can give you a ride home. Just find me." And Marie hurries off, adjusting her mike and switching on her transmitter midstep. I have no time to say thanks.

Jordan steps in front of me, his broad shoulders and the back of his blond head blocking my view. "Can I get some help?"

Without a word, I zip up his mask, clip on his transmitter, and turn it on. It's my job to assist him, but I don't have to talk to him.

Chapter 23

The costume room is dark when I get there, the coats and dresses on the racks like a somber, silent crowd waiting to judge me for my offenses. I clutch the Beast's mask and transmitter with one hand and grope for the light switch with the other, relieved when the ceiling lamp comes on.

The scene wrapped up a while ago, and I expected Jordan to take off the mask right then. I know he saw me waiting in the wing, because he looked right at me. But he turned away and kept the mask on. The actors get director notes after each scene, and once Mrs. Adams launched into her comments, I couldn't interrupt. By the time she finished, Jordan, Marie, and me were the only students left. Everyone else was gone.

Now I hurriedly put the mask in its box, and blindly reach for my backpack.

But my hand comes up empty. My backpack isn't there. Did I move it? I always leave it in the same spot. I nervously glance around me.

There it is. Off the floor and on one of the racks. I grab it and hurry out of the costume room, past the dim stage and out into the hallway. My footsteps echo in the empty building. I take a shortcut past the gym and push through the side door—and then I'm outside.

A sidewalk runs alongside a wire fence to the student parking lot illuminated by tall street lamps. I look around for Marie's car. I was supposed to meet her there. But the lot is empty. Beyond it, inky darkness swallows the fields and the only road.

A chill goes through me, and it's not just the October air.

I dig in my backpack for my phone, but can't find it. *Oh, come on.* I kneel on the cool sidewalk and check my backpack more carefully. Nothing. Did I drop my phone in the costume room? I texted Mom when I got here…

I rush back and yank at the school door—but it's locked. All the doors are at this hour. No way to get in.

"Abby! Took you long enough."

I spin around, relief mixed with annoyance. I'm glad not to be stranded alone at night—but not thrilled with the company.

Jordan leans with his back against the wire fence off to the side. Behind him, the sidewalk stretches past the tennis courts and forks off to the track and the baseball field before looping around the building.

"What're you doing here?" I ask.

He smirks. *"Waiting for you.* Ready to go? I'm

parked in the back."

He's waiting for me? Two weeks ago I'd be ecstatic, but now the smug look on his face only makes me suspicious. "Did you see Marie? I was supposed to ride with her."

Jordan shrugs. "I told her not to wait. I can drive you."

I stare at him. "You *told her* not to wait?"

"Relax. What's the big deal? Wouldn't you rather get a ride with me?" He moves closer, smiling, and tries to slip his arm around my shoulders.

I step away, indignation surging through me. Who does he think he is? He doesn't get to decide for me. "No, actually. I wouldn't."

"So you're going to walk home? Alone at night?" He looks at the dark road and scowls. "Really?"

"She won't be alone."

My heart leaps in my chest as Cory walks out of the shadow. I thought he left hours ago, with the rest of the set crew.

Anger flashes in Jordan's eyes, and an ugly grimace twists his face. "Man, you really don't listen. I told you to get the fuck out of here."

Told him? Jordan told Cory to leave? When? I stand frozen, my body cold and brittle as ice.

Cory keeps walking toward us, his face expressionless, and his hands in the pockets of his hoodie. He stops a few feet away, his gaze fixed on Jordan. "You told me *she asked you* for a ride. But I don't think she did."

Jordan glares at him. "And *I* think you should walk away before you really piss me off."

Cory stays put. "I'm not going anywhere unless she tells me to." He looks over at me.

I meet his eyes. *Don't leave.* I order my tongue to move, my lips to form the words, but no sound comes. My throat is too tight.

Doubt crosses Cory's face.

Jordan barks a laugh, but his eyes are cold and there's an edge of warning in his voice. "Tell him to go to hell, Abby. Before I smash his face in."

I open my mouth to speak, then close it again. This isn't just about me. I don't want Jordan to hurt Cory, so I shouldn't provoke him. If I let him drive me home, Cory will be safe. It's a short ride. What's the worst that can happen? I don't even have to talk to the driver.

But the thought of getting in a car with Jordan makes me shudder. Mom is still out of town, so I'm alone in the house. And now I lost my stupid phone. I don't know if I can do this…

"Abby?" Cory asks.

I don't look at him. I stare at the sidewalk, paralyzed by my own fear and disgusted with myself for letting it control me. I need to be brave. Jordan has been itching to hurt Cory for a while. I can't give him an excuse...

Then Jordan grabs my arm. "Enough of this bullshit. You're riding with me. Let's go."

His touch shocks me into action. My voice returns, and I yank my arm away. "I'm not going anywhere with you!"

Jordan glowers at me. "What the fuck, Abby? You'd rather walk in the dark with this creep than let me drive you? I know you're not that stupid."

He reaches for me again, but I jump away.

Cory steps forward. "Don't do that. Don't touch her."

Jordan turns to face him, his mouth curled with disdain. "Or what? What are you going to do about it, creep? *Fight me?*"

Dread floods me again, icy cold, my muscles freezing instantly. *What have I done?* This is exactly what Jordan wanted.

It's like Cory can hear my pleading thoughts. "I don't want to fight," he says.

Jordan takes a step toward him. "A little too late for that."

There's nothing aggressive about the way he moves—his arms stay loose at his sides, his hands relaxed—but every movement is suddenly more precise and deliberate, and his focus locks on Cory like a cobra ready to strike. He takes another step.

"You know, I could break your arm right now—no, both of your arms—and no one would give a shit?"

Cory's eyes harden. "Maybe—"

And he slams into Jordan.

He moves fast. Metal flashes in his fingers. *A knife?* My heart stops.

"But then you'd have to explain this."

Cory raises his arm—and Jordan's arm jerks up too. They're handcuffed together, their wrists joined by the metal chain.

I gasp in shock.

Jordan jerks on the chain, livid. "What the fuck is this?"

"I don't want to fight," Cory repeats. "This is me not fighting."

"Give me the key." Jordan's voice is a low growl, promising violence.

"This key?" Cory reaches into his pocket. Metal flashes in his fingers, a small object catching the light as he holds it up for half a second. Then he pulls back his arm and throws it far into the field.

Jordan shoves Cory in the chest, all his control, all the haughty self-assurance gone for a moment. "You fucking psycho!"

Cory trips and nearly falls, almost pulling Jordan down with him. Jordan yanks him back to keep his balance, the metal of the handcuffs biting painfully into their wrists. Two more yards, and they would've hit the wire fence.

"Jordan, stop it!" I cry out.

Cory shoots me a warning look. *Stay back, Abby.* He spins Jordan away from me.

But Jordan pays me no attention. His glaring eyes are fixed on Cory, his lips twisted in a cruel snarl. He rolls his free hand into a fist.

"I hope you like pain, because I'm going to fuck you up," he sneers, his voice full of hate, and yanks on the handcuff, again and again, forcing Cory to move in a circle.

"And then what?" Cory's voice is firm, his jaw clenched in determination. "You don't scare me. Like you said, nobody gives a shit what happens to me. *Including me.* Think about that."

I stare at the side of Cory's face, stunned. *What? That's not true.*

Cory's head moves a fraction in my direction, as if he could hear my frantic thoughts. But he never looks at me. He keeps his eyes on Jordan.

"Is that right?" Jordan assesses him.

"Yeah," Cory says. "And that should scare *you*. You have a lot more to lose."

Jordan considers this. "Maybe you don't care—*but she does*."

And he grabs the front of Cory's shirt and slams him against the fence.

Cory groans as his back hits the wire with a sickening thud.

"Cory!" I scream and lunge at them, all hesitation gone as my fear for him spurs me forward.

"See?" Jordan scowls, and I see his fist rising in my direction.

I stare at it, registering every detail as if in slow motion—the tight knuckles, the muscles flexing under the sun-tanned skin. And I'm paralyzed again, unable to believe he'd actually hit me—

Another hand pushes me back, firm but not hurtful, and I'm spinning away before Jordan's knuckles can touch me.

I land on my hands and knees on the cold ground a split second before his punch connects with someone else's flesh and bone somewhere above me, followed by another thud and a hollow ringing of the wire.

The sounds feel surreal, like something in a dream. Then my mind catches up.

Jordan punched Cory. After Cory pushed me out of the way.

The ground spins and buckles under me, and I taste bile in the back of my throat. Was Jordan really going to punch me, or was he just taunting me? I'm sickened and appalled either way.

The wire fence shakes and rings again, and I hear a muffled crack that can only be a hard fist hitting bone, and the guttural, straining sounds of wrestling.

I scramble to my feet, already turning.

Jordan's forearm is crushing Cory's throat, pinning him to the fence, and Cory's lip is split and bleeding.

"What did I tell you?" Jordan sports the arrogant scowl of a victor.

But from my low vantage point, I see Cory's hands working, his free hand doing something to the metal cuff. Soundlessly, the cuff springs open, and Cory pulls his wrist free.

Then he shifts, pretending to struggle, while he pulls Jordan's cuffed wrist back—and snaps the other cuff around the wire in the fence.

Realization hits Jordan a second later. He lifts his arm from Cory's throat, momentarily distracted.

And Cory steps away.

One smooth movement, and he's out of Jordan's reach. He never tries to hit Jordan back, doesn't even look at him.

He hurries over to me. "Abby, are you okay? I'm sorry, I—"

"It's fine. I'm fine," I quickly say. But it's a lie. I'm not fine. "I just want to get out of here."

Cory nods.

"*Fuck!*" Jordan rattles the wire fence he's

handcuffed to, then examines the cuff, looking for a catch. He glares at Cory again. "How did you open it? I saw you threw away the key."

Cory looks at him coldly. "Why would I do that? That would be stupid. The key is right here." And he holds it up.

Jordan slowly turns around. He stares at the key with greed. Then his gaze slides to Cory's face. "I'm not going to ask you again. Give me the key, or you're going to regret it," he threatens.

"I won't regret it." Cory glances at me, then takes a step in Jordan's direction. "But I'll make you a deal."

"About time, you creep," Jordan mutters, misunderstanding what's about to happen.

Because Cory stops after one step. "I want you to leave Abby alone. And in exchange, I'm putting the key… right here." He puts the key down on the ground. Yards away from the fence and from Jordan. "You have your phone. Call for help. And if not, the custodian gets here early. You should have privacy until then."

Jordan yanks on the cuff so hard, he almost dislocates his shoulder, the muscles in his arm and neck taut, the veins standing out. But the cuff holds, and so does the fence. He's not going anywhere. "Fuck you," he says.

Cory leaves the key on the ground and turns to me. "Come on. Let's go."

He picks up my backpack from the sidewalk, and we start across the parking lot, away from the school. I look straight ahead and concentrate on walking, my legs like blocks of wood.

"Cory," Jordan calls after us, his voice calm and controlled again, almost friendly.

Cory stops and looks over his shoulder.

"You're a dead man," Jordan says.

I walk faster, then start running toward the dark road ahead.

Chapter 24

Cory catches up with me just as I turn from the school driveway onto the blacktop—and as the half-moon breaks through the clouds. The blueish light gives off no warmth, but I'm grateful to see the edge of the blacktop and the outlines of the brush and trees alongside it.

I slow to a brisk walk. I'm pretty sure Cory could outrun me even if I sprinted all the way home, and I don't want to fall into the ditch and sprain my ankle.

He falls in step with me, and I extend my hand without quite looking at him. "Can I have my backpack?"

"It's okay. I'll carry it for you." I hear the worry and confusion in his voice. He can sense I'm upset, and that some of it is directed at him, but he doesn't know why.

That makes two of us.

"I can carry it myself."

He hands me the backpack, and I shrug it on and keep walking.

"You don't have to walk me home either." I don't

know why I say that. It's like poking at a fire to see if it collapses or flares up.

"Yes, I do." Cory's voice is firm, but I can hear the tension in it.

"It's a long walk," I say.

He throws me a look but doesn't answer.

Now that we're away from Jordan, the chill and the numbness are gone, and a restless urgency pulses through me, my heart ripped open and my thoughts racing miserably.

I pick up the pace. I don't even know what I'm running from. Surely, it's not Cory, is it? But I can't think clearly right now. I just need to keep moving.

Cory easily matches my pace, never straying from my side.

"Abby?"

"What?"

"I'm sorry I didn't… I wasn't sure if you…" Cory lets out a shaky breath. "Did he… bother you before I got there?"

"No!" Heat burns my face and throat at the idea—and because Cory still doesn't get it.

He's worried about me and trying to protect me, but I never asked him to do that. I'm not scared or helpless. I don't know what happened to me back there—why I didn't scream or punch back or walk away. I can handle Jordan. Cory just never gave me a chance.

I make a mistake of glancing at Cory's face. Even in the faint moonlight, I can see his badly swollen lip and the dark bruise on his jaw.

I stop abruptly, emotions welling up in me. "What were you thinking?"

Cory stops too, and I catch a wary look on his face. He's putting up his guard. "I don't follow."

"What was your plan, exactly? I really want to know. You were going to let him beat you up? Maybe break your arms? Is that it?"

Cory frowns. "What? No. I just—"

"You told him you didn't care what he did to you. Is that why you didn't fight back? You wanted him to hurt you?"

Cory's eyes flash. I hit a nerve. "*Fight back?* You mean punch him? Or throw him down?" He shakes his head. "You think I didn't want to? You have no idea... But I can't do that. *I can't get in a fight.* If I as much as laid a finger on him..." He exhales in frustration. "Doesn't matter."

"*Doesn't matter?* See, you're doing it again. It doesn't matter if he hurts you? Is that what you mean?"

A sound of exasperation escapes Cory's throat. He shakes his head and wrings his hands. "I don't... What's this about, Abby? I don't know what I did wrong. Just tell me what to do, and I'll do it."

We stand at the edge of the blacktop, the thick darkness of the tangled brush and vine-dripping trees like a huge, hungry creature watching and waiting to pounce. A single misstep, and it'll snatch us and carry us off to its lair somewhere, and we'll never see daylight again.

I look into Cory's eyes, and his pain splits me open. The darkness seeps inside me, igniting my fear, kindling the doubts. How can I tell him what to do? I'm in pieces, barely holding myself together. I want to pull him close and kiss him. I want to turn and run away. I want to cry and laugh and scream. It's too much.

"It doesn't work like that, Cory." The words taste bitter in my mouth, and I spit them out in a rush. "It's all wrong, and you can't fix it."

Cory's face changes. "If you wanted to go with him, you should've said so."

"*What?*"

I look away at the dark wall of trees, memories pushing in. I see the cruel glare on Jordan's face, the tight knuckles of his fist, his arm pressing down on Cory's throat. I hear him growl, *You're a dead man.*

And Cory thinks I'm having second thoughts? That I wanted to get in the car with Jordan? I'm stunned and furious. More so because it's true: a part of me wallows in a twisted regret that Jordan wasn't the perfect prince I'd imagined—and blames Cory for it.

"Watch out!"

Cory's arms close around me, and my feet leave the ground as he lifts me up and moves me off the blacktop. I'm suddenly behind him, his body a shield between me and the road.

I dig my toes into the uneven ground and peer over his shoulder. Blinding headlights slice through the night. A car is barreling straight at us.

Alarm shoots through me. *Jordan.*

But the car is too low for a jeep, and it's coming from the wrong direction.

"Tammy!" I recognize the driver and almost step into the car's path in my haste. Cory moves in front of me, blocking my way, and I bump into him instead.

The car passes us, Tammy's frowning face in the window. The brakes shriek, and the car skids to a stop on the side of the road, narrowly avoiding the ditch.

Cory's hands are still on my arms, and I shake them off. "It's okay. Let go."

I head for the passenger side, but Tammy jumps out of the car and rushes to meet me.

"Abby! Oh my God! I'm so sorry! Are you okay?" She scans my body like she expects blood and wounds all over me.

"I'm fine," I assure her, hyperaware of Cory standing behind me.

Tammy doesn't look convinced. "I told Marie to

give you a ride. But then I texted you like ten times, and you didn't respond. Marie said you already had a ride." Tammy glances at Cory behind me, and her eyes narrow in confusion. "What happened?"

"I lost my phone." I can't believe she drove here to check on me, and I'm grateful. But I'm not ready to talk about tonight. I wouldn't even know how to begin. "It was totally my fault."

"Are you kidding? I promised I'd get you home from rehearsals. I feel like a monster. You could've—"

"Tammy, I'm fine, really. Can you take me home?"

Tammy blinks. "Of course. Yes. Sorry." She hurries to the car and gets in the driver seat.

I take two steps after her, then stop, my chest tight. It's like I reached the end of some invisible rope and can go no farther. I turn to face Cory.

He's washed in red, and panic grips me. *How badly did Jordan hurt him? Is that blood?* But it's only the car's red tail lights.

He stands still like a statue, his eyes on me. I expect him to move closer, but he doesn't. I have to go. Tammy's waiting. I was in a hurry to leave a moment ago, but now my feet refuse to move. My throat doesn't work either. When I try to speak, no words come.

"Take care, Abby," Cory says, and he walks away first.

He crosses the road and is gone.

I almost run after him, the invisible rope dragging me forward, but I grit my teeth and turn the other way, walk to Tammy's car and slide into the passenger seat. I clutch my backpack in my lap and try to calm my pounding heart.

Tammy looks at me, then twists in her seat to look out the rear window at the road behind us. "What about him? Doesn't he need a ride home?"

Shame burns my cheeks. She's right. Why didn't I think of that? Selfish, as always.

I drop my backpack on the floor and jump out of the car. "Cory?"

But there's no response, and no sign of him. Even after Tammy executes a three-point turn, and we drive back. The road is empty.

It's like Cory melted into the darkness—or was never here at all.

○○○

But Cory is at school the next morning. We get to the Physics classroom at the same time. His lip is still swollen, and the bruise is darker. He steps forward and holds the door open for me. He looks at me but doesn't quite turn his head, his movements oddly stiff, and for a moment I wonder if he's in pain. But that's not it. He's just careful not to touch me.

After class, I grab my backpack and hurry out the door, my head bent and my eyes down the whole time. If Cory waits for me in the hallway, to walk me to Calculus, I plan to pass him without looking up. He's not there, though, and he doesn't follow me either.

It hurts more than I thought, and I'm starting to think I deserve it. I cringe to think of what I said to Cory. Or worse—what I didn't say.

But I can't dwell on it right now. I have to run to the costume room before class.

Last night, when Tammy drove me home, I used her phone to text Mom. I explained I left my phone at school after the SAT prep class. A lousy lie—but I didn't want Mom to worry or to summon Mrs. Smith for help. I carefully erased the texts from Tammy's phone before I gave it back, and that felt lousy too. Now I really need to find my phone.

My nerves are frayed when I get backstage. I have the keys, and there's no one else here. But I keep expecting to run into Jordan every time I turn a corner or cross a passageway, and I'd really like to avoid that.

I was lucky the bus was early today, and I got inside the building before Jordan ever arrived, judging by the absence of his jeep in the parking lot. I ran up to the second floor to check the back lot as well, just in case. And just before class, my heart in my throat, I snuck up to the side door to see the wire fence. No sign of Jordan or the handcuffs. So someone helped him reach the key and free himself.

But that doesn't mean he's not mad as hell.

As I search the costume room for my phone, I idly wonder who Jordan called and what he told them. Did he make it into a joke? Maybe a dare or a bet he accepted and had to back out of? But most importantly, did he mention Cory's name?

A locker door slams somewhere—a harsh metallic gong that yanks me back to reality. I'm out of time. I already missed the bell. I rush out of the costume room and get to my next class a whole minute late.

Then lunch comes, and I stand on the second floor balcony, debating what to do as I watch the river of students pouring into the cafeteria. I should go back to the costume room and keep searching. My phone must be there, and I need to find it before the weekend. But I could look for it during the rehearsal too, and try to talk to Cory now...

I spot him in the crowd, heading straight for the back door, and it strikes me, for the hundredth time, how alone he is. Other students walk in groups, trail after someone else, or move with the current. But he sets his own path and sticks to it. If all the students were gone, and the hallway was empty, he'd keep walking in exactly the same way.

Suddenly, he looks up straight at me, and I hold my

breath, waiting for a sign—a smile, a nod, anything—that he wants me to follow him. But his gaze doesn't linger, and his face doesn't change. There's no sign, although I know he saw me. He just keeps walking.

Or the sign is there—it's just not what I hoped for. It says: *I want to be alone.*

I hurry to the costume room and spend the lunch hour combing through the racks and searching backstage. Maybe I dropped the phone on my way, and it slid under a bench? I even risk turning on the lights and checking the stage and the wings. Nothing. No trace of my phone.

A footfall startles me nearly out of my skin.

Natasha grins. "Hi, Abby. Sorry about that. I thought we left the lights on or something. I wouldn't want them to burn the whole weekend."

"The whole weekend? Don't we have the rehearsal tonight?"

Natasha shakes her head. "Nope. It was cancelled. Didn't you get Skyler's message?"

Of course I didn't. Skyler uses an app for that, and the app is on my phone. "Why was it cancelled?"

Natasha shrugs. "Jordan can't make it. He's missing school too."

I swallow hard. So he's not here at all today. "Why? Is he hurt?"

"*Hurt?* You mean *sick?*"

"Right, sick."

"Nah. I heard he flew out to California with his dad. Some fancy awards ceremony, and then they're visiting colleges out there on the weekend. Must be nice." Natasha looks at me. "Neon and Patricia sneak in here to rehearse. But what're you doing here?"

"I lost my phone yesterday. I'm not sure where, so I'm checking everywhere." I don't want to sound like I'm making an accusation—like I think someone took it. Our theater group is not that big.

"Bummer." Natasha reflexively pats her own pocket. Her phone is there. "Have you tried the office? They have a lost-and-found box. Maybe someone found it and dropped it off."

A lost-and-found box. I didn't think of that. "I will. Thanks, Natasha."

I rush to the office, trying not to get my hopes up. But what do you know? Sometimes good things happen, and everything works out, because my phone is actually there.

It's not until I'm on the bus home that I remember Cory and my heart sinks. I was going to find him at the rehearsal. Now I won't see him until Monday?

No. I can't wait that long.

Chapter 25

The metal mailbox is the color of dried blood, and vines strangle the wooden pole it sits on. But the number is right, even if no name is printed on it. The mailbox belongs to Walter Brennell, as does the farm I'm standing on. A narrow gravel road breaks off from the main two-lane road I took to bike here.

The gravel road must lead to the house eventually, but it bends sharply up ahead, with thick bushes and tall oaks and maples in flaming foliage lining both sides, obstructing my view. The only way to see what lies at the end is to walk the road.

The sun is high in the sky, a warm breeze rustling the leaves. It must be almost noon. I would've gotten here an hour ago if my bike hadn't broken halfway through. It's the bike from the duplex. All I did was wipe the dust and check the tires. Not very smart, but I was in a rush.

But now that I'm here, doubt pins me in place. *What am I going to say to Cory? What if he doesn't want to see me? What if he's not even here?* I'm tempted to turn back. If I left right now, Cory would never know I was here…

No. I need to see him. I came all this way.

I adjust my backpack, then grip the handlebars of the bike and force my feet to move. The wheels crunch the gravel, and the busted chain clicks, both sounds jarring in the peaceful silence that stretches over the fields and woods around me. I keep my eyes down and focus on avoiding the larger rocks. I haven't faced Cory yet, but I already feel like an intruder. Not a good sign.

A growl raises the hairs on the back of my neck.

I look up and freeze, my blood turned to ice.

A huge black dog blocks my way.

It prowls toward me, its head bent low, the jaw wide enough to bite off my arm, then stops and snarls.

Terror curls around me like smoke. I think of the Beast's mask—and of Jordan. But that's not right. This is Cory's dog, and Cory would never hurt me.

"Hi, doggie." I make my shaking voice friendly. I've never been around dogs much, but people talk to dogs, don't they? "You're a good dog. I know you are."

The dog lifts its head and lets out a series of barks, as if answering. Then it starts in my direction, tracing an arc around me. I slowly turn after it, one hand holding the bike.

"Such a good, smart dog. Where's your owner? Where is Cory? Can you get Cory for me? He did something very brave, and I never told him—"

"*Abby?*"

I spin around to see Cory jogging toward me, soundless as ever.

My cheeks warm. How much did he hear? What did I even say, exactly?

I glance at Cory. A mistake. He stares at me with such intensity my face only gets hotter.

"What're you doing here?"

Mortified, I drop my gaze. *What was I thinking? He doesn't want me here.* "Nothing… I only wanted to say hi… I should go…" I start to turn my bike around.

Cory grips the middle of the handlebar, stopping me. "*No.* Abby. Stay… I just… I can't believe you're here."

I forget about the dog until it bumps its huge head into my thigh before ambling away.

"Sorry. This is Pearl."

"*Pearl?*" I smile, some of my nervousness lifting. I feel Cory watching me but still can't quite meet his gaze.

"Yeah. She's my grandfather's dog. He named her."

Up close, white frosts the dog's muzzle. "How old is she?"

"Pretty old. I'm not sure. Old and stubborn. Jill's allergic, so my grandfather had to leave her here. She mostly ignores me, though."

"She's still company." I glance around me, trying to imagine the woods and the fields after nightfall. The road must be pitch black.

I think back to the scene in the parking lot—the wire fence, the handcuffs, Jordan's arm crushing Cory's throat. And then Cory walking next to me in the dark.

"Your chain has slipped." Cory has moved to the other side of the bike, one hand on the handlebar. There's worry in his voice, and something else I can't quite name. A restlessness. He pushes his hair out of his eyes. "I can fix it for you."

I look into his face, and my chest tightens. His split lip is still swollen, his jaw darkened by a painful bruise.

Before I know what I'm doing, I touch his hand. "I *didn't* want to go with him."

Cory exhales, then nods, his fingers pressing mine. "*Good.*"

And just like that—I feel lighter, a weight lifted off my chest. "So... what's up the road?"

Cory smiles, taking the handlebars from me. "Come on. I'll show you."

He wheels the bike, and I walk next to him.

The house at the end of the gravel road is unlike any house I've seen around here. A tall two-story with white brick walls, a gray tile roof, and blue window shutters. A spacious porch with slender columns wraps around the first floor, with a hanging swing and several rocking chairs. Shrubs and hostas line the front of the house, and more plants spill from hanging baskets. Metal wind chimes sing in the breeze. A large red barn stands up the hill behind it.

"Wow. The house's beautiful."

But I instantly see why Cory's grandfather would have trouble. Several wide steps lead to the porch, which sits high above the ground, as does the whole first floor.

"Thanks. It's a hundred years old, but this isn't the original. They had to rebuild it twice." Cory leans the bike against the wall. He climbs the steps to the porch, and I follow.

"Why?"

"We're in the flood zone." Cory's fingers close around mine, and he leads me around the porch to the back. My pulse speeds up at his touch. But he lets go of my hand and points away from the house. "The creek is right there. Can you hear it?"

A gentle slope ends in a line of oaks, then the land drops off sharply. I can hear the rushing water. I nod. "I hear it."

I turn my head—and Cory's right next to me. He peers into my face, and hair falls into his eyes. He brushes it away impatiently.

I smile. "Your hair's getting long."

He frowns. "I know. I need a haircut."

"I could cut it if you want." *What?* I have no idea why I said that. It must be my nerves.

Cory studies me, his eyes bright. "You cut hair before?"

"Never." It's the truth.

Cory grins, his swollen lip riding up. "Okay. I'm in. Do it."

I blink. Now I have second thoughts. What if I mess it up? "Are you sure?"

"Positive. You need scissors, right?"

I shrug off my backpack and unzip it. "I have mine. In my sewing kit. I always carry it with me." I pull out the kit and fish out the scissors from it. "But we'll need a comb."

"I'll be right back." Instead of walking to the front door, Cory yanks open the nearest window and climbs through it. Through a white lace curtain, I catch a glance of a large flowered sofa and framed photographs on the wall. A moment later, Cory is back with a comb and a tall bar stool.

"Let's go over there on the grass. Less mess to clean up."

I put my sewing kit away, set my backpack on the porch, and follow Cory down the steps, my scissors in hand.

It's happening. *I'm cutting his hair.*

I should be scared, but I'm actually excited. For about a year in middle school, I wanted to be a hairdresser and seriously studied the craft. Now I can finally put it to good use.

Cory puts the bar stool in a patch of sunlight a few yards from the house, and sits down, facing me. "I'm ready."

I circle him, studying his haircut until I can picture it the way it was when he first got it. His hair is thick and straight, with just a little wave to it. "How short do you want it?"

"Whatever *you* want. I trust you," Cory says.

My heart swells up at this, although I did nothing to earn the trust yet.

"Okay." I stop in front of him and lean forward, ready to start. But Cory's eyes are locked on mine, the specks of green shining in the sunlight, and the invisible rope loops around me again, reeling me toward him.

I pull back, blinking. "Close your eyes," I order.

"Why?" Cory doesn't sound happy.

Because I can't focus when you're looking at me. "Do you want a haircut or not?"

Cory's brows knot, but he closes his eyes.

I hesitate, suddenly shy, then reach out and pass my hand through his hair.

The touch is electric—a sweet thrill rushing

through my body.

Cory must feel it too, because his eyes fly open. He slowly rises and takes the scissors from my hand.

"What're you doing?" My voice is a whisper.

"Putting these away before someone gets hurt." The scissors disappear behind him.

My heart hammers in my chest, but time slows, each heartbeat stretching into eternity.

He leans closer, his gaze holding mine. "Can I kiss you?"

Every cell in my body whispers yes, *yes*. But Cory's lip is still swollen and his jaw badly bruised. I let my fingertips brush his face. "I don't want to hurt you."

"You won't."

I already did. It's my fault Jordan hit you. If you hadn't stood up for me—

Cory cups my face in his hands and kisses me, and all my hesitation melts away.

His lips move against mine, warm and soft, searching and giving, his fingers light on my cheeks—and it's like he's opening me up. His mouth tastes sweet, and his skin smells of summer, and I can't get enough of him. But I can feel the cut and the swelling in his lip, so I'm gentle, desperately holding back even as his kiss deepens.

Cory pulls back and looks into my eyes. He sensed

my hesitation and wants to make sure I'm okay. I can read him better now.

I glance at his lip, and he smiles. *Is that why you're holding back? Don't worry. I'm fine.*

So this time, I take his face in my hands and press my mouth to his. Because I already miss him—the touch, the taste, the smell of him. His mouth covers mine, and his arms slip down to my waist, looping behind my lower back. He pulls me close, and warmth bursts in my chest. I've never felt anything like it, and I don't want it to stop.

I push my hands into Cory's hair, and he shivers. This thrills me—but also reminds me.

I reluctantly break the kiss. "I have to cut your hair."

Cory presses his forehead against mine. "Mmm," he murmurs, his breath warm on my face. "True."

I pick up the scissors again, and Cory sits down. But his eyes follow me, bright and alert like he doesn't want to miss anything—or like he's worried I'll vanish if he lets me out of his sight.

I step closer, and his arm lifts, reaching for me, his fingers brushing my waist.

"Cory," I scold, but my heart is drumming. One look, one touch is all it takes.

"Okay, okay." Cory sits on his hands and closes his eyes.

But that doesn't help me as much as I hoped. I want to study every detail of his face, learn every line of his body, and it's easier—not harder—when he's not looking back at me. His chest and shoulders rise and fall as he breathes, and that simple fact delights me. His lips part, and my heart skips a beat. I can't resist. I quietly put the scissors down and step toward him.

I put both hands in his hair and graze my fingers through it until I'm framing his face in my palms.

Cory opens his eyes and leans to meet me just as I press my lips to his smiling mouth.

He hooks his arms around my waist, pulling me closer, and for a moment I'm sure I'm falling—we're both falling, with Cory about to topple backward. But we're fine. His feet stay firmly on the ground, his long legs on both sides of me and his arms wrapped around me like a protective armor.

We were never going to fall—he only did it to make me laugh.

"I thought you were cutting my hair." Light dances in Cory's eyes.

"I'm a little... distracted," I admit.

He chuckles.

"What?"

"You sit in front of me in Physics. You think it's been easy to focus?"

Happiness surges through me, and my face warms.

But the admission surprises me too. "I thought you barely noticed me in class. You always look... like you don't care." I cringe at how harsh that sounds, but it's too late to take it back.

Cory's brows furrow, and his arms tighten around me. "Trust me, when it's about you, *I care.*"

His words take my breath away. But the look in his face, fearless and vulnerable all at once, touches me even deeper. Walls crumble and forces shift inside me, fragments of myself rearranging into a new and stronger whole. My skin feels electric. I stand on new legs, see with new eyes. I travel a great distance in the span of a breath. Even the air smells different. I'm not the same person I was a moment ago.

Eventually, Cory releases me and I start on the haircut. I take my time with it. After a minute or so, Cory opens his eyes and watches me, and I let him. I'm going to be distracted either way. I take the comb from him when I need it, then hand it back.

When I finish, I step back to admire my work. Pearl comes to check on us.

"Hi, Pearl," I say. "What do you think?"

The dog barks, then turns and walks away, her tail smacking my leg.

Cory laughs. "That bad?" His eyes stay on me. If it was my haircut, I'd want to see a mirror, but he seems more interested in my reaction.

"*I* like it."

Cory grins. "Yeah?"

"But I'm not the best judge."

"Why's that?"

Because I already think you're beautiful. Because I care about you a little more every minute. "Because I cut it," I say. "How does it feel?"

Cory puts his hands through his hair and ruffles it. "It feels great. Lighter. Nothing gets in my eyes." He gets up from the stool and wipes at the back of his neck, where cut hairs cling to his skin.

I put down the scissors. "Do you have a towel?"

"I have a better idea." He pulls off his shirt over his head.

I inhale sharply, too surprised to hide my shock.

Scars cover Cory's arms, shoulders, chest, and torso. Short, jagged lines at all angles. I picture a car crash—the windshield shattering, the pieces flying inward and hitting flesh.

"Cory, what happened? Were you in an accident?"

He stops frozen, his face dark and his eyes downcast. "It's nothing. It was a long time ago."

I move closer and take the shirt from his hands. "Let me help you."

He doesn't protest when I use the shirt to wipe the hairs off his neck. I study the scars on his skin, and my heart aches. There are so many. The cuts that caused them had to hurt like hell. Was it a car accident? Or did... someone do it to him? I shudder at the thought.

I gently touch a scar on his chest. "I'm so sorry."

Cory covers my hand with his, but his voice is hollow and distant, like he's suddenly far away. "Don't be. It doesn't matter." He takes the rolled shirt from me and steps away. "I'm going to grab another shirt and then I'll fix your bike."

He wants me to leave. The thought hurts. "Right. I should be going."

Cory frowns. "That's not what I meant."

"I know. But I do have to head back." A strange stubbornness grips me.

Cory's face hardens, light draining from his eyes. "It's up to you."

He runs to the house, using the front door this time. He returns in a fresh shirt and gets right to work on the bike.

I put the scissors away in my sewing kit and bring the backpack down from the porch. "Do you need any help?" I ask coolly.

Cory glances at me. "No. I've got it." He fixes the chain, then adjusts the seat and handlebars for me. "All done. We can go."

I blink in confusion. "*We?*"

Cory's expression is unreadable. "I thought I'd walk you to Highway 15."

To Highway 15? That's almost the whole way. I shake my head. "No. You don't have to do that. I can bike home."

Cory clenches his jaw. "Okay. Then I'll walk you to the main road."

We walk side by side on the gravel, Cory wheeling the bike for me. We reach the main road, and I expect him to hand me the bike. But he leans it against the mailbox and turns to me.

He takes a deep breath. "I... I really like you, Abby. I'm sorry if I did anything to upset you." His voice rings with anxiety, but hope shines in his eyes. "Are we... okay?"

Relief floods me, and I move into him and press my mouth to his. "We're good. I really like you too." I've never said these words to anyone.

Cory exhales and wraps his arms around me, pulling me into a kiss. It's a deeper kiss than those before, as if we lost and found each other again.

I am breathless when I pull back. But I still can't make myself leave, and Cory shows the same reluctance. He laces his fingers through mine and studies our joined hands.

I badly want to see him tomorrow. I want to bike to his farm again. But how do I do this? I can't just show up. I have to say something now. Or should I wait for him to invite me? I know he wants to see me too, and I can't have him over at my place.

"It's supposed to be sunny and warm again tomorrow," I offer. I don't actually care what the weather is like. If the road is still there, that's good enough.

Cory's face brightens, and he squeezes my hand. "Then come back tomorrow. I'll show you the orchard. And you haven't seen the creek yet, or the walking trails in the woods. It's beautiful out there."

The light in his eyes and the pressure of his fingers send a wave of joy through me. He doesn't have to convince me. "What about Physics? We have an exam. I need to study, even if you don't."

"We'll study together. *I promise.*"

"What time?"

"Any time. I'm up at sunrise."

I laugh. "Are you really? *I'm not.*"

Just then, a jeep passes us. It's black and caked with mud, not red and spotless like Jordan's. But it still sends a chill through my body. A bad omen.

A foreboding follows—a sudden certainty that a disaster is heading our way, dark forces conspiring against us, dead set on crushing our dreams and ruining our plans. *Your happiness won't last*, they threaten.

Cory peers at my face, frowning. "Abby? What's wrong?"

I shake my head and manage a smile. I read too

many fairy tales. "Nothing. I'll see you tomorrow."

And I press Cory's fingers one more time before I let him go. Anything more would be tempting fate.

Chapter 26

The next morning, I wake up before my alarm, which never happens, my mind buzzing and my body wired with anticipation. I hurriedly pack my backpack after last night's mostly pointless study attempts. I don't bother with breakfast. I lock the kitchen door behind me, jump on my bike, and I'm off.

The sun is out, but the night chill lingers in the air, biting through my sweatshirt and jeans. I'm not cold for long, though. As soon as I get out of downtown and cross Highway 15, the country road stretches before me, and I step harder on the pedals, my muscles warmed by the effort.

The bike works like a dream after Cory's tune-up, and soon I'm flying down the empty road, the houses and driveways fewer and farther apart, until the sidewalk ends and fields open up on both sides.

The road winds and climbs. When I crest one hill, I catch a glimpse of a red barn up ahead and someone standing on the roof. A few cars pass me, but all trace a wide arc around me, and I'm grateful. The road has no bike lane to speak off, and barely a shoulder sometimes.

I get to Walter Brennell's farm so much faster today that I almost miss the dark red mailbox. I make a sharp turn, gravel popping under my wheels, and skid to a stop.

"Whoa! Are you okay?"

The short haircut confuses me for a second. But it's Cory running in my direction, worry in his eyes.

I get off the bike, breathless and laughing. "I'm fine."

Cory's already next to me, one hand on my arm, steadying me, the other on the handlebar, holding the bike.

I'm still catching my breath, my shins and thighs burning. "Wait. How did you know I was coming?" Then a thought strikes me, and I frown. "Was that *you* on the roof? That's so dangerous."

Cory shakes his head at me, but a smile pulls on the corners of his lips. "Not as dangerous as the speed you were going. So the bike works now? No issues?" He quickly scans the wheels, the chain, then returns his gaze to me.

"It works great. And I was in a hurry."

Cory's eyes are on me. "Why is that?"

I try to keep a straight face. "I need to study. I have a Physics exam tomorrow."

Cory's smile widens. "I thought you came to see

me."

"That too."

I lift my hand to his cheek. His lip looks better today, the swelling almost gone. *Good.* I lean closer, and he does the same, his hand still on my arm, and our mouths collide in a kiss.

When we pull away, he reaches for my backpack. "Let me carry it."

I hand it over, and he chuckles at the weight as he shrugs it on. "What do you have in there?"

"School stuff. Mostly." This includes my polaroid camera. I'd love to take a photo of Cory, but I don't want to freak him out. I'm guessing he's as wary of having his picture taken as I am. I'll have to wait for the right moment.

I wheel the bike and Cory walks next to me.

Halfway to the house, Pearl shows up. I let her sniff my hand, then cautiously pet her head. "Hi, Pearl." She gives a soft bark and ambles away, her guarding and greeting obligations fulfilled.

I glance at Cory, amused. He wasn't joking about the dog ignoring him.

Cory catches it. "She'll remember me when she's hungry. Speaking of—did you have breakfast yet? I have fresh bread and cheese if you like."

My mouth waters. "That sounds great. I'm starving."

Cory laughs. "We'll fix that. Can't study on an empty stomach."

We reach the porch, and I lean the bike against the wall. Cory takes my hand, and my heart flutters in excitement, partly because of his touch, but partly because he lives here, and I long to learn more about him.

Cory pushes open the door and we step inside the house.

The walls in the foyer are painted green, and the floor boards are dark wood. The living room with the flowered sofa is to my right. Two armchairs flank a handsome fireplace. The hallway ahead leads to more rooms in the back, and a steep staircase goes up to the second floor.

I look around me, soaking up the details. The framed photographs in particular draw me like magnets. One wall in the living room is covered with them, and more decorate the hallway. I'd love to inspect them one by one, and search for Cory in them. Some must show him with his parents too…

But Cory turns left, his fingers tight around mine, and ushers me into the kitchen.

The kitchen instantly enchants me. Sunlight pours through two large windows. The cabinets are the same rich dark wood as the floor in the rest of the house, but the floor is cream tiles, and the walls are brick red. A large dark wood table sits in the middle, with chairs on one side and a bench on the other. A matching cupboard hold stacks of white ceramic plates, bowls, and cups, with a collection of painted pottery displayed on the top shelf.

Only the appliances look new—a stainless steel fridge, a microwave, a stove oven.

My mind leaps to Mrs. Smith and her odd comment about being careful, and my face warms. "You have a gas stove too!" I blurt out.

Cory's just setting my backpack on the bench. He raises an eyebrow. "Not a cast iron wood stove, you mean?"

I remember the farmhouse kitchen Skyler painted, and Mike baiting Cory to critique it, and my face gets hotter still. "No, no. I have a neighbor who's obsessed with gas burners causing fires. The last time I saw her, she wanted to know if I'm being careful."

Cory chuckles, his cheeks reddening too. He doesn't miss anything, does he?

"Why're you laughing?" I know perfectly well why, but I want to hear him say it.

"That sounds like… she wasn't talking about fire."

"I know. I was very confused."

Now we're both blushing and cracking up.

But underneath the nerves, I feel another shift inside me—a new idea taking hold in my mind. I've never seriously thought of having sex, nothing beyond idle daydreaming. There's never been anyone I'd let so close to me, anyone I trusted enough to act on my fantasies.

Until I met Cory. Now I want every moment, every touch, to be real. Even if I'm not ready to go all the way.

Cory opens the fridge and starts putting things on the counter: butter in a ceramic dish, sliced cheese wrapped in wax paper, a bowl of blackberries. He pulls out the bread from the bread box. The loaf has a golden crust. He cuts a few slices, the crust crunching and breaking under his knife.

I snatch one slice from the cutting tray.

"Wait," Cory protests. "It's better with butter and cheese."

I lift the bread to my nose. It's still warm and smells of rosemary. I bite into it. It's delicious.

"It's perfect. Did you bake it?"

Cory laughs. "*Me?* No. Jill did. She dropped it off just before you got here."

"She sounds like a good friend." So that's how Cory gets his groceries. I was wondering about that. I finish the bread and lick my fingers.

A shadow crosses Cory's face. "She is." He hurriedly butters the slices and puts cheese on them, then arranges them on a large plate, eyeing me like a thief, which technically I am. He carries the plate and the bowl of berries to the table. I start in that direction, but he intercepts me, shaking his head at my mischief. "Do you drink tea or coffee?"

I shoot him a dirty look. Fine. I'll wait. "Tea, please."

I watch him as he grabs two mugs and drops a tea bag in each. Then fills a teapot and sets it on the front burner. He picks up a long lighter and turns on the gas knob. Blue flames bloom from the burner as the spark hits the gas and devours it.

He turns to me, and the familiar warmth spreads through my body.

"Your lip is better."

"Everything is better," he murmurs, his eyes on mine.

My heartbeat speeds up, but my mind is alert. I catch the front of his shirt and pull him away from the stove. "Careful. Don't start a fire."

His eyes widen at my joke, and he grins, his arms already pulling me close. "I'll try not to. But I feel... very flammable."

I laugh. That's a good way to put it. "Me too."

A shrill, piercing whistle interrupts our kiss. I jump in alarm, and Cory releases me and hurries to the stove. He turns off the burner, and the horrible shriek dies out.

"It was the teapot?" I'm pretty sure the sound will

haunt me in my dreams.

"Sorry. I should've warned you. I'm used to it." Cory lifts the teapot and pours the water into the mugs.

I peer outside the window and spot the hanging swing. "Can we eat on the porch?"

Cory smiles. "Sure. If you want."

He carries the steaming mugs, and I follow with the plate and bowl. The blackberries are lustrous black, and I extract one with my lips. I'm rewarded with a burst of sweetness.

I step on the sunny porch, in the process of stealing another berry, and find Cory watching me with amusement. He sets the steaming mugs on a small table and reaches for my plate and bowl. I surrender the bread but not the berries.

"Really? You're not going to share?" Cory asks.

I take a blackberry in my teeth and offer it to him.

His breath catches. He closes the space between us in one long step, cups my face in his palms, and bites on the berry, his mouth crushing mine. The sweet juice bursts on our tongues.

I take his hand and pull him toward the swing. One by one, the berries disappear from the bowl, each shared between us in a kiss. Fruit has never tasted better.

It's not the quickest way to eat, though, and by now I'm really hungry. So we share the bread and cheese in a less exciting way, the plate on the swing between us and crumbs falling into our laps and onto the floor. I'm sure some brave birds will find them later. I can hear their trills and warbles drifting down from the trees.

We finish sipping our tea, and Cory gets to his feet and collects the dishes. "Come on. Time to study."

I give him a sullen look, but he's right.

We go back into the kitchen. I pull out my Physics textbook, my notebook, and the loose pages with practice problems Mr. Miller gave us to help us review. Cory dashes out the door and returns with his messenger bag. He pulls out his own copy of the textbook, and we sit down across the table from each other.

I push one set of practice problems toward him. Mom's printer can also scan documents, and I made copies at home.

"Thanks." Cory smiles. "Okay. Let's go through the unit section by section. Review the concepts first, then do the problems and discuss the answers. Bonus points for guessing any applications Mr. Miller might ask about. Sounds good?"

"Sounds great." I beam at him, impressed. He could lead a killer study group. I'm lucky.

Cory leafs through his textbook to find the unit we need, and I cringe at the notes scribbled up and down the pages. And not even in pencil—in pen! Mom bought my textbook new for me, but Cory's must be a used rental. So distracting.

Then a pen appears in Cory's fingers, and I realize the notes are his own. I've noticed he never brings a notebook to school. Now I understand why. He reads and takes notes on his own, right in the textbook, and prefers to only listen in class.

We get down to work, and I lose track of time. I've always been good at math and science, but Cory is brilliant at it. Whereas I tend to solve problems by the book, he likes to come up with five unique approaches, each with a different real-life application. I can see why Mr. Miller is a fan. I'm only surprised he doesn't call on Cory more often. But maybe it's because he knows Cory hates showing off. Some teachers are kind like that.

We power through half of the unit before I come up for air, my mind swimming with laws, definitions, and formulas.

I push my book away and stretch my arms until my joints crack. "Can we take a break, please?"

Cory actually hesitates. He frowns at the clock on the wall, as if calculating our average studying speed, efficiency, and energy usage before answering.

I gently kick him under the table, laughing. "*Cory!* A half hour break. I want to see the orchard. You promised."

"True. Come on."

He takes my hand, and we walk out of the house, through the porch, and down the steps to the yard. The gravel road continues to the red barn up on a hill. As we get closer, I crane my neck and shade my eyes to see the high roof.

"How did you climb up there?"

Cory smiles but doesn't stop, pulling me past the red wall and down a foot path that runs along the barn. "I'll show you another time. You said half an hour."

The orchard sits nestled between a corn field and the edge of the woods. It's not very big—just three short rows of trees—but I'm still delighted.

I pull Cory down one green lane overgrown with wildflowers, my head turning from side to side as I examine each tree. So far they are all apple trees, but the apples on each tree look different.

"The apple you brought me. The one I didn't get to eat. Which tree was it from?"

"This way." Cory turns, pulling me behind me.

We cut to the next lane and walk to a tree in the middle. The branches are like a giant, twisted umbrella, hanging lower around the edge.

"Watch your head." Cory steps under the tree, and I follow him.

The air is cooler in the shadow. The leaves are so dark they're almost black, and have sharp, prickly edges. A thick, moss-covered trunk stands on dense roots that dig into the dirt like a monstrous hand trying to free itself. The lowest branches are no higher than my shoulders. I don't see any apples I could reach, though.

Cory jumps up and plucks one for me. "Can you keep a secret?"

"Yes."

He hands me the apple. "Smell it."

I lift it to my nose, and my eyes widen. "It smells like... roses."

Cory looks up at the branches, then at me. "It's magic."

I bite into the apple. It's crisp and sweet, but somehow the hint of roses is still there.

I offer it to Cory, and he takes a bite. We finish the apple between us. I split open the core and shake out the seeds. There's a single one.

"We have to plant it."

We walk to the edge of the orchard and plant the seed there. Cory marks the spot with three rocks, so we can find it later. We're turning into quite the gardeners.

He takes my hand and gives it a tug. "Come on."

"Where're we going now?"

"To study."

I roll my eyes but I'm impressed again. He keeps surprising me—and in the best way. "And when we're done studying? Will you take me up on the roof?"

Cory sighs, not thrilled with the idea. "If you promise to be extra careful, I'll take you up to see the view from the roof. Yes."

I suspect a trick, but I'm too excited to argue. "I promise."

"Okay. It's a deal."

We walk back to the house holding hands.

When we enter the kitchen, I distractedly fish out my phone from my backpack.

Three texts and a missed call from Mom.

"*Shoot.*"

I read the texts and hurriedly type an answer.

Cory watches me with a tense, worried look. "What is it?"

"I have to go. My mom is back early."

He looks relieved. He must have expected worse news. "Back from where?"

"From her trip. She travels for work." I drop the phone back in the backpack, then pack my books, notebook, and problem sets. I wish I knew how long it'll take me to bike back. Hopefully not so long that Mom will get suspicious. "She was supposed to be back tomorrow." Bitterness fills my voice.

"She doesn't know you're here." It's a statement, not a question.

I shake my head. "*Definitely not!*"

Cory's face darkens. "Why not? Would you get in trouble?"

I backpedal. I made it sound like coming here and spending time with him is some terrible offense I have to hide, but that's not what I meant at all. "She just... wouldn't understand."

I know it's not an answer, but I don't have time to explain. I shrug on my backpack and turn to leave.

"Where does your mom think you are?"

"With Heather, this girl from school, studying." But Cory still looks troubled, like he's to blame for my lies, so I add. "My mom doesn't know I do theater either. I just... don't tell stuff like that."

Cory frowns. "You lie to her."

He's just stating a fact, but shame cuts through me like a whip, and I lash out. "Yes, I lie to her. What, you never lie to your mom?"

Pain flashes in Cory's eyes, and he looks away. "I did."

His voice is hollow, and I instantly know his mother died. I suspected his parents were gone. Why else would he come to live with his grandfather? But parents can be out of the picture for many reasons. Just take my dad.

"I'm sorry, I didn't—"

"It's okay," Cory cuts me off. It's clear he doesn't want to talk about it, so I don't ask.

I follow him outside and grab my bike. "I wish I could stay longer."

"You'll review the rest of the unit, right?"

I blink. We're talking about Physics and schoolwork again. "Yes. Sure."

Disappointment cuts through me. Is that all the goodbye I get?

But Cory moves closer. He strokes my hair and peers into my face, then pulls me to him. His kiss is gentle, and his sadness hangs over us like a shadow.

"Be careful on the road. I'll see you tomorrow."

I'm already biking home, racing down the winding road back to town, when I remember my polaroid camera. It's still in my backpack. I never took a picture of Cory.

I'll have to remember next time.

Chapter 27

Monday morning can't come soon enough. I've never been more eager to get to school.

Mom stands at the kitchen counter, clicking through a deck of slides on her laptop, her coffee getting cold and her toast forgotten. She wears her good suit and heels. She's presenting a report to her bosses in an hour, and I can tell she's nervous.

"Mom, you have to go," I remind her.

She looks up. "Yes. You're sure you don't need a ride?"

"I'm sure. Good luck with your report."

She hugs me. "Thanks, honey. Have a good day at school." She slips her laptop in her bag, throws on her coat, and hurries through the backyard to the car.

A minute later, I'm ready to go too. I grab my backpack and step out the kitchen door—only to rush back inside to grab my jacket. I zip it up all the way to my chin and stuff my hands in the pockets, but my teeth are still chattering as I walk to the school bus. It's freezing.

I ride with my cheek pressed to the chilly bus

window, scanning the blacktop for Cory, but I never see him. I hope he's wearing a warm jacket, and the jacket is waterproof. It's not raining yet, but heavy, gray clouds hang low overhead, obscuring the sun. *Please, no rain at lunch.* But I don't get my hopes up. The weather doesn't care what I want.

I step off the bus and join the stream of students heading for the front door.

"Abby!"

My heart leaps, and I turn my head, thinking it's Cory, it must be him. But Jordan catches up with me.

A chill runs down my spine. I forgot all about him.

Blue eyes lock on my face. "How are you?"

I blink. If I didn't know any better, I'd think he was... happy to see me.

I glance at his hands. Bandage wraps each of his wrists like after a tough workout. Clever to do it on both sides.

I keep my voice neutral. "Good. How was California?"

Jordan gives me a slow smile. "Boring. I'm glad to be back. I hope I didn't... *miss anything*."

I look away, my face warming. Does he mean Cory and me? Is he spying on me now? I push the thought away. *Impossible.* Still, the whole conversation unnerves me.

"I have to go." We're already at the door, and I

hurry ahead of Jordan, suddenly anxious to put some distance between us.

But Jordan speeds up too and we enter the building together.

I reflexively scan the crowded hallway for Cory.

There. Leaning against the wall. Elation surges through me when I meet his gaze. He straightens and steps forward—then his eyes slide to Jordan, and his face darkens.

Jordan sees him too. No emotion shows on his face, but his whole body tenses.

I slow my step, suddenly afraid for Cory. "Jordan, about Thursday—"

Jordan turns to me with a smile. "Thursday? Nothing happened on Thursday." He squeezes my arm. "See you at the rehearsal. Oh—and good luck with your exam."

The unwanted touch registers, but I'm too stunned to react. *Nothing happened on Thursday.* Does it mean he's not holding a grudge and won't try to hurt Cory? I desperately want to believe it. But what if it's a trick? And how does he know about my exam?

Jordan heads down the hallway just as Cory moves toward me. They stare at each other, and I hold my breath, expecting them to collide.

But at the last moment, Cory stops and looks down. His shoulders are squared and his jaw clenched, but he lets Jordan pass.

Relief fills me but it's mixed with unease. I think back to Thursday night, and Cory's words echo in my head, bitter and frustrated. *I can't get in a fight. If I as much as laid a finger on him...*

Cory is already next to me. "Hey."

"Hey."

The familiar warmth spreads through me, and I want to step into his arms and kiss him. But I can't. Not here—not with all these people watching.

Cory walks me to my locker. I set my backpack on the floor, take off my jacket and hang it inside the locker, then shrug on my backpack again. I feel Cory's eyes on me but only allow myself a few glances at him. It's hard enough to resist touching him when he stands so close. If I look into his eyes now, I'm done for.

"What did he want?"

The edge in Cory's voice startles me, and I meet his eyes. When my thoughts are on kissing, his mind is stuck on Jordan.

He said nothing happened on Thursday. But I can't tell Cory that. Not right now. It'd be like touching a spark to a gas cloud. Something else. Quick. Anything. What else did Jordan say? "He said hi and... wished me good luck on the exam."

Cory's eyes narrow. "How does he know about that?"

I asked myself the same question, but now I shrug. "Maybe Mr. Miller mentioned it? Who cares." I brush Cory's hand. "Just forget him. It doesn't matter what he knows. *He can't touch us.*"

Cory stares at me, a complicated emotion in his face—and I freeze, terrified he's going to kiss me, right here in front of everyone. A part of me wants him to.

But he looks away. "We should go."

"Right." The exam.

We start down the hallway toward the Physics classroom. Normally, my stomach would be in a knot by now, my panicked mind spinning visions of failure and humiliation. But today, my nerves oscillate between the usual dread and a strange new excitement. Dread because Mr. Miller never asks easy questions, and I need to keep my grades up. Excitement because now every topic in Physics makes me think of Cory.

I pause outside the classroom and take a deep breath.

Cory leans closer. "You've got it, Abby. Have fun."

I shake my head. Fun taking a Physics exam? *No way.* But the light in Cory's eyes wins me over.

"You too."

The oscillations collapse into a cautious confidence as I step through the door.

At lunch, rain pounds the cement patio and the fields outside the cafeteria window. My rotten luck. So much for sneaking out the back door to find Cory. I didn't see him since Physics. He finished his exam early and Mr. Miller sent him on some errand.

I'm looking around the main hallway for him when Heather intercepts me. Her nails dig into my arm. "Abby! Only three weeks left. How can you be so calm? I'm freaking out."

She looks and sounds so distraught, I let her drag me to her table. We spend the lunch hour racing through a hundred SAT problems at a breakneck speed. She's done them all already, and the solutions look fine to me, but she doesn't trust herself, trapped by self-doubt.

I try to help her the way Cory helped me. "Heather, *you've got it*. You're going to do great. Don't worry."

But the encouragement only irks her. She frowns at me with reproach. "You don't know that. Anything can happen. I need to be *certain*."

What if there's no such thing as certain? I muse after Heather's gone, and I'm walking to my next class. *What if some risk is always there, impossible to avoid? The risk you might be wrong or make a mistake or fail altogether. The risk you might get hurt—or you might hurt someone else, even though you don't mean to.*

By the end of classes, I'm really anxious to see Cory. I text Mom I'm staying at school to study and head over to the cafeteria. I sit at my favorite corner booth, pull out my books, and try to focus on my homework.

The rain has stopped, and the sun peeks from behind the clouds, the puddles on the ground shining like mirrors. What if Cory went home, and he's not coming back for the rehearsal? There's little for the set crew to do for the next week or so, until the full run-throughs.

I grab a pencil and lean over the problem set.

"Hey."

Cory slides into the seat across from me, his eyes bright.

My breath catches and my heartbeat speeds up, and I drop my gaze to my homework, suddenly self-conscious. I pretend to read a line, as if I wasn't waiting for him all along. "Hey."

"What's wrong?" Worry rings in Cory's voice.

I look up. "I thought you went home."

Cory's face relaxes. "Why would I do that when *you're here?*" He reaches for my hand across the table and laces his fingers with mine.

Happiness zaps through me, and I can't hold back a smile. It's still a mystery to me how he does it. But a touch, a look, a few words are enough. It's like stepping into the sun.

"I don't know. Maybe you forgot me." I let my fingers wander over his skin, stroking his knuckles, the back of his hand, his wrist.

"Impossible." Cory watches me with bright eyes. "By the way, if you're casting some spell on me, it's working."

I laugh. "*Good.*" What I really want is to lean forward and kiss him. But not here. I'm too afraid some cast or crew member will stroll into the cafeteria and see us. "I should warn you, though. I'm new at this, and I don't really know what I'm doing. So if you suffer some dangerous side effects, that's why."

I meant it as a joke, not a confession. But emotion passes Cory's face, his gaze so intense my cheeks warm. His voice is low and earnest when he answers, "Do whatever you want to me, Abby. For as long as you want."

My heart leaps, but the last part burns like a splinter. He makes it sound like there's an end date to my feelings for him. "*For as long as I want?*"

Cory pales and shakes his head. "How was Physics? Do you want to go over the problems or you'd rather wait for your grade?"

He changed the subject, but I let it go. "Of course I want to go over the problems." I've never been good at waiting, and I do want to see what I got right and what I missed. "But how? We don't have a copy of the exam."

Cory grins, his color returning. "Sure we do. Can I have a pen and paper?"

And he recreates the exam, problem by problem, from memory. Not word for word, and he makes up some values, but it's still impressive. We discuss each answer, then tally the points we'd get. Cory gets a perfect score—better than perfect if you count the extra credit. But I'm just as happy with my A minus.

"Awesome!"

We high-five each other over the table, laughing.

That does it. Longing wells up in me. If I don't kiss him right now, I'm going to burst.

I hurriedly pack my backpack, then shrug it on and get to my feet.

Cory stands up too. "We're going? It's early—"

"I know." For once, I'm ahead of him. But where to? Away from the theater.

Cory follows me out of the cafeteria. "Are we going to watch Neon and Patricia rehearse?"

I hide a smile. We might—after. If there's time. "Come on. This way."

When I start up the stairs instead of turning down the main hallway, Cory falls silent, and I know he's figured it out. The moment we get to the second floor, he takes my hand and pulls me into a nook near the library.

He's smiling when he leans his face close to mine, his arms already wrapped around me. "That was your plan, right?"

"Yes." But I'm too impatient for talk. I cup his face in my hands and press my mouth to his.

※

I rush into the costume room only minutes before the rehearsal, my face still warm and my lips tingling. I drop off my backpack and check my phone, then grab the Beast's mask and hurry out the door. Mrs. Adams wants to do two scenes today to make up for Friday, and Jordan is in both of them.

I run into Tammy in the wing. She gives me a strange look. "Abby. Hi. Jordan's waiting for you. He wants to retest the mike before they start."

"I'm here." Since when does Tammy care what Jordan wants? But Tammy lingers, clearly troubled, and now I'm uneasy too. What if it's not about Jordan at all? "What's up?"

"Umm..." Tammy begins, but a screech of a wheel cuts her off.

We both turn to the stage. Several crew members are just rolling in the set pieces that make up the castle. Cory is among them, pushing the large platform. He nods to me, and I smile.

Tammy glances from Cory to me and frowns. "Never mind. *It's nothing.* You better go." And she slips past me and hurries backstage, shaking her head.

But by the end of the rehearsal, I know it's definitely *not* nothing.

The signs are impossible to miss. A tense silence that falls over the stage when I help Jordan put the mask on or take it off. The whispered conversations that stop as if snipped with scissors when I walk past. The furtive glances and wary, suspicious frowns of the cast and crew. Until the air feels so charged and toxic, I can barely breathe.

What the hell is going on?

Then I get my answer. It comes in sharp, urgent whispers in between Jordan's and Marie's smooth voices booming from the speakers as they rehearse the scene.

"…Handcuffs? Are you serious?"

"…I've never seen him act weird, but…"

"…I know. What if he snaps again?"

I walk away before I recognize the voices. I don't trust myself to keep my temper. It's safer to picture a faceless rumor mill churning out collective hostility.

I thought I was the target. *Wrong.*

The target is Cory—and that makes it worse.

But I have no doubt who's behind it, feeding the

mill and fanning the flames, keen to enjoy the carnage without ever dirtying his hands.

From the shadow of the wing, I stare daggers at his back, the Beast's hideous mask a more truthful depiction of his character than the handsome face underneath it.

So much for *nothing happened on Thursday*, Jordan.

Chapter 28

Every day this week, I go to school hoping the rumors died down. I tell myself to ignore the obnoxious stares and grating whispers that follow Cory and me at every step—in the hallway, in class, during the rehearsal. If we don't let the gossip bother us, surely people will get tired and leave us alone, right?

A naïve wish, and it doesn't work.

Gossip is like trash dumped into a river. Invisible currents snatch bits of it and spread it all over. You have no idea it's even there, or how ugly it is, until it pops up next to you or you step on it and get cut. But by then it's too late—the whole river is polluted.

Cory acts like nothing's going on. I don't know how he does it. He hates being in the spotlight even when it's praise for something he did right, and this is infinitely worse. Still, he shows none of it, his face like a stone.

I don't have that kind of self-control. I get angrier and angrier. By Tuesday, I start returning the stares, so people will get the message. *You have something to say to me? Then say it to my face—or keep your mouth shut*.

How much did Jordan tell them about what had happened in the parking lot? Surely, he never mentioned he'd grabbed me, or the chokehold he'd put on Cory, or the fact that Cory had won without throwing a single punch. What's left, then? Admitting Cory had handcuffed him to the fence would only make Jordan look weak. He wouldn't brag about me choosing to walk home with Cory rather than get a ride from him either.

No. The truth is not in Jordan's favor. The rumors he's spreading are nothing but vengeful lies.

I'm dying to hear them, so I can strike them down one by one and set the record straight. I'm sick of the whole school looking at Cory like he's a criminal. But I refuse to stoop to that level.

It's more than that, though. I have a feeling Cory wants me to ignore the rumors, like he does. Maybe in his mind, if I hear them, Jordan wins. But it's just a guess. We don't talk about it, and I don't have the heart to ask him.

On Wednesday morning, I walk into the Physics classroom a step ahead of Cory. A stack of papers sits on Mr. Miller's desk. He graded the exams!

A nervous anticipation cuts through me. I'm counting on an A minus, after reviewing the answers and tallying the points with Cory, but what if we made a mistake and my grade is worse?

"Good morning, Mr. Miller," Cory says behind me.

Mr. Miller looks up from his computer. "Cory. Abby." He nods to each of us, clearly pleased to see us, and just like that, my worry eases. I know I did well on the exam—and Mr. Miller noticed. Maybe even figured out I studied for it with Cory.

I turn around and glance at the boy behind me. He meets my eyes and smiles, as if guessing my thoughts, and sweetness spreads through me. He's happy I did well, maybe happier than I am. I want to touch him, give him some sign it means a world to me, my fingers already reaching for his hand.

But Mr. Miller turns on the projector and we're caught in the spotlight, so I drop my hand and keep moving. More students file into the room behind us.

I get into my seat and pull out my notebook, still in a blissful haze, only to find Gwen staring at me.

"That apple was for you, wasn't it?"

I blink. What apple? *Oh.* The apple on my desk, which she took. For a moment, I'm back in the orchard, standing under the apple tree with Cory. I hide a smile and shrug. "It's okay. You didn't know."

But Gwen narrows her eyes. She wasn't apologizing. "*Okay?* How was it okay? I *ate* that apple. What if it was drugged or something?" she hisses.

"*Drugged?*" I whisper back, my good mood

evaporating.

Mr. Miller closes the door and dims the lights, and a video starts playing on the screen, but I'm not really paying attention.

"It smelled weird," Gwen insists. She points with her head to the back row. "You should've warned me it was from *him*."

The accusation riles me. She thinks Cory would drug me? I struggle to hold my temper. "Cory left it on *my* desk. A surprise gift. He didn't expect anyone else to take it."

Gwen flinches when I say Cory's name, not hiding her shock. "I figured he had a thing for you. But... you like him back?"

"It's none of your business," I snap, my cheeks hot. A coward's response. Why should I be ashamed of liking Cory? "Actually, you know what? I do like him. *A lot*."

Gwen swallows, then leans closer. She gapes at me with a morbid fascination. "You mean... you're not afraid to be alone with him?"

I let out a furious breath, my blood boiling. "*Afraid?* I trust him with my life. And I'm sick of people spreading stupid rumors."

Gwen's mouth falls open.

"No talking, please!" Mr. Miller pauses the video and steps in front of the screen, squinting in the projector's light. "Unless you're discussing today's topic and want to share your thoughts. In which case we all want to hear them. Anyone?"

A hushed silence falls over the room. Mr. Miller waits another moment, then sighs and returns to his usual spot. He clicks the remote and the video resumes.

I fix my gaze on the screen, my jaw clenched and fury pulsing in my veins. I don't look at Gwen again, and she doesn't say another word to me, which is smart of her.

At the end of class, we get our exams back. My grade is actually an A, since Mr. Miller generously awarded me partial points for the extra credit I attempted but didn't finish. But I can't enjoy it anymore. I stuff the exam in my backpack and rush out of the room, a bad taste in my mouth.

Cory falls in step with me in the hallway, a troubled look in his eyes. "Abby. Is it the exam? How did you do?"

Irritation grips me, and I walk faster. He should be worried about the rumors Jordan is spreading about him, not about my grade. He needs to act, to speak up and defend himself, not turn the other way. Jordan isn't going to stop. And I can't help him if he won't let me.

Cory pales. I still haven't answered his question. He must think I failed. "How bad is it?"

I shake my head. "No, it's fine. I got an A. He gave

me points for the extra credit."

Cory exhales. "Good. That's good. So... you want to tell me what's wrong?"

We reach the staircase and start up. At least there are fewer students to stare at us here. But still no privacy and not enough time to talk. I don't want Cory to be late for class. He's still watching me, though, his brows knotted. I have to tell him something.

"The usual. People getting on my nerves," I mutter.

Cory takes my hand, his touch warm and reassuring. "Ignore them."

I grip his fingers and look him in the eye, the anger and frustration returning. "*I can't!* That's the problem."

Cory's face darkens. We climb to the second floor in silence.

But before we step into the hallway, he turns to me again. "Meet me outside at lunch?"

My heartbeat speeds up. The rain has stopped. I just have to evade Heather. I nod. "Okay."

"Okay." He squeezes my fingers before he lets go of my hand.

03&0

A gust of wind sends a chill through me when I step out the back door at lunch. When did it get so cold? My sweater is way too thin. But getting my jacket from the locker would take too long, and now that I'm here, I'm anxious to see Cory.

I hook my thumbs under the straps of my backpack and hurry to the storage shed.

But he's not here yet.

I step behind the small building. It rained last night. The ground is too wet to sit on. Shallow puddles dot the sidewalk and the staff parking lot, reflecting the overcast sky. But maybe the wall can shield me from the wind. I'm freezing.

Come on, Cory. Where are you?

Another gust of wind makes me shiver. The shed is no protection. I wrap my arms around myself and let my eyes and my mind wander as I wait.

The summer is definitely gone. The mowed grass is still green, but the field beyond it is a patchwork of sage, rust, yellow, and brown. The oaks and maples in the distance sway and shudder in the wind. Some branches are already bare, a few broken off. But the assault isn't over. Each gust snaps another small branch, tears off more leaves, harsh and relentless. I'm watching a torturer at work.

The old questions come back to nag me. Why did Cory carry handcuffs on him? Where did he learn to pick locks? How did he get the scars?

And, most of all, why does he give me this tense, searching look sometimes—like he's waiting for something and dreading it at the same time? The look is gone a moment later, but my heart still aches for him. What is Cory so afraid of? And why won't he tell me about it? I can't stand to see him in pain. But he needs to trust me first.

"Abby. Hey."

Cory comes to a halt next to me, his breath quickened like he ran here. He takes one look at me and frowns. "You're cold."

"I'm fine," I lie.

Cory shrugs off his bag and drops it on a dry patch of ground next to the shed. Then unzips his hoodie and peels it off. He holds it out for me. "Here. Put it on."

I hesitate. "What about you?" He's wearing a flannel shirt underneath, but it can't be warm enough.

But Cory only moves closer. "Come on. Please."

He reaches for my backpack, and I surrender it. He sets it down on the ground next to his bag and practically puts the hoodie on me, guiding each arm into one sleeve.

I can't help a smile. "Are you going to zip me up too?"

It's a joke, but Cory deftly grabs the two parts of the zipper and zips me up to my chin.

I slip away from him, laughing, before he can put the hood over my head. "Okay, okay. I'm good. I'm warm."

And it's true. The hoodie feels wonderful, warmer than it looks. Or maybe it's Cory's body heat. Either way, I love it. It smells like him too. I want to lift the front over my nose and inhale that smell. But I can't do it when he's looking right at me.

I feel the familiar pull, like a rope tightening around me and reeling me in toward him. A part of me tries to resist, or not resist as much as delay. I badly want to kiss him, but I need to talk to him first, and the lunch break is short…

Cory leans closer, his gaze never leaving my face. He takes my hand and laces his fingers with mine. His lip is healed, the cut and swelling gone. He smiles.

And just like that, my heart starts to race in anticipation. I want to kiss him. I *need* to kiss him. We can talk later. I lean toward him.

But at the last moment, Cory turns his head, and instead of kissing my mouth, his lips brush my ear, and he whispers, "I want to show you something."

He tugs on my hand, already turning, and I follow him into the field, stunned at the trick he played on me.

I'm still deciding how to tell him off—maybe I won't kiss him at all today, and see how he likes that—when Cory stops. He lets go of my hand and crouches in the grass. Moves some leaves aside and points at the ground. "Look."

The happiness in his voice gives it away. I crouch

next to him. "The seed we planted?"

"It's a proud *seedling* now." Cory gently touches the tiny green thing that pokes out of the dirt next to the rocks that mark the spot. "It has leaves."

I laugh. "I can't believe it. I didn't think it was going to work."

Cory throws me a reproachful look. "I knew it would."

I marvel at the baby plant. It looks so fragile. But it survived so far. "So what happens now?"

"A couple more years, and it'll be a sapling."

"No way. That long?" I shouldn't be surprised. It takes forever for a tree to grow. But an odd sadness seeps into my thoughts. I get to my feet. "We'll be gone by then. I mean, we'll graduate."

Cory gets up too. "We can come visit."

We both step away from the tiny plant, careful not to crush it, and turn to each other. I see my strange mood reflected in Cory's eyes, and my chest tightens.

The notion of graduating high school and going away to college suddenly terrifies me, even if we're only juniors. How am I going to see Cory after I leave? What if he moves away too, and we end up far away from each other? I try to picture us in two years and draw a blank. Too many forces at work, and I have no control over any of them. Instead of a clear path, the future is a vast, cold unknown.

I take a shuddering breath, and Cory steps closer. He strokes my hair, then cups my face in his hands and peers into my eyes. "Hey. It's going to be okay. *We're going to be okay.*"

I don't know how he does it—read my mind like that. I never thought I'd want anyone to have that power. But I'm glad Cory does. It saves me the frustration of trying to express things I have no words for. I just wish I could read *him* better.

"I know," I say, and I want to believe it.

I want to believe he and I can weather this storm together and be all right. But questions swarm in my head again, and fear crawls up my spine. It was how Cory said—the note of defeat in his voice. Like he's wishing things will work out but has no hope they will.

"I never dreamed I'd meet someone like you, Abby," Cory says. "I don't deserve you."

Tears sting my eyes. This is too much. Why would he say something like that? I grab his shirt and pull him closer. "Are you going to kiss me or not?"

And Cory does. He wraps his arms around me and covers my mouth with his.

The kiss stretches, neither of us wanting to pull away.

Until an odd sensation prickles the back of my neck. I tense, breaking the kiss, and twist around to look at the school building.

Someone's been watching us from the second-floor window. Now they step out of view.

I frown, unnerved. I only caught a glimpse of the face. But I'd recognize it anywhere.

Jordan.

☙❧

I do my best to ignore the rumor mill for the next two days. If that's what Cory wants, I owe him to try. I take extra detailed notes in all my classes, avoid eye contact in the hallways, and keep to the costume room as much as I can during the rehearsals. When I'm too restless to sleep at night, two hours of furious SAT prep knock me out flat.

But my resolve implodes when Jordan strolls into the costume room Friday night, fifteen minutes before the official rehearsal.

"Abby. So that's where you're hiding." He gives me a slow smile, his eyes the dark blue of storm clouds in the dim light.

I'm by myself, attaching bright feathers and fake gemstones to a hat for one of the Sisters. Tammy and Zoe like to watch Neon and Patricia practice their scenes. They're often the only audience and do it partly for moral support, which is sweet of them. Although right now, I selfishly wish they were here, in the costume room, with me.

I freeze, my eyes on Jordan's hands. If he tries to close the door behind him, I'm walking out. I don't want to be near him any more than I have to even with the others around, and definitely not alone.

Jordan's eyes narrow, but he leaves the door open.

I relax a fraction. "What do you want, Jordan?"

"I want this play to be spectacular. I want rave reviews and casting calls. And I want everyone in the audience to still remember my name fifty years from now." He circles the small room, pretending to look around. When he gets to the rack for Beauty and the Beast, he passes his hand over the costumes until he finds his own blue coat.

I roll my eyes. That's not what I was asking, and he knows it. I put away the hat I'm holding. It's not like I can focus on my work right now. "What do you want *from me?*"

But Jordan's face is serious. "I just told you. *You* are the key to our success—to my success. You and the incredible costumes you make." He spots the box with the Beast's mask and picks it up. Opens the lid and admires the mask. Then closes the box and turns his gaze on me. "I hope you know how important you are. I can't do it without you, Abby."

I blink, annoyed, because my cheeks are warm and my heart is hammering, even though I know it's all an act and I can't trust a single word coming out of his mouth.

I get to my feet, cross the small space, and snatch the box from his hands. "I'll be there in a few minutes to help you get ready. But you don't have to come here. Just wait on stage. I'm busy."

A grimace twists Jordan's mouth. "You've definitely been busy."

Does he mean me and Cory? Anger slams into me. "*So have you!* Spreading all the lies about Cory. It must take a lot of effort. Is it worth it? What do you get out of it?"

Jordan's eyes flash. "*Lies?* I never told a single lie about him. I swear it."

He's a great actor. If I didn't know any better, I'd think my accusation hit a nerve. "Right. Sure you didn't. It's always someone else."

Jordan takes a step toward me. "It's not what you think, Abby. I'm your friend. And as your friend, I need to tell you—"

"*Jordan!*"

Tammy stands in the door, staring daggers at him.

Jordan slowly turns his head. "Hi, Tam. Abby and I are in the middle of something. Do you mind?"

Tammy walks right in. "Too bad. The director wants you."

Jordan still doesn't budge. "Now? What is it?"

"I don't know. Why don't you go ask her?"

Jordan's face relaxes into a smile that's just a notch too bright. He starts for the door, his steps unhurried, but stops next to Tammy. "You used to be fun, Tam. What happened?"

Tammy's cheeks turn red but she raises her chin and glares at him. "Get out, Jordan. You have no business here."

Jordan looks back at me. "Actually, I do. I meant to ask Abby. Are the Beast's hands ready yet?"

The gloves. I finished them last week but I've kept him waiting. A small payback. "Not yet. I'll let you know." A lie. But that'll gain me time till Monday.

"You okay?" Tammy asks me after Jordan leaves.

I haven't talked to her in a while. Does she buy into the rumors about Cory? If she's really my friend, she wouldn't, but I don't know for sure. I'm tempted to ask her, but I have to run to help Jordan in a moment.

So I keep my voice neutral. "I'm fine. Thanks for kicking him out."

And I mean it. I'm grateful she stood up for me.

But a part of me regrets Tammy's timing and wonders. *What was Jordan going to tell me when she came in?*

Chapter 29

Saturday morning, I'm up with the sun again. No need for the alarm—the thought of spending time with Cory is enough to wake me. I'm about to throw off my comforter and jump out of the bed when I remember Mom is still at home. She's leaving on another trip this morning, but what time? She mentioned it, but I forgot. I've been distracted this week.

I sit up in semi darkness. My room is small and crammed with furniture meant for a bigger space. A queen bed with a trundle and a side table. An armchair draped with my clothes and holding a pile of day pillows. Several tall bookshelves. A large, cluttered desk sits under a window that overlooks the backyard. Next to it, a low dresser blocks a glass door to a tiny balcony. Not ideal, but it was the only place to put it, and the dresser is solid enough I can sit on it, rotate my legs, and voila—I'm on the balcony.

Faint sunlight filters through the closed blinds, beckoning for me to get up, get dressed, and jump on my bike. Cory is waiting.

Mom must be up by now. If I get up, she'll hear the

old floor boards creaking under the rug and know I'm awake. I want to go downstairs and make her coffee and toast. But what if she asks about my plans for the day? She doesn't know about Cory, and I don't want to lie to her about him.

I'm still sitting on my bed, debating, when I hear a door open and close downstairs.

Mom is leaving!

I don't know where the urgency comes from, but I leap out of bed and race barefoot down the stairs and into the kitchen. I get to the backyard door and throw it open just as Mom gets to the back gate.

"Mom!"

She turns, surprised, the wheels of her suitcase rolling into the grass and getting stuck there.

"Abby? Honey, what is it? I hope I didn't wake you. I left you a note." She's wearing her comfortable pants and a sweatshirt, which means she has a long drive ahead.

I run on my tiptoes to where she's standing, the grass cold under my feet and a chilly air biting through my pajamas. "Wait! I just want to wish you a safe trip."

Mom laughs and pulls me into a hug. "Oh. Thank you, honey. Now get back to bed. It's still early. You can sleep in one day, can't you? You work so hard."

"Not as hard as you."

She kisses my hair. "Go on inside before you catch

a cold. I'll text you when I get to Chicago."

Chicago. That's about ten hours of driving. "I love you, Mom."

"I love you too, honey."

She steps through the gate, loads her suitcase into the trunk of the car, and gets behind the wheel.

As she pulls out of the parking spot, I wave to her. She waves back before driving away.

I chew on my lip as I hurry back to the kitchen, guilt burning in my stomach. Mom thinks I studied with Heather every day last week, but I wasn't. I was at the rehearsals.

I can't keep lying to her like that. About theater—or about Cory. But how would she react if she knew?

Three more weeks before the show. Then I'll tell her the truth. No more excuses.

൞ഌ

A rude truck driver almost clips my back wheel when I bike across Highway 15, even though I have the green light. But after that, there's nothing to slow me down. I step on the pedals and race down the road.

Ranch houses flash past me. Curved pumpkins sit on doorsteps, and fake spider webs cover the windows. Halloween is next week. But it's the backyards that draw my eye. I catch a glimpse of a half-collapsed shed, a rusted car frame on bricks, a large metal cage overgrown with weeds. Weird. I've never noticed them before. I can hear the rumbling of the creek that runs behind the backyards all the way from here.

I pass the blacktop that leads to the school, and soon the houses fall away. Tall, yellowing corn stalks line the road for a while, their leaves sharp like knives. Then those fall behind too, and it's nothing but rolling fields and patches of forest with an occasional house or barn in the distance. I'm getting close.

I pedal harder, climb a hill, then fly down the other side.

By the time I turn into Cory's driveway, sweat dots my hairline and trickles down my back under my backpack, jacket, sweatshirt, and t-shirt. Some of it is the workout. But the weather is warmer than I planned for, and I'm wearing too many layers.

Not that I'm complaining. The sun feels wonderful. It's like the summer is back for a day.

Cory is already waiting for me. His eyes light up. "Hey."

"Hey." I jump off my bike and hand him my backpack. "Take this."

He grabs the strap and shrugs it on his shoulder, smiling. "Okay."

"And this." I hand over my bike.

But I'm not done yet. I peel off my jacket. I pause,

deciding. But I'm still too warm, and Cory's in a t-shirt. I grab my sweatshirt and pull it over my head. "Aww. That's better."

A touch startles me. Cory's hand brushes my lower back, his fingers cool on my hot skin.

My breath catches, and I turn to face him, my arms full of clothes.

Instantly, Cory's hand is gone. His shoulders tense, and his eyes search mine. "Sorry. I was just pulling down your t-shirt."

He's giving me this look again, like he's uncertain if I want him to touch me. Why? Doesn't he know I do? I give him an encouraging smile. "Is it down? Are you sure? You better check."

Cory relaxes. He moves closer and slips his free arm around me, smoothing my t-shirt over my back. His other hand holds the bike. "It's good."

A restlessness grips me. I want his hands on my bare skin, not on top of my t-shirt. And I need my own hands free. I should've tossed my jacket and sweatshirt on the ground. But Cory's face is only inches away. Light dances in his eyes, and a smile pulls on his lips. So I stop worrying and wishing—and instead lean forward and kiss him.

Cory's arm tightens around me, but his kiss is slow and gentle. And careful—like I'm something fragile and valuable he's afraid to break. Then he pulls away and studies my face—my eyes, my forehead, my nose, my lips. It's like he's memorizing my picture to get it right on an exam. But what for? I'm right here. I'm not going anywhere.

A low whine of the engine hits my ears. The car is a dark, blurred shape in my corner vision when it speeds past us.

Cory doesn't react, his mind far away.

"Cory, what is it?"

He blinks, refocusing. He glances at the road behind us. "We shouldn't stand so close to the road. Let's go to the house. I'll make you breakfast."

Then he lifts his hand to my face. His fingertips trace my sweaty hairline. He presses his mouth there.

The kiss is so tender and unexpected, my stomach flutters, and my knees go weak. What is he doing to me?

"Okay," I whisper. He could've asked me anything right now, told me to do anything, and I would've done it.

The house looks different, colder and less inviting somehow, the white walls a stark contrast against the darkening reds and browns of the shrubs in front and the oaks behind it. Some of the blue window shutters are closed, and the rocking chairs and hanging plants are gone from the porch. Fallen leaves litter the roof and the yard.

But the kitchen looks the same, and it feels like coming home, although I've only been here twice. Cory's strange mood must be getting to me.

Today, the breakfast is corn bread, golden yellow and still warm, judging by the delicious smell. Cory puts several slices on a plate, then boils the water and makes two mugs of tea. He's quiet as he works, barely saying a word, although he keeps glancing in my direction.

I move to the kitchen table, not wanting to be in his way. But the longer I watch him, the more uneasy I grow. Why the silence? Clearly, something's bothering him. Is he going to tell me what it is—or keep torturing both of us? I have enough questions rattling in my head already. One more could push me over the edge.

Cory puts the plate and the steaming mugs on a wooden tray, picks it up, and turns to me. "Do you want to eat on the porch?"

"Why did you have the handcuffs?" I didn't mean to ask it now, but I forget myself for a moment, and the question slips out.

Cory's face changes. Slowly, he crosses the kitchen and sets the tray at the end of the table, like he's afraid to drop it and spill the blistering hot tea on both of us. Then he sits down in the chair across from me.

It feels like hours before he speaks. "I bought them online."

That's not an answer. Dread cuts through me, but I have to know. "Why?"

Another long pause. His voice is hollow. "To remind me."

"Of what?"

Pain twists Cory's face, and he bends his head, his hands clenching into fists. "Of who I am."

His emotion slams into me. I've never seen him like this. I can barely breathe, a wordless fear choking me. "I don't... understand..."

Cory looks up at me, and something shifts behind his eyes. He shakes his head, then leans back and slips his hands under the table.

"My father..." He trails off, then tries again, his voice calmer now. "My father was a cop. He was killed on the job. Shot in the back of the head when making an arrest. Right after he handcuffed a guy."

I stare at him, numb and confused. He just told me his father was murdered. So why do I feel relief? This is wrong.

"He wasn't even supposed to be there," Cory continues. "His shift got moved. And the guy he caught was a kid. Thirteen or fourteen. My age then. They were all kids, the whole gang. That's why my father didn't use his gun, I think. He looked at them and saw me."

He lets out a long breath, like a weight is off his

shoulders, and falls silent. The silence stretches.

"I'm sorry you lost your father," I whisper. I don't know what else to say. "Do you miss him?"

Cory's face hardens. "No. Not really. He wasn't home much, and when he was around, he was... harsh." He hesitates. "But I think about him a lot. About how he died, and why."

"My father is alive, but I don't miss him either. He lives in New Zealand now. He remarried. He may even have kids. I don't know, and I don't care. We don't keep in touch."

I cringe when I hear myself say it. I've never shared this with anyone, not even Mom. It sounds awful, even though it's true. What's Cory going to think?

But Cory only nods. "That's okay. I'm sure he deserves it." Then he adds, "But if, at some point, you decide to give him another chance, that's okay too. It's up to you."

My chest tightens. I didn't realize how badly I needed to hear this until Cory said it. I always assumed the fault was mine. What heartless monster wouldn't miss her parent? But Cory gets it. With him, I don't have to pretend.

I frown at the table that separates us—four feet of solid dark wood. Too far to reach across. I need him closer. There's plenty of room on the bench beside me.

But I'm suddenly too self-conscious to ask. What if he doesn't want to sit by me? Or kiss me? I can't force him.

Instead, I look away and reach for my backpack, an obvious diversion, and I'm sure Cory can see through it.

"My mom is on the road today," I explain as I check my phone. No messages.

I put the phone away, and my eyes snag on the SAT prep book. I sigh. I brought it with me for a reason. I need to study, even though it's the last thing I want to do right now.

Cory sits down on the other side of my backpack and peers inside it. I didn't hear him get up, but I'm used to him soundlessly appearing next to me. One of his many talents.

He pulls out my prep book. "Right. You're taking the SAT."

"Hey! You've ever heard of boundaries?"

"I've heard of them." He studies the list of contents, then pages through the book, unfazed. "So when is it?"

I wince. I wish he didn't ask. Saying it makes it real. "Two weeks from now. When are *you* taking it?"

He smiles. "*Not* in two weeks. So let's focus on you first." He sets the book in front of me on the table. Then remembers the breakfast tray and slides it closer, frowning. "You have to eat, though. I'll make another tea." He whisks the two mugs away.

Why are you so nice to me, Cory? But I'm not brave enough to ask him. Not today.

Reluctantly, I pull the book closer and pick up a pencil. Find the spot where I stopped the last time, barely past the middle of the book. My erasing was sloppy, and the page still has faint markings of the previous owner, but I ignore them. If I make mistakes, they'll be my own.

"Sorry to interrupt." I finally get my wish, and Cory sits on the bench beside me. He sets the steaming mug on the table. "Here's your tea. Careful, it's hot."

"Thanks."

He glances at the untouched plate. "If you don't like corn bread, I'll make you something else."

My stomach is still in a knot for several different reasons. But I don't want to pass out and scare him, and I need to bike home later. So I take a piece of corn bread and bite into it, trying to catch all the crumbs.

"No, no. I like it. It's good. What about you? You're not eating either."

Cory blinks, then grabs a piece of corn bread for himself. "Sure I am."

Once the food hits my stomach, my hunger stirs. We clear the plate between us and wash it down with tea, still delightfully hot. Cory takes the empty dishes to the sink.

I wait for him to come back and sit next to me. But he dashes out of the kitchen and returns with a large blanket and a book.

"Want to study in the orchard?"

I'm on my feet at once. I grab my prep book and a pencil. "Of course I do."

Chapter 30

We step outside the house and follow the footpath past the barn to the orchard. The sun is warm on my face and arms, and normally that would cheer me up, and it does a little. But today I don't trust it. The dead leaves rustling under my shoes seem more truthful somehow. The breeze carries a faint, sweet odor of decay.

I keep waiting for Cory to take my hand but his arms are full and he never does.

We weave our way between the apple trees to the edge of the orchard. A large wooden crate sits on the ground, as tall as my waist. Tall grass hugs the bottom and vines are starting to climb the walls. The lid is crooked, the wood buckling from exposure. A loose board leans against one side.

Cory starts to set his book on top of the crate, but I reach for it. "I can hold it."

He hands it to me, smiling. "Thanks."

The book is heavy. I glance at the cover. *Electric Circuits*. It's a used college textbook.

Cory brings over the loose board and props it against the wall, then hangs the blanket over it and spreads it on the grass in front. The blanket is huge and has a leaf pattern. A makeshift outdoor sofa.

He inspects his creation, fixes one corner, then turns to me. "How is that?"

Happiness flutters through me. Did he plan this for me? "It's perfect."

To prove it, I set our books in the middle and settle down with my back against the board and my legs stretched in front of me. I pass my hand over the blanket. It's thicker than I expected, rough and a little itchy, tightly woven. I bet it can last forever.

Cory sits down on the other side, his knees bent. He looks at me, and I hold his gaze. The moment stretches, the tension building, until I'm sure he's going to kiss me. But he only smiles and hands me my book. "If you want any help—"

"I'm fine," I snap, then instantly regret it.

I do want his help. He's a good teacher. But I want other things more. I thought Cory did too, but today I'm not sure. He answered my question and told me about his father. So why do I feel like he's slipping away—like some force is pulling us apart when we try to get closer?

"I have to do it on my own, Cory. But if I get stuck, I'll let you know."

Cory nods. "Okay. I'm right here."

Are you? It feels like you're miles away. "I know."

I bend my knees, copying Cory's position, and put my open prep book on top. It takes a bitter effort to focus on the practice problems, the pencil restless in my fingers, but I force myself to keep my gaze on the page.

I make a deal with myself. Every five problems, I get one glance at the boy next to me. It's not nearly enough, but it seems to work. It helps that each time I look over at Cory, his attention is on his book. It stings a little. But if he can do it, so can I.

A crow screams somewhere behind us—a shrill call of distress.

I glance at Cory. But he doesn't react, engrossed in his book. Maybe I imagined the sound.

I look around me. The orchard, the fields and forests, the barn—the view is as still as a theater backdrop. Peaceful. But the sun is lower in the sky, dipping toward a distant mountain, and the light has the reddish hue of late afternoon. A chill has creeped into the air. How much time before we have to go?

I check my progress. I finished two whole sections. More than I planned. I put the book away and steal a glance at Cory.

He's watching me. "How's it going?"

So he's not completely oblivious of me. Good.

"I'm done." I make my voice firm, just in case he's planning to encourage me to keep going. "But you can keep reading if you want."

Cory's lips twitch, as if the idea amused him. He puts his book down. But when he looks at me, there's no lightness there. His eyes are serious, and his hands stay at his sides.

My cheeks warm, and my heart beats faster. I long to touch him. Why won't he move closer and reach for me? We're less than an arm's length away. Something's still wrong.

But I've been selfish. Worried only about what I want. What if Cory needs something other than a kiss from me?

I don't know where the idea comes from, but I stretch my legs and pat my lap. "You want to lie down? You can put your head in my lap." I feel silly saying this, but I don't care.

Cory's eyes widen. "Okay."

He moves closer and lies down on his back, his legs stretched perpendicular to my own. Propped on both elbows, he slowly lowers his head to my lap.

"Relax." I scoot toward him until his shoulders touch my thighs and gently push him down, my left hand on his chest. "I want you to be comfortable."

He covers my hand with his, trapping it in place, and looks up at me. "I am."

Not yet. The tension is still there. I have to do better.

"Close your eyes."

When he does, I slide my right hand into his hair and lightly graze his scalp.

A low murmur escapes from Cory's throat, and I feel the muscles in his neck relaxing.

Encouraged, I do it again. I graze his scalp and stroke his hair until the tension is gone. Cory's eyes stay closed and his breathing measured. He could be asleep, except for the firm grip of his fingers, pressing my hand to his chest, right over his heart.

There—that's better.

I lift my eyes and take in the view, while my fingers keep working. In the west, the sun almost touches the horizon, the whole sky on fire. In the orchard, the shadows are growing darker under the apple trees.

Under my left palm, Cory's chest shudders and his breath catches—and this time it's not from pleasure.

I look down in alarm. His eyes are squeezed shut, and his mouth is trembling despite his clenched jaw. My fingers brush his cheek—and come away wet.

He's crying.

I freeze. "Cory?"

He lets go of my hand and pushes up to a sitting position, his back to me. He crosses his arms, elbows on his bent knees, and hangs his head.

I kneel behind him. I'm scared for him. I want to help him. I want to put my arms around him and hold him close. But what if he doesn't want to be touched?

"My mom used to do that." His voice is thick with emotion. "Stroke my hair like that."

Oh God. I did this. It's my fault. "I'm sorry. I didn't know."

Cory shakes his head. "It's not you, Abby... You're... It's not you... I just..."

He starts to cry harder, his whole body shaking. His shoulders rise and fall too fast, each breath ragged as if the air burned him. His hands clench into fists.

"*Shit.*"

It's the first I heard him swear, and my mind swings to Jordan. But this is not how Jordan swears. There's more pain than anger in Cory's voice.

I desperately want to soothe that pain, to take some of it for my own if I have to, if he'll share it with me. He might not—he might push me away. But I need him to know he's not alone.

I touch my hand to Cory's back.

He doesn't turn to me or reach for my hand, but he doesn't move away either. So I keep my hand there while he sobs into his bent arms. My heart breaks for him, but I don't tell him to stop. I hope all this pain and anger and sadness can come out. I just keep my palm pressed to his back and wait.

Slowly, Cory's breathing calms, and he stops shaking.

"She had cancer and was in a lot of pain, although she tried to hide it from us," Cory says quietly, and I lean closer to listen. "I read somewhere that stress makes it worse. So I tried to save her all the stress, to protect her from it. *I really tried.*" A sob escapes him, but it's cut short. The muscles in Cory's back tense, and he straightens. He's done with crying, done with pain. Now a bitter anger rings in his voice. "But it made no difference. She still died. And I wasn't even there. I didn't get to say goodbye to her. *It was all for nothing.* Stupid. I was so stupid." He shakes his head, then puts his face in his hands and falls silent.

I have no words to console him. There's still so much I don't understand. *What* was for nothing? What did he do? And how long ago was this? I'm terrified I'll say the wrong thing. So I lift my hand from his back and move even closer, slip both of my arms around him and lean my cheek against his shoulder.

I hold him like this until he turns to face me. I start to pull away when I feel him move, unsure of myself, but he catches my arm and guides it around his neck.

He runs his thumb under my eye, frowning. "You're crying."

I wipe at my cheeks. I didn't realize I was. "What's wrong with crying? Everybody cries."

"Not for me. Only you do that."

Cory's eyes are rimmed with red, but he smiles at

me.

And I'm suddenly giddy with relief, because his face is only inches away and his arms are wrapped around me—and it's not just me; he wants it too—and it's like some invisible barrier vanished between us.

"Well, if I want to cry, you can't stop me. So better get used to it."

It comes out all wrong, but it doesn't matter. Because Cory presses his mouth to mine, and I pour everything I feel for him into the kiss.

Chapter 31

Sunday morning is sunny again, but the temperature has dropped ten degrees. I'm glad I brought my hoodie. I keep it on as I bike to Cory.

I crane my neck to see him as I race down the last hill. He usually waits for me by the mailbox, right near the road. But he's not there when I turn into the driveway.

I skid to a stop and slide off my seat, my sneakers hitting the gravel. I stand there, clutching the handlebars, unsure of what to do. Did Cory change his mind? *No.* I know he wants to see me too. Something must have happened…

I jump back on my bike and race up the driveway, dread propelling me forward.

The sharp smell of burning hits my nostrils as soon as I reach the yard. I don't see any flames, but a column of smoke rises from the roof and more drifts slowly through the air.

I drop my bike and my backpack. I turn and trip on something heavy. Pearl yelps as my knee hits her side. I feel bad but I'm in a rush.

"Cory?" I run up the steps to the porch. I don't bother knocking. I push through the front door and rush into the foyer. "*Cory!*"

He comes running from the kitchen.

"Abby! I was just going to—"

"I think there's a fire!" My heart is pounding. I scan his body for burns but he looks fine. He's holding a knife. No—a metal spatula.

Cory laughs. "No. It's just me. I'm making pancakes. I burned the first two."

I frown. "I'm serious. I think it's in the back. Can't you smell smoke?"

Cory's face grows serious. "Okay. One second."

He dashes into the kitchen, puts the spatula on the counter, and turns off the burners under two pans. The fan over the stove buzzes, and the kitchen reeks of burned oil. None of the windows are open. No wonder Cory didn't notice the smoke.

He grabs a small fire extinguisher from the coat closet and I follow him down the hallway to the back of the house.

I glance at the framed photographs on the walls. In one, a woman in a tank top and shorts sits crossed-legged among wild flowers. A small boy stands behind her, his hands clasped over her eyes. They're both laughing. An ache stings my heart. Is it Cory with his mom? I want to study the photo but I can't linger.

At the end of the hallway is a mud room. I follow Cory out the back door and onto a small, raised patio. I saw no sign of fire inside, which is a relief.

But outside is a different story. Thick, gray smoke like torn, dirty cotton drifts across the backyard, which slopes away from the house. Several tall oak trees cover the slope, the ground between them carpeted with leaves. I hear a rumbling, and remember the creek at the bottom. But where's the smoke coming from?

"I'll be right back. Wait for me?" Cory jumps off the side of the patio, the fire extinguisher clutched in his hand.

I snort. Like I'm going to let him go alone. *No way.* I run down the steps after him.

The creek lies at the bottom of a small canyon. Cory stands at the rocky edge, frowning at the trees on the other side. I catch up to him and squint in the same direction. The smoke is thicker here. My throat itches, and I cough.

Cory gives me a tense look and catches my arm. "Be careful. Not too close. The water is very low right now. You'd fall on the rocks."

"Okay." I let him pull me a step back.

An open field stretches beyond the trees on the opposite side of the creek. A line of tall metal trash cans stand in the field, each can releasing a column of smoke.

"Are they burning leaves?"

Cory frowns. "I'm not sure what they're burning. But they're not supposed to do that."

I glance up. Some of the oak trees on both sides are so tall and their canopies so wide, the branches touch in the air high above the creek, forming an intricate, swaying bridge. "Can the trees catch fire from the smoke? And could the smoke then jump to our side?"

Cory shakes his head. "No. I don't think so. But it's still rude." He turns to me and puts his hand on my back, steering me away from the creek and the smoke. "Come on, let's go inside."

Sounds good to me. My eyes are stinging.

Pearl stands guard halfway up the slope.

"Come here, Pearl. *Come.*" I tap my thigh, but she doesn't budge.

"She never comes near the creek," Cory says. "Fell in as a puppy and almost drowned."

When we reach her, I warily extend my hand, unsure of how she'll react. I kicked her pretty hard. "I'm sorry I almost stepped on you."

The dog sniffs my fingers, then runs her long, wet tongue across my knuckles. I gasp, not expecting the sloppy kiss. I'd be less surprised if she snapped at me.

Cory smiles. "I think you're forgiven. She doesn't hold a grudge."

Pearl turns her head toward the creek and wrinkles

her nose. Then walks over to Cory, gives a short bark, and bumps her head into his thigh, as if urging him to get moving.

Cory pets the dog's head and scratches behind her ears. "Oh, now you remember me? Yes, I don't like the smoke either."

Pearl trots away, and we walk back to the house. I'm hoping to go through the back door and the hallway again, to steal another glimpse at the photograph, but Cory leads me around to the front. He picks up my bike and props it against the wall, then shrugs on my backpack and takes my hand. We climb the steps to the porch, Cory puts away the fire extinguisher, and we're back in the kitchen.

I take off my hoodie and toss it on the bench. The kitchen is warm, and Cory's in a t-shirt too.

He peers into my face, his brows knotted. We're both blinking from the smoke. "How are your eyes? Cold water might help."

He hands me a fresh towel, and I wash my hands and splash water in my face at the sink. He does the same, and I hand him the towel back. He puts his face where my face was a moment ago. It's a small thing, but joy still zaps through me.

We turn to each other.

Cory pushes a wet strand of hair out of my face. "Better?"

"Yes."

"Good. So let's start over." He steps closer, his gaze on mine. "Hey."

My whole body warms. The word is a secret signal between us. "Hey."

I smell the smoke on him, taste it in his kiss, but I don't care.

I lift my hands to his neck and slide my fingers into his hair, pulling his face to mine. His arms slip around my lower back, pressing me closer.

My only regret is too many layers of clothing again. I should've removed my sweatshirt at least. And why is my t-shirt so long, the hem almost reaching my hips? Shorter would be better.

When we move apart, I glance at the stove.

"Did you really make pancakes?"

"I tried. Come." Cory pulls me across the kitchen.

Sure enough, two pancakes sit in the two frying pans. A tall stack of pancakes sits on a round cake tray on the counter, protected with a glass lid. A mixing bowl sits next to the tray, half an inch of cream-colored dough left on the bottom. Looks like I timed my arrival well by a sheer stroke of luck, if you ignore the drama with the smoke.

"Here." Cory hands me three small jars and three spoons on a plate. "They go on the table."

"Jams!" I scan the labels on the jars. "Blackberry,

raspberry, apricot. *Yum*." I put the plate in the middle of the table, then open each jar and stick a spoon in it.

Cory brings the whole tray of pancakes over, sets it down next to the jams, then lifts the lid and puts it aside. A fork lies on top of the pancakes.

"We can't possibly eat all of them!" I laugh, but my mouth waters at the sight.

"I made them for you."

He crosses back to the stove, picks up the metal spatula and slides the two pancakes onto a plate. Both are a little burned on the bottom. He grabs another plate and joins me at the table. He puts the empty plate in front of me, keeping the burned pancakes for himself.

"I can eat one of those. It's okay."

"Absolutely not." He grabs my plate and slides three pancakes onto it, one on top of another. Then scoops up a spoonful of the blackberry jam, spreads it over the top pancake, and rolls it. He repeats the procedure with the raspberry and apricot jams. Then he sets the plate back in front of me.

I lower my head over the plate and inhale. They look delicious and smell like summer.

Cory gets up again. "Tea! I forgot. But don't wait for me. Dig in." He busies himself with the teapot and mugs.

I do wait for him, though.

I pull his plate closer. I don't know which jams he

likes, so I pick two at random, hoping he won't mind if I get it wrong.

Cory comes back with two steaming mugs and some paper napkins. He takes one look at his plate and fixes his eyes on me. "We don't want to fight."

"No, we don't."

"And I can't win anyway."

"Nope."

He sighs. "Okay." But a smile tugs at his lips as he picks up one burned pancake from his plate and takes a bite.

"Okay." I pick up the other burned pancake—now on my plate—and bite into it.

It's still very good, despite the charred patch in the middle. My second and third pancakes—thin, golden yellow, and crispy around the edges—are pure perfection.

"Mmmm," I murmur as I chew.

Cory grins. "You like them?"

"Yes!" I help myself to one more, to prove it. They're light and airy. "Where did you get the recipe?" I don't see any cookbooks around, and I don't think Cory has a smartphone.

Cory's smile falters. "My mom used to make them."

His mom. I'm back in the orchard, my hand on Cory's back as he's crying. "I'm sorry. Forget I asked."

Cory shakes his head. "No, it's okay. I want to remember her. And it doesn't... it doesn't hurt as much."

He holds my gaze when he says it, his eyes intense, as if to say, *thanks to you*, and a wordless emotion surges through me. Is it because of yesterday? Because he told me about her, and telling me lessened his pain a little? The thought takes my breath away.

"She never actually used a recipe," Cory continues. "Not once. She didn't measure the amounts either. The pancakes were a little different each time. She never taught me how to make them, but I remembered the ingredients. Eggs, milk, and flour, plus a pinch of salt."

I find my voice again. "So how did you figure it out?"

"I experimented. This is the third time this week I'm eating pancakes."

My face warms. He did all this for me? My mind can't quite grasp it. "Wow. That's... impressive dedication to science." I point at my empty plate. "Well, the evidence is pretty clear. Your experiments are a *great* success."

Cory considers it. "Four pancakes? That would indicate a *modest* success. Sorry. I don't make the rules."

"Excuse me, who said I was finished?" I slide two more pancakes onto my plate and roll them. No jam this time. "Make it six. A *great* success, and that's final."

Cory laughs. "Okay." And he grabs a few more pancakes himself.

By the time we push our plates away, half of the stack is gone. Cory covers the remaining pancakes with the lid, but leaves the plate on the table. "A snack for later."

He carries our plates and mugs to the sink. I bring the plate with the jams to the counter. I take out the spoons and screw the lids on the jars, and Cory puts them back in the fridge. Then his eyes go to my backpack, and I already know what's coming.

I have to study for the SAT and for a Calculus exam next week. Then I remember one more thing I packed and I'm restless. "Can we go to the orchard before we study? Just a short walk."

Cory crosses to the front window and peers out, frowning. "The smoke is going to be everywhere, and the wind keeps blowing more of it across the creek. Look."

I step next to him and look out the window. He's right. Clouds of smoke drift in the yard.

"*Ugh.*"

Why did the neighbors have to burn that stuff today? Pearl may not hold grudges, but I do.

The disappointment must show in my face, because

Cory looks crestfallen. Then his eyes brighten. "But I know another place I can take you."

"The roof of the barn!" I catch on. "Right?"

"Kind of. Come on. I'll show you."

"Wait." I hurry to my backpack and pull out a small leather bag. I strap it across my chest. The bag, shaped like a cube, hangs at my hip.

Cory eyes it warily. "What's that?"

"Nothing."

Realization dawns in his face, and he tenses, his discomfort tangible. "You want to take a picture of me?"

"It's a polaroid camera. It makes one print, and that's it." When he still looks unconvinced, I coax, "You can take one of me if you want. I'll trade you."

His eyes light up at that. "And I get to keep it?"

"Well, I don't want it. I hate pictures of me."

Cory stares. "*What?* Why? You're so... I mean..." His face darkens, and he drops his gaze and trails off.

My own cheeks burn, and I have an impulse to flee, even as joy fills me. I'm even worse at receiving compliments than he's at giving them. I turn to the door. "I'll do it if you do it. That's the deal. But you don't have to decide yet. Let's go."

Chapter 32

We step out the door, cross the porch, and start across the yard. The smoke is thinner but the burned odor lingers. I lift my hand to cover my nose and mouth and break into a run. Cory runs alongside me.

We reach the barn, and he pulls open the heavy rolling door. The handle is cast iron and painted black, as are the wheels and the rails they move on. The metalwork looks old and ominous against the blood red of the walls. The door could be a set piece for a gothic fairy tale. What's on the other side? Stacks of vicious weapons? A terrifying monster chained in the corner? I picture a dark and gloomy space crawling with spiders and alive with shadows.

But the barn is clean and well lit when we enter. A huge, open space that reminds me of a loft—the kind that costs a fortune to rent in Chicago.

Sunlight filters through long, narrow skylights high above my head. The dust motes stir in the air, sparkling like glitter. Dozens of empty shelves and hooks cover the red walls. The ground is packed dirt but level and swept clean. At the far end, empty stalls with low gates must have held horses once.

I look up. Long, exposed beams line the high ceiling. Except the section to my left, where the barn has another half floor two stories above ground. An open attic? There's no wall—no barrier whatsoever—guarding its edge.

My pulse speeds up in excitement. "Is that where we're going?"

Cory pulls the door shut, then follows my gaze upward and nods. "That's it."

"But how?" I glance around me, perplexed. There's no stairs, no ladder. Do we just climb the wall? Use the shelves and hooks as footholds?

Cory takes my elbow and pulls me off to the side. "Stay right here."

"Where're you going?"

He runs to the far wall under the attic and starts climbing. He quickly reaches the lower ceiling, his movements swift and practiced, and before I have time to worry he'll fall or wonder what's next, he lifts one arm and presses up against the wood.

A small section dislodges, and he slides it out of the way and climbs through the opening. I see his long legs and the soles of his shoes, and then he's gone.

I swallow. He made it look easy. My turn, I guess. I take a step in that direction, but Cory's voice stops me.

"Abby!"

He's standing at the edge of the attic, a tangle of ropes and wooden boards in his hands. Then he drops his load—and a flexible ladder unfolds. The end, heavy like rocks, thuds against the ground.

So there is a ladder. I'm glad. But why keep it hidden?

I reach for it, but Cory starts climbing down, so I pull back my hand and wait.

He jumps down and grabs the ladder, pulling down on it until the rope is taut. "I'll hold it steady for you. Go ahead."

But I'm anything but steady when I step closer. My eyes glide over the flexed muscles in his arms, and my nerves flutter. I want to touch him, to step into his arms. Surely, the climbing can wait…

I meet Cory's gaze, and he smiles, the scar pulling down one corner of his mouth. "I'll see you up there."

A warm shiver runs down my spine. I grab the rung in front of me, lift my foot, and start climbing. In moments, I'm rising over the edge, then leaning over the floor and standing up.

"Wow." I gasp in surprise and delight.

I expected a dim, empty room with bare floor boards. But brilliant sunlight pours through a row of skylights on each side of the slanted roof, illuminating low bookshelves, a desk and chair, an oversized bean bag, and a large mattress covered with a blanket and pillows. Pillows!

The attic isn't small, either. It stretches three lengths of my bedroom, at least. Plenty of room, and all of it completely, wonderfully private. If I could design a perfect hideout, this would be it.

Cory steps next to me, and I feel his hand on my back, nudging me forward.

"Don't stand so close to the edge, okay? I need to make a railing."

I reflexively give in to the pressure of his fingers and take a few steps. But I'm still staring at the bed, thrilled and alarmed, my imagination running wild.

"You sleep here?" I ask.

Cory gives me an uncertain look, but he nods. "Sometimes. You can see the stars at night."

"Ah!" I cross to the mattress. The head of the bed is right under a skylight. I spin to Cory. "I'm never leaving, you know!"

He laughs, relieved, like he wasn't sure of my reaction until this moment. But his voice is earnest when he answers. "Works for me."

Happiness stabs my heart, and the familiar invisible rope loops around my waist, pulling me toward him.

I take a step, and the camera bag bounces on my hip. *The photo*. I better take it now, before Cory distracts me. The light is perfect, and I don't want to forget. I open the bag and pull out the camera. I extend it to Cory. "I can go first."

He sighs but takes the camera from my hands. "Show me how?"

I explain how to use it. "Wait for me, though, okay? I'll let you know when I'm ready." My nerves are getting to me.

I find a good spot, out of direct sunlight, but I'm not ready yet. I wish I had a mirror. I glance down at myself and frown. My t-shirt is ridiculously long. On impulse, I grab the bottom and tie a knot on one side. Now it's shorter. But is that better? I don't know. This was a bad idea.

Cory walks over to me. He holds the camera in one hand and strokes my cheek with the other. "Abby. I was trying to tell you earlier. *You're beautiful.* I hope you know that."

I look at him, stunned—and he quickly steps away and snaps a photo.

The camera hisses, and a square print slides out. Cory catches it and grins. "Wow. Look."

I ignore the photo. I'm still astonished by his shrewdness. I snatch the camera. "My turn."

"Okay." He tenses, his face turning to stone.

I point the lens at him. But this won't do. It's like he's wearing a mask. "Did you mean it? You think I'm beautiful?"

It works. Conviction burns in Cory's eyes. "You are!"

I take the photo.

The camera hisses. I can barely wait. And then I see the print—and my breath catches. It's perfect. "You want to see it?"

Cory shakes his head. He doesn't even glance at it. "You tricked me."

"I guess we're even then."

I carefully slide the photo in the back pocket of the camera bag. I already worry about losing it. It's way too fragile, too easily torn or damaged. I want it to last forever.

I put the camera inside the bag and I'm about to strap the bag on, when Cory catches it. "We don't have to leave yet. Unless you want to."

"*No.* I want to stay here." I eagerly surrender the bag, and he puts it on the desk, smiling.

We face each other, and my heart drums in anticipation. Cory reaches for me, and I step into his arms. I lift my hands to his face, ready to press my mouth to his.

But in that instant, Cory's fingers graze my bare skin. The touch is electric—a sharp jolt of pleasure—and we both gasp.

He glances down at me, and his eyes widen. His finger traces the bottom of my t-shirt, now short enough to expose my waist. Then slowly, gently, his palms press to my sides.

I shiver, and he lifts his gaze to my face. "Is that okay?"

"Yes," I breathe, my heart pounding. This is what I want. I want his hands there, on my bare skin. I move closer.

His eyes darken and his lips part. He slides his hands to my lower back, and then his arms wrap around me, pressing me to him and covering me up.

My insides turn to liquid heat. I can't wait any longer. I hook my fingers in his hair and pull his face to mine. For a second, I smell smoke again and dread cuts through me. But then our mouths collide, and I lose myself in the kiss.

When we surface again, Cory turns his face and bends his head. His mouth travels down the side of my throat and stops at my collarbone, his breath hot and sweet on my skin. His arms never let go of me, and I loop my hands around his neck and press my body to his. We hold each other tight.

I love you.

The words sound so clear in my mind that for a moment I'm terrified I spoke them.

I tense, and Cory pulls away.

"Abby, what is it?"

What would it be like to say these words to him?

"I..."

I imagine the look in his eyes when he hears them. I want to see that look. I want him to know how much I care for him.

Come on. This shouldn't be so hard. I'm not lying for once. It's the truth.

"I... thought I heard something."

I look away. I'm not brave enough.

And I do hear something—several sounds jumbled together, growing louder. Closer.

The roar of an engine and tires crunching the gravel. A dog barking like mad. And then a voice. No—two voices. A man and woman.

Cory pales and his hands drop to his sides. He steps away from me. "It's Jill and my grandfather. We have to go."

I fall a step forward, unbalanced. My skin is cold where his arms kept me warm a moment ago, and I'm instantly annoyed at the visitors.

But that's selfish of me. They just came to check on Cory, even if their timing is terrible. I smooth down my hair and untie the knot in my t-shirt. I want to make a good impression. I give Cory an encouraging smile. "That's okay. I'd love to meet them."

Cory frowns, a troubled look in his eyes. "Just so you know, Jill doesn't..." But he shakes his head and turns away without finishing the sentence. He grabs my camera bag and presses it into my hand. He squeezes my wrist before letting go. "I'm sorry, Abby."

Anxiety slashes through me. "For what?"

But he's already climbing down the ladder. I follow, moving as fast as I can while he holds the ropes taut for me. Then he runs to the back wall and climbs up through the opening again. The heavy end of the ladder lifts off the ground, yanked higher and higher in a jerky rhythm, until it's gone from view.

A moment later, Cory's legs appear in the opening, then his whole body. He pulls the lid in the place, hanging by his arms for a moment, then lets go and drops to the ground.

He jogs to where I'm standing, and we hurry to the door. I see him take a deep breath, like he's bracing himself, before he pulls it open. He steps outside first, and I follow behind.

"*There he is!*" An angry voice yells. A woman's. "What on earth did you do, Cory?"

I'm instantly on edge. The harsh tone and unfair accusation sting like a hundred cuts even before I see the person. Does she blame Cory for the smoke? That makes no sense.

He's still walking ahead of me, as if to shield me from view. But I need to see her face. I lengthen my step to catch up until we walk side by side.

Cory shoots me a warning look. I return his stare.

Is he trying to protect me—or hide me? Neither is going to work.

An older couple are arguing in the yard, their attention on each other for the moment. A bright green SUV is parked behind them, and wisps of smoke drift through the air.

"...Don't tell me I'm overreacting. I'm not!"

"All I'm saying is, we don't know what happened yet..."

The woman—who must be Jill—is tall, slender, and visibly upset. The man, broad-shouldered and thickly built, is trying to pacify her. He must be Walter Brennell, Cory's grandfather. Pearl dances around him, her tail swinging.

We stop a few yards away from them, and Cory clears his throat. He's nervous. "Jill. Grandpa."

They both turn, and their eyes fix on me. But the reactions are very different. Walter's bushy eyebrows rise in surprise, and he smiles under his mustache. Jill frowns, though, and her eyes drill into me like x-ray.

I meet her gaze defiantly, but my stomach knots. She must be over sixty, but only the short silver hair and the wrinkles on her face, throat, and arms betray her age.

"Who's this?" Jill snaps at Cory, her eyes on me.

I speak before Cory can. "I'm Abby. I'm Cory's—" I hesitate, wanting to say *girlfriend* but not sure I should "—friend from school."

Walter steps forward, smiling broadly. He extends his hand. "I'm Walter, Cory's grandfather. Very pleased to meet you."

"Nice to meet you too." I smile back, and we shake hands. His is calloused and large enough to engulf mine.

Walter turns to his grandson and jovially slaps his back, although I catch a note of worry in his voice. "I see why you didn't want to switch to Jill's district and you never have time to visit me. Busy with schoolwork, huh?"

I blush, half embarrassed, half pleased. But Cory doesn't react, his face blank and his body frozen with tension. He doesn't make eye contact either. He stares into the distance.

Dread coils in my gut. What's going on? Is he in trouble? But why? The smoke isn't his fault. Or is it because I'm here?

"I'm Jill," Jill says to me curtly, then rounds on Cory again. She fans the air in front of her face in annoyance. "You're burning leaves so close to the house? What're you thinking?"

Cory blinks. "It's not me. It's coming from the other side of the creek."

Walter looks thoughtful. "That's George's land." Pearl sits by his leg, and he pets her head distractedly.

Jill scowls. "So it's the old George setting fires? And I'm supposed to believe that?"

Walter throws Cory a sidelong glance and shakes his head. "Nah. It wouldn't be George. He's visiting with kids in Pittsburgh for a couple of weeks. And he wouldn't do it where the smoke might drift over to us. Only has a handful of trees, anyway."

I wait for Cory to say something, to defend himself. But he just stands there, his jaw clenched and his eyes empty.

Finally, I can't stand it.

"Maybe it's a stupid prank?" I say. "We saw three metal trash cans. Someone put them there and lit the fire."

Jordan.

My head snaps to Cory. Did the same suspicion just cross his mind? But his face gives nothing away.

Jill's eyes narrow, though. She looks from me to Cory, latching onto the idea. "*A prank?* You mean someone went to all that trouble just to stink up this yard? Brought the trash cans over, filled them with leaves, risked getting caught for trespassing? They must really have it out for you, Cory."

I cringe. I should've kept my mouth shut.

"Jill." There's an edge in Walter's voice for the first time.

"What?"

"*Please.*"

Impatience flashes in Jill's eyes. "He can answer me, Walter. Is that so much to ask?"

Heat rises to Cory's face. "Answer you how? *And what for?* It doesn't matter what I say. You already made up your mind about me. So why should I bother?"

He turns on his heel and stalks away.

I start after him. "Cory, wait!"

But he shoots me a dark look over his shoulder. "Go home, Abby." Then he breaks into a run.

I want to run after him anyway, but my feet refuse to move. All of a sudden, my eyes and throat are burning. It must be the smoke. I've been standing here for too long. Maybe I should be going. If Cory doesn't want me here, I have no reason to stay. But my feet are stuck in place. I can't bring myself to leave either.

Jill's voice yanks me out of my indecision. "You live in town? Come on, I'll give you a ride. Have an errand to run there anyway."

"No, thanks. I have my bike." I thought she's Cory's friend, but she's not.

But Jill is already plucking out her car keys. "We can put it in the back. Did you bring anything else with you?"

"My backpack's in the kitchen."

"Well, go get it."

I glance at Walter for support, but he only sighs. "It was nice to meet you, Abby. I'm glad Cory made a friend. You're always welcome here."

My heart sinks. So he wants me gone too.

I glance past the drifting smoke toward the barn, and memories rush in—the sunlight in the attic, Cory's arms wrapped around my back, the look in his eyes just before he kissed me. My whole body aches with longing, even though I'm mad at him too. Where did he go? Not to the barn. He ran in the opposite direction.

The roar of the engine startles me. Walter is already lifting my bike into the back of the car. Jill sits behind the wheel, giving me a stern look. *Hurry up.*

I wish I was braver. But I'm not. I run to the kitchen to get my things.

In the car, Jill asks my address, and I tell her to drop me off in the small park downtown. It's only two blocks from my apartment, and she doesn't need to know where I live. I know it's petty. She probably doesn't care anyway. But I hate how she treated Cory.

I turn to the window, determined to keep a grudging silence until we get there. But Jill has another agenda.

"So, Abby. How do you know Cory, exactly?"

I bristle, tempted to tell her it's none of her business. She's as nosey as Mrs. Smith. "We're in Physics together. Cory is the best student in that class."

I don't mention the fall play.

Jill eyes me shrewdly. "You seem to know him pretty well."

I don't fall for the bait, but it still annoys me. "And you don't seem to know him at all!"

Jill throws me a sharp glance. "I know he needs to keep his head down and stay out of trouble."

I grit my teeth. I picture Cory in class. I picture him with Jordan's arm choking his throat. "*He already is!* I don't think he spoke a single word in class all semester. And he never stands up for himself, not even when other students are mean to him or try to pick a fight!"

Jill purses her lips. "Well. I'm sorry to hear that. I didn't know he's having a hard time." Her voice softens. "But… this isn't easy on his grandfather either. There's been a lot of pain in this family already, a lot of heartbreak, and I want to spare Walter any more."

I think of Cory's mother and father, and my chest tightens, my anger fading. "I know."

I meet Jill's eyes, and an understanding passes between us. I know why she's harsh on Cory. It's the same reason why I was harsh on her just now. We're both protecting someone we care about. For me, it's Cory, and her for, it's Walter.

"I'm glad Cory found one good friend," Jill says, echoing Walter's words, as we drive into town and pull into a parking spot near the park. "Just… be careful. He can't afford another mistake."

A chill runs down my spine. *What mistake?* What is she talking about?

But Jill has just spotted someone she knows. She pops open the back door and gets out of the car. She waves to a woman across the street, and the woman waves back and steps to the curb, waiting for several huge delivery trucks to crawl past so she can cross.

Is it… Mrs. Smith? *Great.* The last thing I need is these two women chatting about me.

I grab my bike, mutter a thank you to Jill, and hurry away.

Chapter 33

The Beast's gloves lie on red paper in a long plastic box like the corpses of two small, strange animals. I remove the lid and hold the box out for Jordan. We're standing on the side of the stage, next to the center wing.

His eyes flash with excitement, and he grabs one and slips it on his left hand. It's long, reaching halfway up his forearm, brown fur on top and a matching fabric underneath. A long, discreet zipper runs along the inner side.

Jordan works each finger of the glove in place until the claws sticks out. I replaced the plastic with leather, so they can't scratch or break. He flexes his fingers and rotates his wrist, testing and admiring my creation.

"Wow, Abby. This is amazing. So soft."

"Thanks." I didn't spend so much time on them just for him. They're for my portfolio.

Jordan grabs the second glove. "What's this?"

I look at where he's pointing, and my cheeks warm. It's the polaroid photo I took of him in the blue tailcoat. I completely forgot about it.

"I don't need it anymore." I flip the photo face down and close the lid on the box.

Jordan presses his Beast's hand over his heart. "*Ouch.* That hurts. You don't mean it."

I roll my eyes, but my face gets a little hotter. It's infuriating but I can't help it.

Jordan laughs and starts to put on the second glove. The task is harder without an ungloved hand. Serves him right.

I glance around me as I wait.

It's Monday, and the rehearsal is about to begin. The set crew are busy setting up, but Cory still isn't here.

I scan the theater every few seconds, searching for him. Where is he? I haven't seen him all day. The last time I saw him was yesterday—and he told me to go home. I haven't forgotten that. But I'm still anxious to see him. What if he's not coming at all?

"Abby?" Jordan's voice yanks me back.

"What?"

"A little help." He extends his right hand to me. The fur and fabric of the glove are comically twisted and bunched up, the claws pointing in odd directions, and Jordan is grinning. He did it on purpose and doesn't even hide it.

Seriously? He's getting on my nerves, but I have no choice. He's the star of the show, and my job is to get him in costume.

I put the box down on the bench, and help him fit the glove on each finger until the fur and the fabric are smooth. Then I carefully close the zipper on each glove.

"What would I do without you?" Jordan murmurs.

I turn away from him, furious with myself for blushing so easily. I grab the Beast's mask from the bench and pretend to check the mike, waiting for my cheeks to cool off.

"I meant to ask you last week," Jordan says casually, addressing my back. "Did you ever get your phone back?"

I spin around and stare at him, my fingers digging into the Beast's mask. He has a nerve to ask about my phone when we both know it was him who took it. But I sense a trap and hold my temper. "Yes. I got it back. Why?"

Jordan shrugs. "I was just wondering. But sounds like someone found it and returned it, so that's good. Do you know who it was?" And his eyes narrow almost greedily.

"I don't. I picked it up from the office."

"And you're not curious? If it was me, I'd want to know. So I can... thank them."

Unease stirs in me. It's a trap. Jordan is egging me on for a reason. But now I wonder.

"All right! Where is my Beast?" The director's

voice booms. "Is my Beast ready?"

I hold the mask out for Jordan. But he can't put it on with his gloved hands, and there's no time to take the gloves off. I'll have to put the mask on him.

Jordan smiles, his face only inches from mine, and my arms looped around his neck as I get the mask in place. "Thanks, Abby."

ॐ

Who returned my phone? The question nettles me when I ride the school bus the next morning. Rain slashes against the window, blurring my view. I know it's a mistake to listen to Jordan, but I can't get it out of my head, so I might as well find out the answer.

The office is off the main hallway, right past the double front door. I hurry inside as soon as I enter the building, water dripping from my raincoat.

Our secretary, Mrs. Pearson, looks up from her computer. "Hi. You need a pass?"

"Good morning." I shake my head. "No pass. I have a question."

"What do you need?"

"I lost my phone last week, and someone returned it here."

Mrs. Pearson squints. "Oh, yes. I remember you."

"I was wondering who dropped it off." I swallow,

suddenly nervous. What if she can't tell me? There may be some rule against it. "I just wanted to thank them. I was really worried about my phone."

"I bet. It was the new student."

My heart stops. "The new student?"

"You're a junior, right? He's a junior too. What's his name?"

No. That's impossible. "Cory?"

"Yes! That's it. Cory. He returned your phone."

I stand frozen in place, my mind spinning. *Cory found my phone?* But why didn't he tell me? And why would he bring it to the office when he could just give it to me? Unless he didn't want me to know…

"You okay? You're going to be late for class."

"Thank you." I step out the door and start walking. The hallways are nearly empty, the last students slamming their lockers shut and rushing to their classes. If I don't hurry up, I'll be late for Physics.

Physics. *Cory.*

Cory found my phone and never told me. Why didn't he? And where did he find it?

"Abby." Mr. Miller spots me through the open door. He gives me a worried look and beckons me in. "Come in, come in."

I keep my gaze on the floor as I walk to my seat. I know Cory is there, in his usual seat in the back row. But I don't let myself look at him.

I pull out my notebook and grab my pen. Mr. Miller starts his lecture, and I order myself to focus. But it's hopeless. By the end of class, I still haven't written down a single word.

I get up from my seat and walk out of the classroom the same way I came in—my gaze fixed on the floor. I get to the staircase but instead of turning, I walk past it. I follow the main hallway to the back of the building.

I'm aware of someone walking behind me, but never turn to look. I don't have to. I know who it is. But I still don't know what to say to him.

I hesitate when I reach the back door. I have Calculus. I've never skipped class in my life.

Cory steps next to me. "Abby, wait—"

A desperate urgency propels me, and I push past him and out the door.

Rain hits my face, but I keep going until I'm behind the shed.

"Abby!"

I turn, and he's right in front of me, his face framed by the dark green hood of his jacket.

He reaches for my hood and pulls it up over my head.

The motion startles me, and I shrink from his touch. "Don't!"

Blood drains from Cory's face. "I'm sorry." He

takes a step back. "I won't touch you… I just want to talk."

Talk. But I still don't know what to say to him. He found my phone and didn't tell me. He kept it from me. What else did he keep from me?

We stand in silence, the rain beating down on us.

Cory studies my face anxiously. "Jill drove you home yesterday."

"Yes."

He takes a shuddering breath. "What… what did she say about me?"

I frown. That's not what I want to talk about. Maybe later—but not now.

"You found my phone?"

Cory blinks and doesn't answer, only stares at me, and for a moment hope fills me. *It wasn't him. He would've told me.*

Then he hangs his head.

I'm stunned all over again. "You found my phone and returned it to the office? And never said a word about it?"

"Yes."

The wind picks up, and the rain changes direction, hitting at a sharp angle. My legs are ice cold, probably because my jeans are already soaked, but I barely notice.

There's something I need to know. "Did you really

find it? Or did you… take it from my backpack? Tell me the truth."

Cory moves closer, his eyes blazing. *"Take it?* You think I stole your phone? Abby, why would I do that?"

Guilt stings me. Do I really believe he could've stolen it—or am I just being cruel? Punishing him for sending me away yesterday? I think back to that night—to the empty parking lot, all the other cars gone. I picture Cory walking next to me on the dark road.

"I don't know… To be alone with me?" I regret the words as soon as I say them. "I don't know. I'm asking."

Cory clenches his jaw. "I didn't steal your phone. I found it." He pauses. But we both know what my next question is going to be. "It was in my locker."

"In your locker," I echo.

And just like that, relief washes over me. I'm not sure why. Maybe because his locker is the worst place he could've named, so I know he's telling the truth.

Water drips from the edge of my hood and into my eyes. I wipe the water off. "Okay. So someone took my phone and put it in your locker to frame you. I say it was Jordan."

Cory's face relaxes a little, but he still watches me warily. "Maybe he took it. But I don't think Jordan could pick a lock to save his life. How would he open my locker?"

I'm thinking fast, grasping at possibilities. "What about the custodian? He might know how. He fixes the locks at school if any get jammed. If Jordan asked him a favor or paid him—"

Cory cringes and shakes his head. "We don't know that."

Shame burns the back of my throat. I just accused Cory of a whole bunch of awful things, but he won't accuse a stranger of one to defend himself.

"Why didn't you tell me about the phone?" I ask.

Cory doesn't answer right away. He just watches me, his eyes intense, his jaw clenching and unclenching like he's battling with himself. "Okay. The truth." He takes a breath. "I wasn't sure you'd believe me. It was… easier not to tell you."

I stare at him. It's like a punch to the gut.

He wasn't sure I'd believe him? So he'd rather lie to me? Doesn't he trust me at all?

I'm suddenly grateful for the rain, for the water dripping into my eyes. It hides the angry tears I can't hold back. "You should've told me."

Regret crosses Cory's face, and he opens his mouth to speak. But I turn away and hurry to the back door. I stand there, waiting, my body numb but my mind screaming and my heart breaking. I have more questions but no guts to ask them.

Why did you tell me to go home? Do you have any

idea how much it hurt? What are you so afraid of?

I don't have to wait long. Cory unlocks the door and moves out of my way, and I go inside.

I take three steps and stop, misery clawing at my insides. What am I supposed to do now? I push back my hood and wipe at my face. Water drips from my jacket and pools on the floor. My jeans and sneakers are drenched. The class period hasn't ended yet, so the hallways are empty, but that could change any moment. I need to get out of here.

I look behind me. The door is closed but no sign of Cory. He stayed outside.

Furious, I march back to the door and grab the handle, ready to rush back outside to get him. What is he thinking? He must be drenched too.

But I don't.

He told me to leave after I almost told him I loved him.

I need to move. But where can I go? *Come on, think.* The costume room. Tammy keeps spare clothes there. I can sneak in and borrow some.

I push back my hood and start walking. I don't look behind me again.

Chapter 34

"Turn around. Let me see you." Tammy looks me over and smiles approvingly. "They fit you really well. Better than me, actually."

We're in the costume room, and I'm wearing the sweatpants she's letting me borrow. "Thanks, Tammy. I appreciate it."

I mean both lending me dry clothes and spending her lunch break here. I debated with myself if I should text her or not, but finally caved in. It wasn't just the clothes, although that was a big help. I didn't want to be alone to brood over Cory, my thoughts running in frantic circles without getting anywhere.

Tammy's good company. She made small talk and cheered me up. But she never pressed me why my eyes were red and I was soaked from the rain in the middle of a school day. Although I could tell she was both worried and curious.

I don't blame her. I would be too.

Actually, I'd love to tell her about Cory. It'd be a relief to open up and get her advice.

But I can't. Not yet. I wouldn't know what to say. I

don't understand it myself yet.

I put my hands in the pockets of the sweatpants. The fabric is soft and warm, and the pockets are deep. I've never worn a more comfortable and more comforting piece of clothing.

Tammy grins at me. "The pockets are great, aren't they? You know, you should keep them. The pants, I mean."

"That's really sweet of you, but I can't—"

"Sure you can. I want you to keep them. Seriously. I never wear them anyway."

I grin back, disarmed. "Okay. I've got to say, I love them already."

She laughs. "See! I knew it. Nothing like a nasty downpour that ends in true love."

Memories flash through my mind, all involving the rain and Cory, and my chest tightens. I must look like I just saw a ghost.

Tammy frowns with sympathy, but she doesn't ask, and I'm grateful. Instead, she glances at her phone to check the time. "Anyway. We should be going. The lunch break is almost over."

"You're right." I shrug on my backpack and grab my raincoat from the hanger. It's almost dry, unlike my sneakers, which are still damp and make horrid squeaking noises on the floor.

Tammy glances down at my feet. "Sorry I don't

have an extra pair to lend you. Are you going to be okay?" And I know she doesn't just mean my shoes.

"I'll live." She's been a good friend, though I've done little to earn that friendship. I've barely talked to her or Zoe for weeks. I'll have to do better in the future. "See you and Zoe at the rehearsal?"

Tammy shakes her head. "Not today. We don't need to be there. Skyler sent a message."

"I missed it." Again. I really need to check my phone more often. Except now my phone reminds me of things I don't want to dwell on. "Why no rehearsal? What's going on?"

Tammy shrugs. "Some special guest who's going to talk to the actors only. Don't remember the name." Then her eyes brighten. "But if you don't have plans, you should come with us!"

My heart sinks. No rehearsal for the crew, so I won't see Cory.

I shake myself. It doesn't matter. I don't want to see him.

"I have to study for the SAT. But where are you two going?"

Tammy giggles nervously. "Okay. If we didn't have to go right now, I'd totally make you guess. But you're not going to believe—"

"You're going thrifting."

Tammy smacks my arm, laughing. "How did you

know? But yes! We want to go thrifting."

"But we're all set for the costumes." I vaguely remember doing another solo shopping trip at some point, when Mom was in town.

"Oh, it's not for the play. It's for the contest." I give her a blank look, so she adds. "Hello? This Friday? *Halloween in the Park?* Tell me you're coming. Everybody's going to be there!"

I sigh. For Tammy and Zoe, a crowded party outdoors means fun. But my first impulse is to run and hide.

"I'll go thrifting with you," I offer, and we agree to meet in the main hallway after school.

I don't learn much in the rest of my classes that day. My body is in the seat, my eyes on the teacher, and my notebook in front of me. But my mind isn't there. It stumbles in time and space between events that don't fit together—the attic washed in warm sunlight and the back of the shed in chilly rain, the happy smile on Cory's face just before he pulls me close, and the cold, withdrawn look in his eyes before he stalks away.

Memories rush at me, cut up and jumbled together. Cory taking the scissors from my hand... Smoke drifting through the yard... A bowl of blackberries... Cory walking next to me on the dark road... The apple trees in the orchard... The scars on Cory's arms and chest... Pearl prowling toward me in the driveway...

Cory's head in my lap, my fingers stroking his hair... The red paint on the barn... Cory's eyes on mine as he leans in to kiss me... Handcuffs hitting the floor...

My brain seems to contain an endless supply of these moments, and today it keeps replaying them stubbornly and tirelessly. I can't get Cory out of mind, no matter how hard I try.

Why was he so shaken that Jill drove me home? What could she tell me about him that scares him so much? And what makes him think I'd believe her or care?

Outside, the wind hisses and moans, the rain slashes at the windows. It matches my mood perfectly. The only thing missing is a few trees snapping in half or the roof being torn off.

At last, the classes end for the day, and I race alongside Tammy and Zoe to Tammy's car. We jump in, slam the doors, and just sit there for a minute while rainwater drips from our jackets and shoes on the floor. Then Tammy turns on the engine and merges into the stream of cars leaving the parking lot, and we're off.

I scan the blacktop for the familiar green jacket, but don't see it. Did Cory ever go back inside after our fight? I hope he did. He must have. He wouldn't just take off. It's not like him to skip classes. But then, how well do I really know him?

Zoe is riding up front. She turns to me and smiles.

"Hi, Abby. How're things going?"

She sounds timid and unsure, like we just met for the first time and she's testing the waters. I don't blame her. I've spoken to her even less than to Tammy. I'm really bad at being friends.

"Good. You know. I've been busy with the SAT prep." A lousy excuse, and not really true, but it slides smoothly off my tongue. "So you're thrifting for Halloween? Looking for anything in particular?"

Zoe perks up. She glances at our driver, but Tammy is watching the road like a hawk and doesn't react. I can see her eyes in the rear view mirror. The rain is still coming down hard, the wipers slicing back and forth across the windshield to keep up.

"We have an idea. But it's going to be a surprise. You have to wait till Friday to see it."

Friday. *Halloween in the Park*. I'm not really planning to attend, but I nod. I don't want to spoil her fun.

"Are you talking about our costumes?" Tammy pipes in. She turns her head to her girlfriend, but her eyes stay on the road. "*Zoe.* Don't tell her anything. She has to come and see us."

"I know, Tam!" Zoe protests. "I wasn't."

I don't think they're teasing me on purpose. But it's working. Curiosity stirs inside me, and I already half regret not going. I hope they'll take pictures.

We go to a small thrift store at the edge of downtown, one block from the bridge over the Susquehanna River. Tammy parks on the street, and we leave our rain jackets in the car, and dash inside. The small space is crowded, and I spot at least ten other girls from school, all seniors and juniors. They must've been speeding to get here so fast. They stare at us coldly when we come in, and Tammy and Zoe stare back. I guess the costume competition is a big deal.

The store is full of treasures, and normally I'd be thrilled to comb through the racks and shelves. I spot a light green sweater and a cute black skirt, both great quality and practically new. A steal compared to department store prices.

But I'm not here to shop, and I've got too much on my mind anyway. Instead, I shadow Tammy. I need to ask her something, if I can find enough courage.

Like the best tactical team, Tammy and Zoe split up and start at the opposite ends of the store, moving toward the center. In seconds, a stack of clothes is dangling over Tammy's arm, the plastic hangers swaying as she quickly searches through the rack.

"I can hold these for you," I offer.

Tammy smiles gratefully. "You're sure? Okay. But... don't try to guess! Don't even look at them."

"I won't. Cross my heart."

We transfer the clothes to my bent arm, and

Tammy resumes her rapid inspection of the first circular rack, then moves on to the adjacent one. Every so often, she looks up and exchanges a signal with Zoe. It looks like they have a whole secret code for high-stakes, competitive shopping. I'm impressed and a little envious. I've always been a lone hunter.

"Is your arm okay?" Tammy asks me after she adds several more garments to the stack I carry.

"Fine," I lie, although my arm is already sore. "You know, I missed you and Zoe."

Tammy turns to me and smiles. "We missed you too! We should hang out more often. But I know you have a… I mean, you have a lot going on."

Heat rushes to my cheeks. Was she going to say a *boyfriend?*

Is Cory my boyfriend? I thought he was. I was sure of it when he kissed me in the attic on Sunday. But maybe I only imagined it. He can't be my boyfriend if he doesn't want to be.

I shake my head miserably. "I'm not sure if I do anymore."

Tammy sighs, and her eyes are kind. "Oh, Abby. Did you guys… break up?"

A sharp pain cuts through me, my chest too tight to breathe. *Break up.* I picture a tree snapping in two. The phrase is so final, so definitive—a sharp before and after. It doesn't match my feelings, which are tangled and confused and swing from one extreme to another. But maybe it's only me who's lost. Maybe it's all crystal clear to Cory.

"I don't know…"

Tammy waits for me to elaborate. She's just being a good friend, but I still get restless. I move a few hangers on the rack and pull out a dark, flowing blouse.

Tammy's eyes widen. "Oh! Can I have it?"

"Sure."

She snatches it and admires it, then narrows her eyes at me. "*Wait.* You weren't supposed to be guessing."

"I'm not. I just liked it." I take the blouse from her and add it to the pile over my arm. But my muscles have gone to sleep, and the layers of fabric start to slide. I catch them at the last moment, and flip them to my other arm.

Tammy frowns. "You okay? It looks heavy."

"I've got it."

Tammy cranes her neck to see the end of the store. "I'm almost done. Zoe's real close."

Close to what? I follow her gaze. Zoe is third in the long line to the only fitting room. *Smart.*

It also means I'm out of time. If I want to talk to Tammy alone, I better hurry.

"Can I ask you something?"

Tammy moves to another rack, her fingers deftly

sliding the hangers. "Sure."

I swallow, my throat tight. "What are people saying about Cory?"

Tammy's hand stops. "What does it matter? People always talk. None of it may be true."

"Please. I know you've heard things. *Tell me.*"

She chews on her lip and wrings her hands, her discomfort palpable. She hates gossip as much as I do. But she must know I'm desperate. There's no one else I can ask.

"Okay. I heard that… he has a history. Behavioral problems, violence. Serious stuff."

I think of the scars on Cory's body, and dread slams into me. "What serious stuff?"

Tammy winces and shakes her head. "Don't ask me, Abby! You know how people are. They love to make shit up."

I have more questions, but Zoe is urgently waving us over. She's next in line for the fitting room.

Tammy waves back, then scoops up the clothes from me. "None of it could be true."

Frustration wells up in me. "But that makes it worse. I need to know…"

She gives me a pointed look. "You could ask *him*."

Ask Cory? I start to shake my head. He'd never answer. He never tells me anything.

Wait. That's not true. He did tell me things about

himself—difficult, personal things. He told me about his mother and father.

Tammy's right. I should ask Cory and give him a chance to explain. If the roles were reversed, I hope he'd do the same for me.

I glance out the store windows. The rain has slowed to a drizzle. "Tammy, I'm going to head out. You don't want me to see the costumes anyway. Can you unlock your car, so I can grab my stuff?"

"Sure." Tammy digs in her pocket, and her electronic key beeps. Then she surprises me with a hug. "Hang in there, friend. I'll see you tomorrow."

I smile. "See you. Say bye to Zoe."

But as I head out the door, unease gnaws at me. Tammy means well. I know she's got my back, no matter what happens with Cory, and I'm grateful. But I can't shake the feeling she knows more than she's letting on. Why hide it from me, though?

How bad is it?

Chapter 35

The classroom is tucked away at the end of the hallway on the second floor, eerily quiet after hours. Maps, travel photos, and handwritten words in different languages decorate the walls. Spanish, French, Chinese, and other languages I don't recognize.

I'm the only person here, and it's possible I'm breaking some rule. Are students allowed to enter and use the classrooms? I don't know. But the door was unlocked, and I needed a place to study before the rehearsal—a place where no one would bother me.

I sit at a desk in the back corner, the SAT prep book open in front of me. Two-thirds of the monster are covered in my handwriting already, one-third still to go.

A long bookshelf lines the back of the room. A collection of miniature buildings and bridges in solid colors crowds the top shelf, all coated with dust. An old class project. At least they didn't have to destroy their work and recycle the materials, the way we'll have to take apart the set after the final *Beauty and the Beast* show.

This reminds me. I have something I get to keep

too. I pull it out of the inside pocket of my backpack and study the small square print. A piece of cardboard is attached to the back to protect it.

Cory's photo.

In it, he looks straight at me, his eyes bright and his lips parted. Telling me he meant what he said earlier—that I was beautiful.

An ache pinches my heart, and I'm suddenly restless. What time is it? Outside the windows, the sky is darkening. But the wall clock says I still have thirty minutes.

Enough time to talk to Cory, if I can find him.

I carefully put the photo away. Then pack my book, shrug on my backpack, and rush out the door. I pause on the bridge and scan the main hallway. No sign of him.

I check the cafeteria next, half expecting to see him in the corner booth, head bent over a textbook. But he's not there either.

I hurry down the main hallway, heading for the theater door. I cross a smaller hallway, and movement catches my eye. There—at the far end! Someone's unlocking a door. His back is to me, but I instantly know it's Cory.

He must sense my presence, because he turns my way. I hesitate, and for a few moments, we just look at each other across the long hallway. Then I start walking toward him. He waits.

His eyes stay on me, and my heartbeat quickens. I'm both impatient to reach him and desperate to delay. Time and space stretch with my every step, then snap like a rubber band, and I'm suddenly there, facing him.

He's holding the door open a crack. I glance at the sign, and my eyes widen.

It's the storage room.

The custodian keeps his stuff here.

Suspicion prickles my skin. This room is off limits. Cory must have picked the lock. "What are you doing?"

Cory looks me in the eye. "Guess."

I stare back, unnerved. Does he think it's a game? "No. I don't want to guess. You're not supposed to go in there. That's why the door stays locked."

Cory shows no expression. He simply turns away, pulls open the door, and goes in.

I huff and clutch the straps of my backpack. *Fine.* I get it. It's none of my business what he does. I should walk away right now.

But I can't. The door is open. I step inside after him.

Shelves line the small space, full of detergents, mops, tools, and spare hardware. A single caged lightbulb hangs overhead. The air reeks of pine, the scent too intense to be natural.

Cory bends over the wheeled bucket, empty and

dry for the moment. Then he grips the handle and flips the heavy contraption on its side.

He raises his foot—and realization hits me. It's payback for my phone.

I spring forward and grab his arm. "Don't break it!"

Cory's face darkens and he throws me a sharp look. Then he reaches into his pocket and pulls out a small wrench and some screws. "I'm not going to break it. I'm going to *fix it*."

My cheeks flush with shame, and I drop my hand from his arm.

He slowly steps over the bucket, then kneels on the other side and examines the wheel.

I kneel across from him. Each time I think I know what he's going to do, he surprises me. Why do I keep expecting him to turn bad and do something terrible? He never gave me a reason. Maybe it's me who needs more trust.

Cory looks up at me. "What are you doing?" His voice is quiet and almost sad.

"Watching you."

He sighs. "Why?"

Because I miss you. The thought is unhelpful, and I try to shake it off. I should be mad at him for pushing me away and hiding things from me. But the hard edge is gone, and what I feel is more like grief.

"Does it bother you?" I ask.

Cory frowns and shakes his head. And I don't know if he means it doesn't bother him or something else, but I stay where I am.

He works quietly, his eyes on the wheel he's repairing. I watch his fingers, his arms, his face. His hair is getting long again. It falls into his eyes. How long has it been since I cut it? It feels like years. Would he let me cut it again if I offered? Would he distract me with kisses, like he did last time? I miss being with him. I miss seeing him happy. Did I do something wrong? What happened to us?

Cory extends his hand in my direction. "Can you hold this?"

"Sure." I open my palm, and he drops a screw into it.

I lift it to my eyes. It's broken. A deep ridge runs across it top to bottom, splitting it nearly in half. I didn't know a piece of metal could break like this. Isn't metal supposed to be strong? For some reason, the idea upsets me. No wonder the wheel didn't work.

Cory finishes the job, and we both get up. He sets the bucket upright and rolls it back and forth a few times, testing the wheel. It turns smoothly. The rattling sound is gone.

I turn to Cory, the broken screw still in my fist. "He'll wonder who fixed it."

"I hope not. I could get in trouble." The corners of Cory's mouth lift slightly, one side higher. A hint of a smile, gone a second later.

"True." The smile unlocks something inside me. I want to see it again, bigger. I want to hear him laugh.

We stand two feet apart. Close enough that if I lifted my arm, I could press my palm to his chest, right over his heart. Is his beating faster too, like mine is?

I'm still holding the broken screw. "Here."

He opens his hand, and I drop it in.

"Thanks." He pockets it. "We should go."

But he doesn't move from his spot. Neither do I.

I think back to Sunday. I picture his face when he yelled at me to go home. The words hurt, but I don't think he meant them. So why push me away? Does it have to do with the rumors about him? Are any of them true, and he's afraid I'll find out? Is that why he didn't want me to talk to Jill? I still don't understand the reason—but it hangs over us like a storm cloud, poisons the air like smoke. Why won't he trust me? He'll have to tell me sometime. What is he waiting for?

Impatience burns under my skin. But I can't give up. I won't.

"They have *Halloween in the Park* downtown this Friday. Food, music, a costume competition."

Cory gives me a strange look. "We have a rehearsal on Friday."

"It ends early, so everyone can go." I take a deep breath. *Come on. Be brave.* I think of the drop at the edge of the backyard, the sharp rocks on the bottom of the creek. But I'm not going to fall. I'm going to jump. "Do you want to go with me?"

Cory doesn't answer right away, only studies me, his brows knotted. "I'm not big on dressing up…"

"I'm not dressing up either. I'm just going to watch."

"Everyone from school is going to be there…"

I stare at him, my heart pounding angrily. Why is he doing this? It's a simple question. "Yes or no, Cory? If you don't want to go with me, just say it."

His eyes flash. "Of course I want to go with you." He exhales, then shakes his head. "But it's not about me. Are *you* sure you want to do this?"

The relief is so great, my body feels weightless, all the tension gone at once. *He wants to go with me.*

Then his question registers. Is he worried people will see us together? So what? Let them see us. I'm tired of hiding. And if they don't like it, that's their problem. They can't get between us. Even Jordan won't be able to touch us. Not when everyone is watching.

"Yes! I'm sure."

Cory sighs. "Okay."

I want to step forward and close the space between us. What would happen if I did? Would he pull me close and kiss me?

But Cory stands still like a statue, his face tense and his arms at his sides, and I've used up all my courage. So I only nod and turn to the door.

"Okay."

Chapter 36

The rehearsal on Friday is a mess, one stupid mistake after another. Natasha's finger slips on the sound board, and Beauty's whisper turns into a scream. Adam misses his cue, and the Beast disappears from the stage as the spotlight swings in the wrong direction. And most dangerous of all, the huge platform that forms the second floor of the castle starts rolling away in the middle of the scene, after one of the Beast's Servants bumps into it.

Thankfully, someone from the set crew grabs the back frame and kicks the safety lock down before the platform crashes into the backdrop. It happens fast, and from where I'm standing in the wing, I never see the person. But I'm pretty sure it's Cory.

It gets worse, though. The actors are as distracted as the crew. After Jordan, of all people, butchers his lines something awful, the director throws up her hands.

"*Enough!* This rehearsal is over. Get out of my sight. Go enjoy Halloween." She waves us off the stage. "Just don't get hurt. I need everyone back here on Monday in one piece."

The theater empties as people rush off, and I'm suddenly worried Cory will change his mind and leave. Where is he? I also need to find Tammy. I'm hoping she'll give us a ride.

Jordan walks up to me, his eyes alarmingly blue against the dark fur of the mask, and I reflexively reach for his hand to help him with the glove. But he moves his arm away.

"I'm keeping them on. I'm going as the Beast tonight."

I grab his wrist. "No, you're not!" It's bad luck, not to mention against the rules. What if the costume got damaged? Skyler would tear our heads off.

Jordan laughs. "I'm kidding." He extends both arms toward me, and I hurriedly help him take off the gloves, then step behind him and unclip the transmitter for his mike and unzip the back of the mask. He pulls off the mask and shakes his blond locks before handing me the mask. "Thanks, Abby. So I'll see you in the park, right?"

The question unnerves me, and I shrug, hoping my cheeks aren't as warm as they feel. What does he care? If I come to the park, it'll be with Cory. I'd prefer Jordan didn't pay attention.

"Maybe." And I hurry backstage, clutching the Beast's mask and gloves in my hands.

In the costume room, Tammy and Zoe are giggling. Did I interrupt something? But Tammy smiles at me. "Here you are. Ready to go?"

I put the Beast's mask and gloves in their boxes and grab my backpack, my thoughts racing. I can't leave without Cory. But if he's already gone… No, he wouldn't. "Give me five minutes? I have to find—"

"Hi," Cory says behind me, and relief washes over me. His face is somber when I meet his gaze, but I don't care. He came.

I turn back to my costume mates. "Can Cory get a ride too?"

Tammy and Zoe trade a sharp glance. Surprised? Worried? I don't quite catch the meaning, but I still bristle. Every second of hesitation hurts, and Cory doesn't deserve it. He hasn't done anything to them.

They must reach an agreement, though, because Tammy nods. "Sure. We can drop you off at your house or at the park."

"My house." Mom doesn't come back until tomorrow. The place is empty.

I turn to Cory. I picture stepping into the dark, quiet kitchen with him, and my heartbeat speeds up. "We can leave the school stuff there and grab a bite to eat?"

I don't know why I feel the need to explain. It sounds like I'm apologizing. But for what? And why am I suddenly nervous, my palms sweaty? I've been alone with him before. I trust him.

Cory's not carrying his school bag. He must have left it in his locker. He studies me. "We can do whatever you want, Abby."

I should be thrilled. I know he means it. But the answer bothers me. It sounds like I'm twisting his arm, like he's only going because I asked him. "No. It's about what *you* want too."

Cory only frowns, as if trying to solve an impossible problem.

Zoe's eyes flicker from him to me in alarm. "Why would you eat inside? There'll be plenty of food at the park."

Tammy's face is tense too. "Okay, you guys ready? Let's go. We don't want to be late and miss all the fun." She gives me a pointed look.

It's like they're both trying to tell me something without actually saying it. But what exactly? And why can't they just say it? I'm not good at riddles.

I turn to the door, frustrated. "I'm ready."

Outside, the sun has set and dusk is falling, as if someone was dimming the stage lights. The air is chilly but not cold, and when I look up, faint dots of light flicker in the darkening sky. It's going to be a starry night.

We cross the empty parking lot to Tammy's car.

We're the last ones here. Tammy and Zoe sit in the front. Cory and I get in the back seat.

The car starts moving, and I switch my backpack to my lap and glance over at Cory. He sits with his back straight and his hands on his thighs, his face turned to the window and his whole body radiating tension. He's not comfortable here, and the awkward silence doesn't help.

I clear my throat and lean forward. "So how does the contest work?"

Tammy catches my eyes in the rearview mirror, but it's Zoe who answers, turning round in her seat to face me. "The costume contest? Oh, it's great! There's one for small kids, but that's earlier in the day, so it's already done. And then the main one later tonight. At nine, I think?" She glances at the driver. "Tam, do you remember?"

Tammy keeps her eyes on the road. "The voting ends at eight-thirty. At nine, they announce the winners."

"Right." Zoe turns back to me. "Anyone can enter—you just have to fill out a tiny form and let them take your picture. There's a bunch of categories, including the funniest, the scariest, the most creative, and the most popular costume overall. Everyone gets a ballot and writes in their picks for each category."

"Good to know." I nod, though I'm only half

listening. At least Cory turned this way. I wish Zoe looked at him more often, instead of mostly at me.

We're already downtown and turning into my street. Somehow, night has fallen. The street lamps are on. Each has three glowing white spheres on top of a slender green column. Pretty except for a thick cloud of bugs buzzing around each lamp. Porch lights are on too in most houses, and small figures hurry from door to door, swinging their plastic baskets—a ladybug, a ghost, a princess, a fire fighter. The adults hover behind.

Looks like trick-or-treating is in full swing.

Up ahead, a kid in a green, boxy costume skips down the sidewalk. I grab Cory's arm and point at my window. "Look!"

Cory leans toward me and peers outside. "A circuit board. Nice."

He smiles at me, his face only inches away from mine, and longing cuts through me. I want to pull him close and kiss that smile. I miss him. Does he miss me too? The look in his eyes says he does, but I need to know for sure. He and I need to sort things out.

Not right now, though. We're almost there. I need to wait a little longer. Cory leans back in his seat, and I look out the window.

Blinking lights catch my eye. A witch in a pointy black hat sits in a chair on a small porch. A glass ball flashes with color by her elbow, and a huge drawing of a black cat covers the door behind her. Kids step forward, squealing with delight, and she drops candy in their baskets, cackling and twirling her long, fake nails.

The witch looks familiar... Mrs. Smith!

My house is next door, and Tammy is already pulling over, when I grab the back of her seat. "*No!* Keep going." Tammy jumps up and throws me a dark look in the rearview mirror, so I quickly add, "Sorry. Can you let us out round the corner, please?"

Tammy turns the corner, pulls over, and Cory and I get out.

"See you there. You're going to love our costumes." Zoe smiles at me and me only before the car drives off.

I turn into the back alley, and Cory follows. The sounds of the trick-or-treaters fade to a distant hum, and music drifts from the direction of the park. Fences, garage doors, and trashcans are all blurry patches of gray in the dim light.

"This is it. We can get in through the back door." I unlock the gate and we enter the backyard. The grass and the stone path are a dull gray, the tree in the corner and the vines choking the fence almost black. Only the light walls of the house stand out.

Cory peers into the narrow alley that runs alongside the house, connecting to the street. Flashing color lights lick the pavement at the far end. There's a cackle, and a bunch of kids trot across the opening, swinging their candy baskets.

Cory turns to me. "The witch is your next door neighbor. You didn't want to run into her."

"That's right. She's very nosey." I'm glad he figured it out.

I fumble with my house key, half expecting him to offer to pick the lock. But he patiently waits. Finally, I open the door, and we step into the kitchen.

I reach for the light switch but hesitate. The kitchen isn't overly dark, and the bright lights will be visible from the street and draw Mrs. Smith like a moth. And what if any trick-or-treaters knock on the door? Not part of my plans.

"I think I'm going to keep the lights off."

Cory nods, so I drop my backpack on a chair and pocket my key. I'm suddenly nervous again. My mouth feels parched.

I cross to the sink and pour two glasses of water. I offer one to Cory. "Water?"

He steps closer to take it from me, and his fingers brush mine. "Thanks."

We both empty our glasses, and I put them in the sink, careful not to make noise. "Do you want anything to eat? Like a sandwich?"

Cory shakes his head. "I'm fine. But you go

ahead."

"No. I'm okay." I know I should eat, but I'm not hungry, my stomach in a knot.

Why all the nerves? Is it because I'm alone with him? That's part of it. He affects me more than anyone ever before. But that's not the main reason.

I have some questions to ask him. They've been haunting me and tearing me up. They're harsh, cruel questions. I don't know how to ask them without hurting him, and hurting him is the last thing I want.

Why are people talking about you? Where do the rumors come from? Did you do something? What did you do, Cory? Please tell me. I need to know.

Cory watches me, his brows furrowed. I forgot he can read me like an open book.

And suddenly I realize—he already knows what I'm going to ask, and he's waiting. He's been waiting for the questions for a while now. I just haven't had the courage to ask them.

Dread grips me like a cold fist, squeezing air from my lungs, crushing my muscles. I cannot speak. I can barely stand. I've changed my mind. I don't want to know. It doesn't matter. I want things to stay the way they are.

Cory pales, and frustration glints in his eyes. He's not okay with my decision. He takes a shaky breath.

"Abby, I need to tell you something—"

While dread felt like ice, panic is fire. It flares inside me, scorching hot, and I can't stay still another second, can't listen to another word.

I grab Cory's hand. "Tell me later, okay? After the contest? We should go. We don't want to miss it."

Cory swallows, and I sense relief in him. He's braver than me, but that doesn't mean he's not afraid. He's dreading whatever he's going to tell me too.

His fingers tighten around mine. "Okay."

We leave the same way we came in—through the back door.

Chapter 37

The small park is milling with people when we get there. Under a starry night sky, zombies and mermaids, ninjas and punk rockers, Viking warriors and Egyptian goddesses, werewolves and ghosts and cabaret dancers mingle. The crowd is a clashing mix of characters that don't belong in the same story. Voices, dance music, and the smell of fried food fill the air.

Cory and I cross Market Street and stop at the top of the stairs to take in the view. He's still holding my hand, and I have no intention of letting go.

For a moment, I wish we were wearing masks too. Everyone else is. But I push the thought away. I don't want to hide my face right now. I want people to see me with Cory.

The park takes up two town blocks. Old, gnarly trees surround a network of stairs, sidewalks, lawns, shrubs, and benches. A creek borders the park on one side, and a long parking lot, right now occupied by several food trucks, on the other. And in the center, a large wooden gazebo serves as the stage for events, framed by a half circle of stone benches built into the hillside for the audience. Right now, that area is packed with people and awash with throbbing lights.

I crane my neck and scan the crowd, searching for Tammy and Zoe. They must be here already. But with everyone masked and costumed, it's impossible to tell from the distance.

"Do you see them?" I ask Cory.

"No. It's too far. We have to go down to the gazebo." He looks into my eyes. "That's what you want, right?"

"Yes. I want to find them and see all the costumes." That's not the only reason, but I don't have to explain. He knows. "Don't you?"

"We'll be the only ones not dressed up."

"So? They should be grateful. If we did, our costumes would be awesome, and we'd win."

Cory chuckles. "You'd win for sure. But not me. I'm terrible at it."

"I'd make your costume for you!" I protest. "*Next year*. I'm serious. We should do it."

Cory's face grows serious, his eyes intense as he leans toward me. I hold perfectly still, certain he's going to kiss me. But he only lifts his hand and runs his thumb along my jawline. "Sounds good to me, Abby."

"Okay. It's a deal then." My tone is matter-of-fact, but warmth floods my body and electricity dances on my skin. How does he do that? Ignite me like that with one touch? Maybe it should scare me more—as much as what I don't know about him scares me. But it only draws me in. I don't feel weak when he does it, I feel stronger. I feel alive and wide awake.

We descend the short flight of stairs and start down the sidewalk toward the gazebo, weaving our way through the crowd. It's mostly high school students. I recognize the way they stand, act, and talk, even if I can't see their faces. Everyone holds a phone in their hand, and a flash goes off every few seconds like a silent explosion.

A group in front of us—vampires with red eyes and sharp fangs—all turn and race into the lawn, almost knocking me down. Cory pulls me back at the last moment.

They cluster around a festive couple standing there, while one vampire snaps photos.

I turn after them. "Wait. Are these—?"

"Scarecrows," Cory says.

He's right. Adult-sized scarecrows in full outfits stand scattered all over the lawn. The vampires pose with the bride and groom. There's also a police officer arresting a robber. A lumberjack holding an ax. A librarian with a stack of books. A butcher with a blood-stained apron. A businesswoman with a coffee mug. Even a small kid on a bicycle.

They look almost realistic until you look closely

and see the cloth-sewn faces and straw sticking out of the sleeves. Creepy is an understatement.

"Do you want a picture with any of them?" Cory teases.

I shudder. "No, thanks."

I didn't even bring my phone, I realize. It's still in my backpack. I'll have to text Mom later. Or is she already on the road heading home? Maybe I got the days wrong, and she comes back tonight. I can't remember.

Cory's gaze lingers on the scarecrow in a police uniform, and my chest tightens in sympathy. Is he thinking about his father? The robber scarecrow looks broken, his head bent to the side and one shoulder sagging. The wind and rain must have damaged it.

I step toward Cory and touch my lips to his cheek.

He blinks and smiles at me, surprised. But his voice is full of sadness. "What was that for?"

"Nothing. I'm glad you're here. I'm glad you came with me. That's all."

Cory shakes his head like he disagrees, but he leans toward me, his gaze locked on mine. He doesn't say a word—only lifts my hand to his chest and presses it over his heart.

The gesture takes my breath away, and for a moment I feel lightheaded, like after biking down a steep hill. Cory's heartbeat drums under my fingers, strong and fast, and his face fills my vision. Everything else recedes. The masked people, the flashing cameras, the music, the twisted trees under a night sky. They're nothing but moving shadows. Cory is the only real thing.

"Abby! You made it."

Jordan's voice.

I turn, startled, and yank my hand from Cory's grasp.

I instantly regret it. Why did I do that? I don't care if Jordan sees us. I want him to. But Cory turns as well, his arms stiff at his sides, and it's too late. The moment is ruined. Jordan ruined it, and I know he did it on purpose.

I'm about to snap at him, but the man blocking my way looks so striking, his eyes so impossibly blue in the dramatic makeup, my tongue turns to cotton and I can only stare.

Jordan is a pirate prince. Despite the October night chill, he's wearing only a loose white shirt and brown leather pants and boots. Thick golden chains hang around his neck, leather cuffs cover his wrists, and a heavy-looking sword with a wide, crooked blade hangs from a holder at his belt.

He smiles at me from under his tricorn hat, no doubt pleased with my reaction. He completely ignores Cory.

Anger rolls over me, bringing me to my senses. I can't control how my stupid body reacts to Jordan. But I won't play his twisted games. I don't know what he wants from me. I don't believe for one second that he's serious about me. But whatever it is, he's going to be disappointed. I'm here with Cory, and the sooner this sinks in, the better.

I grab Cory's hand and lift my chin. "*We're* just passing through." I put extra emphasis on *we*. I step onto the dead grass that used to be the lawn, intending to walk around Jordan. But I don't get far.

An ugly grimace twists his face, and he steps on the lawn too, blocking my path. Casually, he pulls the sword from his belt and flexes his wrist, his motions smooth and practiced. The blade traces a slow infinity pattern in front of me, the metal catching the lights.

Cory's grip on my fingers tightens, and he steps past me, his eyes fixed on Jordan and his voice low. "Careful, or you could hurt someone. Even if it's not a real sword."

"Not real?" Jordan's eyes flash with malice.

Slowly, his sword tracing the same graceful pattern, he turns to a shrub next to him. He pauses with the sword raised, the tip pointing at the stars—and then swings it down so fast the blade blurs.

There is a faint click when the metal scrapes the ground—followed by a dry rustling as the cut twigs start to fall.

I stifle a gasp. Jordan... brought a weapon with him? How does he get away with this?

I glance around the park. Shouldn't the cops be around for a public event, keeping an eye on things? I thought I saw a parked police car earlier, but I don't see one now. What if something happens?

Jordan slides the sword back into the holder in one swift motion. His eyes drill into Cory's face. "That's the problem with you, Brennell. You can't tell what's real and what's not anymore. And I feel bad for you, man. I do." Mockery rings in Jordan's voice. "But you can't change facts to suit you. That's just delusional."

Cory's face darkens. "You've got me all figured out, huh?"

Jordan sneers, then moves closer. He lowers his voice to a hateful growl. "Wasn't very hard. And, honestly, I don't give a shit what you do. But you need to stop fucking with other people's heads." Jordan throws me a look, then turns back to Cory. "It won't end well, Brennell."

Cory stares back at him, his scars painfully visible against his flushed skin. But this time his jaw is clenched and no sound comes out, like he's biting down the answer.

I can't stand it. Cory isn't bothering anyone. We just want to have a good time. Why can't Jordan leave him alone?

I glare at Jordan. "If you don't give a shit, then stop following us around."

His blue eyes snap to me. "I meant him. Not you." He rips off his pirate hat, his blond locks tussled, and frowns in frustration. "Honestly, Abby. What are you doing with him? You have no idea—"

"Shut up, Jordan!" My chest constricts, and the words come out hollow and breathless. "It's none of your business!" He's a good actor, but the trick doesn't work on me anymore. I know he doesn't care about me, and I won't be a prop in his hands. He won't use me to hurt Cory.

All around us, masked faces turn toward us, their eyes bright and hungry, excited to watch me lose my temper. I bet some would love a violent fight even more. The thought makes me sick.

I grab Cory's hand and pull him behind me. "Come on, let's go to the gazebo." We have to get away from Jordan.

The crowd gets thicker and the lights brighter, the beat of the music like a restless heartbeat. A large flat screen has been installed next to the gazebo, facing the stone benches built into the hillside.

"Look. It's Neon!" I squeeze Cory's fingers, and we stop to watch.

A stunning android poses on the screen, all silvery

alloy, streamlined form, and high-tech gear with hookup ports and control panels. The makeup alone is incredible—the face outlined and shifted slightly like a lid cracked open, the neck and parts of the hands segmented at the joints. There's nothing to indicate gender, but that makes sense. An android doesn't need one. A caption underneath the photo reads, *Presenting NEON as... NEON 2.1 ANDROID.*

Cory perks up. Or maybe pretends to, for my benefit. "Nice."

The screen shows a moving carousal of photos, three at a time. A new image slides into view from the right every few seconds, moves to the center and pops forward, then slides to the third position and recedes, before dropping out of frame on the left.

FOR YOUR CONSIDERATION IN ALL CATEGORIES screams a headline at the top of the screen. It's off center to accommodate a large sponsor logo in the corner. I bristle at the name. It's the real estate company that pressured Mom to sell them the duplex.

The next contestant on the screen is a fierce-looking Batman in a black mask, full body suit, and flowing cape. The tall figure looks familiar. I glance at the caption. *Presenting HARPER as... BATMAN.* I blink. Harper? I'd never recognize her. But maybe that's the point. Today everyone gets to be someone else.

The next costume on the screen reverses the colors from black to white. A majestic Snow Queen in an elaborate tiara and a magnificent, full-length gown. Even her skin and waist-long, silvery hair glitters like fresh snow. *Presenting PATRICIA as... SNOW QUEEN.* Wow. Another surprise. Patricia looks nothing like herself. But maybe it's the other way around—this is who she always was, and I just didn't notice.

The carousel advances, and another photo moves to the center. *Presenting MIKE as... CONSTRUCTION WORKER.* Mike sports a yellow hard hat, a matching vest over a flannel shirt, jeans, and steel-toe work boots, all believably smudged with dirt. In the photo, he poses with his hands on his hips and grins a little too brightly, which spoils the effect. But it's still a good costume.

People push past me and Cory to get to the gazebo and enter the contest. A man and a woman supervise the process. Both wear ugly sweatshirts with the sponsor's logo on them and tacky plastic masks—he is a clown, and she is a cat. New arrivals who want to compete in the contest fill out a card, take it to the woman to have their picture taken, and then walk up to the man, who works on the computer.

Flashes go off all around us, everyone taking

pictures of everyone else, not bothering to ask permission. A flash blinds me a few times, but I ignore it. It's not worth it.

"Watch out." Cory alerts me a second before I sense movement behind me and hands grip my shoulders.

"Boo!"

Cory lets go of my hand, and I spin around, my heart in my throat—only to see two beautiful flapper girls beaming at me.

"Tammy! Zoe!" I breathe with relief and gawk at their costumes. "You look amazing!"

They both giggle, the long feathers in their headbands shaking. "Really?"

"Yes! Turn around. Let me see you."

They're both wearing cocktail dresses in *The Great Gatsby* style. Tammy's dress is midnight blue, with silver sequins and long tassels that shimmy when she moves, with long silk gloves to match. She has pearls in her ears, a long strand of pearls around her neck, and more pearls on her gloved fingers.

Gorgeous—but I like Zoe's dress even more. Emerald green, with intricate beaded designs and long tassels along the hem. Instead of pearls, she's wearing green and black gems. They dangle from her ears, loop around her neck, and hug her wrists on top of her long black gloves.

Tammy and Zoe wait patiently as I study their dresses, touch the fabrics, marvel at the seams, stitches, and hidden zippers, sighing in admiration the whole time. For a moment, I regret not dressing up. It would've been fun. But I had other things on my mind.

The dresses are sleeveless, but both Tammy and Zoe wear long sleeves and tights underneath. Smart. Otherwise they'd be freezing. What about the shoes?

I start to look down, but Zoe groans, "No, no, no," and Tammy lifts my chin in her gloved hand and gives me a stern look. "Uh-uh. We *do not* look at the shoes. The shoes *are not*—"

How could I resist? I push Tammy's hand away and glance down.

Laughter bubbles in my throat when I see their feet. "You're wearing sneakers?"

Tammy hides a smile and frowns. "I'm sorry. Look at the sidewalks. See the cracks? You try walking in high heels on that for three hours."

Zoe grabs her arm and spins her around. "Tam— look! It's us!"

Us?

We all turn to look at the screen just as the next photo moves to the center. And sure enough, it shows them both posing together—and they look happy and absolutely dazzling. *Presenting TAMMY AND ZOE as… FLAPPERS*, the caption reads.

"It's a great picture!" I gush. "So you can enter as a couple?"

But Zoe and Tammy exchange a grim look.

"What?" I snap, instantly on edge. If they have a problem with me and Cory, I'm out of here and never speaking to them again.

"The Cat Lady didn't cut off the shoes like we asked," Tammy mutters. "She said she would, but she didn't. Dammit." There's no anger in her voice, just disappointment.

The shoes. I didn't even notice them in the photo. But when I look back at the screen, the carousel has shifted, and the Flappers' photo is gone.

"Who cares about the shoes? Your costumes are fantastic. I'll vote for you right now. How do I do that? I need a ballot, right?" I glance toward the gazebo, and see Jordan staring right at me, his face tense with anticipation. What does he want?

I sense the change around me before I know the source—a wave of shocked gasps and spiteful chuckles, all somehow aimed in our direction.

"Abby." Tammy touches my arm, and I spin to Cory first. He stands frozen, his eyes fixed on the screen. I follow his gaze and blink in confusion.

Cory's photo is in the center of the screen. A hasty, awkward, unposed snapshot. But why would they show his photo at all? He never entered the contest. He's not even wearing a costume. It must be a mistake.

Then I read the caption, and anger chokes me.

Presenting CORY as... THE GOOD GUY.

I'm in motion, stalking toward the gazebo, before I consciously decide to act. Jordan sees me and walks down the steps to meet me, a hint of smile on his lips.

I grind my teeth, my face hot. I knew it was him, and this confirms it. I run the last few steps, heading straight for him.

"Abby!" Cory is right behind me, but he's too late to stop me.

I ram my hands against Jordan's chest and use my momentum to shove him back.

"You asshole!" My voice is a hoarse whisper, my throat too tight to scream.

But Jordan doesn't budge, and my body slams into his, my arms folding in front of me. I barely manage to twist my head and avoid ramming my face into his. I panic and recoil from him, unsteady on my feet, and nearly topple backward.

Jordan's hands grip my wrists. "Calm down. It's just a joke." He glances over my shoulder. "You never know. He might win."

"Let go of me!" I try to wrench away, but his fingers clasp my wrists like iron.

Cory steps next to me. His voice choked with fury. "You heard her. Take your hands off her."

Jordan releases me with a laugh. "Okay, okay. Take it easy." He's using his stage voice. Performing for the audience. "She collided with me. I caught her. What's the big deal?" He looks Cory in the eye and scowls. "It's not like I've never touched her before."

What?

I have no time to react.

Cory's eyes flash, and his arm shoots forward, his clenched fist aimed at Jordan's face.

But Jordan blocks the punch. He expected it. He grips Cory's wrist the way he gripped mine.

"Careful. I can't have a swollen lip. I'm the star, remember?"

He lets go of Cory's wrist just as the music cuts off and a stern voice booms.

"What's going on here?"

A heavyset, mean-looking cop stands three yards away. His hands are at his belt, like he's ready to reach for something.

He's staring daggers at Cory.

Chapter 38

With the music off and the crowd hushed, a charged, heavy silence fills the park. I can feel the weight of it pressing down on me.

I glance at Cory. He stands frozen, his eyes on the cop and his jaw set.

The cop frowns, clearly displeased. "Young man. I asked you a question."

Dread licks my spine. What is Cory doing? *Come on*, I urge him in my thoughts. *Say something. Answer him. Please.*

But Cory only stares back, his mouth stubbornly closed.

It's Jordan who speaks, his tone suitably respectful. "Good evening, officer. Everything is fine. Just a... small disagreement between friends. No harm done."

Jordan catches my eye, and I look away, unnerved. He's trying to defuse the tension and appease the cop, and a part of me is grateful. But the other part resents him for it. As always, he's twisting the story to make himself look good—better than he deserves—and to make Cory look bad.

The cop looks at Jordan, an eyebrow raised in surprise. He saw trouble and came over to exert his authority and put an end to it. He's not quite sure how to handle a teenager doing his job for him. "I appreciate it, son. But I still need to hear it from your *friend*." The cop doesn't hide the sarcasm as he turns back to Cory. "You threw the first punch. Why?"

"No, he didn't!" the words rush from my mouth, though I never decided to speak. "I did. I hit Jordan. Cory was just defending me."

Cory throws me a sharp look. "Abby, don't."

The sharpness hurts, but I try not to show it. "What? It's true!"

The cop's reaction is not what I expected. He narrows his eyes at Cory, his face and voice even more severe than before. "Cory. Cory Brennell. I remember you." He nods gravely, as if now everything made sense. "Well, that didn't take long, did it?"

Cory pales, and I have a sinking feeling.

What have I done? I wanted to help him, not to make things worse. It's like the cop didn't hear anything I said except Cory's name. How do I make him listen?

I glance at the crowd around me. They all stand watching and waiting. But waiting for what? I want to yell at them to go away. We're not putting on a show to entertain them. This is real. Cory is in trouble, and I don't know what to do.

A witch in a pointy hat stares at me with disapproval.

I cringe. It's Mrs. Smith, with a phone in her hand. *Great.* Did she already report on me to my mom, or is she about to? As if tonight wasn't terrible enough.

The cop walks over to Cory. "You've got anything to say for yourself?"

"No." Cory bends his head, but there's no hint of remorse or apology in his voice. It's more like he can't stand the sight of the man and would rather stare at his shoes.

The cop's face darkens in offense. "Okay, Brennell. Suit yourself. I respect your grandfather, but you're giving me no option. I'm taking you to the station and filing a report. You can explain it to your prob—"

"Just do it already!" Cory cuts him off, a note of panic in his voice. "Take me to the station, file your report. Whatever. Just get it over with."

"That's enough. I don't like your attitude." The cop grabs Cory's arm with one hand and reaches back for something with the other.

Handcuffs? My heart stops.

Cory's eyes meet mine for a second, and the shame and defeat in them splits me open.

I spring forward, reaching for the cop's arm. "No! I

told you it wasn't his fault. I started it. You can't arrest him."

The cop blinks at me. Car keys—not handcuffs—dangle from his fingers, which is a relief. "I can and I will, miss. And you're not helping him by interfering. Unless you want me to write you up as well." He gives me a warning look.

I'm already taking my breath to say, *Go ahead*, when a hand grabs me and yanks me back.

I spin around, certain it's Jordan and ready to lash out at him. But a scary insect mask stares back at me.

I flinch, then reflexively scan the costume. Patches of brown fur cover the body suit, and thick, triangular wings with intricate designs extend from the arms. A Moth!

The Moth pulls off the mask—and Skyler looks me in the eye. "He's right, Abby. Don't push it." Skyler's fingers dig into my arm, pinning me in place. "The cop is already pissed off, and you'll only piss him off more. You don't want to do that. If he writes you up, it'll go into your record and follow you forever. Wreck your college plans big time. Trust me. I've seen it happen."

I stare back at Skyler, my head spinning as I process the information. A record? As in, *a criminal record?* Then another thought crashes through. Is that what's going to happen to Cory?

Cory!

I turn around just in time to see the cop shut the back door of the police car and get behind the wheel. I squint at the back window as the car pulls out of the parking spot and drives off. Cory must be in the back seat, though I can't see him through the darkened glass. Can he see me? How did this happen? I should've tried harder. But I lost my chance.

The realization hits me, and I spin back to Skyler. I wrench my arm away. "You did this on purpose! You distracted me!"

"Yes, I did. You can thank me later."

"Which way is the station?" I've lived here for over a year but barely know the town. I never made the effort.

There's no sympathy in Skyler's voice. "Just stay out of it, Abby. I'm serious."

Bitterness fills me. "You mean, stay away from Cory?"

"That would be smart too." And Skyler puts the insect mask back on and walks away.

A grating sound rents the silence as the speakers click back.

"All right!" The man in the Clown mask stands on the steps to the gazebo, awkwardly clutching a microphone. "Can everyone hear me? Yes? Great!" The woman in the Cat mask hands him a ballot box, and he almost drops it, trying to hold it with one hand. "Oops.

I got it. Not to worry. Anyway. Who hasn't voted yet? You have five more minutes to get your ballot into this box!"

The Clown guy lowers his microphone and turns to Jordan, unaware we can still hear him. A rookie mistake. "Are we waiting for your father? Is he coming?"

Jordan's lips curl angrily, but he covers it up with a bright smile for everyone watching. "My father is in London this weekend, so probably not?"

Confusion registers in the man's face. "But he's the sponsor. Who's going to give out the awards?"

Jordan's smile grows a little too wide to be genuine. He walks up the steps, playing up his pirate persona, and jovially smacks the Clown on the back. *"You will!* A promotion!" Then he snatches the microphone from him and turns it off.

I glare at Jordan, although he's not looking at me. So his father is the sponsor. The pushy real estate guy who keeps pestering Mom to sell the duplex.

Good. I'm glad. Now I have one more reason to hate Jordan.

The music resumes, even louder than before.

I glance around me. Most of the crowd has lost interest in me. They stand in groups, laughing and posing for photos, checking the large screen every few seconds for the contest announcements that must be coming. But I spot two familiar faces.

Tammy and Zoe watch me anxiously. They start in my direction, still looking unsure.

I hesitate. I don't really want to talk to them. I don't want to talk to anyone. But maybe they know the way to the station. I really should've brought my phone.

But someone else hurries toward me, and a chill grips me when we make eye contact.

Mom.

Tammy and Zoe must see my alarm because they stop, so my mom reaches me first.

"Abby!" She's out of breath, like she ran all the way here from our house. Straight from the car, too, judging by the sweatpants and sweatshirt she's wearing—her driving-all-day outfit.

"You're back," I say weakly.

My mom scans me up and down, a frantic look in her eyes, like she expects knife wounds or bullet holes. "Are you hurt? Mrs. Smith called me. She said you got in a fight!?" Mom's voice is choked and her hands are shaking.

I knew it. The nosey neighbor ratted me out. I search the crowd for the pointy black hat. *There*. The Witch is still spying on us.

"I'm okay, Mom. It wasn't really a fight." I say crossly. "Mrs. Smith likes to exaggerate."

Mom frowns. She looks exhausted, her skin gray and dark circles under her eyes. But her voice is sharp, her worry for me turning into anger.

"*Exaggerate?* She also said you talked back to a police officer. That you tried to stop him from arresting the troublemaker who started it! Did she exaggerate about that too?"

The troublemaker who started it.

She means Cory.

Heat rises to my cheeks. "*The troublemaker?*" I glare at my mother. "You don't know anything about him! But you're ready to blame him anyway, just like everyone else!"

A few people turn our way, attracted by my outburst.

Mom's eyes widen with a hurt astonishment. I just yelled at her in a public place. I've never done anything like it before. But she collects herself and touches my arm. "All right. We're leaving. I'm not going to argue with you in front of these people. Or do you want to make a scene? They're your friends, not mine."

They're *not* my friends. At least not most of them. And after tonight, maybe none. But I don't want an audience either.

I start walking, and Mom matches my stride. We walk side by side in silence, ignoring the masked faces and the whispers that follow us.

We reach the top of the stairs at the edge of the park when I grab my mother's arm, remembering. "Wait! I have to go to the police station!"

Mom turns to me, her patience clearly running out. "And do what, Abby?"

"Talk to the cop that arrested him? Explain everything? I don't know." Desperation wells up in me. "But it's not fair. It wasn't his fault. Jordan provoked him. He's hated Cory ever since…" I clamp my mouth shut and shake my head. I almost blurted out about the play, the rehearsals, and the parking lot. I can't get carried away like this. "Anyway. If the cop writes that report, Cory will have a criminal record."

Mom hesitates. "Abby. This boy you're talking about. Cory. His last name is Brennell?"

Dread twists my insides. I shrug to hide it. "Yes. So?"

Mom opens her mouth, then closes it. Takes a deep breath. When she finally speaks, her voice is gentle and cautious. "Honey, I know this may be hard for you to hear, but—"

"But what?" I cut in. "Did Mrs. Smith fill you in on him too?"

As soon as I say it, I realize she did. She's friends with Jill. Of course they talked.

"Abby. It doesn't matter how I know. But I need you to listen to me." Mom sounds almost sad. *"Cory*

Brennell already has a criminal record. Do you understand?"

Misery slams into me, and my eyes burn. "No. I don't understand."

It's not completely true. I've had the pieces for a while, but refused to put them together and look at what they said—the rumors, the hints, the anxious looks Cory gave me. And just tonight, he was trying to tell me something, and I let my fear get in the way.

"He was in juvenile prison. He's on probation now."

Cory was in prison?

My mind rejects the idea. It's not possible. I cannot accept it.

"It's serious, Abby. That's why they took him to the station. That's why they have to file a report. It's for the best."

"For the best? You sound like he's some dangerous criminal. He's not, Mom!" I'm almost pleading with her, desperate to convince her. If I can convince her, I can convince the others too. "I know him, and he's smart and brave and kind. He's a good person!"

But my mother is unmoved. "People are not always what they seem, Abby." Her face becomes stern. "You are *not* going to see this boy anymore. Is that understood?"

"What? No!" I almost say, *he's my boyfriend.* But I

don't have to say it. She knows.

"Abby!" A warning rings in my mother's voice. "I set very few rules. Normally, I let you be independent and make your own decisions because that's the only way to learn. But this is different, and it's not up for discussion. I cannot worry about your safety every time I'm out of town."

"My safety!?" I recoil as if she hit me, my whole body reacting in shock. "Mom! Cory would never—"

"He would never *what*, Abby? Keep you in the dark about who he is? Pretend to be a nice guy to make you like him and trust him?" My mother's tone is cold and bitter, no trace of sympathy left. "I was a teenager once. I get it. But you need to be honest with yourself. How well do you know him? Is he really the person you think he is—or do you just want him to be, and you want it so badly that you believe it? Because here's the thing: if someone cares about you—truly cares about you, and not just tries to use you—they wouldn't lie to you. And Cory lied to you, Abby."

I stare at her, taken aback. Who is this harsh and cruel stranger? I barely recognize her. Is she hurting me on purpose? Because it's working. Every word cuts like a razor, the pain sharp and hot. I want to yell at her and argue with her, refute everything she said and show her she's wrong. Wrong about me, about Cory, about everything.

But instead, I turn on my heel and run home, angry and heartbroken, my face wet with tears.

Because she's right.

Cory lied to me.

Chapter 39

That night, after exhaustion and anguish pull me under, my dreams are restless.

I dream that I sit alone in the dark audience of the theater, the only person watching the show. The set design is familiar and so beautiful my heart aches: an enchanted forest washed in a silvery moonlight. Whispers and footsteps rustle at the threshold of my hearing, and I hold my breath in anticipation. It's the climax of the play, and I know what's coming. The Beast is wounded and dying, and Beauty is searching for him.

But moments pass, and the stage remains empty. Where are the actors? Instead, curls of smoke drift between the trees.

If there's a fire, I should be hurrying out the door, toward safety. Instead, I fidget in my seat. It's hard and cold to the touch, no longer a padded chair but a stone bench.

The smoke finds me. Wisps of it brush my face, stroke my hair, wrap around me. Dread mixed with longing surges through me. The touch is a reminder. I have to find the Beast before it's too late.

I get to my feet and hurry down the aisle. Layers of fabric tangle around my legs, slowing my movements, and I look down, frustrated.

I'm wearing a full, dusty pink gown that reaches my ankles. Beauty's gown. It feels wrong, not something I'd ever wear, but I don't have time to worry about it. I grab the front of the skirt in my fists and rush up the side steps and on to the stage.

The stage is deeper than I remember, the back end of it far away and blurred with smoke. I start walking between the flat, painted trees. Except they're neither. The trunks are round and the branches extend in all directions. The roots dig into the wooden floor, splintering the boards. The smoke is coming from underneath the floor, seeping through the cracks. I move a branch out of the way. Small black apples hide under the pointed, waxy leaves that reflect the moonlight.

How strange. I thought the set design was a forest, but it's… an orchard.

A gust of wind makes me shiver, and I look up. The roof is gone, and a night sky stretches above me. One by one, the stars blink out, and the darkness thickens, pressing closer.

Where is he? Where is the Beast? I'm almost out of time.

I start running.

The wind chases the smoke, growling and hissing, but more seeps through the floor boards. The wind is freezing, and the smoke burns. Two equal and opposite forces locked in a battle, but neither is my ally. Shadows shift between the trees and fall across my path, and harsh whispers follow me, but when I turn around, I can't see anyone.

I know they're there, though, hiding from sight, taunting me. They captured the Beast and want to hurt him. And I know it's my fault, somehow, and if he dies, it'll be my fault too. And I couldn't survive that.

The darkness presses closer, quieting the wind and putting out the smoke, and for a moment I rejoice. It's killing my enemies, so it must be my friend, and I could really use one. Someone who can help me find the Beast. But the joy dies when I look up at the top of the trees. They are vanishing. Any branches the darkness touches fade and flicker, and then dissolve to nothing, a silent but unstoppable destruction.

The same fate awaits me if I don't hurry. The darkness will not spare me. It destroys everything in its path without purpose or passion. It's not just above my head anymore either. My gown is already lighter, the top skirt threadbare and turning to ash. A dark smudge appears over my bare wrist, the skin neither cold nor burning but numb.

My Beast, where are you?

And then I see him.

He stands with his back to me, in his blue tailcoat. His furry head is bent and his shoulders slouched, but relief still fills me. I expected him wounded and bleeding on the ground. But he looks fine. Unharmed. We can still make it. We can get out of here.

He turns to me and rips off his mask—and I want to run to him and throw my arms around him.

But the tense, uncertain look in his dark eyes stops me, his face pitted with acne scars grim and achingly familiar, and I remember I need an answer first.

"Why did you lie to me, Cory?"

Darkness closes around us, swallowing all but the path we stand on and a few nearby trees. The Beast's mask fades in Cory's hand. His long coat turns gray and vanishes. He must know we're running out time. But he only stands there, in his sweatshirt and jeans, his gaze locked on me.

I wake up with my face wet, still waiting for him to speak.

◊

Later this morning, the breakfast is quiet. Mom and I sit at the kitchen table. She sips her coffee, and I pick at my toast. I keep my gaze fixed on my plate, but I can feel her eyes on me. The only sounds are the hum of the refrigerator and an occasional screech of the breaks when a truck stops on the lights on Market Street.

I finish my toast and get up, my plate in hand. Mom's mug is still half full, but I'm eager to slip away and be alone with my thoughts. "If you're done, I can wash it."

Mom smiles and hands me the mug. "I am. Thanks."

I carry the dishes to the sink and wash them. From the corner of my eye, I see Mom wipe the table, and I expect her to pull out her laptop and work on her emails. But instead she walks up to me.

"I'm going grocery shopping. Do you want to come? Looks like you're out of snacks for school." Her tone is casual, but she's watching me closely.

I'm completely out because the play rehearsals make for long days at school, not to mention I've been sharing with Cory. The thought of him sends a jolt of misery through me. I glance out of the window at the backyard and the alley.

"I'm fine. I have a stash in my locker," I lie. "But could I take the car later?"

Mom's lips press into a stern line. "Abby ..."

My face warms. She doesn't even have to say it. I know what she's thinking. And the most annoying thing? She's right again. I want the car to drive to

Cory's place.

How else can I find out what happened at the station? Did the cop tell the school? If Cory got detention, he couldn't do theater and be on the set crew anymore. And what if it's worse than that? Could the school kick him out for this? What does probation mean, exactly, if you've been in juvie? What happens if you slip up? Do they send you back? I have no clue how any of that works, so I imagine the worst.

Skyler might know. But I haven't forgotten they distracted me when the cop was arresting Cory. Or the dig they made about how I'd be smart to stay away from him. I'm still mad about that too.

"Forget it. I don't need the car," I snap at my mother. "I have to study."

Even if I had the car, I'm not sure I should go to see Cory. What if the cop kept him in jail overnight, and he's not home yet? Or he's home, on the farm, but Walter and Jill are with him and not keen on me barging in during a family crisis? And what about Cory? I know what I want. I'm anxious to see him, despite everything that happened. But does Cory want to see me?

The question burns like a fresh cut. Because to be honest, I can't be sure. I swing back and forth on this. I never doubt him when I'm with him, but when he's away, the doubts return.

Why do I always come to him, and he never comes to me? Now he knows where I live, of course. But even before last night, he'd have no trouble finding my address if he tried. Is it just the distance, and how long it takes to walk it or bike it? Or is it something else? And why doesn't he have a phone? If he wanted an easy way to reach me and for me to reach him, wouldn't he get one by now?

I start up the stairs, in a hurry to get to my room and dissect my sorrows in private.

But my mom's voice stops me.

"Before you go. I talked to Mrs. Smith."

I turn back to face her, my thoughts racing and my heart in my throat. Did Mrs. Smith find out about the play? *Please, no...*

I grip the rail for support, not trusting my balance. "What about?"

"I gave her a spare house key. Just in case."

I breathe with relief. But that doesn't mean I like the news. "In case *what?*"

My mother frowns at me, clearly put off by my tone. "In case anything happens when I'm not here. You'll have an adult nearby who can check in on you and help you if you need it."

"Check in on me? Right. You mean *spy on me and report to you?*"

This time I crossed the line. My mother's eyes

flash with hurt and disapproval. "Well, that depends on whether you have anything to hide, Abby, doesn't it?" She slips on her shoes and grabs her coat, purse, and car key. "If you remember anything you need from Weis, text me." And she walks out the back door.

I bite my lip. *Spy on me and report to you?* What an awful thing to say. Not to mention stupid, since now my mother will surely suspect I have things to hide.

I'll have to watch out for Mrs. Smith. She knows too much about everyone's business.

But that means... she might have news of Cory! For a second, I'm tempted to knock on her door and ask. She would never answer, though—not without drilling me first, not without poking through my most private thoughts and turning my heart inside out.

No. I can't do it. The less I interact with her, the better. I want her to forget all about me for at least two more weeks, until the play is done.

I'll have to wait till Monday to get an explanation—when I see Cory.

Chapter 40

Monday morning is chilly and gray. The sky is overcast, the clouds passing so low over the three-story houses downtown, they seem to touch the roofs. In the dim daylight, the houses look dull and flat, like set pieces that badly need a fresh coat of paint. The wind chases the fallen leaves along the curb, sweeps them off the street and tosses them in their air. They sound like hushed, gossiping voices.

I stand close to the wall, my arms wrapped around me for warmth, waiting for Tammy to pick me up. What if she doesn't come? The bus already left, and Mom took the car to work early. I could bike to school, but I'd miss Physics, and I really need to see Cory.

Tammy's car pulls up to the curb in front of me, metal scraping on cement.

By habit, I get into the back seat before I notice Zoe isn't here.

"Sorry I'm late." Tammy is already turning the wheel to merge back into traffic. Her purple hair looks frazzled. "Zoe is down with a cold. It's pretty bad. My poor baby."

Normally, the endearment would make me cringe. But Tammy's affection is fearless and loyal, and she's not shy about showing it. I feel a sting of envy. Why do I always question things? "Oh no. I hope she gets better."

Tammy sighs. "Me too. I picked up some meds for her. She promised to stay in bed and rest."

We both fall silent, lost in our separate worries. It's selfish of me, but I'm glad Zoe isn't here. A question for Tammy burns on my tongue. If I only knew how to ask it.

We turn into Market Street. Pass the old high school. Merge into the morning traffic on Highway 15.

Tammy catches my eyes in the rearview mirror. "Do you want to know who won? Or do you already know?"

Won what? I draw a blank for a moment. Then it hits me. The costume contest! "I don't know. Tell me! I hope you and Zoe won. You deserved it." Guilt flickers in me. I never cast my vote.

"We got third place in the Funniest category because of the shoes." Tammy rolls her eyes. "But guess what? Skyler won the Most Creative, and Neon got the second place for Best Overall." She grins, genuinely happy about both. "Isn't it great?"

"It is!" A thrill travels up my spine. Neon is super talented, and the recognition is long overdue. And I don't begrudge Skyler their win either. The Moth costume was amazing. "Who got the first place for Best Overall?"

Tammy's expression sours. "Jordan. Who else?"

Any lightness I felt evaporates at the sound of the name.

I'm back in the park on Friday night, masked faces gawking at me as I rush at Jordan, my arms slamming into his chest and then folding against it. And he never budges, his face shaded by his pirate hat and his blue eyes staring at me as his fingers close around my wrists like vice.

It's Jordan's fault Cory got arrested. And he did it on purpose. He must have known…

My heart is heavy again, and suddenly I can't hold the sadness in any longer.

"Cory was in juvie," I tell Tammy.

I catch a startled look on her face. She's as shocked as I was when I found out, and I'm grateful. She didn't know either. If she'd known, she'd told me…

But Tammy winces. "I'm sorry, Abby. You just… seemed so happy. I… didn't want to ruin it for you."

It's like punch in the chest. "So… you knew? For how long?"

"A while? I'm not sure. You know how rumors spread. Our school is so small, it's hard to avoid them."

I turn my face to the window. My lungs burn, and

it hurts to breathe. I can't quite get enough air. I close my eyes, trying to get my rising panic under control.

They all knew this whole time. Everyone in the school knew.

Except me.

They say ignorance is bliss. But it's a lie. Bliss is forever. While ignorance means that at some point the truth catches up to you, and you crash.

The car jerks to a halt, and the engine cuts off. I open my eyes. We're here.

"You okay?" Tammy asks when we get out of the car and she pops the trunk to get her backpack.

"Fine. I have to... I'll see you later." And I hurry ahead of her across the school parking lot and into the building.

Heads turn and whispers follow me, but I clench my jaw and keep my gaze fixed straight ahead. I'm not even going to stop by my locker. I can keep my jacket with me. If I can just get to my Physics class without blowing up or breaking down, I'm going to be okay.

But as soon as I cross the double doors and enter the main hallway, I see Cory.

He stands motionless against the wall, his face grim.

A jolt goes through him when he meets my eyes. He straightens and starts in my direction. He was waiting for me.

I'm on the opposite side of the hallway, and I reflexively step back, closer to the wall and out of the flow of people, never breaking eye contact with Cory.

I should keep walking. I can't talk to him right now. Not here, with everyone watching. But I can't seem to leave or look away. Only wait for him to reach me.

Cory clears his throat, his voice tense and low when he speaks. "Abby, I need to—"

But his gaze swings past me, and his lips clamp shut, a flash of anger in his eyes.

"You have a nerve, Brennell," a voice says, and Jordan steps next to me.

Cory ignores him and returns his gaze to me. But his breathing is too fast, his hands crammed into the pockets of his jeans, and I can tell he's struggling to hold his temper.

"I need to talk to you."

"It's too late for that," Jordan cuts in again, his voice calm and smooth. "You blew it. Just drop the act and walk away, man. You've hurt her enough."

Cory's eyes burn into mine. "Abby?"

I hear the urgency in his voice, and my heart aches for him. Every second of delay must be torture. But the words refuse to come. I'm too stunned and confused. Because Jordan's taunting echoes my own angry thoughts. And how is that possible?

I turn to him now, and he turns to me. I gaze into his blue eyes, puzzling it over. What is his deal? How can someone so beautiful be so cruel and hateful at the same time—a monster hiding under a pleasing mask? And what does it say about me that he can guess my thoughts?

I glare at Jordan. "Maybe you didn't hear me the last time. But you're *an asshole.* Don't act like you know me or care about me, because I'm not buying it for one second. And neither is Cory."

I aim to insult him, but Jordan only laughs, his eyes glinting. "Oh, I don't know. He might, finally."

My breath catches, and I spin around to Cory.

But he's gone.

Guilt rips through me. When did he leave? He walks so quietly I missed it. He never got my answer. All he got was me staring at Jordan.

But a part of me blames him too. Why did he walk away? Is he ready to give up so easily?

Because I'm not. At least not until I hear what he has to say.

I get to my Physics class seconds before Mr. Miller starts his lecture, the last student to arrive. I do my best to focus and take notes. But it's pointless. I'm too worried and distracted.

Because Cory's seat in the back is empty. He never came to class.

Where is he?

My next class is Calculus, and as soon as it's over, I hurry down the stairs and push out the back door. The cold wind stings my face, and I'm glad I kept my jacket on as I rush to the back of the storage shed.

Cory isn't here either.

I turn toward the wild grass field. In the distance, the trees sway and bend in the wind, shaking their bare branches. But what I want is closer. I walk into the field and search for the three rocks marking the spot. The apple tree we planted.

I gasp when I see it, anger slashing through me like a whip.

Someone yanked the sapling from the soil.

I kneel on the ground and pick up the torn plant. It hangs lifeless like a piece of two-colored string, the leaves green and the roots brown. But the damage is fresh, the small hole in the ground still visible.

Did Cory do this? Did he rush out here after Jordan provoked him? But killing the sapling wouldn't hurt Jordan—it would hurt me.

No. Cory wouldn't do that.

Would he?

※

My chance to confront Cory doesn't come until the

rehearsal on Tuesday—and I almost lose my nerve when I see him heading straight for me backstage.

I didn't make it to the rehearsal yesterday. My mom was still in town, and I didn't want to risk it. I'd trained both Tammy and Zoe on how to help Jordan with the Beast mask and gloves, just in case I couldn't make it. Since Zoe was out with a cold, the job fell to Tammy. She wasn't thrilled about it, but she got it done. Tammy is good like that.

The best thing about tonight is that Jordan isn't here. The Beast isn't in any of the scenes. It's Beauty visiting with her family. And compared to Jordan, Marie and the other actors barely need help with their costumes, and when they do, they're much easier to work with.

So when I face Cory in the narrow corridor, at least Jordan can't interrupt us.

We are directly behind the stage, and muffled voices cut through the wall. Beauty's Sisters scheming to make her break her promise to the Beast and delay her return. Do the Sisters realize this will kill him? Does Beauty? For some reason, I can't recall how it works in the play or in the original story. But it makes all the difference, doesn't it?

I mean to ask Cory about the sapling, but the look he gives me is so vulnerable, the shame so raw, my heart breaks for him. I don't even care if he did it. I forgive him on the spot.

"Abby, about Friday. I... I... " Cory's brows knot, and he takes a shuddering breath, then another. Like he's on the edge of a cliff and bracing himself to jump. "I'm sorry I dragged you into this. You... deserve better."

I frown. There's a lot to unpack there, but I can't get distracted. "You were in... juvenile prison?"

Pain crosses Cory's face, but no surprise. He expected the question. "I was."

I swallow. "For... how long?"

His voice is hollow. "Ten months."

I clasp my hand over my mouth in shock. *Ten months!* A whole school year. Almost a year of his life. I can't imagine it. My throat tightens, and my eyes burn. Not in blame but in sympathy. Or maybe both. I don't know anymore.

"Why didn't you tell me?" I whisper.

Cory moves half a step closer, his gaze locked on mine. "You know why," he murmurs.

I shiver. Because I *do* know. Maybe I've always known.

He didn't tell me because he didn't want to scare me away. Because he was afraid to lose me.

Cory's chest rises and falls, his breathing too fast again, as if he just sprinted, and I want to press my palm over his chest and feel his heartbeat. I want to slip my hands around his neck, hook my fingers in his hair, and pull his face to mine. I've never missed anyone more than I miss him right now, even though he's only two feet away.

But a voice in my mind intrudes. And it's not Jordan's this time. It's my mother's.

He pretended to be a nice guy to make you like him and trust him.

If he cared about you, he wouldn't lie to you.

These aren't her exact words, but the harsh, bitter warning makes me shrink back.

Cory notices, and the light drains from his eyes. "Abby ..."

"Were you ever going to tell me?" My voice shakes. *"Be honest."*

"I tried..." He clenches his jaw, battling with himself, then makes a decision. A hard edge creeps into his voice. "But if I could keep it from you forever, I would."

I blink, stunned. *Keep it from me?* He means lying to me. And he admits it?

Running footsteps startle me.

"Abby? Are you back here?"

Alarm rings in Marie's voice. I spin around just as she rushes into the corridor toward me.

"I broke it! Can you come?"

"Broke what?" I ask.

Marie sees Cory behind me and stops short, looking stricken. But collects herself and turns back to me. "The zipper on the dress. Tammy can't fix it. She told me to find you."

She's back in her regular clothes, a sweater and leggings. Is the rehearsal over? How long have I been here, backstage, with Cory? It feels like no time at all.

Marie's chin is trembling. "Please. Can you help me? Tomorrow is the picture day."

The picture day! A chill goes through me. Is it tomorrow already?

The official photo shoot of all the actors in full costumes is a big deal. The photos are used in the program and printed in the local paper. And if anything goes wrong with the costumes, guess who is responsible? Me.

I turn to Cory. "I have to go."

It comes out harsher and more final than I intend.

Cory's face falls, but he nods and steps back.

I hesitate, suddenly reluctant to leave. Does he think this is my answer? It's not. I don't have an answer for him yet. But I also don't have time to explain.

Cory holds my gaze for another moment, looking like he wants to tell me something. But he doesn't. He only turns and walks away, vanishing into the shadows.

My breath catches, the disappointment a sharp ache in my chest.

He's doing it again. Acting like he's ready to give up—like he already lost, and it's all over.

I hate it. I need him to fight for us. If he cared about me, he would keep trying. I can't be the only one.

I spin to Marie, my tone sharp, though it's not her I'm mad at. "Where's the dress? Show me."

Chapter 41

The Fabrics & Sewing Supplies section of Walmart is deserted when Marie and I get there, the attendant long gone for the day, and I'm glad. I'm still silently fuming at Cory, and I'd rather search the messy shelves and racks alone. Marie hovers anxiously by my elbow, but stays quiet, sensing my mood.

I hold the broken zipper in my fist. It's beyond repair, several dainty teeth on one side broken right off. I undid the stitching and cut it out of the dress back in the costume room, with Tammy and Marie looking grimly on. My only hope is to find a match in color and length. If I can't fix the zipper before the cast photo shoot tomorrow, we're all in trouble.

Marie drove me here. Beauty's dress lies neatly folded in a garment bag on the back seat of her SUV, which is by far the nicest car in the Walmart parking lot at this hour.

I think of the awful night in the school parking lot, almost a month ago. The night Jordan tried to bully me into letting him drive me home after the rehearsal. The night Cory stood up for me and got punched in the face—before he outsmarted Jordan and handcuffed him to the wire fence.

Marie was supposed to give me a ride that night. If she had—if she'd waited in the parking lot for me, instead of taking Jordan's word for it and leaving—none of the awful things would've happened. I wouldn't have been stuck alone with Jordan; I wouldn't have needed Cory's help. Cory wouldn't have defended me and earned a busted lip.

None of the full-price zippers hanging on the racks match the broken one I'm holding. Not even close.

I move down the aisle until I find the clearance bin. It's on the bottom shelf, only inches above the floor. About the most uncomfortable placement ever, but at least the bin overflows with zippers of all kinds tangled together like a nest of snakes.

I huff with annoyance, kneel next to the bin, and start digging. Marie kneels next to me, and I'm tempted to snap at her to get up. I don't need her help now. Where was she when I needed a ride home? But I know that's unfair, so I bite my tongue and ignore her.

My thoughts keep churning, though. I picture the empty parking lot again… Jordan's arm crushing Cory's throat… Cory reaching for the handcuffs in his pocket… Putting the small key on the sidewalk… Walking next to me on the dark road, shielding me in case a car drove by…

If Jordan never cornered me in the parking lot that night, and Cory didn't challenge him to protect me, would things really be better now?

The more I mull over it, the more I doubt it. Jordan would find other reasons to hate Cory, other excuses to put him down. It was never about me. Jordan's been using me all along.

And what about me and Cory? Would I still go to see him on his grandfather's farm? I can hardly believe I did it. I only went to thank him and to assure him I hadn't wanted to go with Jordan, no matter what Jordan claimed. And if I never biked to Cory's farm that morning, would he still kiss me? Because I'm pretty sure I'd never have the courage to kiss him…

The thought sends a chill through me. How can I regret what happened that awful night in the parking lot if it brought me closer to Cory?

I can't. Not if I'm honest.

But that's selfish and messed up. It's like wishing Cory trouble. Maybe I should worry less about myself and more about him. Would he be better off if he'd left right after the rehearsal that night, instead of waiting for me?

No.

Something deep inside me rejects the idea.

Cory and I are good together. We have each other's backs. We make each other stronger.

Maybe that's what most enrages Jordan. He helped to bring us together, and he hates the idea. So he keeps trying to break us apart and pitch us against each other.

But it won't work.

I don't realize I stopped moving until next to me Marie exclaims, "Here! *Look!*"

She yanks her hand from the bin, and a light pink zipper dangles from her fingers. She's been busy digging in the bin alongside me while my mind drifted to Cory.

"Can I see?" I snatch the zipper from her and stretch it out against with the broken one I'm holding. The new one is a brighter shade of pink, but the length matches. I nod to Marie. "It should work."

She sighs with relief. "Really? Oh, good." Then gives me a nervous look. "And you know how to sew it back on, right?"

I tense. I'll need my sewing machine, and Marie will probably want to watch. She might also need to try on the dress when I'm done. Which means I have to invite her over.

I stand up, both zippers clasped in my fist, and Marie gets up as well, her eyes still on me and her expression growing anxious.

"Yes. I can reattach it," I tell her. "I have a sewing machine at home."

Marie's eyes brighten. "Is it okay if I come over? I

know it's late, but I really want to see how you do it. Would your parents mind?"

My parents. Embarrassment stings me. I forgot Marie doesn't know much about me.

"Sure, you can come over." I shrug, trying to sound casual. "It's just my mom and me, anyway, and she's out of town right now."

"Oh." Marie frowns, processing the information, and I can practically see the questions forming in her mind. "You mean—"

"We should be going." I turn on my heel and hurry to the register. Marie trots behind me in silence, her curiosity held back for now.

We pay for the zipper, then head outside and get in the car. Thankfully, it's a short drive to my apartment, and I spend it piloting Marie, who seldom drives downtown, through the maze of narrow, one-way streets, cars parked bumper to bumper on both sides.

I expect resistance and more frowning when I tell Marie to turn into the poorly lit back alley and park in my mom's spot. This must be nothing like the house she lives in—no private driveway leading to a spacious garage, with neatly trimmed lawn on both sides.

But she only beams at me. "Phew. I was worried I'd have to park on the street. My parallel parking sucks."

Unraked leaves rustle under our shoes when we

cross the back yard. The linden tree with its bare branches is a sorry sight in the corner. Only the rose bush near the window still looks striking, black flowers on thick gray stalks with vicious thorns. How long do roses bloom? All the other flowers are long dead.

As I fidget with my house key to unlock the back door, memories of Cory flood my mind again. *Halloween in the Park* was only a week ago, but it feels like months.

"Come in." I usher Marie into our small kitchen and close the blinds before I flick on the lights.

I hope Mrs. Smith has better things to do than spy on me tonight, although the wish is probably in vain. If she is watching, I wonder what she'll make of the fancy SUV parked out the back, and of me bringing over a girl late at night. And what will my mom think when she gets the report? Will she be okay with it, as long it's not Cory? The thought makes me bristle, so I push it away.

Marie takes two steps into the kitchen and stops, unsure of what to do. At least she's not gawking at the old cabinets, crooked floor, and mismatched chairs. The way she's holding the garment bag in her arms, Beauty's dress could be some wounded fairy creature we have to save before it dissolves into pink mist.

I point at the table. "I do all my sewing here. The kitchen has the best light. Just give me a second."

Marie nods, and I grab a towel. I move swiftly, to distract myself from feeling self-conscious. I scrub the table until the surface is spotless. Then I unlatch the door to the secret staircase and retrieve my sewing machine and other supplies I'll need.

Marie's eyes widen when she sees the steep, dark stairs, and I rush to explain before she can ask. "It used to be a staircase, but we use it for storage. It's an old house." I set up my sewing machine, fish out the new zipper out of the bag, and reach for the dress. "Okay. Can I have it?"

We take the dress out of the bag, and I lay it on the table and start pinning the new zipper in place.

Marie hovers over me for a moment, then slides into a chair next to me. She folds the bag in her lap and becomes perfectly still. But I can feel her watching me.

Once the long zipper is pinned to the dress, I turn on my sewing machine, load a matching color thread from my supplies, and carefully start attaching the zipper.

In the back of my mind, I know I'm a lousy host. I should at least offer my guest a glass of water. But wariness coils inside me, and my guard is up. Marie and I aren't friends, and this isn't a social visit. We have a job to do. No time to talk.

I'm halfway done—one side of the zipper safely attached, one left to go—when Marie breaks the silence.

"So are you and Cory... dating?"

My cheeks flush, betraying me before I can speak. My relationships with Cory is the last topic I want to discuss, and I'm too tired to be polite about it. I look Marie in the eye and make my voice sharp. "Listen, do you want me to fix this dress or not? Because I need to focus."

She quickly backtracks. "You're right. Sorry. It's none of my business. I just wanted to say... I think you're very brave."

A jolt goes through me, and I sit up. I know I should let it go. But I can't help myself, a dark energy itching under my skin. "*Brave?*"

"Well, you know... *To be alone with him.*"

I clench my teeth. She must think she paid me a compliment. But it makes me want to grab the gorgeous gown I'm mending and tear it in half.

"*Why?* Because he was in juvie? Not everyone who goes to juvie is a monster."

I have more to say to her, but the look in Marie's eyes stops me cold.

It's not about Cory serving time in juvie. It's the reason *why* he was sent there. The crime he committed. And I realize I have no idea what it is. I assumed theft, since he can pick locks. But is that serious enough to earn him ten months in prison?

I don't know the answer. But Marie does. I can tell from her panicked expression.

"What did he do?" I demand, my heart hammering.

Blood drains her Marie's face. "You...don't know?"

"I don't." I stare her down. *Tell me.*

Marie blinks, and her hands start to fidget, twisting and rolling the garment bag in her lap. "Oh, Abby... I'd rather not..."

"*Marie.*" My voice is a growl. I can't stand not knowing another second. "Either you tell me, or I rip the zipper right out. I mean it!"

Marie gasps. "You wouldn't!"

I grab the scissors—and more memories of Cory rush in.

The haircut... His split lip... Our first kiss...

Tears sting my eyes. I touch the blades to the fabric. A part of me recoils in shock. I can't destroy the dress. It's unthinkable. But I'm not in control. Something dark rises inside me, ready to take over.

"Stop! I'll tell you!" Marie cries. "He stabbed a guy."

The scissors fall from my fingers and hit the floor.

"*What?*" My throat is so tight, the sound barely makes it out.

Marie swallows. "He stabbed a guy with a knife. The guy survived but it was close... That's all I know. I swear."

I shake my head. Cory... *stabbed someone?* I don't believe it. It's not possible.

"Who told you this? *Jordan?*"

Marie blinks. "Jordan?"

"It sure sounds like him! A stupid lie to hurt Cory." My face is hot, my whole body burning up. "Jordan has hated him from the start."

"Jordan can be... unpleasant," Marie admits cautiously, dropping her gaze. "But it wasn't him. And it's not a lie, Abby."

"How do you know?" I press, although dread gnaws at me. "Did Cory tell you himself?"

Marie hesitates. "I overheard my dad tell my mom. He's a lawyer and on the school board. They had an emergency meeting after Cory got arrested on Halloween."

I stare at her, dumb with shock.

So it's true. Cory stabbed a man. Almost killed him.

But how is it possible? He'd never do that. I know him.

"I don't think other students know," Marie assures me anxiously. "I never told anyone. Just you right now." She takes a deep breath. "Because, honestly... I'm worried. I know you like him. But I don't want anything to happen to you. What if snaps again? I mean, he's—"

Violent… Dangerous… A murderer…

"Don't!" I'm on my feet so fast, the chair topples behind me. "Just—don't say it. Don't talk about him at all."

"Okay. Okay." Marie gets up too, alarmed. "I won't. I'm sorry. Are you all right?"

I'm not all right. I stumble, suddenly lightheaded, my insides twisted in a knot and a bitter taste in my mouth like I'm going to be sick.

Marie drops the garment bag on her chair and reaches for me, but I wave her off.

"I just… need some water." I cross to the sink, pour some tap water into a glass, and force myself to drink it.

Cory *stabbed* a person. Stuck *a knife* into them.

My mind can't accept the idea, can't even comprehend it.

Then a memory surfaces—Cory pulling off his shirt after the haircut—and I shudder.

The scars. So many scars. Like thick pieces of rope carved into his shoulders, chest, and torso. The type of scars you earn in knife fights.

It fits. It's terrible, and I hate it. But it fits.

I turn to Marie without meeting her eyes, struggling to keep my voice steady. "Listen, the dress is almost done… I'll have it ready for you tomorrow…

But it's late…"

She takes the hint. "You're right. I should go." She hurries to the back door before I can see her out. Turns to me one more time before stepping outside. "Abby, I… I'll see you tomorrow." She was going to say something else but changed her mind. The door closes behind her.

I watch through the window as she crosses the backyard and exits through the gate. A moment later, the headlights come on, and the SUV pulls out of the spot and drives off.

By then, misery wells up in me, and tears blur my vision.

I thought I knew Cory. Really knew him. I was sure of it.

But I don't.

Maybe all of them are right—Tammy, Skyler, Marie. Jill. My mom. Even Jordan.

Maybe it's all an awful mistake, and I should stay away from Cory before things go too far.

Chapter 42

The prep for the photo shoot starts right after school, to take advantage of the last hour of daylight before the early November dusk. When I get backstage, the set crew is already hard at work constructing three temporary dressing rooms, plus a separate makeup and hair station.

Emotion slams into me the moment I see Cory, a bruising blow of grief and anger that knocks the breath out of me. I turn away before he meets my eyes. We're both too busy, anyway, even if I wanted to talk to him. And I don't.

With Zoe still out sick, the costume crew is sorely short-handed. Tammy and I need to hustle to prep all the costumes and get every actor ready in time. The clock is ticking, the daylight fading with every moment we delay. Or is it the darkness pushing in, like in my dream?

Beauty and the Beast are first up, the stars of the show and the photographer's priority.

Jordan heads straight for me, and normally, I'd swallow my resentment and do my job. But the smug look on his face, like he owns me and expects me to adore him, rankles me more than ever.

On impulse, I grab Beauty's dress, still in the garment bag, and step toward Marie.

Tammy shoots me a dark look, but I only say, "The new zipper gets stuck."

She heaves a sigh and nods in understanding, snatching the Beast's costume, mask, and gloves. "You come with me," she snaps at Jordan.

He snorts with displeasure, and his stare burns the side of my face when he passes me. My whole body tenses, but I ignore him. Even if he was right about Cory, Jordan is still a jerk. I haven't forgotten what he did, and I don't blame him any less for it. He won't be getting any adoration from me.

We dispatch Beauty's Father, Sisters, and Brothers, and the Witch in record time. Only the Beast's Servants are still left, getting their makeup, when Natasha comes running. "Abby? We need some safety pins. Or you better come."

"Tammy, you're okay to finish?" I ask my crew mate, who nods and waves me off. I grab a whole sewing kit, just in case, and follow Natasha out into the main hallway. "What happened?"

She rolls her eyes. "Mike was showing off and ripped out his sleeve."

"Showing off how?"

She rolls her eyes. "Pretending to attack Jordan. You know, Beauty's Brother killing the Beast. Only Jordan grabbed his sword and kind of spun him around. It's lucky he didn't break his arm."

I grit my teeth. "Jordan really likes hurting people, doesn't he?"

Natasha throws me a nervous look and shrugs. "It was more Mike's fault. He shouldn't have surprised him like that."

"Right," I snap. "It's never Jordan's fault. It's always someone else's."

What is it with all of them? Do they really not see how spiteful and vicious their idol is—or do they see it just fine, but are afraid to admit it? Jordan can hurt them and humiliate them, he can pretend to be their friend and then walk all over them, and no one ever calls him out on it or stands up to him.

Except Cory.

Not that I care anymore.

I'm so caught up in my thoughts, I don't notice where we're heading until Natasha stops at the familiar back door. "Nobody has the key, so don't let it lock," she instructs me, pointing with her toe to a door stop. "Or we'll have to run to the front."

I almost say, *I know*.

Outside, a dramatic sunset in pink, magenta, and purple blazes in the sky. The back of the school faces

West, and the photographer set up the shoot in the wild grass field. The background is perfect, and I'm sure the photos will be too. But if the young apple tree wasn't already dead, it would've gotten trampled on right now.

I shiver, and it's not just from the chilly November air.

The photographer, a middle-aged person in a black unisex jumpsuit, shoots Beauty and her Sisters against the setting sun, while Mrs. Adams directs, gesturing with animation.

I glance around, searching for Mike and his damaged sleeve, but Jordan, in the full Beast costume, gets to me first.

"Abby!" He hooks his arm around my shoulders, tight like a vice, and pulls me toward the photo set. "Could we have a picture with Abby? She takes credit for all the costumes."

"Maybe later. I'm here to fix Mike's shirt." I push an elbow into Jordan's side as hard as I can. He chuckles, as if I tickled him, but lets me twist out of his grip.

I spot Patricia and Neon standing forlornly off to the side, in regular clothes, and the injustice of it stings me. I've watched some of their rehearsals, and they're both great actors. Too bad they won't get a chance to show it. And it looks like they won't be in the pictures either.

"You want to impress everyone? Invite the understudies," I hiss at Jordan.

His blue eyes flash at me from behind the hideous mask. "You're fucking brilliant." Then louder, in his charming voice. "Marie! We need a picture with Patricia and Neon. Come on, you two." He makes a sweeping motion with his arm, urging them forward.

Mike finds me and hands me his sleeve. Thankfully, it's not truly torn but only detached at the seam. I can sew it back on later. But for now, four safety pins will do the job.

"Thanks, Abby," Mike says after I'm done. He holds his arm away from his body, cringing. "I hope the safety pins don't open and poke me. I hate needles."

"Why do you let him treat you like this?" I snap.

Mike blinks at me. "Who? *Jordan?* It was an accident. He didn't mean it. We were just goofing around."

I shake my head. If that's what he wants to believe, I won't argue with him. What's the point?

I watch with a mix of disgust and amazement as Jordan the Beast puts one arm around Patricia and the other around Neon, as if they were his best friends and he was thrilled to have them close. Marie trots to take her place next to Neon, and they all pose for the camera.

But Jordan isn't done yet. As soon as the

photographer lowers the lens, he dashes off the set, walks up to the director, and offers his arm. A perfect gentleman. "Mrs. Adams, will you join us, please?"

Mrs. Adams nods her permission, visibly flattered, and Jordan escorts her in front of the camera, her hand never leaving his arm. While the five of them pose for the pictures, the back door flies open, and the Beast's Servants arrive.

Jordan spots them and calls out, "Come on, everyone! A group picture with our director before we lose the light." And all the actors rush over and take their places around him, as if it was only natural that Jordan must be the center, the brightly shining star for them to orbit around.

I pick up my sewing kit and slip back inside the school through the back door. I'm tempted to knock out the door stop and let the door lock behind me, so Jordan has to run around the building to get back in. But it would punish everyone, not just him, so I resist the impulse.

My fight is with the Beast alone.

Waves of annoyance roll over me as I half walk, half run down the main hallway, push through the door leading backstage, and rush into the costume room. I remember—too late—not to scare Tammy. "Sorry, it's just me."

But the room is empty. Tammy isn't here.

I put the sewing kit away and stand still for a moment, listening. Voices, footsteps, and the sounds of heavy objects being moved into place come from the stage. The set crew must be prepping the sets for the second part of the photo shoot, indoors.

I feel the familiar pull, like an invisible rope loops around my waist, and someone is pulling on it. If I snuck into the wing, could I catch a glimpse of Cory?

No, I tell myself sternly. *Bad idea.* I should stay here, away from him. Tammy will come fetch me if they need me on the set.

Sure enough, not a minute later, I hear a footfall. I've been pacing the room. I stop and turn to the door.

But it's Cory who stands there.

He meets my gaze and takes a slow, uncertain step toward me. "Hey."

My breath catches, and I reflexively step back. "Don't."

Cory pales. "You're not... afraid of me? Are you?" I can hear the fear in his voice. "Abby, whatever you've heard, I would never hurt you. *Never*. I'd rather—"

"You already did."

"You're right, and I'm sorry, but... *Please*... Can we talk?"

I want to yell at him to leave, to get the hell out of this room and stay away from me. But the words are stuck in my throat, and the rope is still pulling me in, even now.

I need to get out of here.

"I can't… right now."

And I slip past him and out of the room.

I catch a glimpse of relief in his face. It should've been a hard *no*, but it wasn't.

Because I'm still hopelessly torn—one part of me trying to slam a door shut, while the other fights to keep it open.

Chapter 43

The indoor portion of the photo shoot proceeds at the same brisk pace. The actors pose alone and in groups against one set and backdrop after another, with Adam assisting on the lights, and Skyler directing the set crew as they swiftly roll the different set pieces on and off the stage.

Then the photographer puts away their camera, and the actors disperse to the makeshift dressing rooms and the school bathrooms to change out of their costumes. I help Marie out of her Beauty's gown, while Tammy grudgingly helps the Beast transform back into Jordan.

It takes Tammy and I another hour to properly put all the costumes away. By the time we're done, the theater is dark and silent, and all the actors and crew have gone.

Disappointment stings me when I don't see Cory, although it makes no sense. I'm glad he's not waiting for me. Or I should be glad. Even if I can't get him out of my thoughts.

In fact, the harder I try not to think about him, the more my mind plays tricks on me. I imagine him standing at the edge of the parking lot as I cross with Tammy to her car; walking on the dark road as we drive past; sitting on my doorstep when Tammy drops me off. It's like his picture has been seared into my retinas. He's everywhere I look, whether I like it or not.

It's almost midnight, and I'm getting ready for bed, when a text pings on my phone.

My mom already texted me good night, so it's not her.

My heart skips a beat. Did Cory get a phone?

But it's Heather.

Are you up? It's important, the text says.

I hesitate. What are the chances it's about Cory? She's not part of the theater group, but still. Has Marie tattled? Rumors travel fast.

Heather doesn't wait for my answer, though. *I'm calling you now.*

It's a video call too. I glance around my small, messy room, and irritation flickers in me. I move to my bed, so there's only a blank wall behind me, before I accept the call.

"I need you to study with me tomorrow." Heather stares right at me and speaks so fast, I can barely keep up. She doesn't bother with pleasantries.

"Um… You mean at lunch or after school?"

"I mean all day."

I blink. I must have misheard her. Tomorrow is

Thursday. "All day?"

"Yes. In my house. My parents work late and have a department dinner. We'll have at least twelve hours to study without interruption."

I'm stunned. Heather is planning to cut a whole day of classes? I ask the obvious question. "What about school?"

Heather huffs with impatience. "If I bomb the SAT, it could literally ruin my future. A sick day won't even show up on my transcripts. I'm prioritizing."

I doubt Heather could bomb the SAT even if she tried. But the notion of missing school tomorrow is tempting. A fail proof way to avoid running into Cory until I'm ready to talk to him, until I had time to think. All I have to do is leave a message on the school's answering machine and say I'm not feeling well. They'd rather you stay home than infect the whole school.

"If I say yes—" I start, but Heather cuts me off.

"Great! I'll pick you up at seven-thirty. I made a schedule for us already, with stretching breaks and healthy snacks. If we stay focused, we can review half of the units and do one full practice test."

I sigh. "Okay."

So much for having time to think. But maybe that's better. I need to spend less time thinking about Cory, not more. Not to mention, I'm way behind in my SAT prep and could use a solid cramming session.

"We're going to keep each other accountable," Heather rattles on, more to herself than to me. "No texting, no social media, no chitchat. We can't get distracted or slack off." A new intensity creeps into her voice. "No matter how sick and tired we are of studying. Because anything is better than quitting and regretting it later. That's the absolute worst."

My mind swings to Cory. If I stay away from him, is that quitting? Will I regret it later?

I push the thought away, annoyed with myself. That's not what Heather meant at all.

She's thinking about college and her career plans, not about some boy. For the first time, I wonder if she likes anyone. I'm guessing not. At least I've never seen any sign of it. She has more important things to worry about, loftier goals to accomplish, better ways to spend her time. Dating would only be a distraction. Getting entangled with someone like Cory? Out of the question.

I almost envy her.

My life would be so much simpler if I was more like her.

Actually, I used to be, not long ago. Focused and driven. Even if my ambitions have always been more modest, aimed at a professional theater program, not a prestigious med school. I was just fine alone, without all the drama and heartache. Maybe I wasn't happy, exactly, but I knew what I wanted.

But since I met Cory, everything changed.

I'm not sure of anything, least of all what I want. I do things I'd never dreamed of doing, say things I'd never said before. Some days, I barely recognize my face in the mirror.

But the part that scares me the most? I feel more like myself when I'm with him than alone.

"What about Friday?" I ask Heather. A challenge. "We could review twice as much in two days."

Heather narrows her eyes, no doubt recalculating the risks and benefits of cutting two days of school instead of one. Then she nods. "You're right. I'll update the schedule and find another practice test for Friday. I wouldn't be able to focus in my classes anyway."

My plans with Heather settled, I text Tammy next.

I tell her the truth, or part of it, anyway. That I'm cutting school to cram for the SAT, but if anyone asks, I called in sick.

Seconds tick, and Tammy doesn't respond, so I add, *You can tell Zoe.*

What about C? Tammy finally texts.

My chest tightens. He's the whole reason I'm skipping. I don't trust myself to face him. It's easier to run and hide.

Don't tell him anything, I fire back.

Another silence from Tammy. Then she texts, *How*

bad is the zipper?

The zipper? I blank out for a moment. Then it comes back to me. The new zipper on Beauty's dress. I told her it gets stuck. A lie.

If you miss school, you're not allowed to attend the extracurriculars that day, so I'm off the hook for the rehearsals too. Although Tammy must be really unhappy with me. It's a recap of Beauty's scenes with the Beast. She'll have to help both Marie and Jordan.

The zipper worked fine yesterday. Just be careful with it. I'm glad we're texting and she can't see my face. *Are you going to be okay by yourself?*

Do I have a choice? Tammy snaps back. Definitely not happy with me, and I don't blame her.

Thanks, Tammy.

No response. Looks like she already signed off.

Regret cuts through me. She's the best friend I have, and I've been lousy to her. She may not put up with that for much longer. I'm tempted to call her and explain everything. Tell her what Marie told me about Cory and pour out all my heartache. Maybe Tammy can tell me what to do, because I have no idea.

But after staring at my phone for a long time, I never call her.

I need to make my own decision. Or maybe I'm scared of what she'd say.

Heather picks me the next morning, seven-thirty sharp, as promised. Her car, a white Mazda, is spotless, not a drop of mud outside or a spec of dust inside, and her bedroom, when we get there, is the neatest and most organized I've ever seen. The bed flawlessly made, the books perfectly aligned, not a single piece of clothing in sight.

"You have two desks," I observe.

Heather doesn't miss a beat. "I switch between them. It helps my productivity." She points to the one near the window. "You can work at this one until lunch, and then we'll swap."

She wasn't kidding about a strict schedule either.

But it works. We get a lot done, including not one but two full practice tests. By the time we finish the second practice test, discuss our answers, and compare them against the key that came with the mega SAT prep package Heather uses, it's ten-thirty at night, and my brain is mush.

Heather drives me home, and I'm out as soon as my head hits the pillow.

Friday, we repeat the routine with one small variation. We wrap up by nine o'clock, which is still twelve solid hours of studying, even with meals and stretching breaks.

Heather is so pleased with me, she hugs me before she drops me off. She also offers to pick me up Saturday morning, so we can drive together to the test. I gratefully accept. The test location is a middle school in another town, about twenty minutes away, and I can't get there without a car.

I should be exhausted, like I was yesterday, but instead I'm anxious and restless. And it's not just the stress of an important test tomorrow. I pace the kitchen, sit at the table, pace the kitchen some more. It's like I can't find a place for myself.

Then I make the mistake of rummaging in my backpack... and pluck out a polaroid photo.

One glance—and memories rush in.

Cory looks straight at me, his gaze intense. We were in the attic when I took the photo. I remember the secret ladder, the skylights, the bed. I remember his smell when he pulled me close, the warmth of his hands on my bare waist, the taste of his mouth when he kissed me. I almost told him I loved him...

Stop it. I want to shake myself. *What are you doing?*

He almost killed a person. He lied to me. I need to stay away from him.

I should rip the photo to pieces. I grip the corners in both hands, ready to do it.

But I can't. It's the only photo I have of him. I let

go of it, and it drops on the table.

A text pings, and I grab my phone with shaking hands, convinced something terrible has happened.

How did your studying go? Tammy asks.

I breathe with relief. *Fine. Thanks. How were the rehearsals?*

Also fine, Tammy types. *Though Jordan was pissed you weren't there.*

I grit my teeth. *Ugh. I'm sorry, Tam. What's his problem?*

He's a selfish asshole? But... The typing pauses. *It's weird. I've never seen him act like this.*

A chill runs down my spine. *Like what?* I type.

Like he has a thing for you. Only sick and possessive.

My stomach twists. *No, he doesn't. He's just using me to get to C.*

Maybe, maybe not. Could be both. Dunno. I picture Tammy frowning as she types. *But you should be careful.*

I think back to that night in the parking lot—to Jordan throwing a punch and Cory pushing me out of the way. Was the punch aimed at me? Would Jordan really hit me? Maybe it's naïve of me to think he wouldn't. I saw him slam Cory against the wire fence and almost crush his throat. Underneath the handsome face, Jordan has a nasty temper.

One more thing, Tammy types.
What?
C took the bus after school. I'm guessing to look for you.

My heart gives a painful thud. *Today?* I type.
Today and yesterday.

Cory came downtown to see me. Twice. And I wasn't there. *Why didn't you tell me earlier?*

You cut school to study, remember? Tammy types. *I thought you wanted to focus.*

You're right. Sorry. I backtrack.
So he didn't find you?

I studied with Heather at her place. I'm just surprised C came to see me.

Are you really? Tammy types, and the reproach is hard to miss. There's so much I haven't told her, and I know she must be worried and wondering.

It's a long story, Tam. I'll tell you another time.

Tell me when you know the ending, Tammy types before signing off.

But what if I don't want it to end?

Chapter 44

Saturday morning is gloomy and cold. Thick, ominous clouds the color of lead cover the sky and choke the sunlight as Heather and I drive down a country road to take the SAT. The road is unfamiliar, and leads nowhere near our school. Still, every farm we pass, every red barn and gravel driveway, makes me think of Cory. What is he doing right now? Does he think about me too?

"It doesn't matter," Heather says firmly.

I turn to her, startled. Does she mean Cory? "What?"

"If I fail today." Heather grips the steering wheel so hard, her knuckles are white. "I can just take it again. I have time. Today is just another practice test."

"You're going to do great," I assure her. "I know you will."

I mean it as an encouragement, but Heather shoots me an alarmed look. "Don't say that! What's wrong with you? You'll jinx it."

"Sorry."

The first raindrops start to fall when we pull into

the parking lot, splashing against the windshield. Heather parks the car, and we hurry inside the brick school building, then follow the signs down a maze of hallways to the check-in station outside the gym.

A small crowd of high school students is already waiting, some with their noses in their prep books, others bouncing their leg nervously. I recognize one group from our school. I catch a spark of excitement in their eyes when they see me, and they lean closer and start whispering. Unease washes over me. How much do they know? Will I always have to worry about that?

It's a relief when the gym doors open and we can find our tables. Each table has a number that matches a student's check-in number, assigned so that no students from the same school sit close together. The first few rows of tables are straight and neat, but toward the back, the pattern gets more haphazard, as if whoever did the set up was in a rush.

My table is in the middle of the room, not that I care. Heather's table is in the back row, and sticks out a good foot. She pulls it back in line, frowning, before she takes her seat.

My last thought before I start my test is of Cory again. Sitting across the table from me in his kitchen. The day we studied for a Physics exam together. Strangely, the memory helps me focus.

The rain drums on the roof above my head as I

work my way through the SAT problems. Some are challenging, but nothing truly surprises or thwarts me, which is more than I hoped for. Before I know it, the time is up, and we are asked to put our pencils down. A group of proctors collects our tests, and we're free to leave.

Outside, Heather and I run through the downpour to her car, splashing through quickly growing puddles. The rain is really coming down now.

"I don't want to talk about the test," she warns me as she turns on the wipers and backs out of the parking spot, nearly crashing into another car. A teenage driver slams on the breaks and flips us a finger. Heather glares at them in the rearview mirror.

"That's fine," I say. I don't want to talk about the test either.

We're back on the country road, halfway to our town, the rain slashing at the windshield and blurring the view, when a shrill ringing makes me jump. *Beep-beep-beep. Beep-beep-beep.*

"What is it?"

Heather taps the GPS screen on the dashboard, and the alarm cuts off, replaced by a recorded message. *"Attention! Flash flood warning is in effect for parts of the Union County. Seek high ground and avoid areas near waterways."*

Areas near waterways. The creek along Cory's

farm!

Does Cory know about the warning?

I make a decision. "Heather, could you drop me off somewhere else?"

Heather blinks at me. "What? Where?"

"Um... A little past the school? I'll show you how to get there."

"Past the school? No way." Heather jabs her finger at the corner of the GPS screen, and the map expands to show our town and the surrounding farmlands. Flashing red patches indicate the highest danger, and sure enough, the country roads West and Southwest of the school are dotted with red. "They always get the worst floods. I'm dropping you off at your place."

"You're right. Thanks, Heather." I don't press it. It was too much to ask. I just hope we get there quickly.

Five minutes after Heather drops me off, I'm on my bike, my raincoat zipped up to my chin, the hood low over my eyes, and my jeans tucked into tall rain boots. My phone and house keys are in a small backpack on my back, under my raincoat. I race my bike down the sidewalks and streets downtown until I get to Highway 15 and cross it. After that, it's a single country road, and I know all the landmarks by heart, even in the pouring rain.

The road climbs and dips. Biking uphill is painfully slow, but I fly downhill, speeding through the water gushing across the low points. The last valley is the most treacherous, the water almost knee deep. The current yanks on my wheels, trying to drag me off the road, but I make it across.

After that, the road is too sleek with rain, and I have to get off the bike and walk it the last stretch to Cory's driveway. But I make it.

I keep an eye out for Pearl, but she must prefer to stay dry and warm somewhere. Smart dog. I don't blame her. Didn't Cory say she almost drowned as a pup and was afraid of the water?

A brisk stream of water flows down the driveway too, getting stronger. I round the bend and slosh toward the house, pushing my bike next to me. I should hurry up and crest the hill before the creek completely floods over. Instead, my steps slow. Every time I glance at the barn, I get more nervous and self-conscious. What am I doing here? It's not like Cory can't see the flood.

"Abby!"

For once, I hear his footsteps, his rain boots splashing in the water as he runs toward me. He grabs the handlebars of my bike and peers into my face, his brows knotted with worry. "What are you doing here? It's not safe on the roads."

I glare at him. "Why don't you have a phone like everyone else?"

He shakes his head, confused. "Because it's a

tracking device, and I don't care to be tracked. Why weren't you at school?"

I ignore his question. "It's also a communication device. You know, in case a flood is coming, and someone needs to reach you."

He frowns. "I have a radio… Wait." His eyes widen. "You came to warn me. Oh, Abby."

His hand covers my own, but I yank mine away, the mix of emotions sparked by his touch more than I can handle right now.

He turns to walk alongside me and glances toward the barn. He wants us to go inside. But I dig in my heels. I'm staying right here. I'm not going anywhere with him.

He sighs. "I came by your house to see you."

Warmth rushes through me, and some of my resistance melts. "I know."

His face darkens. "You were there, and you didn't—?"

"No! I wasn't home. Tammy told me last night."

"Tammy?"

"She saw you take the school bus and guessed."

Cory nods. "Ah."

"I was at Heather's both days, studying." I don't know why I tell him that. It's none of his business.

Cory's shoulders relax a little. "How did the SAT go?"

"I don't really care," I snap, because I'm not going to stand here and chat with him like everything is fine. It's not. Nothing is fine. It's one big mess. I shouldn't be here.

Cory falls silent, and we just stare at each other across the pouring rain. We seem to do that a lot.

"Abby," he says softly.

"What?"

"Can we at least go inside the barn? Out of the rain?"

Grudgingly, I start walking, and Cory falls into step next to me. When we approach the barn, he lengthens his stride and opens the door for us. He ushers me inside, then lifts my bike over the doorstep. I expect him to pull the door closed but he leaves it ajar.

The barn is dimly lit, the air cool and humid. But I'm grateful to be out of the rain.

I push back my hood and turn around, taking in the dirt floor and wooden walls. The ladder is out. I glance up at the attic, and my chest tightens. I miss this place. I shouldn't, but I do.

When I turn back to Cory, he's kneeling by my bike, wiping off the seat, the frame, and the wheels with a rag. His rain jacket hangs from a hook on the wall, dripping water.

I step toward him, embarrassed. "You don't have to do that, really."

He glances up at me, but doesn't stop. "I want to. Besides, it's done."

"Thanks," I mutter.

Cory puts the rag away and leans my bike against the wall. "Can I ask you something?"

I brace myself. "What?"

"Did you drive up here yesterday by any chance? Maybe got a ride from someone?"

"No. I told you. I was studying. Why?" It's not the question I expected, and that's a relief.

Cory shakes his head. "Never mind. I thought I saw strange tire tracks in the yard. Must have been a car turning around."

I think of what Tammy said about Jordan acting weird, and fear prickles my spine. Would he try to hurt Cory? No one at school would believe it, but I've seen the darkness in Jordan, and I know he's got it in him.

I turn around me, scanning the open space of the barn, then walk up to the door and peer out into the yard. Sheets of rain blur the outline of the house. Runoff water gushes around the foundation, tugging at the shrubs and hostas, and tumbling down the driveway.

I meet Cory's eyes. "Where's Pearl?"

He shakes his head. "I don't know. I haven't seen her all day."

"What do you mean? Then we have to look for

her!"

"I already did," Cory protests. "Abby, wait—"

But I'm already out the door. Icy rain drenches my head, and I yank my hood up. But my hair and face are already wet, and cold water drips down my back under my sweater, making me shiver.

A hand grabs my sleeve, and I turn. Cory has caught up to me. He frowns at me from under his hood. "Please go back inside. I'll look for Pearl. You don't have to come with me."

I shrug his hand off me. "*No way.* I'm going to look for her too."

The truth is, I'm desperate for something to keep me busy. Anything to delay the question I have to ask him. I swore to myself, I won't let him get away with silence or excuses this time. Everything depends on his answer, and I'm dreading it.

Exasperation flashes in Cory's eyes. "Come on, Abby! This is…" But he stops himself. Exhales. "Okay. But we stick together. People vanish in flash floods all the time."

"Fine."

We head down the hill to the house first. The yard is quickly turning into a swamp. The mud pulls on my rain boots. Water cascades down the front steps. I check the wrap-around porch while Cory runs inside. I hear him kick off his rain boots, then calling Pearl's name as he checks each room.

"She's not here," he reports a few moments later, his face grim.

"What about the backyard?"

"She wouldn't go near the creek."

"We should still check."

Cory nods, and we circle to the back of the house and start up the hill. The rain shows no sign of relenting, a deluge of water falling straight down. If anything, the sky is darker, the light fading as if it was dusk instead of early afternoon.

We are two feet away from the edge of the creek when I slip on the grass, bent flat and smooth as ice under the flowing water.

Cory's arm closes around me, breaking my fall and yanking me back from the cliff.

I start to push his arm away when I find my footing, but his fingers grip my hand instead.

My pulse speeds up, and I'm about to protest, but the look in Cory's eyes stop me. "I'm not going to let you fall in."

I tell myself it works both ways. If he trips, I can save him too. But the truth is, I'm weak. I love how his hand fits into mine, the warmth of his skin, the strong grip of his fingers. I miss holding hands with him. Or maybe I just miss him.

We make our way along the edge of the creek,

Cory's hand wrapped around mine. He walks closer to the edge and slightly ahead of me, his body a barrier between me and the creek. It all feels achingly familiar.

I glance down the small canyon in awe every few steps. The creek churns and froths angrily as it rushes forward, the surface at least a yard higher than I remember it. Broken branches roll and tumble in the waves, tearing out chunks of soil and ripping out small plants when they slam into the embankment.

I sense Cory's alarm a second before he stops—his fingers involuntarily squeezing mine so hard it hurts.

"What is it?"

He quickly relaxes his grip and turns to face me. "Nothing. We should go back."

But I'm not buying it. His stance is too deliberate, his shoulders too tense. He's blocking my view of something.

"Abby, no—"

He tries to stop me, but I'm faster. I sidestep him, and my gaze sweeps the creek up ahead.

I gasp when I see it.

A black shape caught in a heavy branch, limp and half submerged in the rushing water.

We found Pearl.

Chapter 45

Cory moves closer. "Abby. We can't stay here." He tugs on my hand, turning me away from the creek.

But my feet refuse to move, shock pinning me in place. I'm still staring at the lifeless black shape trapped down there in the branches, taking a beating from the icy rain and the violent current. My stomach churns, but I can't tear my gaze away. I think of Pearl ambling toward me in the driveway, her wet nose brushing my hand, her large head nudging my thigh. It can't be her down there. She can't be dead.

"I don't understand..."

Cory's voice is hollow. "She slipped and fell in."

"But her head..." The shape is wrong, half smashed, one eye gone. Or is it the rain and poor light messing with my vision?

"She hit a rock." The same empty tone.

Hit a rock? The rocks are at the bottom, and the creek looks twice as deep. But it's the coldness in his voice that gets to me.

Angry tears sting my eyes, and I yank my hand from his grip. "So that's it? You're just going to leave her here? You don't care?"

Cory's calm evaporates. "She's dead, Abby! There's nothing I can do. I'll come back for her later. But right now, I need to get *you* inside. It's not safe here." He pushes his hood back, letting the rain drench him as he stares into my eyes. "I know you're angry with me, but can we please get back to the barn?"

I suck in my breath, guilt slashing through me. I've been cruel. It's not his fault Pearl drowned. And it's not the reason I'm angry with him either.

The rain pounds on Cory's head, dripping into his eyes, but he doesn't move, only stares at me, waiting. Until I can't stand it anymore. I want to pull his hood back up, I'm already raising my arm toward him. But I stop myself.

Instead, I spin on my heel and hurry back to the barn, knowing Cory is right behind me.

Water covers every inch of the ground, rushing down the hill toward the house and the yard, pooling into large puddles. There's no place for it to go, the soil already choking on it, too swollen with it to absorb any more. As I walk, my rain boots sink to my ankles. But the downpour continues, the grim, heavy clouds shrouding the sky in every direction. It's definitely getting darker too. How long before nightfall?

The barn is even darker and colder than before. But it's still a relief to escape the merciless rain. I walk several steps before turning around.

Cory is just closing the door behind us. His hood is still down, his hair and face drenched.

I bite my lip. Is he doing this to upset me? But he seems distracted, like his mind is somewhere else.

Until I push down my own hood. The movement wakes him up, and his gaze locks on me.

He shrugs off his rain jacket and hangs it on a hook by the door. Then wipes the water from his face with his sleeve, looking embarrassed, and takes a step in my direction. "Do you want to take off your coat?" he offers.

I take a step back. "No."

"If you're cold, I have sweaters and blankets upstairs." He glances up at the attic. "Do you want to go up there? You'll be more comfortable."

I follow his gaze, and my heart aches. I think of our kiss up there. Did it even happen? It feels like a dream. I shake my head. "No."

Cory frowns. "Are you hungry? The power is out but I could—"

"Stop! I don't want anything."

We both fall silent, and the silence stretches, tense and unbearable.

I should speak. I should ask him what I need to ask. This is why I came here.

Misery fills Cory's face. "Please, Abby. I know I

messed up. I never should've lied to you. But I'm still hoping…" His voice breaks, and he swallows hard. "Just tell me what to do, and I'll do it. Anything. Just tell me how to fix it. I don't want to lose you."

I stare at him.

How do I do this? I am undone, my whole body fragile as glass.

I don't want to lose you either. But I have to know.

I press my nails into my palms. "You stabbed a man."

Blood drains from Cory's face. "What… How did you…"

"That's why they sent you to juvie? For stabbing a man?"

Cory looks away. He takes a deep breath, then lets it out. He's still pale but calmer when he meets my eyes again. "Yes."

I don't know what I expected. But this short, simple answer rips me open. "You… did? You… stabbed a man?" I didn't believe it until now. A part of me still doesn't believe it and maybe it never will.

"Abby—" Cory starts, but I cut him off.

"*Why?*" I demand. I don't want excuses or apologies. I need facts. "Why did you do it?"

Cory opens his mouth, then clenches it shut. He doesn't answer.

"Was it in self-defense? Did he attack you first? Is

that why?"

Still no response.

"Or did you start the fight? Is that what you used to do? Carry a knife and get into fights? Would you do it again if you got angry? Would you stab someone again?" I know I'm pushing too hard, but I'm desperate. "Would you stab *me?*"

Cory's face darkens. "*No!* God, Abby."

"Then tell me what happened. Help me understand."

He grinds his teeth in frustration, like he's battling with himself. "I want to, believe me… But I don't know how… And I don't want to lie to you."

"What does that mean? Just tell me the truth."

"I will. I just… need time. *Please.* Can you trust me?"

I stare at him, stunned. He won't tell me what happened. He was never planning to tell me. I'm such an idiot. All the pain and doubt break loose inside me. "No! I can't trust you. Not anymore. I'm done! *We're* done!"

Cory recoils as if I hit him, and something shifts behind his eyes, a light going out.

And suddenly, I can't stand the sight of him. It hurts too much. I need to get out of here.

I stalk past him, grab my bike, and turn to the door.

Cory blocks my path, alarmed. His hands grip the

metal frame between the handlebars. "What are you doing?"

"Leaving!"

He blinks and shakes his head. "Now? The roads are flooded. It's not—"

"I don't care. Let go!" My eyes burn.

"You can't bike in this rain."

"Fine, then I'll walk!" I let him have the bike and rush around him for the door.

But Cory beats me to it. Spreads his arms to block my exit.

The bike clatters to the ground behind me.

"I understand you don't want to be here." Cory's voice is strained. "But I can't let you leave right now. It's too dangerous. If anything… if anything happened to you…" He trails off.

"You can't stop me," I warn.

Actually, he probably could. He's stronger. I try to hold on to my anger. I close my hands into fists. Could I punch him if I had to? Hurt him? I can't even imagine it.

Cory's gaze slides to my hands, and anguish fills his face.

"I'll make you a deal." He stares at the ground as he speaks. "I'll leave you alone. If that's what you want. I won't touch you or speak to you or bother you ever again." He looks up at me, and his eyes are wet.

"Just… stay here tonight. Okay?"

My own vision blurs with tears. Is it really what I want? For him to leave me alone? If it is, why is my heart breaking?

But I look Cory in the eye and nod. "Okay. It's a deal."

We stand there awkwardly for a few moments, as if neither of us knows what to do next.

Then Cory walks over to my bike and picks it up. I shrug off my raincoat and hang it on a hook next to his. My small backpack is still on my back, and I keep it on.

I cross to the hanging ladder and grip the rung in front of my face. But I hesitate. Will the ladder twist away from me when my feet leave the ground?

Cory appears next to me. He grips one rope and pulls it taut. "Go ahead."

"Thanks." I quickly climb to the attic.

The space is cold and full of shadows, nothing like the happy, sun-washed oasis I remember. Rain drums angrily on the slanted roof and the two skylights.

Cory turns on a portable light, then pulls out a stack of blankets and spreads them out on the bed. "Here. The bed is yours."

"What about you?" I ask.

He crosses to the armchair in the corner. "I'll be over here. Is that okay?"

"It's fine." Sadness wells up in me again, and I turn

away to hide my face.

I need something to do, something to distract me. I pull off my rain boots and sit down on the bed. I shrug off my backpack and pull out my phone.

I have several texts from Mom, but, thankfully, all about the SATs. Wishing me luck, then asking how the test went, and finally telling me to rest. Nothing about the flood. I quickly text back, giving her the highlights. I tell her I took a nap as soon as I got home, and will be turning in soon. I don't mention the weather or where I am.

Then I wait for her answer. But it doesn't come.

I move to the middle of the bed, bend my legs, and hug my knees, my phone still in my hand. Why isn't my mom answering? Didn't my texts go through? If not, she might get worried and ask Mrs. Smith to check on me. That would be bad.

I glance around me, getting anxious. And that's when I see it, hidden by my own shadow—something tucked to the wall next to the head of the bed. I lean closer, lifting my phone to light it—and my chest tightens.

My own smiling face looks back at me from a polaroid photo.

So this is where Cory keeps it. By his bed. The thought sends a new ache through me.

My phone buzzes, and I sit up on the bed to check

it. It's a text from Mom, telling me she's proud of me and wishing me good night. I sigh with relief.

I reach for my backpack, but I'm clumsy and knock it off the bed. It clatters to the floor.

I grasp for it, but Cory is already kneeling next to me. We touch it at the same time.

"I got it." I pull my backpack closer and, on impulse, offer him my phone. "Do you need to call anyone? You can use my phone."

He shakes his head. "No. You should save your battery."

He gets to his feet but lingers, his gaze locked on mine. And all I want is to grab his hand and pull him closer, make him sit next to me. He could sleep here. The bed is more than big enough...

I tear my gaze away. "Then... can we turn off the light? I want to try and get some sleep."

CBSO

I wake up to darkness... and an eerie silence.

Careful not to make noise, I move the blanket off me and get to my feet, then tiptoe to the slanted ceiling and peer out the skylight. The rain has stopped, and the last shreds of clouds drift across the night sky. But it's too dark to see the ground.

I glance to my side. Cory sleeps in the armchair,

sitting up, his arms on the armrests and his knees bent. A single blanket covers his torso and thighs. His eyes are closed, his chest rising and falling in a steady rhythm. But even when asleep, worry is etched into his face, his brows knotted and his jaw clenched. His rest is not peaceful.

I watch him, and my heart swells up with sorrow, like the ground after the rain.

A floor board creaks under my foot, and Cory opens his eyes.

I turn my face to the skylight, my cheeks warming. Maybe if I hold perfectly still, he won't come here. But he's already standing up and walking over. He stops three feet from me.

"Abby?" A soft whisper, like he's afraid to scare me away.

I look at him. "It stopped raining."

He barely glances out the skylight, his gaze on me. "Do you need anything?"

We used the bathroom in the house earlier, and ate cereal bars for dinner. I have a bottle of water by the bed. The blankets keep me warm. My basic needs are met.

But when I look into Cory's eyes, pitch black in the night, a deep longing stirs in me. It'd be so easy to give in. Two short steps, and I could be in his arms, my body pressed against him. And I know it's not just me.

He stands perfectly still, his lips parted, waiting for my signal.

I can't give in, though. Whatever was between us, it won't work anymore. Not if he still won't trust me.

"No. I'm fine."

I turn away from him and hurry back to bed before my resolve crumbles.

※

When I open my eyes, a weak dawn light pours through the skylights. No rain.

Time for me to go.

The cold bites sharply when I push back the blankets. I forgot there's no heating in the barn. I clench my jaw to keep my teeth from chattering. Slowly, so slowly, I pull on my rain boots, slip on my backpack, and rise to my feet.

I glance at Cory. He's asleep in the armchair, in his jeans and sweatshirt, his arms wrapped around him.

Where's his blanket? I look back at the bed. Sure enough, it tops the pile of blankets that covered me. Cory must have put it there after I fell asleep.

I frown, annoyed. Why would he do that? I was already warm enough, and he must have been freezing. I'm tempted to cover him now, but I can't risk waking him up. I need to get out of here.

I keep my breathing shallow and my steps soundless as I cross to the edge and start to climb down the ladder.

"Abby?"

I don't look up. I dip my head and hurry down, my hands and rain boots slapping the rungs, and the ladder twisting under me. No point in being quiet anymore. Haste is more important.

"Abby, wait!"

I jump to the ground, yank the door open, and grab my bike. I don't bother with the raincoat.

I lift my bike over the doorstep and jump on as soon as I'm outside. The ground is still soft, and my wheels skid in the mud, but I manage not to fall.

The yard is a mess, muddy and littered with weeds and branches. I'm already past the house, when I hear Cory running behind me.

"Abby, please! Just hold on. You forgot—"

"Leave me alone, Cory!" I yell over my shoulder, and step harder on the pedals.

I race down the driveway and burst onto the road. Deep puddles stretch across it, and water fills the ditch, but the road is passable. My heart pounds and my muscles scream, but I don't slow down until I'm on my street.

It's only when I get off my bike and dig in my backpack that I realize my error.

My house key is gone. It must have slipped out when I dropped my pack.

So this is why Cory chased after me. He must have found it by the bed. Too late now.

I check my phone, but the battery died. What time is it, anyway? Seven o'clock? It can't be later than that. Not that it would help me if it was.

I look at my own reflection in the kitchen window. Rain boots and jeans splashed with mud, hair unbrushed. It's obvious I didn't sleep at home last night.

But I have no choice. No one else has a spare key, and I can't go back to Cory.

I walk up to Mrs. Smith's door, take a deep breath, and ring the doorbell.

Chapter 46

The morning is freezing when I take the bus to school on Monday. Early frost covers the dead grass and the bare trees, and a thin layer of ice floats on the puddles left by the rain.

My seat is cold to the touch, the chill spreading through me until my whole body is numb. But to be honest, I don't mind it. Once the discomfort wears off, the numbness isn't so bad. I wish I could turn off all my feelings that easily.

When I open my locker, my raincoat hangs inside it, and my house key is on the shelf.

My heart skips a beat, and I cast a quick glance around me. But Cory is nowhere in sight.

Thanks for nothing, I think bitterly, as I slam my locker shut, even though it's not his fault I dropped my key in his attic. Maybe none of this is his fault. It's mine.

A huge poster advertising the show hangs in the main hallway. One third of it is a stunning shot of Jordan as the Beast and Marie as Beauty posing against a flaming sunset.

Excitement buzzes through me. The opening night is on Friday, and the show will be magical. But the thrill quickly fades, drowned by unease. There are only three rehearsals left. A tech rehearsal tomorrow, and two dress rehearsals on Wednesday and Thursday. Then three shows on the weekend—and the play is over.

What am I going to do then? And why do I have a nagging sense that something awful is about to happen and I'm missing all the signs?

Later that day, I'm hurrying to my last class, when I see Cory heading my way in the hallway. I almost turn around and flee, but that would make me late, so I brace myself and keep going, my heart rate climbing the closer he gets. What if he asks to talk to me? What should I do?

But Cory barely looks at me and doesn't say a word, his face unreadable. He walks past me like we're strangers.

I know he's only doing what I told him. Leaving me alone.

But it still hurts.

༺༻

As if today wasn't awful enough, my mother is waiting for me when I get home from school. She sits at the kitchen table, still in her travel clothes, her unpacked suitcase next to her chair. And from the cold look she gives me when I walk in the door, I know I'm in serious trouble.

"Mom, you're back."

"Sit down, Abby."

I take off my backpack and sit in the chair, dread coursing through me.

"I talked to Mrs. Smith—" my mother starts.

"Right." Bitterness fills me.

My mother frowns. "And I can't believe what I'm hearing, Abby. The Brennell boy comes over to see you? And you... you spent the night in his house the other day?"

My cheeks flush. "It's not what you think."

"Well, obviously not." Her voice is stern. "Since I thought you were at home. Isn't that what you told me? That you were taking a nap after the SAT, and then turning in early?" She pales. "Did you even take the SAT, or was that a lie too?"

"Yes, I took it! And I studied for it with Heather."

A half-truth, since most of my after-school study sessions were a cover for the rehearsals. But I'm desperate to reassure her and avoid further questions. Especially about Cory.

My mother isn't done, though. "Now, about that boy. I give you plenty of freedom, Abby, and I don't set many rules. But this is different. I was very clear about that. So explain to me why you're still seeing him after I specifically told you not to."

"I'm not!" Emotion rips through me, and tears well up in my eyes. "We... broke up. Okay? So you don't have to worry about him."

My mother purses her lips. I get no sympathy. If anything, she looks skeptical. "All right. I'll take your word for it."

I bristle. "Good. Because it's true. Can I go now?"

She's just like everyone else—treating Cory like he's a monster, when she doesn't know a thing about him, because she never gave him a chance.

My mother narrows her eyes at me. "Not yet. Is there anything else you haven't told me, Abby?"

I swallow. There's a whole list of things I've kept from her. The play... My work on the costumes... The summer theater program I want to apply for...

But it's only another week until the play is over. I can tell her afterward.

"No."

A mistake.

My mother's expression hardens. She gets up without a word, crosses to the secret staircase and opens the latch. She returns with my sewing machine and puts it on the table. Then pulls out her laptop, opens it, and turns it to me.

My breath catches. A digital poster for the *Beauty and the Beast* show fills the screen.

"I got an email invitation to the play. The theater program sends it out to all students and parents," my mother explains in an icy voice. "The poster was impressive, so I clicked on the link to visit the website." She scrolls down the list of cast and crew, and stops on my name. "And guess who I learned made the costumes?"

I stare at the table. There's nothing I can say. I just hope she doesn't scroll to the bottom of the list and find Cory's name under the set crew.

"Theater costumes?" My mother pulls the laptop close and swipes through a photo roll of the play's characters. "When did you even learn to sew? And why on earth would you hide it from me?"

"*Why?* Because you'd never let me do it! You'd say I need to focus on the academics, on all the science and math classes, and not waste my time on theater. I know you would!"

My mother blinks, taken aback by my intensity. "Well, to be fair, theater is a huge time commitment. There are other opportunities that would help you get into the best neuroscience programs when you apply to college. So, yes, I wish you'd asked my advice first."

I should bite my tongue. It's the worst time to get in a fight with her. But my temper gets the better of me.

"What if I don't want to get into a neuroscience program?"

"What are you talking about?" She sounds confused. "Of course, you do. You have a brilliant, analytical mind, and you've always been gifted in quantitative subjects. Neuroscience is a perfect match for you."

"No, Mom! *I really don't!* And I don't want to do medical research after that either. These are your plans. Not mine. You can't force me to be someone I'm not."

"Abby, no one is forcing you to do anything. I just… I had no idea." My mother stares at me in dismay. "Then... what do you want to do?"

My chest tightens. How long have I waited for her to ask me? "I… don't know yet," I admit. "But I need to figure it out for myself."

My mother looks shaken, but tries to collect herself. "All right. Well. You still have time, and I hope you'll keep your options open. But regardless, we'll have to make some changes around here."

A chill goes through me. "What changes?"

"I'm sorry to have to do that, Abby, but you leave me no choice. I'm your mother, and I'm responsible for you."

"Mom?"

A pained look crosses my mother's face. "You are grounded, Abby."

I spring to my feet. "*What?* You can't do that! The play—"

"You can still finish the play," my mother says. "I respect that you made a commitment and the group relies on you. But you're coming straight home after that. And I need to know where you are at all times when you're not at school. Is that clear?"

"Yes." I grab my backpack from the floor, and rush up the stairs to my bedroom, this new humiliation adding to my misery.

But it's not like I have anywhere to go or anyone to see, anyway, so what does it matter?

Chapter 47

My favorite thing about the tech rehearsal on Tuesday are the lights. I haven't had a chance to sit in the audience and watch the finished sequences until now, but Adam has outdone himself.

He even designed a light motif just for Neon, a sort of sparkling rainbow twirl that says *hello, gorgeous*, or maybe *I see you, and you're doing great*. He plays it whenever Neon is onstage. It's subtle enough that I wouldn't have noticed if Tammy didn't point it out. Anyway, it's incredibly sweet, and I hope it makes Neon feel a little better that, despite all the work they've done rehearsing for the Beast, they won't actually be in the play.

If I focus on the lights, on the colors shifting and blending in the air above the stage, I can almost forget the people. Especially the set crew, as they hustle to assemble the set pieces for each scene, and then take them apart. Especially Cory.

There's nothing for the costume crew to do today, since all the actors are in regular clothes. It's not a true rehearsal. The goal is to test all the tech—particularly the lights and sounds, but the set pieces and props too—and troubleshoot any problems. The rhythm is a choppy stop-and-go, with the actors skipping most of their lines to get through the blocking.

Honestly, I have no reason to be here. Except for a vague sense that something is wrong, forces are out of balance and about to clash, and I need to pay attention. Or maybe it's the anguish that things are ending in the worst possible way.

The actors sit in the front rows of the audience, alone or in small groups, quietly waiting for their cue. Most seem nervous when not on stage, even Mike and Nate, and I don't blame them. The opening night is in three days.

Only Jordan looks perfectly relaxed, gliding from person to person as if bestowing his royal grace on them.

A misgiving stirs in me when he slides into the chair next to Marie. I watch him casually put his arm around her shoulders, resting it on the back of her chair. Marie tenses, but doesn't pull back. They sit like this for a few moments before she bends her head and whispers in his ear.

Jordan's head snaps toward her, like he's just heard the best news, and my heart sinks. *No, Marie. You promised you wouldn't tell.* But then Jordan jumps to his feet and strolls up the ramp to the wing, and I know what I have to do. I slip out of my seat and follow him backstage.

I'm too late to warn Cory, though.

Jordan gets to him first. "Brennell, wait up."

I slip behind an old backdrop and watch from the shadows.

Cory puts away the set piece he was carrying and turns back. "I'm busy."

But Jordan blocks his way. He waves his hand dismissively. "Relax, they'll be fine without you. But I just heard the craziest shit. You... *stabbed a guy?*" He sounds positively gleeful.

Cory freezes.

"Fuck me!" Jordan laughs, and mock punches Cory in the arm. "Man, I would've loved to see that fight. Or was it more of an accident? Did you trip, Brennell? Is that what happened?"

Cory still doesn't move. "Get out of my way."

"Or what? You'll stab me too?" Jordan circles around him. More mock punches land on Cory's ribs and back. "You have a blade on you now? Let's see it. I bet I can still take you with my bare hands." He throws another punch, a real one. It connects with Cory's chest, twisting him backward.

Anger flashes in Cory's eyes, but he shakes his head. "I'm not going to fight you."

"Right. I forgot. You're a coward." Jordan rolls up

his sleeve, revealing a bandage on his forearm. "Your stupid dog had more balls than you. The bitch fucking bit me. Before I cracked her skull. Can you believe it?"

I clasp my hand over my mouth to stifle a gasp of shock. *Pearl.*

So she didn't drown. Jordan smashed her head in and threw her in the creek.

Cory's face darkens. "You sick bastard. I knew it..."

"Yeah?" Jordan sneers. "Then what are you going to do about it?"

Cory's hands close into fists, and he steps forward. And I almost want him to keep going, to slam his fist into Jordan's smug and hateful face and make him pay for what he's done.

But Cory's better than me, and he stops himself. "You're going to miss your cue."

Disappointment twists Jordan's mouth. "Okay, Brennell. We've got to wrap this up, so here's what's going to happen. You're fucking done here. Your theater career is over. You're going to quit the crew after tonight."

I catch a trace of worry in Cory's eyes. "And if I don't?"

"If you don't—if I see your face here again—I'll tell everyone what you are. A big fucking reveal." Jordan's voice is a growl. "Starting with Abby. Maybe you'll finally get the message and leave her the fuck alone. Because I'm sick of you following her around."

"I'm sick of you pretending you care about her," Cory says.

Jordan laughs. "I don't. But you do, Brennell. That's the whole point."

I shudder, a searing anger rushing through my veins. I suspected Jordan only used me to hurt Cory, but now I know for sure. And I hate it.

ଓଃ୨

If the tech rehearsal meant a downtime for the costume crew, a dress rehearsal is nonstop work, even with Zoe back. From the moment we step backstage, we are rushing to get the actors in costume for their first scene. Luke and his helpers on makeup and hair are just as busy.

Tammy and I work side by side, putting the finishing touches on Beauty's Sisters, when a thought pops into my mind. Something she said to me when we first met.

"Tammy?"

"Yeah?" She doesn't look up from fluffing the oldest Sister's skirt.

"Why did you switch to costumes? I thought you loved working the lights."

"I did." Tammy shrugs like it's not a big deal. "But we didn't have enough people on costumes. So…"

"So you did what was best for the play."

"Well, sure. It's all about the play, right?"

"Right," I echo, but shame itches on my skin.

She makes it sound so simple, like putting aside your ego for the good of the project is the most natural thing to do. But it's not—at least not for me. My reason for doing the play has always been selfish: to build my portfolio and earn recommendation letters. And I've definitely let my feelings interfere with my work…

A familiar hum of the wheels comes from the stage. The set crew are rolling in the set pieces and locking them in place.

I remember Jordan's threat, and dread licks my spine. For Cory's sake, I hope he listened. The crew will be short-handed without him, but they'll manage. He needs to worry about himself. Jordan wasn't joking.

"I'll be right back," I tell Tammy and dash out.

I hurry behind the stage and step inside the wing on the other side.

The whole crew, including me, is dressed in black. On the dimly lit stage, the set crew move swiftly and quietly like shadows. I scan their faces. Then one person turns and meets my gaze.

Cory.

A jolt goes through me, and I stare at him, my

thoughts racing.

Confusion registers in his face, and he walks over.

"What's wrong?" he asks me.

"What are you doing here?" I snap. "You can't be here."

Because I know that look. He's still worried about me, when it's the last thing he should be doing.

Cory's face falls, the hurt in his eyes unmistakable.

Pain pierces through me. He doesn't know I heard Jordan threaten him.

But there's Jordan crossing the stage, still in his regular clothes and heading for the costume room. I need to be there to help him. Maybe I can stop him.

"Forget it," I tell Cory and hurry away.

I burst into the costume room a moment after Jordan.

"I'll help him!" I exclaim, grabbing his costume, mask, and gloves off the rack. I sound eager and breathless, like a star struck fan ready to throw herself at his feet, and my face flushes from embarrassment.

Tammy and Zoe stare at me in confusion, but Jordan only laughs. "Whoa. Easy, Abby. Slow down. I don't want you to hurt yourself."

He looks so damn pleased with himself, my hand itches. I've never slapped anyone in my life, but if my arms weren't full of the Beast's costume, I might slap him right now. I imagine the red burn across his face and the shock in his eyes, and the image cheers me up. If he thinks he won me back, he's got it all wrong.

"Let's go to a dressing room," I offer, turning to leave. "We'll have more privacy."

Jordan's eyes flash, and a shrewd smile curls his lips. "Sounds good to me." He steps closer and puts his arm around my shoulders as we go out the door.

I suck in my breath and almost trip in surprise. My skin crawls underneath my sweater, the need to push him away overwhelming.

But I grit my teeth and endure his touch. If his attention is on me, he won't have a chance to hurt Cory. I'm just glad I can't see Tammy's and Zoe's reaction.

I don't let Jordan out of my sight for the rest of the rehearsal, and I do it again on Thursday. I take longer than necessary to hook up his mike, I fuss over his mask and gloves, I wait in the wing when he's on stage. I even fetch him a bottle of water when he asks, running to and from the vending machine in the hallways, just in case it's a trick to get rid of me.

I catch the same wounded look in Cory's eyes a few times, but I ignore it. I don't care what he thinks of me. If I can shield him from Jordan's cruelty, it's worth it. A few more days, and the play will be over. Maybe Jordan will forget the whole thing.

If I had one wish, I'd wish for that.

Chapter 48

And then it's finally Friday.

My classes pass like in a dream. I go through the motions—walk from room to room, sit down at my desk, take out my notebook—but my thoughts run in restless loops, and an anxious energy flows through me.

More posters for the play hang in the hallways, and every time I walk by one, the Beast's glare follows me. And it's like Jordan is looking straight at me, his eyes an icy blue behind the hideous mask, savoring my fear and mocking my hope. Because it doesn't matter what I do, does it? He'll still expose Cory and make everyone hate him. He won't stop until he ruins Cory's life.

The classes end, and I reluctantly make my way to the cafeteria, where a handful of doting parents have set up an early dinner for the cast and crew. The space is already crowded, the air buzzing with chatter and laughter.

Tammy and Zoe intercept me and we stand in line together. I scoop some salad and a small slice of pizza on my paper plate, plain water in a cup. Then we find a table to sit down. I skipped lunch, so I force myself to eat, though my stomach is in a knot.

I glance around the cafeteria. The set crew sit at one table, several extra chairs crammed so tight together, they bump elbows as they eat.

But Cory isn't with them. He could be eating off by himself somewhere. Or… he's not coming.

Like on cue, Jordan strolls up to that table, a friendly smile on his face. He chats with the set crew for a bit, and although I can't hear the words, I catch the exact moment he asks about Cory. The group shake their heads, looking grim. They don't know where he is, confirming my suspicion. And, for a second, Jordan's eyes blaze with triumph before he fakes concern.

Guilt slashes through me. Cory is part of the crew and deserves to be here.

But I tell myself it's a good thing. He made a smart decision. He doesn't want to set off Jordan.

When the dinner is over, I follow the crowd out of the cafeteria and into the theater. We gather on the stage to hear the director's last-moment instructions and encouragements. And then it's time to get ready for the show.

There's a moment, right after I enter the costume room, when all my anger and anguish and helplessness slam into me, and I want to grab the Beast's mask, hurl it against the floor, and storm out.

But Tammy's words echo in my head. It doesn't matter what I want or how I feel. This isn't about me or Cory or Jordan. *It's about the play*—and I have a job to do. I cling to that as I throw myself into the work.

Jordan doesn't make it easy, though.

Tammy and Zoe are helping Marie and the Sisters in the costume room, so Jordan and I are in a makeshift dressing area backstage. He already changed into his costume. Now I'm helping him with the mask.

We barely speak and I avoid meeting his gaze, but my throat burns and my skin crawls just from being so close to him. It's like standing in a toxic fog. Jordan radiates a malicious satisfaction.

Then, as soon as the Beast's mask is on and zipped up in the back, he speaks.

"Looks like Brennell didn't make it."

Resentment cuts through me, but I won't let him provoke me. I pick up the first glove and put it on him. But when I grab the second glove and reach for his hand, Jordan yanks his arm away.

"You know why he was in juvie? He stabbed a guy with a knife."

I shudder and look up, my calm gone.

Jordan has no idea I already knew. His blue eyes glow with excitement. "He's a fucking psychopath, Abby. And I'm going to tell everyone. I just haven't decided when yet. What do you think? Tonight after the show—or tomorrow night at the cast-and-crew party?"

I stare at him, speechless. Cory gave him what he wanted—he quit the crew, and he's missing the play—but it makes no difference. Jordan never intended to let it go.

"Here is good."

Skyler's voice makes me turn—and my heart gives a painful thud.

Cory and Mr. Miller carry an antique mirror between them. Skyler points out a spot against the wall, and they gingerly set it down.

Skyler immediately hurries away, but Mr. Miller turns to Cory and squeezes his shoulder. "Thanks for your help, Cory. This thing is heavier than it looks. I'm sorry you missed dinner."

"No problem," Cory says, and the teacher smiles and hurries away too.

Cory turns to us, and his eyes stop on me.

I stand frozen, but Jordan the Beast takes a step in his direction. Rage simmers in his voice. "I thought I told you to stay the fuck away, Brennell. *But he never listens, does he?*"

A shadow crosses Cory's face, and I suck in my breath. Jordan made it sound like I'm on his side. *I'm not.*

But before I can protest, Cory walks up to me, bends down, and hands me the Beast's glove. I didn't even notice I dropped it. I take it with shaking fingers.

Jordan glares at him. "Get ready for your big reveal after the show, Brennell. It's time everyone knew what a fucking psycho you are. So don't even think about sneaking out."

Cory finally looks at him, his face stone cold. "Don't worry. I'm not going anywhere."

Jordan sneers, but there's an edge of rage underneath it. He was hoping to rattle Cory and failed. "You're even more fucked up than I thought."

"Have a good show, Abby," Cory says to me before walking away.

Heat rushes to my face, because for a mortifying second, I'm not sure which one he meant. The play—or what Jordan is planning for him afterward? Does he really think I could enjoy the latter? But Cory doesn't have a cruel streak. His good wishes were genuine, even if I don't deserve them.

Jordan sticks out his hand, and I force myself to take it and put the second glove on it.

He flexes his fingers, the fake claws slashing the air. "Good? The show's going to be great. And then we'll have real fun. He's going to wish they never let him out of juvie."

A bell rings three times, and Jordan and I hurry to our places, as do all the cast and crew.

Rushing steps, banging chairs, and a cacophony of

voices come from the other side of the curtain, as the patrons settle in their seats. We have a full house. All the tickets for tonight sold out.

The lights in the theater dim and a hush falls over the audience.

Then the curtain rises—and the first scene begins. I shiver over and over as I watch from the wing. It doesn't matter that I made the costumes, painted the sets, and watched hours of rehearsal. The play comes to life in front of me, and the magic of theater fills my heart.

But the feeling doesn't last. Every time I help Jordan get ready for his scene, some of the magic sours and wears off. His threats rattle in my head. *Get ready for your big reveal after the show, Brennell... It's time everyone knew what a fucking psycho you are... We'll have real fun...*

Until a resolve grows in me. I can't let Jordan do this. I won't.

And then it hits me—I'm not over Cory, and I don't want to be.

I think of the hundred things he did that moved me, delighted me, impressed me. I know he's not perfect; I know there's darkness in him. But he's braver, kinder, and smarter than anyone I've met.

And a better person than Jordan, no matter what their records say.

Suddenly, the play onstage moves too swiftly, the scenes rushing forward when I need them to slow down. What do I do? How do I stop Jordan? I'm running out of time.

From the wing where I stand, I scan the theater, looking for familiar faces. The actors on stage. Neon and Patricia watching from the wing on the other side. And I know others are around too, even if I can't see them. Tammy and Zoe. Skyler, Natasha, and Adam. The set crew.

They all know Cory by now. If only I had time to talk to them first, to warn them of what Jordan is planning, I could convince them Cory is not a monster.

But there's no time—only minutes to the final scene of the play.

Despair grips me. Is there anything worse than knowing something awful is coming and being powerless to stop it? Than knowing someone you care about is about to get hurt, and you can do nothing to help them?

My time is up, though.

Beauty kisses the dying Beast, confessing her love for him and begging him to survive, and darkness envelops them both.

I slip onto the stage under the cover of dramatic lightning and thunder.

I'm here to help Jordan get off his mask and

gloves—the Beast transforming into a Prince.

I take my place behind him and turn off his mike. "Mask off. Ready?"

"Yeah. Let's show them my real face."

That's it.

Maybe I can't save Cory, but I can show everyone what Jordan is really like.

I reach for the back of his mask—and twist off the flimsy pull tab on the zipper.

"Go to hell," I mutter.

And I turn on his mike and step away.

Jordan spins around, his mean temper flaring.

He yanks at his mask, trying to grasp the zipper through the gloves. *"What the fuck, Abby?* Are you shitting me? What is this? Get that fucking mask off me!" The speakers distort his voice into a vicious growl before his sound cuts off.

The thunder booms and the lightning flashes over my head.

What have I done? I ruined the play.

Jordan is still cursing and flailing, blind in his skewed mask, when he trips. He's at the edge of the stage and about to tumble down, head first, into the deep orchestra pit.

Marie scrambles out of the way as I spring toward him.

But another crew member moves faster.

He dives from the wing and across the stage, slamming painfully into a set piece in the process. Grabs Jordan's arm and swings him around, changing his trajectory and saving him from plummeting off the stage.

I catch a glimpse of his face when he shoves Jordan into the wing.

Cory.

Emotion rushes through me.

Cory… saved Jordan. No, not just Jordan. If Jordan fell and broke his neck…

Cory saved me too. He didn't hesitate.

I hear Skyler's voice. "Your coat and scarf. *Quick.*"

The lightning sequence continues, but now there's a hint of color in it. A rainbow twirl.

"Neon, you're up. Put it on." Skyler again. Then, "Natasha? Mike them."

The moment I slip into the back wing, a romantic spotlight blooms over the stage—with Neon standing opposite Marie.

My knees go weak with relief. I did something horribly rash and selfish, and I'm sure I'll have to pay for it. But at least the audience will still see the ending.

I can't linger to watch, though. I have to find Cory.

Chapter 49

I find Cory backstage. He leans with his back against the wall. He touches his arm and winces. He drops his arm when he sees me.

I want to run to him, but the look on his face—guarded and wary, as if he wasn't sure he should talk to me at all—unnerves me, and I slow down to a walk. "How is your hand?"

"It's fine." He clears his throat and looks down at the floor. "Just a bruise."

"It's my fault," I say miserably, because it's true. It's my fault he hurt his hand. And because a new fear grips me. What if he doesn't feel the same way about me anymore?

Cory looks up at me, frowning. "No, it isn't. His mask got stuck. It happens. And then... it was all him."

I take a deep breath. "It got stuck because I broke the zipper. On purpose."

Cory blinks. "What? *Why?*"

All the emotions return, and words pour from my mouth. "Because I'm sick of how he treats you! Always threatening you and putting you down. Using me against you." I shake my head. "I couldn't let him get away with it." My voice hardens. "He thinks he's better than you. But he's not. And now everyone knows it."

Cory looks at me sharply. "You did this... for me?"

This isn't the reaction I expected. But it's too late to take it back. Misery wells up in me, but I nod.

"Abby. *No*." Cory's hand closes around my arm. I don't think he's even aware of it. Not hard enough to hurt me, but the tension in his fingers tells me plenty. He's upset with me.

"It's done. Okay?"

"Well, it was stupid," he snaps. "Don't you get it? This is serious. It's sabotage and reckless endangerment. You could get in trouble for this. What about that summer program you want to apply for? What about the recommendation letters?" His brows knot, and he sounds angry. "Why would you throw it away... for me? I'm not... I'm not worth it, Abby."

"Yes, you are!" I say with conviction.

But Cory only shakes his head. "No, I'm not. You know what I did. You know why they sent me to juvie. That's all I am."

"That's not true." I look deep into his eyes. His fingers are still around my arm. I cover his hand with my own, pressing it in place. "I know you, Cory, and you're so much more than that."

Cory's eyes darken, and his voice gets quiet. "What

are you saying?"

Terror grips me. No more hiding. I need to be honest. "I'm sorry I pushed you away. I'm sorry I didn't trust you. I was wrong." I take a shaky breath. "You don't have to tell me what happened. If you need time, that's fine. I'll wait. But… I don't want you to stay away anymore."

Cory doesn't answer right away. He takes my hand in his and studies it, as if it held the answers. But when he looks up at me, his eyes are bright. "Are you sure?"

I move closer, my heart pounding. "Yes. I want to be with you. If you… want to be with me."

Cory frowns, and for a moment, I'm terrified he'll say no. But he brings my hand to his lips and kisses my fingers. "*If?* There's no if for me, Abby. You're all I think about. I've never wanted anything more in my life."

I can't wait any longer. I pull his face to mine, and he wraps his arms around me. We kiss, and then hold each other.

"I missed you," I whisper into his neck.

Cory lowers his face to my collarbone, his breath warm on my skin. "You have no idea."

Clapping startles us. The applause grows louder until the whole theater reverberates with it. I feel it in the soles of my shoes.

I jump up. "The mask!" I forgot all about it. I need

it back. "Did anyone help Jordan take it off?"

Cory shakes his head. "I don't know. His father came to get him."

"His father?"

"Yeah. He was furious." Cory grabs my hand. "Come on. I know where they are."

We rush into the main hallway, then turn into a side hallway lined with lockers.

And there's Jordan. He stands next to his locker, his head bent, clutching the Beast's mask and gloves.

An angry-looking man in an elegant suit is yelling at him. "...Do you have any idea how much damage you've done to my business just now? I need these people to respect me, Jordan, and I can't do that if you humiliate yourself in front of them."

So that's Jordan's father.

A slender woman in a black dress, pearls, and high heels stands off to the side, holding a tiny purse. A fake smile is plastered on her face. Jordan's mother. I'm guessing she helped him unzip the mask and gloves. At least I hope so. I hope he didn't just rip them off.

"Dad, please…" Jordan sounds scared. He's like a different person.

"I said, empty your locker, Jordan. No discussion. You're not coming back." His father grimaces at the Beast's mask and gloves. "And get these disgusting things away from me."

I react without thinking. I hurry over and extend my hands. "I'll take them."

Jordan looks at me, then at Cory behind me, and his face turns red. His fingers dig into the mask, and I hold my breath. Is he angry enough to destroy it right now? *Please, no.*

But Jordan hands over his load without looking me in the eye.

"And you can forget theater or UCLA," his father continues as if Cory and I weren't here. Or maybe it's part of the punishment. "I gave you too much freedom. I see that now. What you need is a discipline and a real job."

Jordan shudders. "Dad. No. Come on." He tries to smile. "It was just a silly joke. I got carried away, but it'll never happen again. I'll make you proud, I swear it."

His father sneers with distaste. "Spare me the pathetic acting, Jordan. The locker. Now."

"Okay." Jordan turns and starts fumbling with the lock. A tear flows down his cheek, and he wipes it with the back of his hand. "Dad, I can't... Please, don't make me transfer... It's my senior year. I have friends here..."

The father crosses his arms. "You have ten seconds to open the locker, or I'm taking the jeep."

Jordan grabs the lock again. He's really trying this

time, but his hands are shaking, and it's not going well.

Cory walks over. "Let me do it."

Jordan steps aside, and Cory opens the lock for him.

Jordan looks up at him, then over at me. "I'm sorry."

Cory nods, but I'm not that quick to forgive. Now that I've met his parents, I almost feel sorry for Jordan. But not quite.

"Dammit, Jordan," his father growls. "Hurry up. I'm not going to tell you again."

A crowd of patrons fills the main hallway, leaving after the show, so Cory and I use a side door to sneak backstage. I head for the costume room, eager to inspect my load. But Tammy intercepts us and steers us toward the stage.

"Come on. A debrief meeting. We're only waiting for you."

Dread licks my spine. This is it. They're going to kick me out. It's only fair after the stunt I pulled.

Cory gives me an encouraging look, but I can tell he's nervous for me too.

"I found them," Tammy announces, and all eyes turn to us when we step onstage. All cast and crew stand or sit in a half circle facing Skyler who presides over the meeting.

I meet Skyler's eyes, and brace myself for what's

coming.

But the stage manager points to the garments in my hands. "Any damage?"

I check the mask first. The pull tab on the slider is broken, but the zipper still works, and the mask looks intact. I hand it to Cory and inspect the gloves next. "A zipper is broken on one glove."

"Can you fix it before the matinee show tomorrow?"

My throat is tight. Is that all? I almost ruined the opening night. And no one is going to yell at me for what happened? "I can fix it."

Skyler nods. "All right. Listen up, everyone. Good work tonight. We hit a few snags, but we worked them out and still gave a good show. Which brings me to two announcements." They pause and glance around. "Announcement number one. Jordan resigned his role." Whispers fill the stage, but no one seems surprised. "Which brings me to announcement number two."

In that instant, dancing lights fill the stage. I recognize the rainbow twirl and have to smile.

Skyler rolls their eyes and looks over their shoulder up at Adam's booth over the audience. "Okay. Nice. Thanks for that." Skyler scans the faces. "Neon? Where are you?" Neon gets to their feet, and the lights shift over them. "You're the new Beast. Congratulations."

This brings out a chorus of cheers and clapping.

"Yeah, Neon!"

"Woo-hoo!"

"Slay!"

Skyler smiles. "All right. That's all for tonight. I'll see you all bright and early tomorrow."

Everyone gets to their feet. Tammy and Zoe come over to us.

"We're driving you home, right?" Tammy asks me, then looks over at Cory without asking for my answer. "We can drop you off first."

Cory sounds surprised. "You don't have to—"

But Tammy only frowns. It wasn't a question. "We're dropping you off."

She and Zoe look ready to leave now, their backpacks already on. But I need to do one more thing. I gesture at the Beast's mask in Cory's hands. "Let me just put it away and grab my staff."

Cory follows me to the costume room, and I put the mask in its box and pack the gloves in my backpack to take home. But I don't pick up my backpack yet. Instead, I turn to him.

"How much time do we have?" he murmurs, his arms already pulling me close.

"Not enough," I whisper back, slipping my hands around his neck and pressing my mouth to his.

And it's true. The time is so short, it's torture. But we make every second count.

Chapter 50

After a hectic and thrilling Saturday, with one show in the morning and the closing show in the evening, Sunday is slower and bittersweet.

It takes only six hours to tear down the set for *Beauty and the Beast*—nothing compared to how long it took to design and create it. The cast and crew work side by side, disassembling the larger set pieces, collecting the screws, and moving everything into storage. Some backdrops for the play will be used again, others will be painted over for new productions. The borrowed props will return to the owners, and the costumes will be dry cleaned and added to the wardrobe, carefully labeled with the play and character names.

We linger after the work is done. Graduating seniors take turns giving speeches, some solemn and heartfelt, others over-the-top silly. Lots of hugs, handshakes, and back slaps are exchanged, and by the end, more than a few people are crying, including the director.

Jordan is absent, and no one mentions his name. I

feel bad for him for a second, but then I remember his arm crushing Cory's throat, and Pearl's limp body in the creek, and all the ugly threats that came out of his mouth. I don't trust his apology. I'm glad he's not here today.

I'm standing with Cory when Mr. Miller walks over. "Great work, you two." He beams at us, a sparkle of genuine pride in his eye. "We were lucky to have you both."

My face warms, and Cory's cheeks redden to match. If Mr. Miller hadn't invited Cory to join the crew that day in Physics class, and hadn't asked me to answer Cory's questions, would Cory and I ever speak to each other? Maybe a few words about the exam. But anything more? Anything deeper? I doubt it.

"Thanks, Mr. Miller," Cory and I say at the same time.

And then it's time to leave. The fall play is officially over.

Happiness dances on my skin when I walk with Cory to the parking lot. We're holding hands, his fingers lightly interlaced with mine. It's such a simple thing, but I can't stop smiling.

Mom let me take the car in the morning. I'm still grounded, and she expects me back right away after the set strike is done. But I can't go home yet.

I get behind the wheel, Cory slides into the

passenger seat, and we're off. And the sense of freedom is so exhilarating, we look at each other and laugh.

After today, without the rehearsals or SAT study sessions as my cover, I'll only see Cory at school. But that's not enough. I desperately want to be alone with him. It's not like I can just ask my mom's permission. She doesn't know I'm back with Cory, and she'd never approve.

So although I feel bad about hiding things from her again, and I know I'm taking a risk if I get caught, I turn on the road to Cory's farm.

It's not like we're hurting anyone or committing a crime. We care about each other and want to be together, that's all. Is an hour or two so much to ask?

The yard around the house is a sorry sight. Someone cleared a path from the driveway to the house and from the house to the barn, but the rest of the yard is strewn with broken branches and torn out plants left over by the flash flood.

"I can help you clean up," I offer after we get out of the car.

But Cory shakes his head, embarrassed. "No, I've got it. I was just... distracted."

"What about Pearl? Did you—?"

Cory takes my hand. "Yeah. Do you want to see her grave?"

I nod, and he leads me to a lovely, wooded spot

behind the barn. A simple stone marks the grave. I should've been here to help Cory, instead of fighting with him, but it's too late now.

The old anger stirs in me, and I squeeze his fingers. "I know it was Jordan."

Cory frowns. "How? Did he tell you?"

"No. I overheard him threatening you backstage. The sick bastard."

"Don't worry about him."

We stand over Pearl's grave for a few more moments, the air cold on our faces. Then Cory tugs on my hand. "Come on. I want to show you something."

He leads me to the edge of the orchard, and kneels on the ground. He parts the grass to reveal three stones marking the spot. A skinny seedling with dark leaves sticks out of the dirt. I kneel down to see it better.

"Is it the magical tree we planted?" I laugh in disbelief. "The apples that smell like roses?"

"Yep. And it's tougher than it looks. It survived the flash flood."

We walk through the orchard, holding hands, and it's wonderful. Except by now, I'm really cold and mad with myself for not planning better. The light jacket I brought is fine to cross the parking lot but not to hang outside. I clench my jaw to keep my teeth from chattering.

"You're cold," Cory says with reproach, and he

shrugs off his heavy jacket and wraps it around my shoulders.

"No, don't... Thanks." But now he's wearing only a sweater, and I feel guilty. We need a place where we can both be warm. "Can we go to the barn?"

He smiles. "Sure."

The barn looks exactly the same, a wide open space full of light, as if it patiently waited for my return and held no grudges for my mistakes. I almost want to say thanks as I cross the threshold.

Cory climbs to the attic to drop down the ladder, and then jumps down to hold it for me as I climb up.

My chest tightens as I take in the skylights, the armchair, the bed. My photo is still tucked to the wall. Nothing changed up here either, and I'm grateful.

Cory walks over to the shelf. "I got something for you."

I'm stunned. "You got me a gift?"

Cory flusters. "I mean, it's technically for me to use... But I got it for you... Because of you."

My face flushes. Does he mean... a condom?

Cory opens his hand... and he's holding a phone.

"It's a phone!" I can't help it—a nervous giggle bubbles up my throat. "Okay. It's a phone."

"What did you think it was? Oh." Now Cory's face turns red too.

"No, I love it. Really. I'm glad you got it." My

giggles get worse. "I can finally call you, and you can call me."

He's struggling to keep a straight face too. "It's a simple model, but I'm only going to use it to talk to you, so…"

"It's perfect." I clear my throat to get my glee under control. "So… do you want my number?"

"Yes! Yes, I do."

I give him my number, and he punches it into his contacts. I'm the first and only name in his contacts. Then he puts the phone away and turns me.

"When do you have to be back?" He's not laughing anymore, his gaze locked on me.

I bristle. Will we always have to watch the clock and count the minutes now? I already resent it.

But it's not Cory's fault. He's just looking out for me.

"We still have time."

We move toward each other, the familiar invisible force pulling as close.

I lift my hands and let my fingers stroke his face. He slips his arms around me.

The kiss tastes like a perfect summer day, the sweetest berries, and electricity. It also feels like coming home. My whole body hums with how right it feels.

And I make myself a promise about Cory.

I'll never doubt him or give him up again.
No matter what.

About the Author

Vera Brook is a bookworm and
a multi-genre fiction writer
who gets way too attached to fictional characters.

To learn more about Vera's writing,
including new book releases and exclusive sales,
visit her website, sign up for her newsletter,
and follow her on social media.

www.verabrook.com

Newsletter: http://eepurl.com/cTQmKD

Made in the USA
Middletown, DE
24 June 2023

33443816R00285